WHAT WE SALVAGE

David Baillie

ChiZine Publications

FIRST EDITION

Distributed in Canada by
Publishers Group Canada
76 Stafford Street, Unit 300
Toronto, Ontario, M6J 2S1
Toll Free: 800-747-8147
e-mail: info@pgcbooks.ca

Distributed in the U.S. by
Diamond Comic Distributors, Inc.
10150 York Road, Suite 300
Hunt Valley, MD 21030
Phone: (443) 318-8500
e-mail: books@diamondbookdistributors.com

Library and Archives Canada Cataloguing in Publication
Baillie, David, 1969-, author
What we salvage / David Baillie.

Issued in print and electronic formats.
ISBN 978-1-77148-322-3 (pbk.).--ISBN 978-1-77148-323-0 (ebook)

I. Title.

PS8603.A44386W43 2015 C813'.6 C2015-900088-2
C2015-900089-0

CHIZINE PUBLICATIONS
Toronto, Canada
www.chizinepub.com
info@chizinepub.com

Edited by Sandra Kasturi
Copyedited and proofread by Gemma Files

We acknowledge the support of the Canada Council for the Arts which last year invested $20.1 million in writing and publishing throughout Canada.

Published with the generous assistance of the Ontario Arts Council.

Printed in Canada

for Jay MacDonald,
to whom I owe so much

and

for Nina DeVilliers,
1971-1991

Sorry it took this long to keep that promise;
rest in peace, little sister.

PART ONE

Chapter One

"How many?"

"Five that I can see."

"Who?"

My brother, Tribal, turns his head slowly, glancing down the street through that curtain of hair. Couple streetlamps are out, but the occasional late-night driver lights up the shadows long enough to put a few pieces together.

"Hard to tell. Glasgow and Sean D for sure . . ."

Not a good start, but not surprising either. After all, we're deep in their pissing grounds. And not that it matters at this point, but I ask anyway.

"Anyone else we know?"

"Yeah," Tribal says. "I think that's Billy leaning against a car."

"Hardcore, or that other prick?"

"Nah, Billy Hardcore. And a couple guys we don't know. Definitely skinheads, though. Toronto foot soldiers, maybe. Funhouse said Sean D was recruiting."

"Oi oi oi. Fun and fucking games."

Tribal smiles, grim and humourless.

"Clearly Cannon is closed. We'll have to cut over a block," he says.

I consider.

"We could aim for the corner of Catharine and King. Tina's pretty close to there—we could ride it out at her place until morning." Not the most ideal plan, but better than the alternative.

Tribal doesn't like it. He has a lot of enemies downtown—at least here he's anonymous at a distance. Not me, though. Army parka shell (American M-51 Fishtail, Korean War vintage), bull's-eye sewn on the back, 10-hole Doc Martens—street mod battle standards, a ticket to ride. I make the pointless gesture, just for propriety.

"Or we could split up, meet at . . ."

"Fuck off," he mumbles absently. Our options are limited and pretty grim. Tribal's right hand is badly swollen, probably broken. I still have the short aluminum bat that I carried concealed under my shell, but I lost my knife in the initial scuffle earlier on. Embarrassing, but there it is.

"Keep that peace pipe out of sight and let's shog it." He turns north.

"Why north, eh? Faster down Victoria and then west west west."

"Yeah," Tribal says, "past, what, two squat houses? Plus that's cutting through 2-Tone territory."

"Exactly! Rudeboys'll help, not hinder, eh?"

"No fuckin' way. We don't know where anyone stands right now. Plus, you're the one in the parka shell and bull's-eye, mate. If we end up in the middle of James jackets and Northern-Soul-keep-the-fucking-faith hard-liners, I'm the one with long hair and leather, not you, eh? Your Docs are safe—mine, not so much. It's the long and winding road for us, brother. Barton west then south on Queen."

"That's a long fucking walk, eh?"

"Right. So let's get started."

We shog north, eyes prying into each black gap between buildings. Despite the unknowns, we are half tempted to slip into one of those narrow chasms in the street-front façade, avoid altogether the night stalking of the other denizens of this place. We pause to discuss it, taking shelter by hunching down below street level in the murky recesses of a concrete stairway leading to a basement apartment with a faded and weathered "To Let" sign on the steel door.

And not a minute too soon. A white cargo van creeps around the corner behind us, the low, sputtering growl from its cancerous undercarriage marking its steady progress. That and the slow drag of metal on asphalt—the exhaust pipe dangling below like a lifeless limb, bouncing gently along until whatever connective tissue that still holds it in place finally rusts through. Its windowless, rust-pocked side is an ominous billboard, crudely decorated with a red swastika that has bled down its surface.

The van prowls along slowly, a drifting den of rabid wolves, hungry and alert. Maybe more like hyenas. Carrion eaters, scavengers, opportunists.

Fucking Nazi skins.

"Red lace turf," I murmur. "Great."

"White lace, red lace. What the fuck's the difference?" Tribal whispers viciously, gently squeezing his wrist between tentative fingers, wincing through the pain. "From what we saw tonight, I think the skins've put aside the finer points of their fucking politics. At least for now."

"Yeah. Wanna try the alleys? Could cut at an angle that way. The fucking Hitler Youth out there aren't turning in anytime soon, eh?"

Tonight, mods are scattered all over the north end of the Hammer—Hamilton, that is, our steel city home wrapping around the western tip of Lake Ontario. The north end is mostly industrial, but there are a few haunts scattered throughout. We were collectively vomited out of one recently, in fact, forced to make our way back to calmer waters by slogging through unfamiliar terrain. A shite portage, but you play the hand you're dealt, I guess.

Or just don't play the game at all, but that never occurred to us until later. When you're sixteen, a carefully constructed identity is everything.

Which was the initial reason for the dance—such as it was. There were others there, too, just preppie little fucks—yuppie larvae spawned in west-end neighbourhoods—making a show of toughing it out at an industrial sector north-end gathering. And, of course, a healthy cross-section of stoned skids (long hair, jean jackets and high-tops—invisible: they fit in anywhere), tight nervous pockets of black-clad cavers, the occasional thrash punk, and a pretty solid contingent of rudeboys. It was at a place called the Cinder Block North, a low-end, low-ceilinged basement convention hall owned by some down-and-out lodge and rented cheaply to whoever wanted it.

It started out all right because, although skinheads travel in packs, the numbers are usually low—four or five, six at most. But groups drifted in for over two hours. One minute it was a comforting sea of army green and bull's-eyes, Union Jacks and black lace Doc Martens. Then through the haze appeared rugged and bulky islands of braces and flight jackets, 24-hole red-laced gladiators and oxblood white-laced 14s. If you paid attention, you could watch the tectonic shift, islands merging into larger and more ominous landmasses. Teutonic tectonics, eh? Christ.

The rest was inevitable. Skins picked a target—a Jamaican rudeboy, predictably—and began taunting him. Couple of mods (and I mean street mods, not the fringe posers in their Carnaby Street mail-order 8-holes or store-bought desert boots and Fred Perry shirts) came to the rudeboy's defence. Words were exchanged, then punches, then a knife appeared and all fucking hell broke loose. Full-fledged boot party.

But Hamilton cops are pretty good. They weren't far away, they have a good nose for this sort of thing. They stormed the building, blocked the doors, and figured they could sort it out from there. Situation under control.

What a farcical disaster.

It was Sean D himself who dropped the first cop, steel toe to the balls and then, as the poor fuck folded in on himself, a heavy knee to the face. Out came a small forest of nightsticks in retaliation and then it was every man for himself.

Nice reaction time on the cop convergence, but whatever great white father planned this raid sure as shit didn't compensate for numbers. We exploded out of every doorway, scattering the blue-clad portal guardians like chaff in the wind, and the small pockets of fierce fighting began to merge into a riotous sea of heady violence. Fun and games, brothers and sisters, fun and games.

Insanity, really. Fifteen or twenty skins rolled a paddy wagon. A trio of cops were clubbing the living fuck out of some white-laced monster pinned up against a fence. I tripped over a girl—couldn't have been fifteen—curled up on the pavement and crying hysterically, blood pouring from a gash across her forehead. Tribal was suddenly there hauling me to my feet, into fists and boots, cops, mods, skins, shouting, screaming, running, pressed, pushed, punched—mosh-pit madness.

We fought through to the outer edge. Cops had more of a presence out there, a more unified front, but they were beyond damage control—they were in that myopic mode of seek and destroy, furiously scanning for the worst offenders of the civil code and then concentrating their efforts. Tribal and I passed right through them with maybe a dozen others, too insignificant to bother with, like silt through the sieve. I was a bit insulted, but they were after something specific.

It was back to isolated street scraps beyond the cop-lined border, but that was familiar territory for both of us. I'd lost my lot in the chaos—there'd been six of us, all street mods (except Tribal, of course), no girlfriends on this excursion. We were there to see what was what, anticipating the end result. Anyway, just my brother and me left and no way to make contact with the others.

We made the corner, into a narrow parking lot with three metres of chain link to climb at the end of it. Between two cars a pair of skins were laying the boots to some poor bastard, and I saw a bull's-eye on the way by. Kid was curled up to protect as much as he could, but these two assholes weren't stopping anytime soon.

I took a quick look around—none of their brethren within sight—and pulled my bat out, swinging hard at the one on the left.

The metal caught him just below his right ear, caving in his jaw with a satisfying crunch. Joints to jellyfish, he collapsed on the spot and then kind of kicked sporadically in pathetic little spasms.

Tribal must have turned when he heard me hit the skin—it was an audible thump of bone and meat—and sprung at the second one.

Who also had a bat. He was in mid-swing but Tribal intercepted, deflected the hickory with his hand, the crazy fuck.

Saved me, though. His bat smashed into the car instead of my head, and I had a second to slide my hand halfway down the shaft of my own and bayonet the fat end into his mug. This skin was a pug-faced bastard with cauliflower ears and a wiry mono-brow above two sunken, pig-dumb eyes.

I caught him mostly on the upper lip and nose. There was a muffled crack, like stepping on a piece of glass folded in a sodden newspaper. Split his palate, I think, or at least sent most of his front teeth down his throat and broke his nose. He fell back on his ass like a drunken bear.

"Get up!" I yelled at the mod, but he was pretty shaken. Ribs were probably cracked, too, but Tribal hauled him to his feet anyway with his good hand. He was young, scared shitless. Skinny little puke, maybe fourteen, just a wannabe who found out the hard way why you travel with mates. And he wore brand new 8-holes. At the time, so did my girlfriend.

Hardly worth the time, really, but what was done was done. Like I said, I'd lost my knife, so slitting laces was out of the question. It'd take too long to unlace the skins' boots—too bad, too, because they were both in black 14s.

Tribal wasn't as sentimental.

"C'mon, let's get over that fucking fence!" Good advice, of course, we weren't going to remain alone for much longer.

I don't know how Tribal managed it with his hand, but we were up and over pretty fast. We ran down the alley and cut across a rubbish-strewn patch of cracked concrete and weeds before finding a comfortably dark side street that headed south. For a bit, anyway.

From there we aimed cautiously for Cannon Street, but as I said, by the time we got there, that way was closed.

The van passes us by and turns down a side street eastward. Time to move. We spring up and out, Docs thumping hard on the pavement, a hard left and we slip into the narrow darkness between a bar (closed) and a high-rise tenement. We stop and listen.

The alley reeks of stale urine and, deeper in, that pungent, aggressively sharp stink of dumpster. We're alone, good time to reassess. Tribal's hand is pretty fucked, swollen and mottled and crooked.

"We need to get you seen, eh?" I say, mastering the obvious.

Tribal gives a noncommittal shrug. He hasn't mentioned his hand once—he's a tough bastard, even at fifteen.

"Cheers, by the way," I say. "For running interference, I mean. Sorry about the hand—I shoulda hit that ape-faced fuck on the right first . . . I didn't see the bat."

He holds his hand up, pokes it gently, contemplating it as if it were an interesting growth he'd recently discovered. Then he shrugs again.

"Don't matter, mate. It'll heal."

He offers no opinion on my decision to break up a private boot party, but he knows I couldn't let that go by. That's one thing about Tribal: he never interferes with anyone else's personal sense of justice.

But the next little wee-hours encounter we stumble upon . . . ah, that one neither of us can let go.

We cross Bristol and make Barton, turning west but keeping to the north side of the street. Shadows are deeper on that side, on account of the park. It stretches dark and inviting from Stanford to Wentworth.

We aren't too far in from the outer edge when we hear it: struggling, muffled crying, and harsh whispers eager and urgent. They come from just beyond an empty stretch of parking lot, by a picnic area cloaked in shadows. Dim moonlight reveals a little, but all the streetlights within fifty metres are out, broken for the purpose.

It's an old trick.

We look at each other askance, incredulity marking both our faces. Of all fucking times and of all fucking places. Tribal scans quickly, picks up a nearby beer bottle and hands it to me.

"Gimme that bat," he snarls. We stalk forward.

They have her pinned on her back, gagged with something black and crumpled—a torn strip of her leggings, maybe. Mini-skirt up around her belly. One of them squats above her head, holding down her frail shoulders with meaty paws, fingers digging into fragile flesh. Her body is so tiny, so immobile compared to her thin, pale legs that still kick and thrash fiercely against the fuck who works at cutting off her panties with a knife.

Three. Not skins—just night drifters, concert tees and running shoes. Could be worse. But they're focused, heady with whisky or beer, drunk on her terror, on her utter inability to stop the inevitable, empowered by the night, by the immensity of their scheme—that sort of thing is dangerously infectious, addictive.

And as we close in, outraged beyond reason, I understand: they are entrenched in this act, they couldn't see us if they'd wanted to at this moment, the reward is too near—they've cut through the meagre bits that cling pathetically to her hips, pulling her legs apart, opening her up to the cold indifferent night.

They breathe in heavy, rasping gasps, urgent and as yet unfulfilled, now only living mechanisms of obscene and deliberate intent, the central one tugging down his jeans, clumsy and urgent and one-handed, the other hand pawing, groping and digging between the girl's stick-like legs. The others holding her, more animal at this moment than human, jockeying for position, impatient.

That poor thing on the ground, hyperventilating and detaching, cutting the mooring lines as fast as possible. Bracing for unfathomable impact.

Jesus, I think.

We strike, silent and battered night gods wreaking vengeance, dispensing swift and brutal justice. But we are just as obscene, just as guilty, in our own way.

I sweep in from the right, coming up behind the guy pinning down her shoulders and ram my steel toe into his exposed groin as he squats above her, following with another kick that catches his cheekbone and sends him sprawling to the right. I save the bottle for follow-through.

Tribal does for the guy with the knife, crowning him with my bat—a loud and hollow knock, like the sound of one of those big blue plastic kid bats hitting a Wiffle ball. Comical, except for the circumstances.

The third fuck rolls out of the way and gains his feet, startled and enraged at our interference. He dodges right and left, as if he has to fake us out to get by. There's an entire empty field behind him, but that doesn't seem to occur to him. Reluctant to leave his mates, guilt-torn, who the fuck knows what keeps him there?

Then Tribal has an idea.

He points at the one he crowned. Soon-to-be victim of a backfire in natural selection. Ah, slipping from the alpha male position is a bitch. The prick is groggy, half-conscious, curled up on his side with blood welling up between the fingers pressed against the rap he received. His jeans are already around his knees. He had the knife, after all. He was going first.

The one I've dropped is regaining his breath, so we put the boots to him for a bit to settle him down again. Number three's still there, a few metres farther back now, still tensed up to bolt, still at a loss as to what he should do.

Tribal trades me bat for bottle and returns to the first would-be rapist, wary eye still trained on the third. As he leans down to pick up the knife, he lines the lip of the bottle up with the exposed ass of our fetal friend and almost gently inserts it. Then he stands up and savagely kicks it into place.

This next bit's disturbing, but I respect Tribal's sense of justice. He holds his hand out for the bat.

Smash.

But like I said, I feel guilty. The girl we've saved—and that's a relative term, because I'm sure some of the damage already done is irreparable—is the exact same kid I'd tripped over outside of the Cinder Block. Honest to God—you can't make this shit up. It's the cut on her forehead that gives it away, jagged and mostly crusted over, though bleeding through again due to recent duress. If I'd just picked her up like Tribal had done for me, she could've travelled with us. It's a small fucking world, but nothing short of a miracle she'd made it this far down Barton by herself.

Tribal doesn't buy it, though. She never would've even made the fence, he says.

Maybe, but I feel that karma is at work on some level.

We do our best to put her back together, but she's enduring some sort of silent, wide-eyed hysteria, waking night terrors, whimpering out loud only when one of us approaches her.

Tribal's little demonstration of rectal violence is enough for the third member of this little rapist triumvirate—he takes off into the park in a panic. My brother briefly discusses the possibility of stuffing the retrievable shards into the other fuck's mouth and kicking him in the chops, but the moment of crisis has passed. Just idle threats now.

I pick up the remains of the girl's leggings and sort of brush them off, an automatic and idiotic gesture, offering them to her. But it's like trying to coax a feral cat into the open. Tribal finally grabs the leggings and throws them at her.

"We don't have time for this," he snaps. "Look, we helped you, see? We ain't gonna hurt you, but we're not hanging around here either. None of us are safe out here, skin turf, eh? And it's still three hours til dawn."

She watches him with terrified eyes, her small fingers now grasping the ruined fabric in two tiny trembling fists. I can see Tribal's hand is really starting to bother him. Post-scrap lethargy is setting in, and without the adrenaline to keep him alert and vital, it must throb like a bastard.

Then I have a sudden revelation. I take off my shell and turn it inside out to hide the bull's-eye, holding it up like you do a beach towel for a child. She just sort of sinks right into it, wrapping it tight around her thin frame.

"Okay," Tribal says, "let's go."

Just under a kilometre down Barton on the far side of Victoria Avenue is Hamilton General Hospital. The anonymity certainly helps, and we make it in eleven or twelve minutes with our wayward waif following obediently in profound silence. We're already halfway to Victoria when Tribal nudges me and points at the girl's feet. One shoe. Too late to go back for it, though.

Tribal has put some thought into this on the walk—we can't dump her at a hospital in her condition without coming clean on our own recent nocturnal doings in the park. Can't just say we chased off some drunken would-be rapists, either. After all, when the trio sorts themselves out, this would be the logical next stop for them, too, and someone's bound to put two and two together.

I mean, a beating you can nurse yourself, but an ass full of glass? Cops and questions—no fucking thank you. And if we say nothing, just hand-deliver her to the E.R., it will look like we're a pair of conscience-ridden would-be's ourselves. And, of course, I need my shell back.

Standing outside the E.R. entrance, I put together a crude plan.

"Gimme five minutes," I say.

The E.R. is a fucking zoo, even at 3:00 a.m., so it isn't too hard to goop a jacket off one of the racks. I take a trench coat and meander out the way I came.

Our girl still waits in stunned silence with Tribal around the corner.

"She ain't much of a talker, eh?" Tribal notes.

I can't begin to fathom what she's feeling, but something is clearly broken. Nonetheless, the shell is just on loan.

"Here," I say, "I got you a coat. I'm gonna need the shell, eh?"

She complies immediately, not so much as a moment's hesitation. What a mess. The skirt hangs low and crooked on her naked hips, the blouse doesn't have a button left on it, they even cut her bra open. Fucking animals. I wrap her up and take her face in my hands gently but firmly, look her straight in those shell-shocked eyes.

"Get yourself inside and find a nurse, eh? Don't mention us—just tell them that some guys chased off those three assholes and you walked here yourself, understand?"

I know I'm getting through. She nods.

"Good girl. Here's some dosh to call your mom," I press a handful of change into her trembling hand, "and remember, little sister—you never saw us."

As I turn to leave she starts to sob. Jesus Christ. I take her thin shoulders, turn her toward the opening and point to the payphones. "Go call your mom," I whisper and give her a gentle push forward. She obeys, moving woodenly toward them.

Tribal sighs. "C'mon. Let's get the fuck outa here."

"What about your hand?"

"Let's get to Tina's—her boyfriend'll drive us to the Henderson." That was the hospital up on the Escarpment, three kilometres southeast, if you're a goddamn bird.

And the two of us discussing this ten metres from an emergency room.

Unfuckingbelievable.

Tina lives in a squalid little dump above a pawnshop on Catharine Street. Like the three other girls who share the second-storey hovel, Tina's a runaway, at thirteen the youngest by at least a couple years.

Pretty late for a visit, but under the circumstances we don't hesitate. Tribal kicks the street door a few times. Then a few more. Above us, someone opens a window.

"Who the hell's banging on the door? It's four in the morning!"

"Tina," I say, stepping away from the wall and into the dull light of the street lamp, "it's just us. Tribal's hurt. Let us in, eh?"

"Shit. Okay, just a minute."

Soon we hear the heavy turn-bolt click and Tina opens the door wearing nothing but an oversized Duran Duran T-shirt. We slip past her and up the stairs while she locks up.

The small room at the top of the stairs is drafty, but it still stinks of mildew and stale smoke. Jimmy lounges against the wall opposite the window, his lit cigarette contributing to the general lack of air quality. I shoot him a weary smile—he's a welcome surprise on this miserable bastard of a night.

"What happened to your brother?" Jimmy asks. He reads us quickly, assesses, even though the room is barely lit by the residual glow of the street lamp—unless you count Jimmy's cigarette heater. That's his way, though, streetwise far beyond his sixteen years. Jimmy just seems to know things.

"Nothing," Tribal says. "Just my hand."

"Cinder Block North," I add.

Jimmy nods sagely, pushes his mop of hair out of the way. Despite the cool weather, his thin frame is clad only in a T-shirt bearing the image of a

Tibetan prayer flag, some retro and ratty bellbottom jeans, and worn-out sandals. He offers us each a smoke from his pack as Tina finally comes in from the stairwell. She looks worried, agitated.

"She's never this late," she mutters.

Jimmy enlightens us. "Tina's worried about Jillian, and I'm the moral support. She was supposed to be home two hours ago."

Like Tina's other roommates, Jillian turns tricks to make ends meet. She's been like a big sister to Tina, more so than the other two roommates, but it's only a matter of time. Before Tina starts too, I mean. I see it now in Jimmy's eyes, not prediction but prophecy—he watches her fidget and pace. Jimmy sighs and lights another smoke.

Then Tina clues in, notices Tribal cradling his broken hand. "Jesus, Tribal! What happened?"

But Tribal, exhausted and irritable, slumps down on one of the thin mattresses with his back against the wall, and closes his eyes.

"Skin tried to take my head off with a bat," I interject. "Tribal deflected it with his hand."

"Wow, really?"

Sometimes it's easy to forget that Tina is only thirteen. But now she scrounges a bit for details, and no Jillian home to remind her that we don't ask each other for more than is offered. It's just not done. Same way she acts about Chris, her boyfriend—he's meant to be a secret because he's seventeen, but none of us would interfere.

Tina tries another angle. "I don't get it. You're a mod, but Derek's a skinhead, and you guys play gigs together! And Seamus, he's a skin, but you hang out with him and his friends."

"*Trojan* skins," I say, but I'm really looking for a mattress, too. Jimmy's on one, Tribal's on the other. Must be a couple more in the second room. "Derek, Seamus—they're Trojan skins. There's a difference."

Jimmy interrupts. "Tina, why don't you give Chris a call? Tribal's going to need a ride."

Chris is a harmless kid from the suburbs with two parents and his own car. Useful and easy to manipulate. Tina thinks the relationship's a secret because of the four-year difference—"People wouldn't understand," he tells her—but we know the truth. After all, what would mommy and daddy and the neighbours and his fucking math teacher say if they found out he was working every angle under the sun to have sex with a thirteen-year-old runaway living with teenage prostitutes in a Catharine Street squat house? Which was exactly what Tribal asked him the *last* time he needed a ride.

But Tina's confusion? Understandable. Skinhead street politics are a bit muddled—to say the least.

As for the Cinder Block North—well, in retrospect, it was a huge fucking mistake and the catalyst for what would be a solid year of boot culture infighting, but what could we do? Had to be there—every fucking face and ticket, skin and skaboy from east Toronto to Windsor showed up for that one.

What a right bloody mess.

Later, we'd reminisce every once in a while, Tribal and me, about those Hamilton street days, recalling our random acts of senseless folly. And there were many. All of us, we wore our teenage pride like flags, and for my lot they were bull's-eye battle standards of rootless stupidity.

Still, one good thing came out of it all: our little altercation with the authorities got enough negative media attention to piss off some heavy-hitting Trojan skins from Toronto—*real* skinheads, that is, followers of the original movement. They started probing about, showing up downtown on weekends in small groups and mixed, too, with street mods and sometimes rudeboys. Always a race mix. They were SHARPs—Skinheads Against Racial Prejudice, that is, real Spirit of '69 street soldiers.

The media had put a neo-Nazi spin on the Hamilton skinhead movement and, although not far off, it sure as shit wasn't true of the movement's origins. These skins were here to make right sure the local white- and red-lace crews knew they had their attention. They didn't convert too many skins from the Hamilton scene, but over the next year most of the north- and east-end mods traded parka shells for braces and 10-holes for 14s.

Evolution, I suppose.

Chapter Two

Glasgow, Aberdeen, Bristol, Birmingham, Cardiff, Belfast—many of us are right off the boat, or were raised by those who were. And, of course, there's no one as rabid as the expatriate. Hamilton's replete with pubs that echo those of homelands left behind: dark wood and close quarters, house darts and cribbage board behind the bar, Belhaven and Tartan and Boddingtons and a dozen others on tap. Much of our own vocabulary, just echoes of street slang imported, too, unapologetically mixed with Canadian vernacular.

The line in the sand's been imported, too, boot culture divided neatly: mods, rudeboys and Trojan skinheads on one side, and a menagerie of racist bigots on the other.

Not that lines aren't crossed.

—

Summer now, and hot. Ten months since the Cinder Block North night and things have settled down a bit.

As for the crossed lines, I blame my guitar. And maybe my lack of foresight the night before.

I met her while busking in Gore Park, that small wedge of green that runs along King Street. Noticed her boots first, actually. Steel toes, for kicking, she'd explained. Small girl, but a chelsea nonetheless, inanimate property of some skinhead or other. The city's still full of them—lurking in squat houses hidden away in the dank corners of two- and three-storey buildings, above record shops and bars and strip clubs, even ethnic restaurants (Chinese, Indian). Fucking hypocrites, the lot. She wasn't all that interested in my opinion, though. To her, I was just another busker, a street musician accessory. Temporary, not like the permanent installments—bus shelter vagrants, pigeons, refuse, traffic, shoppers. I told her I liked her boots. Skinheads love talking about them, the stupid bastards. I did, though—oxblood 14-hole rangers, real AirWair elite. What was I supposed to do? She stopped, listened to a song and threw a couple bones in the guitar case. Got to be polite, I suppose.

Sleeping with a chelsea isn't like sleeping with a normal girl. The thing is the politics. Not the standard ebb and flow bullshit, but the logical fallout when it gets back to whatever kennel has her in leash. She got pissed afterwards, too, because she saw the RAF bull's-eye sewn onto the back of my army parka shell (the same American M-51) and she put the pieces together. Thought she would duck out for a quick intermission and found herself quite literally in the wrong scene, the enemy camp—the last guy a self-respecting skinhead girl wants to be caught with is a mod, even a street mod like me (and us more skinhead than not). But what the hell did I care?

She wasn't as convincing as she tried to be, though. Angry, sure, but maybe not so much at me. And that ludicrous swastika in the small of her back, exactly where a butterfly or heart or something playful should be. I watched it as she stormed around, collecting her shit. Sharp-tongued little thing, but the words were spit out as if they were foreign objects, stored there in her tiny mouth for safekeeping by someone else. Feculent constructs of hate, the sort of terms you'd expect to read in underground sub-culture magazines, or lyrics scribbled onto the album jacket of some pro-Aryan Nation LP.

Funny observation, as it turned out—the leash for this particular chelsea was held by the drummer of a white power band called the MA-1 Flights. We'd actually played a gig about two months ago at the same venue, I only remember because the sneaky bastards had stolen a patch cord and a couple of power strips from us after the show.

Karma, eh? Amazing.

The chelsea's rage expended, she stormed out into the dawn and I followed not long after. Already the heat was filling the silent streets. We'd spent the night in one of the many abandoned or forgotten corners of this city, squalid and murky storerooms or weatherworn attics you shared with pigeons, mice. Easy enough to find if you knew where to look.

But Sunday morning in last night's clothes is the most depressing way to face the corner of King and James. No buses, hardly any traffic at all. And the people. A scattering of old men emerging from their ritual of shuffling around the dead corridors of the underground mall, street preacher toting a yellow wad of soggy newspaper rank with his own urine and a styrofoam cup for change, some strung-out thrash punk foraging the sidewalk ashtrays for enough butts to roll himself a cigarette.

And one girl, coming out of a narrow door that leads to the tenements above the street. Young, bleach-blonde and self-conscious, but no makeup. Even in the voluminous ratty sweatshirt that falls almost to her knees I recognize her—my brother brought her around once months ago. Stripper, I'd guessed and she'd corrected me, of course. *Exotic dancer*, she'd snarled. Exotic, right. Still, we know one another immediately, but pretend not to by unspoken agreement. That's something I've done too many times and still don't understand. Politics, maybe.

A shower. Agenda item number one, I decide. Tina lives close by, but things aren't great right now. By which I mean Jimmy was right, these streets are consuming her. She now shares Jillian's profession. And often her regulars. I decide to give Stephanie a call instead. She's not too far away, Westdale, maybe an hour on foot.

Westdale's a nice neighbourhood, mostly wooded streets and old houses owned by landlords who rent rooms out to university students. Some families too, like Steph's. She still lives at home, but her parents are never there. Absentee landlords, she calls them. I don't know where they go—she's never said and I've never asked. There's a pay phone in a plaza partway down King Street, so I begin the trudge.

I prefer a hard guitar case for the sake of the instrument because I'm not gentle with things by nature, but the goddamned thing gets heavy after a while. Doc Martens are probably the most comfortable walking boot ever invented, though, especially with the ranger soles.

Funny about that chelsea—she saw I was wearing black lace 10-holes, but she didn't say anything. Usually you hunt around for the ties—there are only a handful of possibilities with Docs, and I obviously wasn't a skinhead. Or maybe that was obvious only to me.

"Hello?" Pretty groggy. I feel bad about it but I like Steph's company.

I've never been sure why—she's pretty apathetic about everything. Callous, maybe, is more accurate.

"Hey, Steph. It's just me. I'm in the neighbourhood. Are you alone?" Always polite to ask, just to give her the chance to say no, even though we both know the truth. She never lets a guy stay over. She used to, she told me once when we were drunk, out at the Point, but she always got this 2:00 a.m. anxiety attack about it—she'd wake up convinced that he was breathing all of her air, as if you only got doled out so much per room per night. Stephanie and her surreptitiously anonymous air-hogging flings. Jesus Christ.

"Whaddaya say? Can I drop by?"

"Mmm."

"Cheers. I'll be about an hour."

"Make it two, will you?" She needs two hours to do anything. I'd forgot.

"Two it is," I say, and hang up.

—

Hamilton's a steel town. Even the nice parts are tainted by the omnipresent factories and mills, the ominous call of foghorns from the lakers as they drift into the harbour like impossibly slow leviathans. The harbour never has less than six or eight of them, those Great Lakes cargo ships that seem to take thirty minutes and more to crawl under the lift bridge. They feed the fires, as it were, carrying slag and coal, coke and pig iron to the yawning furnaces, sacrificial fodder for the industrial gods. And, of course, the rail lines. Dozens of rusted and weatherworn roads that lead to one place: the north end. The rest of the city is bound by a common sense of oneness, blindly tied into those immense steel mills that squat like idle, mountainous, fire-belching dragons beside the water.

Except Westdale. It's like its own self-contained town within the Hammer itself, an intellectual retreat somehow removed from its own surroundings. It lounges comfortably below the escarpment, hemmed in by the university and Coote's Paradise, an inlet bird sanctuary with a wooded point that juts out into the water. That's the only part of the place we use. It's all Crown land, but the cops can't be bothered to hike out to the end, even when we have a fire going. Stupid of us, really: there's only one way in or out.

Stephanie won't go again, anyway. She's not the night-hiking type. Takes her self-image very seriously, like spending a night in the woods will somehow leave a mark visible only to the clairvoyant eyes of the shallow yuppie larvae-swarm of which she, I am sorry to say, is an integral member. She doesn't see it, of course. She dumped her last boyfriend, Gavin, about six months ago. I was confused—Steph never complained about Gavin and both of them were equally infatuated with her, so there wasn't any conflict of interest there.

Jimmy puts it into perspective, as he always does. "He no longer matched her skirt," he says in that deadpan tone he always uses when talking about her.

"Where'd he go?" I ask. It's like Gavin fell off the face of the planet.

"She probably gave him to the fucking Salvation Army," Jimmy says.

No one knew why Jimmy and I were so close. Didn't stand to reason, really. The history was there, though, rooted deep in things neither of us was obliged to explain or defend. He introduced me to Stephanie, actually. It was a while ago. She was in a state of indignation—Jimmy had insulted her dignity by refusing to sell her Benzedrine on account of her age. Told her to stick with east-coast shrooms if she wanted the extra kick.

"Ethics," he told me later. I laughed at him, but he was serious. "I deal by my rules," he said, as if that explained it all. It did, too.

Jimmy was my closest friend, but I didn't do drugs (yet). Still, I hung out with a guy who never carried less than a half quad of pot and a hundred hits. I wasn't against them. I just didn't do drugs myself for the exact same reason I spent so much time with actual dealers—it was one of those things that separated me from the rest of them.

Tina always laughed and called me a hypocrite. You know what my defence was? Ethics. Fuck it—it was all a matter of semantics anyway.

—

Stephanie opens the door a bit too quickly, as if she's been waiting for me. "Hi! Come in, come in," she says, pulling me across the threshold by my sleeve. Once inside with the door safely shut, though, everything goes back into slow motion, her standard operating speed.

"What the fuck, Steph?" I'm a little offended, but it's mostly for show. I respect her priorities. She knows this, but feels the need to offer up the obligatory explanation.

"Listen, this isn't downtown or the north end. If you're going to walk around dressed like that, I'd prefer it if you used my back door."

The obvious response crosses my mind, but it's too early in the conversation and I stay serious. Not exactly my forte, to be perfectly honest, but she's not the type. I used to think it was a façade, but not anymore. I mean, it is, but she's woven so much of herself into the fabrication of the sophisticate that it would be a shame to ruin it.

Anyway, she's put the last couple of hours to good use. Painted, primped and pressed—"height of fashion," as the saying goes.

Stephanie's short and just a touch heavy for her size. Not that you'd know unless you're looking. Long auburn hair, pretty face, pouting lips, and the eyes—good Christ. Green. Actual green, not hazel with greenish tinge or that oh-look-her-eyes-are-kind-of-green-in-the-sunlight green. I mean *green.*

I offer to take off my boots but she just shrugs, so I don't bother. We pass through to the kitchen ("breakfast nook," she calls it), and I have to smile. In the hall is an African mask, some sort of tribal abstract painting, a couple of carefully placed *objets* . . . an anti-apartheid fashion statement. It's perfect: trite, pointless, ephemeral. Global politics reduced to five or six essentially unrelated items that'll eventually end up in a box at the Salvation Army. Probably right beside Gavin, the poor bastard.

Honest to God, Stephanie kills me. The last time I was here it was all *glasnost* and *perestroika* on these same walls. Jimmy was with me. It wasn't long after Steph and I first met. Hard to forget: she felt the need to point out to me that one of the framed and matted posters was a reproduction of a painting done by a Polish *worker*. She stressed the word, as if it were a cryptic riddle to which I was a mere initiate. *Proletariat finger painting*, I'd said, joking. She laughed and so did Jimmy, but for different reasons.

Later, while we were getting coffee, Jimmy said that he once convinced

Steph that Brezhnev was an anti-Soviet jewelry manufacturer, making earrings and pendants for the downtrodden comrades of the CCCP to keep their spirits up. Apparently, she had regurgitated said information to a select group of university students as an icebreaker.

Steph drifts slowly down the hall in front of me, consciously on display. Always practising.

I can't help myself, still lamenting the loss of the back door joke. "Hey—where's the Polish poster? The perestroika art?"

"My God," she drawls, as if pitying me. "We got rid of that thing *ages* ago!"

"Too bad, eh? You should have kept it. It was the ultimate fashion statement."

She doesn't commit herself to more than a suspicious glance over her shoulder and a smirk. She doesn't get it, of course, but Jimmy would.

Thing is, I mean it: for her, it *is* the ultimate standard, the banner of her kind—well, for all of us, really.

Perestroika. Restructuring.

Hey, who among us doesn't?

Chapter Three

I collect fragments, remnants of rag and bone of sorts. *Old fires to ashes and ashes to the earth*, right? Collecting bones of man and beast, we all collect something. To this, I add a phone call (collect), four years later—in 1989—from Tel Aviv.

I saw it falling, shit, farewell to the empire, man. From up on the rooftops, we could see it all falling.

What fell? Where?

It all fell. Into the sands, into the sea. East, west. What does it matter?

But what? What fell? Jimmy? Jimmy, where's Deb?

We'd been above ground too long, man. From up there, up on the rooftops, you could see it all falling.

But where? Where is she?

Down. Gone. I lost her. In a crowd.

What do you mean, gone? Deb's there, right? I mean, she's fine, isn't she?

Swallowed. Sea and sand, I told you.

Swallowed by what? For fuck's sake, lost her where?

You aren't listening. It swallowed her! Tel Aviv. It swallowed her. This place, this place swallows everything.

How? What the fuck are you talking about? Hello? You still there, man? Hello?

Jimmy! Hello—

Hello?

Fuck.

—

Stephanie and I are just friends. It's never been any different, and I hope that's the way it stays. We don't really know each other very well, to be quite honest. I mean, we've revealed things to each other under the influence (me, more so than her) but if that's your medium for honesty, then forget it.

Jimmy's the real reason. He introduced us and there's some tension between them. Not sure what kind—I'm not very good at the details—so to be on the safe side I just assume they were once together. I could ask Jimmy, I guess, but *him* I know: deep down, he'd assume that I was either interested or had already slept with her.

That's a road I don't want to walk again, although the first (and last) time a girl came between us I was so goddamned naïve I didn't realize that I'd even crossed a line. There's the measure of a friend. He forgave. He forgot. We moved on.

Still, the tension is there, palpable and lurking. I've been with some of Stephanie's friends, Jimmy's been with a couple too, and there was (inevitably perhaps) some crossover.

Jimmy watches when Steph and I talk, reading the signs, divining the portents. No need—as far as I can tell, Steph isn't interested in coming between us. Or maybe she just genuinely isn't interested in me at all.

'Course, the irony is that he shows up at Steph's door as I'm coming out of her shower. What the hell can I do? I act casual, say *oi*, finish pulling on my shirt.

"Heard you were in the neighbourhood. Thought I'd drop by," he says. He doesn't even act surprised to see me. Pleased, is more the word.

"Right, cheers. Glad you're here—it'll save me the walk over to your place." Which is true.

Stephanie looks up at me with that tragically bored expression on her face. "I called Jimmy about an hour ago to let him know you'd be around. I figured that was your next stop anyway."

Disaster averted. Damn, she's clever.

The coffee shop is about a ten-minute walk from Steph's, but she doesn't come with us. First, it's outside her self-proclaimed perimeter of acceptable walking distance. Second, she's mortified to be seen with us in

Westdale. Downtown it's fine—in fact, she makes a spectacle of herself when she's with us. Her prissy crowd's terrified of the main strip. They dart from the front entrance of Jackson Square to the taxi like neurotic field mice. As if packs of mods or skinheads are looking for the opportunity to jump them for their fucking penny loafers. She'll waylay some guy with a name like Joshua or Wesley in mid-bolt and talk about anything. I guess we're supposed to eye him menacingly and lick our chops or something. Fucking ridiculous.

But here amongst her own tribe, forget it. In the world according to Steph, we've illegally transcended the social barrier. Well, for now. We're on the bildungsroman express like everyone else, right?

There's an old guy and his wife in our regular seats, so we take the table next to them. You can only smoke at the one end, and Jimmy can't go more than ten minutes without.

It's a clean place, a far cry from the fetid receptacles for the flotsam and jetsam of wasted humanity that you find downtown. I should know—Jimmy's on a first-name basis with most of them. Not me, though. Yours Truly is now an outsider because of the present demographics—skins, punks, skids, cavers, Asian tongs, that's your cross-section *du jour* (Steph's expression). My kind aren't welcome since the incident in the north end, but that's another story. Still, I'm more or less fine. Jimmy's the metaphorical peace pipe. I've become his nameless avatar, an extension of his consciousness. Even among the red-lace Nazi skins. Very strange arrangement, but there are reasons for everything.

"So," he begins, and I cringe a bit. I'm still feeling guilty about Jimmy arriving as I finished showering at Steph's, though I shouldn't. "Did you tell Steph who you were with last night?"

How the hell could he possibly know that? He smiles, just a bit, and a trickle of smoke slips out of the corner of his mouth and creeps up his face. I, for my part, am completely thrown off guard.

"How—where—who the hell told you?"

He takes a leisurely drag, savouring my confusion. He tugs playfully on one of his dreads, opens his mouth as if to speak, and then blows a stream of smoke at me with a cunning smile. Fucking catfish, he is.

"Speak, you silly sod! Who?"

"Tiny Sue, of course," he says smugly.

I'm confused however. It must show in the stupid blank stare which is the sole crop of his little revelation.

"Tiny Sue," he repeats, slowly and a bit louder, as if I were a bit daft, slow to process the spoken word. I just shake my head and lift my hands palms up.

Jimmy looks at me with sudden comprehension. He's discovered the problem.

"That's the chelsea's *name*," he offers.

Ah. Names weren't exchanged, circumstances being what they were. I just nod slowly to let him know that all the wires are now connected. "Hmm," I mumble, "small world." Jimmy's mentioned her name before in passing, but usually in conversations to which I was a third-party observer. Invisible voyeur, actually.

"Well? Did you?" he persists.

"What, tell Steph? Are you fucking mad?"

Too much foul language for the old folks, apparently. They get up in a huff and make a big deal about cleaning off their table, as if this applied lesson in responsible public behaviour will turn us from already predetermined paths of destruction. Then, in the middle of the not-quite-under-her-breath "kids these days" bit with which the old lady must leave us, she farts.

Jimmy's eyebrows shoot upwards, arched in mock alarm. I laugh, rude bastard that I am. The couple makes an undignified and hasty escape, perhaps further compelled to abandon the field by Jimmy announcing, "Thus endeth the lesson!"

We occupy the table immediately, of course.

Flatulent old women aside, I'm still curious why Jimmy would even ask the question. Two years ago, another chelsea split Steph's lip open in a fight. Well, it was more of an argument about racial tolerance that ended in a pretty decent punch. This was all before I knew her, but I've heard the story about three hundred times. Stephanie still has a tiny scar—she's very self-conscious about it.

"So," Jimmy says, tapping ash onto the floor, "the chelsea didn't come up."

"You know me better than that, brother," I say, picking up the loose ends. "Steph's sensitive enough about the present, eh? Why dredge up the past?"

Jimmy just smiles in his furtive way. "Just asking, brother, just asking. You're not always in tune with the scene, you know. You forget that we live between the strata, not just on the top layer."

"Fuck off," I offer, as a point of principle. He's right, though. I have a terrible time with the big picture. Thus the chelsea. Tiny Sue I mean.

"Hey, I'm not telling you anything you don't already know, eh?"

"Yeah, yeah. Well, don't worry. I didn't tell her anything. And she didn't ask, come to think of it." That bit is weird—Steph is the proverbial crossroads for insignificant gossip. A tidbit from my sex life is exactly the type of crap she files away for the future. Which is how she knows quite a bit about me, but I know hardly anything about her.

"Did you busk yesterday?" he suddenly asks.

"Mmm. Only a couple of hours."

"Make much?'

I shrug. "Touch over thirty bones, I guess. Gave a bit to Teddy. I busked on his corner."

"Ah. Well, we all collect something, I guess. Try anything new?"

He wants to know about a song he'd written last week. Not a bad advertising method, really. Busk some material downtown and have a small stack of flyers available advertising the next gig. "I did about half of the new playlist," I say. "It went all right, I guess. Flyers taken, anyway."

"Good, good," he says, nodding absently. "We'll give it another hour and then phone the others. I want to change some shite around on a couple songs."

"Great," I say flatly. "Ewan loves when you do that. Should be good for a right proper scrap." Ewan's our drummer. I don't care about changes, personally. Neither does the lead guitarist, Derek, although he bitches every time, just to be an asshole.

"Hey, while we're on the topic," Jimmy continues, "how'd the new song do, far as you can tell?"

"Well," I smile, "it's mostly popular with the chelseas."

Jimmy rolls his eyes, lights another smoke.

"Look, here's the thing," I say after a pause. "You're right, I mean about the chel—Tiny Sue, that is—and the big picture shite. But that's not the whole problem."

"Okay," he concedes, curiously. "Then what else?"

"Well," I begin, but I don't really know what I'm trying to say. Thing is, it's all tied in to the strata—me, Jimmy, the scene, everything—and I get sick of it. Lost in the layers, I guess. I give it a shot anyway.

"It's like this. When I add up the shite I'm sure of, you know, feel instinctively, and then take into account all the crap that people—" Stuck. Fuck.

"Project upon you?" he offers.

"Right! Project upon me—and you, and all of it, really—then this messes up my perception of, well, me."

Sounds hackneyed as hell, all the comforts of a cliché, but Jimmy doesn't laugh. Instead, he sighs, and says, "Look, I don't care if you sleep with Stephanie."

I don't know how I react, but it must be a pretty funny sight, because Jimmy can't hold it together for too long. He starts guffawing like an idiot. "I'm kidding! I'm just fucking with you!" Tears actually come to his eyes, he's laughing so hard.

"Fuck you—that's not funny." But I smile, in spite of myself.

Jimmy does take me seriously, though, and I love him for it. He pulls himself together and says, "Look, brother, you just have to be the chameleon to a point, you know? Look at me—what am I?"

Dreads, Hendrix t-shirt (with the obligatory pinhole burns, so sayeth the prophet), green combats, oxblood 14s. I don't really know what to say, so I try what comes to mind.

"You're, you know, Jimmy."

"Exactly!" He punctuates it with a finger, as if keeping score. "But you're biased. See, you know more, we've been through too much for you to answer any other way." He sometimes jokes with casual acquaintances, calling me his chronicler. Which is technically true. "So, I'd answer the same way if you asked me the same question—we're friends, right? I don't identify you by bull's-eyes or 10-holes, or the fact your whole demeanour changes anytime you're in contact with a pack of mods—" (It's true, I'm embarrassed to admit.) "You—all of you, mods, skins, rudeboys, even punks, your whole *Oi!* culture—you have some sort of alpha wolf sixth sense as soon as you're in company! Fucking amazing—within five seconds, you've determined pecking order into . . . what do you mods call it?"

"Faces numbers tickets," I mumble.

"Faces, numbers, and tickets," he repeats, and another finger rises in triumph. Then he looks at his hand and frowns, as if this second finger leapt out joyfully of its own accord, distracting him with tangents. It retreats and he returns to his original point. "Look, man, *this* is the thing, if I might borrow your expression—remember that time last year when we found Teddy? The skins? The alley?"

I nod. He means last autumn when we came across this homeless wreck off of James street, and I, moron that I am, stood my ground between a couple of skins and Jimmy.

"Well, that's it. That's who you are. Music, scene, pretenses all aside, that's it." He sits back, smug, and taps his smoke on the table.

"What, too stupid to keep off the beaten track? Letting those two assholes get that close? That wasn't exactly my shining moment."

"Don't talk shite! You were willing to take a hit for me, you silly fuck!"

"You would have done the same—you *have*, in point of fact." He can't argue with that. Jimmy's bailed my ass out of more situations than I care to remember. Running interference was the least I could do, even back then, never mind since.

"Not the point. Defining moments, brother. That's what it's all about, for all of us."

The Polish paintings, that day I first met Steph, rush back upon me. Then their African replacements, I say to myself. And then I say it to him.

"Ah," Jimmy says, and he smiles that furtive catfish smile, his mouth curling up in the way of his kind: ageless, wise, and reckless. "I'll see you at practice. I don't think that bull's-eye and you have much more of a future together, though."

And then he's gone.

So, yeah. Tiny Sue. Looking at her, I guess the name fit in some weird way.

—

The evening before, in Gore Park, I'd been on Teddy's corner with my guitar. Saturday night and no gig isn't a good sign, so you do what you can.

Teddy's corner was a good one for busking, but you had to mind the street ethics. What I mean is, much of downtown was claimed, the unofficial territory of that homeless tribe of panhandlers and sad-eyed street installments who depended (equally) on human sympathy and mild weather. It was good form to fork over some dosh if you set up shop on someone's turf, and we'd known Teddy for a while—almost a year, in fact.

I met him maybe a month or so after the Cinder Block scrap, me still sixteen and he not too old—maybe in his early thirties—down behind James Street, a homeless wreck who'd just had the boots put to him by a couple of skinheads: Billy Hardcore and one of his goon sidekicks, to be precise. I knew because I saw that pair of fuckwits sprawled out on the steps by the entrance to Jackson Square, guffawing their dumb-shit white supremacist asses off and imitating the poor bastard's attempts to defend himself.

Jimmy was with me, the two of us heading east along King to hook a left on James. We passed pretty close to where they were sitting—well within bat swing range—and I wasn't exactly trying for inconspicuous: my M-51 army shell was a proverbial street mod battle flag, massive RAF bull's-eye in the dead centre of my back and my jeans rolled to show off the heavy steel-toe oxblood 14s (new acquisition), vertical scars all the way up each tongue from slitting the laces. But they were laced now and right proper—ladder style, not crossed—with Doc Marten traditional black.

Hardcore and I made eye contact, his drifting down to what was once clearly *Oi!* culture property and then back up to the inviting sneer on my mug. I'd been waiting for the opportunity to scrap with this piece of dog shit for a while, and I think he shared the sentiment. There are just certain people you instinctively detest.

So I was fine with it and so was he—a cool autumn afternoon, plenty of privacy on the flat roof of Jackson Square just up the stairs, sirens down toward Catharine Street guaranteed that beat cops were otherwise occupied. Two-to-one was an obvious disadvantage, but my reputation for street fighting was well-earned (he said modestly) and Hardcore knew it.

But now was not the time. It was Jimmy's presence that postponed these festivities—never fuck with the Source or his companions, a standing order of Sean D himself.

That's what Sean D called Jimmy: the Source. A nickname sardonically bequeathed, not to be mistaken for a sign of familiarity or friendship. The self-proclaimed street lord of Hamilton was a stone-cold skinhead ex-con who ran a white-lace crew of about twenty. White Power skins were plentiful back in the day, but Sean D kept his crew to a set number. Even red-lace Nazi crews and the Anarchy skins knew better than to break this commandment: nobody wanted to fuck with him, he was a right proper savage bastard and there was no place in this city you could go if you were stupid enough to cross him. Sean D's lieutenants—a pair of hulking monsters named Glasgow and Will—were relentless war dogs when let off their leashes. And they could find anyone.

Jimmy's own revered status was a direct result of supply-and-demand street economics. Even when every well in the city and beyond ran dry, Jimmy could conjure up at least the necessities if not the luxuries. Mostly this was because he skimmed and stashed for the droughts. Always keep the three D's, Jimmy said—Dexedrine, Durophet, and Drinamyl. Only the tragically oblivious fucked with Jimmy, but that's why one of us—me or Tribal or Funhouse or even Derek—always went with him when he headed downtown. Every once in a while some strung-out junkie would grow overenthusiastic at the sight of Jimmy and assault him in some way or another.

Still, neither Billy nor I could let things pass in silence, decorum demanding at least a polite exchange of opinions. Since King and James was technically skin territory, he was the one who started. "Nice boots, asshole. Don't plan on keeping them too long."

"Yeah?" I returned. "If you want a piece of them now stand up and I'll kick you in the cunt."

But Jimmy cut us off.

"Civil words, gentlemen—no need for further pleasantries," his unassuming tone reminding Hardcore and his mate of the Baldur's charm arranged by their own angry Odin.

We nonetheless exchanged a few more epithets and insults, all unoriginal and predictable, before moving out of range.

In those days it was difficult for a mod to navigate the flow of downtown foot traffic safely—too close to the north end incident at the Cinder Block, skinhead factions were still under an uneasy truce and happily waging war on the tolerant side of boot culture: mods and rudeboys, primarily, but the occasional Trojan skin fell victim—hacking away mindlessly at the very roots of their own movement. After all, the entire boot culture scene started with our lot, our cultural ancestors. Twenty-five years before, I mean, in the East End London of the '60s. Racist skinheads were offshoots, sub-species mutations. "Abortions," was how our mate Derek put it once, the standard Trojan skin opinion.

So around the corner we went, Jimmy contemplating Benzedrine and me raging at the unfairness of things downtown, when Jimmy suddenly cut across James Street and headed toward an alley opening. I followed out of habit, oblivious to his motive and absorbed in my own petty world. I awakened to our new surroundings when the dumpster stench suddenly struck me. It was a cool afternoon and the smell didn't carry, so we were twenty metres in before I was aware.

And at Jimmy's feet was the cause of his sudden swerve into the alley, a skeletal wretch crying into the snot and blood-smeared sleeve of a filthy winter jacket. He was in his thirties and clearly homeless, though unfamiliar, given we all knew the regular street installments by sight and often by name.

A right fucking mess he was, too: half-moon welt on his grimy forehead where he'd taken a steel toe, one side of his face all torn up because they'd ground his head into the sewage-covered pavement of the alley floor, right eye swollen completely shut, still curled up fetus-style from the boot party to his ribs and gut. He was clawing away at the ground, trying to reach a trampled paper bag just out of range. The knuckles and tops of his fingers on that hand were all raw and bloody, too, and his little finger jutted out at a gruesome angle.

The bag he was vainly reaching for was covered in colourful bits of trash—he'd decorated it with scraps of shiny paper and those fake feathers you find on kids' toys like souvenir tomahawks and big chief headdresses. I nudged it toward the outstretched hand with my boot, but he suddenly snatched his arm back as if he'd just noticed a scorpion coming toward him, tucking his battered face into the crook of his elbow and whimpering loudly. I stood there in mild confusion.

"You're wearing Docs," Jimmy pointed out.

Oh yeah. I gently kicked the bag toward him anyway, then stepped back to survey. He scooped it into his body, hugging it while he cried. At sixteen, I wasn't exactly the model of sympathy, but I did feel bad for this poor bastard.

"Maybe we could call an ambulance or something," I suggested.

Jimmy was angry, though. He may have been a chameleon in terms of image—mohawk to dreads to shaved head to shag—but he never approved of violence, even on the rare occasions when we had to fight on his behalf. He assessed, then squatted down, talked quietly to the guy until the sobbing ceased. For my part, it began to dawn on me that this alley was just enough off the beaten track for certain elements to make exceptions to Sean D's regulations. I had my bat under the shell, that was some assurance, and a decent blade in one of the deep side pockets, but alone was still alone. I kept a weather eye on the street end.

Jimmy took too long. Couldn't get the wreck to his feet, too scared, babbling nonsensically about losing his bed and his room and almost losing his treasure. The bag, I supposed. And I watched, the wyrd fluttering about me on ominous crow wings, as Billy Hardcore and his sidekick sauntered into the alley, bored, for round two.

They stopped short, hardly believing their luck. Then, with wolfish grins and eyes of malice, they stalked forward. Billy unwound the length of chain around his waist, heavy padlock at its end falling with a clunk onto the ground and dragging behind with a dull metallic scrape. Sidekick didn't have anything, that I could see. I pulled my knife out and opened it, slipping the blade into the top of my boot. I'd start with the bat and see where things went.

In the confines of the alley, I wasn't feeling the reckless confidence that you get out on the street proper. But that was just shite, doubt being your worst enemy—outthink and you can outfight. We all knew that, in principle.

"Oi, Jimmy," I said, quiet and tight, "clear off, mate."

Jimmy looked up then, taking in everything. He said something to me in a casual tone, but the words didn't penetrate—ears roaring, planning the best swing to guarantee a follow-through, adjusting stance, my mind flying through the scenario: *stay close to the left wall and under the pull-down fire escape Billy's right-handed eliminate a sweep from his good side chain's too damn long for overhand with the pull-down above me the other one's a pussy too small to be more than a crutch for Billy's ego he'll wait to see what's what, me, I'll exaggerate high but arc low and into the kneecap, old trick but he's a stupid fuck it just might work—*

—but before I could, Jimmy was already in motion, cigarette hanging carelessly from the side of his mouth, one hand in his pocket. Walking toward them as if they were no more than lost King Street shoppers.

Damn it, I thought, *if I have to give up position I'm screwed. Can't think on the fly, not like Tribal can.* But Jimmy removed his hand from its pocket and brought it up slowly, accusatory finger stretching out from the clenched fist until it (I swear to God) stopped them dead in their tracks.

"Billy Hardcore!" Jimmy thundered with all the zeal of a mad-eyed prophet. "You and Angel turn around, or find a way of explaining to the entire skinhead scene why the only things available in the dry season are glue and over-the-counter Gravol!"

There he stood, drug-rug poncho draped about him like a windblown and sand-battered desert robe, vintage sandals almost hidden in the trash strewn at his feet, finger frozen in space and cloaked in the terrible shadow of Consequence.

Hardcore blinked, as if emerging from some reverie to find himself in a compromising position. He mumbled something, a sub-moronic attempt at appearing nonchalant, and did exactly that: turned around and wandered out the way he came, the oddly named skinhead Angel at his heels.

I shook my head, amazed, and replaced my gear.

Jimmy, eh? My fucking hero.

And this wreck in the alley? That was Teddy.

We cleaned him up—nothing broken, cuts were superficial, finger just dislocated—and got him out of there. I popped his finger back in for him (fingers, broken noses, cracked ribs—these things we could fix ourselves) and we headed for Gore Park.

He'd been released from an institution a couple days before, "outpatient status" or some such shite, and then refused re-admittance. I didn't understand why: I mean, I was only sixteen, but I didn't need a degree in psychiatry to tell that Teddy was about as cat-shit crazy as they came.

"Jesus, Jimmy," I said, as Teddy was working on a burger we bought for him on the way to the park, "look at him. I don't know if ground control ever had contact with that space shot, but if they did, he flew out of radio range a while ago. Why the extended interest?"

But Jimmy just smiled at me in that way of his that made me feel so much younger than him, even though we were the same age. Catfish smile, even then.

"You need to learn how to read," he explained. "Words are everywhere, information readily available, accessible. . . ."

"Now just a fucking—"

"No, don't take it literally, you know better than that. I mean signs. Collect enough of them, and you have it!"

"Have what?"

"Vision, my brother, Vision."

Teddy finished folding the wrapper, wet with condiments and condensation, and stuck it in his pocket, who the hell knows why. He looked at Jimmy and signalled him over, witless smile across his mess of a face, all scabs and mustard, working at the paper bag opening with the fingers of his good hand.

But Teddy's bench was by invitation only. I still frightened him, he kept Jimmy between us. I'd even paid for the burger to show him what a trustworthy stand-up bastard I was, but no go. Worse, I was pissed off by Teddy's avoidance without knowing why—which, in turn, made me angrier. Course, army shell aside, I guess I looked as much like a skinhead as any of them. But to Teddy—or pretty much anyone else—what the hell was the real difference?

I stood off to the side feeling a bit hard done by as Jimmy oohed and aahed over Teddy's bag of who the fuck knows what. Probably a dead pigeon or a pet sandwich, I snarled to myself.

Then, show over, Jimmy got up.

"Right. We're off," he said, and off we went.

"What about him?" I asked, a bit peevishly.

"Hmm? Oh, he'll settle into a niche. Gore Park is a good place for him to start—good karma there."

"Ah. What was in the bag?"

Jimmy smiled.

"Butterflies."

"Butterflies? Like, real ones?"

"Yeah. Dead, of course, but yeah, real ones."

I contemplated this for half a block.

"Butterflies, eh?"

Jimmy offered me a smoke and then lit one himself, taking a long and leisurely drag. He always let the world slip by a bit for the first full drag after lighting it, an almost unnoticeable ritual unless you really knew him well. Then he smiled again, somehow cosmically fulfilled.

"Yep," he said, happily. "Butterflies."

—

Jimmy knows me well. My issues with what he calls the strata, I mean—he knows that I just need time to sort things out, collect my thoughts and put everything in order.

Teddy, for instance. Woven into Jimmy's cosmic tapestry, one more signpost on the road. Raving mad he was, but a collector nonetheless—members of that ragged tribe tend to be so, fervently. Or at least more so than the rest of us.

For a long time, it was that incongruous image that gnawed away at me—a homeless, friendless, witless butterfly collector, carrying his precious and desiccated specimens around in a decorated paper bag. That's what bothered me that day, from what was in hindsight really an encounter not worth recalling at all, since naught but shite came of it. We would have our day, Hardcore and me, but it was nothing either of us could have predicted. It never is.

So, daft and blind. Jimmy was right: I didn't see for years what was so immediately clear to him, my brother of circumstance and collector of visions. *Nothing is incongruous*, Jimmy once said, *all things rise and converge.* Even as he hinted at its place in the sequence later, my frustration, my spiritual impotence, was overwhelming as we sat together in this very Westdale coffee shop, tranquil oasis far from the unpredictability of the dirty downtown streets.

"So fucking what, Jimmy! Butterflies?" My voice carried, my anger unfit for this quiet part of the city. Other patrons, already irritated or intimidated by the bull's-eye and boots and utter disregard for Westdale conventions, were murmuring or staring or finishing up quicker than they'd like.

"Relax, brother, relax! You're upsetting the natives. No need for that—this is a nice little hideaway still off the radar, eh? Let's not wear out our welcome. When you're irritated, you remind me of Tribal, you know."

True enough. My brother could be dangerously impulsive, mostly because he loved the challenge of getting himself out of tight corners. Enviable skill, but one I didn't share.

"Right, right, right," I grumbled. Then, raising my voice, a bit out of character. "Apologies, ladies and gentlemen, apologies! A bit upset just then, no more profanity, I promise."

Jimmy shook his head and laughed.

"You're an idiot."

"Yeah—sorry, mate. We were discussing butterflies."

"All right," he conceded, settling back. "Think about it—Teddy, as he calls himself, is in a state of flux. He's trapped outside of whatever world produced him, as well as the world he got used to—an institution. Both worlds have rejected him, and now he's forced to join the ranks of vagrants and alley scroungers and panhandlers. Unforgiving sort of life, and with winter almost here, too."

"Okay, so the bag of insects . . ."

"He's saved them—that's the term he used, anyway. I assume he meant from returning to an ugly state of being. You know, awkward larval stage to butterfly and then, eventually, to death and decay. He's preserved them at the best point in the journey."

"So," I ventured, "you're saying that the butterflies are the mental hospital, the 'best point in his journey'?"

Jimmy considered this, tugging thoughtfully on his goatee as he lit another smoke. "That's one way to see it, I suppose. Just words, though. All I really meant is that he has a bag of words that only he can read. He didn't write them, but he's sure as shit read them and they're telling him something."

"Yeah, great. Instruction manual for the clinically insane, written in dead insects and kept inside a paper sack."

But Jimmy just shook his head, smile sad and mocking and mysterious. "With all the reading you do"—only Tribal and Jimmy knew—"you'd think this would be second nature. This façade of yours, your illusion of ignorance, works with the others, my friend, but not with me."

Sixteen. What did we know? Not a goddamn thing. Everything was still a game where the objective was to stumble upon a rule and then find fifty ways to break it while convincing yourself you're being original. But following the rules—ah, that's the real challenge.

But not for the Catfish. At sixteen, Jimmy seemed as old as the stars, ready to go supernova. Collapse imminent, if only we could have read it then—penetrated the constellations' crypsis, cold mockery hidden behind a system that appeared mechanical and—

(*words, then—the butterflies are words—beautiful but utterly inert, just dead symbols, inviting the artifice of animation, purpose infused only through active participation as if we reach into that ragged and tragic vessel to take up a dead insect, wings still scintillating and sun-dappled, and simulate flight. But of course, the object remains devoid of life, devoid of purpose, it—like words—utterly*)

—meaningless.

Doesn't matter.

Dead is dead.

Chapter Four

Jimmy and I meet downtown Monday morning, a right bloody hot July day, though cloudy. It's nineteen hours since our coffee shop heart-to-heart about Tiny Sue. I know because I've been counting. I'm a little wary of running into her, and say so, but Jimmy laughs.

"It's 10:00 a.m., man. Nothing in her den stirs until at least midafternoon." Then he shoots me a quizzical look. "You okay?"

"Yeah," I say.

"All right. Let's sit for a bit."

We make our way into the park and look for a bench that isn't occupied.

And there he is: Jonah—Jimmy's mad-eyed dispenser of street corner prophecies. Still wearing the same ratty winter coat he's had for the three years I've known him—well, known *of* him—and knee-deep in the fountain, pointing up vaguely at Queen Victoria above him, glaring down at him with that frozen disapproval with which she regards us all. Jonah's yelling. Screeching, even. Something about the buses—he's pretty upset. Most of his grievances are addressed upwards. At God himself, I figure at first. But as it turns out he's mostly talking to Victoria, even if he keeps calling her Mary.

We sit on a park bench, watching him. Then Jimmy retrieves his cigarette pack and pulls out a sizable joint.

I make a quick sweep for cops. "Are you fucking crazy?"

But Jimmy lights up anyway, intent on Jonah. Something's different—he never smokes dope in public when I'm around. Not because I disapprove, but because he doesn't want me around if he gets nabbed at it. He's a good friend that way.

Jonah bellows at passersby, much of it just incoherent babbling. It's mostly older people this time of day, a generation of men who still wear suit jackets and fedoras even in the summer heat. They shuffle about, caught between Jonah and Jimmy. And here, I suddenly realize, are the parameters of their old-age fears: dementia awaiting them on the short and shadowy road ahead, while behind them our indolent generation already regards them as ghosts.

After the buses, Jonah turns on the birds. Jimmy takes a heavy drag and leans forward like he's watching the last seconds of a power play. The old man begins naming the fucking things—not actual names, mind, but numbers. He stares hard at each pigeon, furrows his brow, and mumbles something at it, as if it's disappointed him on a vague cosmic level. Then, with all the finality of an Old-Testament prophet, he points a gnarled, sallow, nicotine-stained claw at one bird and condemns it to a numerical designation.

"Sixteen!" he screams.

All the other pigeons take to the air in startled chaos, as Jonah curls that claw up like a withering corn stalk until it joins his bony fist. . . .

Except Sixteen.

I'll be damned if the fucking thing doesn't *pause*, as if held in thrall by this ridiculous old hobgoblin knee-deep in a public fountain. Then, spell broken, it comes to, joining its brethren in the treetops.

I, for my part, am speechless.

Jimmy, however, is all business. "Right," he says. "Sixteen it is."

"What the fuck are you—and he—talking about?" I ask, thoroughly lost.

"Sixteen!" Jimmy repeats. "That's what we take!"

Now, by this point in our friendship I've learned when to stop asking questions and just watch events unfold. Jimmy quickly pinches off the heater, stows the finger-thick spliff for later, and gets to his feet.

"C'mon!" He turns and heads at an angle toward Rebecca Street. I jump up and follow, jogging a bit to catch up.

Within minutes we're at the bus depot. And before fifteen minutes have passed since a madman in a park startled pigeons, old age pensioners and Yours Truly, we're on Bus 16 and heading into the north end.

I hate the north end.

—

I was little when we emigrated from Glasgow, my mum and Tribal and me. Hamilton was a logical choice for Glaswegians, with a significant population of Scots already, and many of its streets and landmarks bearing Scottish names, including the city itself.

I remember some of it, but not too much. Tribal even less. We came to Canada soon after our baby sister Maggie died in her sleep.

SIDS, they called it.

I was six when she died, Tribal a year younger, and all our mum did for that first month was cry. And drink, but we were used to that. Our da had already buggered off before Maggie was even born, so we were on our own quite a bit.

Don't remember too much about how I dealt with it. I think mostly I yelled and cried a lot and broke things. I remember getting into a fight at school with this freckly, red-headed fuck-ugly kid because he had a little sister and I didn't anymore. But I do remember what Tribal did.

It was our mum's fault, though not directly, she telling us in slurred sobs over and over how Jesus had come in the night and taken away our Maggie, and that was the first time we'd ever heard the name Jesus, coming down and slipping away with our baby sister.

Tribal had been the first to find her, still and blue, skin like translucent porcelain. Jesus—thief in the night, a zephyric vampire who stole the breath of babies—*Jesus blessed Jesus came doon an' ha' ta'en oor poor Maggie awee ah!*—but how were we to understand, still grappling with the sudden and unexplained disappearance of our da one night not too long before Maggie was born?

So one evening, Tribal fetched a knife from the drawer and hid it beneath his pillow. He'd be damned if this Jesus was going to get him, too. And it was at least a week before the poor drunken woman noticed that her five-year-old was glazed over and staggering into things, numb and exhausted from his night vigils. Confused and frightened by what fragments our mum could pry from Tribal, she called a fucking priest in a drunken panic, though she wasn't even Catholic and hadn't seen the inside of a church herself since her own dark childhood.

The priest arrived after our evening forage for food in the squalid kitchen cupboards. The sun had set an hour earlier, and the father opened the door to find Mum out cold in her chair. A flaccid and soft pawed man, stalking forward, sad-eyed and whispering at us like we were feral urban scavengers.

Which was true, I suppose. Tribal bolted to our small room and ran out again a moment later, knife in hand. He caught the priest in the flabby tissue between ribs and hip, barely more than a shallow prick. Must have felt like a wasp sting, because the father howled and stumbled back into the flimsy card table in the kitchen, knocking it over and sending greasy plates and empty stout bottles crashing down. Our mum woke with a scream and found me howling, two little fists pounding, Tribal still wielding his knife wildly and the priest furious. Tenement neighbours started materializing, just curious ghosts sadly amused at the clownish antics of the local drunk and her unfortunate offspring.

We emigrated soon after that, a surreal adventure for such small children and maybe even for her too. Thinking back, I don't even know how we could have left—how could our mum have afforded it? Help must have come from somewhere, the three of us suddenly in this strange city across the Atlantic, she even sober for a while and working a night shift job at a machine shop. Her thick Glaswegian brogue made her popular in our little corner of Hamilton. The drinking, though—she couldn't stay sober for long. Or hold a job.

—

Jimmy arrived in Hamilton around the same time, also a child, reeling from similarly senseless circumstances beyond control and comprehension. Jimmy's dad was from northern Ontario, some little mining town or other. He came to Hamilton under protest, dragged here because his wife—Jimmy's stepmother—couldn't take the isolation anymore. So down they came, the three of them, and for a while he found work in a foundry. Then she ran off with somebody and he started drinking. Heavily. Even stopped talking. Jimmy was seven.

And, like our mum, Jimmy's dad couldn't hold a job, either.

Jimmy and me, we met when we were both fourteen and still living at home, Jimmy with his dad and me with my mum. And Tribal, of course. Our parents had a lot in common: both from somewhere else, both heavy drinkers, both out of work, both abandoned . . . and about to be abandoned again. Jimmy left home first, three months shy of his fifteenth birthday. Tribal and I followed suit.

At fourteen I was already in the mod scene—or I thought I was—and spent a lot of time loitering around downtown with friends, all of us indolent and bitter, mischievous enough to find ourselves on the fringes of authority's radar.

I knew of Jimmy because he dealt downtown, uppers and a little weed, selling out of the inner pockets of an oversized motorcycle jacket. But street vending was a competitive business, and Jimmy had to mind his step.

Which was exactly how we met, Jimmy slipping out of the current by ducking into a music store on King. I was already inside, digging through the used cassette bin and contemplating petty larceny, palmed Who tape already half concealed by the sleeve of my shell. Jimmy wasn't that subtle, spidery fingers crawling across the jagged plastic landscape until they came to a copy of The Doors' *Strange Days*. Up it went and into his jacket, he didn't even look up.

I smiled. "You don't even look around?"

"No need, man. Clerk's too busy watching you."

I looked over his shoulder. He was right: longhaired guy in his late twenties, looked like he might have peaked during the Disco era. Glaring. I made like I didn't realize the cassette was in hand, inspected it dramatically, dropped it back in.

"Uh, cheers," I mumbled.

"Happy to help, brother. You looking for anything for later?"

"Nah, sorry mate. Not my scene, eh? Unless you got whiskey." Back then, I thought a whiskey bottle made me look tough.

He beamed. "I could arrange that! Not *my* scene, but I have the means."

Between Jimmy's giant green mohawk (he had one at the time) and my bull's-eye, we weren't exactly going for inconspicuous. Kids, though—clueless.

We started toward the door, but another pimply employee, gangly and maybe eighteen, blocked the way. He was the brawn of this high-end sting operation—Disco was the brains, calling to us from behind the counter, smug.

"Where you two think you're going? Cops wanna talk to you about shoplifting." And he held up the phone.

My new companion's shoulders dropped, crestfallen. Apparently, he considered Stock Boy Security an immovable object. But even back then I was a scrappy shit—had to be. I stepped up and kicked the poor bastard square in the nuts, dropping him.

Right across the door. That pulled inward.

I grabbed Jimmy's shoulder. "C'mon, mate—out the back!" And we bolted, Disco howling from the sidelines—down an alley, around an industrial dumpster, into a trash can (my fault), out into the daylight and away from King and James.

"Guess I wasn't as smooth as I thought," my companion said, panting. "Jimmy, by the way." He held out his hand.

"Sorry about my, uh, solution," I offered. "Guess neither of us should drift too close to King and James for a bit, eh?"

"I wouldn't worry about it," he returned, serenely. "Mohawks and bull's-eyes are pretty common downtown." Then he grinned. "Maybe just avoid music shopping for a while. Nice kick, by the way. Not that I condone violence."

He led the way, weaving through the grid until he reached a muddy green steel door flush with an old brick wall, rust pushing through the weathered paint and not a handle in sight.

"Whiskey, right?"

"Uh, yeah."

Jimmy took a flat rectangle of steel maybe six inches long out of an inner pocket, slipped it into the crack between door and frame, and pried. The door gave way, popping open to reveal a dark and narrow corridor.

"Come on in," he said cheerfully, ushering me into the hall and pulling the door closed behind us. Not too far down, the passageway widened into a little alcove, strewn with trash and covered in graffiti. The air was stale and stunk of urine, mildew. A payphone clung haphazardly to the wall, its coin reservoir torn open. Narrow sagging stairs led up to a second floor.

"Still works," Jimmy informed me, picking up the receiver. "Don't know why. Forgotten, I guess. Like this place."

"Where are we?" I asked.

Jimmy paused, considering. Amusement bloomed on his face, he grinned foolishly. "You know, I have no idea what this place was. There's a couple squat houses above us. I got friends up there, so it's cool to use their phone."

"You're gonna phone for whiskey?"

"No, man—I'm gonna phone for a taxi. Got some dosh? You get it back."

He dropped the coins I gave him into the slot and caught them as they rolled out. Then he punched in the number scrawled on the wall.

"Hey, yeah. Hi. I need a cab. Address? Yeah—but on the way, could you ask him to swing by the liquor store? I need some whiskey."

It was that easy.

—

"Fate," I claim years later, looking back. But Tribal sneers and Jimmy smiles and the others shrug indifferently, the word "fate" no more to them than the sound of a car horn two blocks away, or a siren, or thunder. A month later, though, Jimmy introduced me to one of its harbingers, if you're willing to buy into cosmic currency—his guru, Jonah.

Jimmy would never put it that way, of course, too pretentious, he'd claim. But the bottom line is the bottom line. Same Jonah as in the park. That's what I think his name is at least, since he refers to himself in the third person about half the time. A wild-eyed old timer in a ratty winter coat even in summer, whose only accommodation for the relentless city heat is to take off his boots and stand barefoot in the fountain.

So, a month after Jimmy and I first met, he was scrounging around for buyers downtown, mohawk still in place and Yours Truly in clueless tow, when Jonah lurched into view and just walked into traffic without so much as a sideways glance. Right into Main Street, filthy coat flapping about like the broken wing of some ugly and monstrous condor.

Miraculously, he didn't get clipped—or us either, seeing how Jimmy took off after him, me still in his wake.

We followed Jonah as he wove his way through Gore Park until he stopped short where the gravel path split.

Then he sat down, a shapeless mound of brown and grey. Jimmy manoeuvred so he could see Jonah's weather-blasted face, those dark and narrow eyes glaring straight ahead at nothing, and I joined him.

"What are we—"

"Shhh. Just wait."

I did, for several long and confusing minutes. Then Jonah's feral eyes shifted to the left fork and Jimmy smiled.

"Okay," he said. "Let's go."

Later that afternoon, Jimmy and I caught a ride with Siobhan and her girlfriend Kathleen back to Jimmy's place in Dundas, the town just west of Hamilton. Jimmy's house, a tiny brick cube still technically owned by his stepmother's parents, was on the far side of Dundas Driving Park. As we came up to the park entrance, Jimmy leaned forward to shout at Siobhan over the music blasting from the tape deck.

"Hey, you mind making a left here?"

"Why?" she snapped. "Quicker through the park." Siobhan was a hefty Irish girl with balls of steel and an Ulster brogue. Everything was a confrontation.

"Seriously, I really want to go around it. I saw Jonah—"

"That crazy old man? Cut the shite, Jimmy!"

And straight ahead we went, until the cop in the cruiser in front of us threw on his lights as we approached a fork. He anticipated (correctly) that we would do the obvious and choose the road less travelled by. I wasn't worried—it was early, we didn't even have any beer on us.

I made some snide comment, but Jimmy was pretty busy: he popped a marble-sized lump of hash into his mouth and pulled out a bag of beans (blues—the mod pill of choice), ready to drop it on the car floor.

The cop approached Jimmy's side first. I grabbed the bag, but the cop saw me move.

"Out of the car!" he yelled. Fuck. Busted, and I didn't even use the goddamn things. But the stupid bastard did a very silly thing: he passed behind the car to come up on my side. A downtown cop would never make that mistake, breaking eye contact. Jimmy snagged the beans, even as I stepped out and assumed the position.

"What's with the knife?" the cop asked. I carried one even back then. Standard mod gear, of course. You fought like a bastard to protect your AirWair (Doc Martens, that is), and mine were nice: black steel toe 10-hole rangers, in fact. Street scrap regulation.

"It's legal," I snapped, truly believing we were all going to the cop-shop anyway.

"Are you trying to tell me what's legal, punk?" Punk. What an asshole. He was exactly the kind of arrogant moron who watched too many cop movies. I liked to think that one day he'd come across a dime bag of high-grade uncut heroin, mistake it for coke and taste a fingerful, just like his snarly-faced American celluloid cop heroes. Then he'd end up in a padded room beside that rookie you always hear about from Floyd fans—you know, the guy who thinks he's a fucking banana and rolls around begging people not to peel him.

He was right, though. I was being a punk about it. "Hey, I can read, *constable*—" He had a couple bars on his sleeve, they hate when you miss the rank. "It's legal."

Thing is, there was no way those beans were staying hidden. Ten centuries of fatalist Pictish blood roaring through my veins—the Norns had spun, all was predetermined, the wyrd was upon me.

Then, enter the Valkyrie. Siobhan actually got out of the car. "Hey!" she bellowed. "Why don't ye go find something useful t'do?"

"Get back in the car!"

"Fuck you!" Like I said, everything was a confrontation. She wasn't particular.

Kathleen called to her, just a few gentle words: *Calm down.* She was the only one could get Siobhan to do anything. Siobhan complied with an angry sigh. Left the door open, though.

The cop had to respond, even at fourteen I could see that. Still, he never frisked Siobhan right proper. Dug through her purse and made a vague show of rummaging through the jacket pockets he could reach, but never touched her. Probably smarter than he looked. One way or the other, he didn't notice when Jimmy took advantage, opened his own door a bit, and dropped the bag of beans behind the rear wheel.

Just in time, too, because the cop turned on him next: "You with the mohawk, come over here."

Jimmy stepped out, sauntering over to be frisked and fondled. The cop was pretty thorough, kind of rough, but the hash was already swallowed and Jimmy countered my insolence and Siobhan's aggression with politeness,

9-inch electric green mohawk and black-laced oxblood 14-holes aside.

The cop knew he was missing something, you could tell. It was probably my fault, for being a smartass. Thing is, it was the first and last time I ever got belligerent with a cop, at least, without good reason.

Long story short, beans were recovered and we drove on.

I bet he was a real asshole to the next poor bastard he ran into.

Chapter Five

The summer nights grow colder and then autumn creeps in, ominous and threatening. Some of the newly homeless start to ask the old hands questions, along with the younger street kids who have managed to slip through the System's net. *Where do you go when it gets really cold*? *Are people more generous if you panhandle in the snow*? Questions about alleys and side streets. About predators. About cops. About good dumpsters and bad. About where to get cardboard and plastic and dry socks, a hit, and maybe a bowl of soup.

A few of the older vagrants, weatherworn and wise, predict a mild winter. But these are just words, the young and inexperienced ones have not yet learned to listen.

For those of us already entrenched in squat houses, cold weather is just an inconvenience. Navigating the dangerous street politics, ebb and flow, this task consumes us instead.

But then there is Jackson Square, *pax* in our hooligan street games, of sorts. The labyrinthine mall has sanctuary status, mostly because of its few and easily blocked exits, Hamilton's Finest being quite adept at casting their nets for wayward salmon swimming against the current status quo. So its food court becomes the winter watering hole, where wary lambs and lions gather in relative harmony amongst the oblivious mob of downtown shoppers. Still, you have to exercise caution, common sense being too much to ask—grudges and feuds get the better of all of us, every now and then.

But Jimmy revels in anonymity here, blending easily into the fabric. Patchwork, he calls it, societal cross-section blanket where every piece is interwoven without interacting. What he means is, you can be most invisible in plain sight. And with a couple reliable pairs of eyes to mind the flanks, casual people watchers won't stare for fear of sustained eye contact. That's our job—casually block from view Jimmy's nimble hands as they take stock of his clandestine inventory, while staring down those few who take a prolonged interest.

We'd originally gone in—Tribal and me—to grab something to eat. Scrounged around that morning for dosh and felt right cocky when Tribal discovered ten bones folded up in his pack of smokes. Providence, we'd decided, and headed out. But Jimmy had been loitering about in Gore Park, dealing under his harmless vagrant veneer. Peckish himself, he'd joined us, sensing—in his way—that it was time to slip out of the circuitry for a bit.

We navigate to the food court, not overly crowded though a Saturday and overcast. Jimmy chooses the table and we settle in.

"If you don't mind," Jimmy says, "I need to count tabs. I think I'm running low."

I turn my chair back to Jimmy to block one side, Tribal standing indolent and seemingly indifferent on the other. Jimmy's fingers start their dance through lysergic confetti.

Then Wally lumbers into view, that slack-jawed fat fuck, sees us, and sets a collision course.

"Christ," I growl in warning, "here comes Walrus."

We tolerate him, like almost everyone else does. Don't know why any of us bother: he's loud, ignorant, stupid, oblivious—those are his good qualities.

And a real flashflood temper, Tribal's favourite food court conversation topic, because he maintains it's unnatural. Somewhere along the proverbial road, Tribal's picked up the notion that fat people are supposed to be jolly, thus making Walrus an oddity, physiology and psychology somehow misaligned. Myself, I can't name one fat person who isn't as miserable as the rest of us.

"Hey," Wally bellows. He bellows everything. "Whatcha doin'?"

"What's it look like, you moron?" This from me, savage and terse. "Sit down, and shut that monstrous cavern of a mouth."

"Jesus fuck, what's your problem? Can't say fuckin' hi?"

"Fuckin' hi," hisses Tribal. "Keep your voice down, Walrus."

"Don't fuckin' call me that!"

"Perhaps," says Jimmy in a disarming tone, "Wally is hungry. Maybe one of you could oblige." Clever, Jimmy is. Better for the vacuous sack of fat to stay still now he's seated, since he makes such a goddamn spectacle of himself every time he comes or goes. Besides, for reasons never adequately explained, he always has money.

Tribal sneers and sighs, volunteering.

"Whaddya want to eat?"

Wally ponders the myriad possibilities, while digging for dosh. "Gimme a hotdog," he eventually says.

"A *hot*dog? What are you, fucking five?"

"Piss off! I like 'em. Hey, get me two, eh?"

Tribal rolls his eyes and takes the dosh from Wally's meaty hand. "Fine, you porky bastard. Two it is. What ya want on 'em?"

"Nothin', just plain."

Jimmy looks up suddenly from his lap and raises an eyebrow, glaring at Wally in mock disapproval. "Walrus," he says, "do you not partake in condiments?"

"Don't fuckin' call me that, and no I fuckin' don't!"

"You *always* eat plain hotdogs? No condom-ents at all?"

"Yeah! What the hell I just say?"

But Jimmy lifts one hand, disarmingly. "Hey, man, I'm just looking out for you. No condom-ents is a choice—as far as I'm concerned you can bareback wieners all day long."

We laugh like idiots, but Walrus gets pissed.

"Fuck you, Jimmy! Fuck all o'you! Why you assholes always pricks to me, eh?"

"There he goes again," Jimmy sighs. "Pricks and assholes—a sad obsession. Well, not me, Walrus, not me. If we're going to have relations, *I'm* using mustard."

Walrus turns red and starts to get up, the ill-tempered bastard. But he really is a fat fuck and it takes some time, so Tribal and I don't let him get that far—hand on each shoulder, we push his ass back into his chair.

"Lemme go! I'm gonna fuckin' kill him!"

I've had enough.

"Keep your voice down, you tubby sack of shit. No one invited you over, so don't whine if you don't like the company."

He tries to get up again, but Tribal kicks the back of his lumpy foot so his leg shoots out from under him. He falls with a crash back into the chair.

"What'd we just say?" Tribal hisses, close and personal.

Jimmy finishes what he's doing, and takes a casual look around us, frowning.

"Bit too conspicuous for my liking, gentlemen. I'm done counting, if you two are done socializing. Hate to deprive myself of your company, Wally m'boy, but we're off."

And we're ten metres off the port(ly) bow, before Wally puts the pieces together.

"Hey! *Hey*! What about my hotdogs!"

Not what about my money, but what about my *hotdogs*. Amazing.

In our defence, Tribal does give him a friendly parting wave.

We exit at the corner of King and James.

"Well," sighs Jimmy, "back to the office." He nods toward a small crowd of kids, loitering part way down the block toward Hughson. We agree to meet up again in thirty minutes at Carnaby Street Imports, a dumpy little head shop on John Street North, after which Tribal slips off to make one of his own clandestine deals, since Jimmy's all out of weed at present.

I mill about inside for a bit, looking over patches and pins, knives and pewter rings. Then I go outside to talk with Seamus and Brent, a couple of Trojan skinheads from an east end crew. We engage in a favourite pastime—arguing about music. We're all equally pig-headed. And probably equally misinformed, but that's a matter of opinion.

"*Quadrophenia!*" I insist. "Come up with one thing—*one thing*—that equals that in quality or depth."

Seamus stabs a meaty finger into my chest. "Trojan has—" But I'm on a ranting roll, and I cut Seamus off. He insulted Pete Townshend, cardinal sin.

"Trojan Records? Look, man, I like ska and rocksteady as much as the next bastard, but—"

"But what? *Quadrophenia*, always fuckin' *Quadrophenia*! That whole album of yours is too—" and here he stammers, casting about for what he means "—too fuckin' confusing!"

But that's weak and he knows it. Brent throws in an oar, being a bit more informed than Seamus, and a touch smarter.

"Hey, brother, I seen the movie. I got the LP, too. It's good. But didn't Townshend also do that album—what's it called—*Empty Glass*? Not exactly a street scrap soundtrack. Well, maybe for a mod."

"Fuck you," I offer. I love *Empty Glass*. I have four copies of it.

Tribal arrives on time, working on the last puffs of a death stick he gets by the carton from a smoke shop on the Six Nations Reservation. DG's, they're called—about nine times the carcinogens of regular cigarettes, and the heater falls off sometimes because the fucking things are all floor sweepings with the occasional woodchip—but Tribal loves the goddamn taste. Even wraps the filter with a strip of tape to trap everything in, the crazy bastard.

Metal-head named Steve and a couple of his mates swerve suddenly to cut off Tribal, just before he reaches us. Didn't notice them at all until they move, their kind are sort of invisible to us. Real skid row elite—mullets and acid wash, three-quarter sleeve concert tees and high-tops. Tribal knows Steve and the sidekick—Shane—from before we agreed to disagree with the inner city Hamilton school system's insistence that we attend, back when Tribal had racked up so many suspensions and absences that not one teacher even knew him, and I wasn't too far behind. Plus that pending expulsion for breaking a kid's jaw.

The third metal-head has a girl with him, huge hair feathered and bleached. They all somehow look like scrawny bipedal lions, but it's the mid-eighties and that's standard. And to Tribal's credit, he tries his best to ignore the fact that they're looking for a confrontation, sidestepping—no go, though, since Steve and his mate Shane echo the move. In all fairness, Tribal *had* slept with Steve's girlfriend a couple weeks before.

There's also the hard truth that the two of us took a right savage beating in the north end just under three months ago, neither of us fully healed yet. Tribal still can't close his left hand completely. Still, he gives them an innocent and disarming smile, like a playful viper.

"You mind, brother? You're in my way."

Steve's having none of it. He's been looking for Tribal for a fiddler's fucking fortnight (Jimmy's expression).

"Not this time, asshole," he says. "You're goin' *down*."

Tribal, malicious grin barely in check, slides his left hand up under his leather to the small of his back.

"Gee whiz, pookie, that's a *real* nice offer, but I don't *wanna* go down on you. Maybe you could ask one of the other Thunder Cats. Not Shaney, though—I hear he's all teeth and gag reflex."

"That's it, you're fuckin' dead!"

Steve and Shane are pretty incensed, coming straight at Tribal with right proper tunnel vision. The third one detaches himself from his girl and moves to the left, clearly not all that interested, but a good mate. Shows some common sense by flanking Tribal, too.

They all slow down, however, when Tribal's hand re-emerges from behind him gripping an SS dagger. Replica, of course. None of us knew where he got it or why the hell he kept it.

I let out an audible sigh and push off the wall, as Seamus and Brent do the same.

"Whoa—hold it, jus'a minute!" Steve shouts as we drift into his narrow line of sight. "We got nothin' against mods, or skins. This is between me and this asshole here!"

"That asshole's with us," Seamus says simply, pulling out his own lace slitter.

But Tribal goes into full-scale mockery. "Ahhhh, now Stevie gotta be bwave an' fight *weal* hard!" Then he turns serious. "Hold on, man, I might have something to help you . . ." He starts patting himself down, digging dramatically through pockets, before shrugging in resignation.

"Oh well. Sorry, Stevie—I'm all out of pussy cream. I guess you'll just have to suck it up."

Then he fakes high with the blade, and kicks Steve in the nuts.

That's the whole fight, one steel-toe to the groin. The other two collect up their mate and beat a hasty retreat. Intelligent, really—they're outnumbered and have nothing to gain, not even reputation.

—

But, as they say, what comes around, right?

Truth, then: to the casual observer, this is all mere madness, the fruitless ramblings of a Hamilton Hieronymo, yet peace (*why then Ile fit you*) comes with comprehension. But only if you watch the periphery. Because—and here I too fear that *Hieronymo's mad againe*—we all look for patterns, comforting ourselves with the repetitions that emerge from observable data.

And life? Just a petty fucking revenge tragedy, nothing more (and now I think *Datta. Dayadhvam. Damyata.* This is what I want, not the *shite shite shite* I've come to expect) or sometimes less.

Too vague? Too cerebral? Maybe, even if I can't be accused of originality.

A case in point, then.

It happened a while ago, during the summer. Maybe a week after Jimmy and I got on a bus bound for the north end selected by a decrepit maniac in a Gore Park fountain, and at a piece of shit north-end restaurant-bar named McMahon's.

Because, as I said, what comes around.

—

"Alright—enough! You two gotta go."

This from McMahon's bartender. McMahon's is the kind of place with clusters of replicated shit nailed to the walls, designed to produce vague and artificial nostalgia in its regular trough feeders. Or maybe it's for the benefit of the forty-something newly divorced guy, out on that awkward first date and struggling not to talk about his ex, because all his buddies around the water cooler or at the gym he just joined warned him not to. But, of course, dumbass is too nervous to remember and brings the bitch up anyway, only recalling the sage words of his friends halfway through a sentence about how she cannibalized his fucking stock portfolio and making a sudden and clumsy transition to a Three Stooges poster or a hurley that he mistakes for a cricket bat, because he doesn't know shit about either sport.

Which is what's actually happening in the booth across from the stools where we're both perched, Tribal and me, drunk and cheerfully heckling the poor bastard while calling down the bar for another round. You can't blame us—they look like twins, this dumpy and tragically unattractive pair. I mean, for Christ's sake, they both showed up for a first date in denim shirts and khakis—her too, and even at seventeen, I know a divorcee sure as shit better have a short black dress handy for when her idiot sister or hairdresser or who-fucking-ever sets her up for a blind date. By unspoken agreement, though, we don't say too much about the woman—not cricket, really. Instead, seeing we've expended our ammunition about fashion, we switch to offering up advice for conversation topics instead.

"Pssst! Hey, buddy, tell her more about your ex! She loved that bit, I could tell!"

"Yeah," adds Tribal, "and your ex's ball skills—you know, like when she played with your cricket bat!"

And idiotic shit like that.

But there comes that point when you've had a few pints too many, in exactly the wrong place to have a few too many pints. At any of the regular pubs—I mean the ones liberal enough not to check our fake IDs—or at the Cave or the Four Nine Four, this sort of thing just wouldn't happen. Faced with the unfamiliar politics of this older and foreign crowd, however, I guess we just don't know what else to do.

Anyway, like I said.

"Alright—enough! You two gotta go."

The bartender was getting right fucking pissed, too, burly Italian looking guy with shaggy forearms and too much loose skin on his sweaty forehead. It all kind of folds downward into a natural scowl, a sagging V bordered by giant bushy eyebrows. He storms over, snatches the empty pint glasses off the bar and stands there glowering at us.

"Aright brother, relax," I say. "We're jus' offering some advice to Casafuckingnova over there. No harm meant."

"I don't give a shit what you're doing—time for you two assholes to hit the road! How old are you little pricks, anyway?"

"Hey, fuck you," Tribal growls. "You're the greasy cocksucker who checked us when we first got here."

And then he's off and running—Tribal never half-asses anything.

"You north-end ginos are all the fuckin' same, eh? I mean, what happened? Roman Empire, Julius fucking Caesar, whole world by the balls. And now what? Your entire culture's been reduced to wearing bikini briefs and driving Z-28s."

The barkeep's beefy neck turns an unpleasant purple colour, but to his credit, he maintains. Just a hard, toothy grin, eyes cold and knowing. But, of course, Tribal can't stop. "C'mon, what you got out back? You go for the Trans Am, you original fuck?"

As it turned out, the bartender doesn't have a Z-28 or a Trans Am. What he does have is a bunch of mates who also happen to be off-duty Hamilton cops. And they've overheard most of Tribal's rant. In a drunken flash, our asses are out back in the dark parking lot where we get the boots put to us cop-style. Proper, too, sticks and all.

Back slammed into brick, I lodge a slurred complaint. "Now just a fucking—"

Or part of one, because a fist catches me full in the sternum.

I double over, heave a bit. Follow-through gets me in the side of the head and sends me sprawling into the asphalt. Tribal's down there already, bleeding from a gash in his scalp and struggling to get to his feet.

Then they really start. A baton flashes to my right and I throw up my hand up to deflect, but it smashes into the base of my little finger and pops it out of joint, impact numbing me arm to elbow. Boot suddenly on my forearm and the baton comes down viper-quick onto my first two fingers, breaking them both.

I kick out blindly, hoping for a knee or at least a shin. I get a steel-toe cop boot in the ribs instead and I can't breathe all that much anymore.

Another one hovers above me, knee on my chest as he punches me in the face piston-like. Half blinded then by the sudden swelling and blood and agonizing pain, the third punch crushing my nose.

Then our cold-eyed host emerges, carrying a beer bottle.

"Not so cocky now, huh? You little fuckin' bastards."

And he breaks it over my gourd. I barely feel the blow, just the warmth as blood trickles its way into my ear and down my neck.

I watch in a dim haze as the vicious bastard jams the jagged end into Tribal's face, catching his upper lip and slicing a flap loose just below his right eye. I reach for my knife, all reason lost, figuring *fuck it I'll take this prick's marbles with me at least*, but I take another blow to the head and black out a bit, groggy and bloody and probably weepy, I can't rightly remember.

—

What a right fucking mess we were after they'd finished: forty stitches and five busted fingers between us, Tribal lost a couple teeth and got his collar bone smashed besides, I got three cracked ribs and (another) broken nose, plus all the bruises and abrasions and bloody pulpwork that comes with a right savage beating.

Could have been worse, but cops always know when enough is enough.

We got ourselves to our feet after a rest there in that cold and indifferent north-end parking lot, fight beaten right out of us. I still couldn't breathe, and both of Tribal's eyes were swollen shut. We set off, lead-footed and staggering along like inebriated deep-sea divers, to get ourselves patched.

Not too far from Barton, as it turned out, so we made our way to the same emergency room we had to walk away from a year before and Karma, that whore, finally got her way. Cops and questions. The very thing we tried to avoid the first time came at us with a vengeance.

But we didn't say shit. Blamed it all on a small crowd of drunken Argos fans on their way back to Toronto, after a football game at Ivor Wynn Stadium. I mean, what the fuck was the point of telling the truth? After all, we weren't rats—we knew you take your beats when they come and move on. It happens to everyone, eventually. Even cops, on occasion.

Besides, it was the whole inept joke of a System we despised, not its enforcers. None of us trusted the Anointed Provincial They to do a goddamn thing properly—we learned that right quick, when we tried to split home the first time.

There's only us. To rely on, I mean—and even this is pointless because we're all witless victims of whatever cosmic machinery runs this meagre shit show. Tribal and me, Derek, Tina—all of us. We try not to think of anything too deeply, sticking to cause and effect only. Because beyond the simple day-to-day litany of petty victories in the midst of overwhelming injustices is Consequence.

That's Jimmy's domain. And Jonah's, I suppose, unraveling each mystery by way of buses and birds.

Here's the thing, though: each one of Jonah's buses leads to a different destination, but it's all interwoven by the grid, an immense Celtic interlace of steel and stone, with crazy bastards just like him as your personal cosmic tour guides. They're all over this city, that invisible tribe of nameless, shiftless urban refuse, dirty heaps of rag and bone.

Signposts, Jimmy called them, and I guess this is why. Because I did ride that fucking bus with him that Sunday afternoon—Bus 16—and it went deep into the north end. We were two errant explorers riding the nameless rapids into a nameless country, a green and grey wilderness of steel mills and warehouses and thousands of tightly packed four-room houses, the dwellings of every cog needed to work the Machine.

Then the bus came to the end of its route. The driver lit a cigarette, turned off the sign light, and opened the door, waiting for his last three passengers to exit—just me, Tribal, and some skinny nervous kid in flannel. We stepped out into this foreign world of longshoremen and mill workers, thrift shops and corner bars with neon tube signs advertising American beer.

And the Salvation Army. There in the window was a framed poster, leaning crookedly against a headless mannequin wearing a Leafs jersey. I grabbed Jimmy's arm and pointed.

"Holy fuck, look at that," he said, and laughed.

It was Steph's *perestroika* poster. Made by the Polish worker.

And now I think, why not? Maybe that really *is* the key: regrouping, renewing.

Restructuring.

Hey, like I said, who among us doesn't?

PART TWO

Chapter One

But when you're still part of that ebb and flow, raging pointlessly against it all (or against nothing), sixteen months is a long time. You forget.

Or you selectively remember.

And so, January—bitterly cold and ruthless. The old men in the park were wrong about the weather, but none of us jest. This is a steel city winter, a Canadian winter. There will be vacant corners for begging come spring.

Derek saw the first one. After a gig at a second floor club, he went outside for some air on the fire escape just off the back storeroom where bands were meant to stow their drum covers, guitar cases. When he came back in, he mentioned it as we were packing up.

"Noticed a bunch of them gathered around what I thought was a heap of black garbage bags," he said.

"Bunch of who?" asked Jimmy.

"You know, homeless types. Raggedy fuckin' lot all crowded around this pile of garbage." Derek kept as neutral as he could. He had no use for that particular street tribe, but he knew of Jimmy's affinity for any creature of misfortune.

Jimmy paused, bass half in the case. Then he handed it wordlessly to Ewan, grabbed his coat, and headed for the door.

I helped Derek and Ewan load Derek's van and saw them off. They left me with Jimmy's bass, but at least they took Jimmy's amp and P.A. and his crate of chords and pedals. I waited outside the club entrance, freezing because it was a right savage bastard of a night.

Jimmy reappeared soon after.

"Well?" I asked.

I knew already, though—I could see it in his eyes, haunted and lost. Jonah.

But Jimmy is resilient, we all are. It comes of living side-by-side with necessity for so long. And so.

January.

Sixteen months after a night of mid-September madness when Tribal and I brought a girl with one shoe to a hospital, and six months after we returned to that same emergency room, stumbling in blindly after a north end beating, we finally converge—we come together for what is in fact the third time.

The first two times happened within two hours of one another—a frightened girl bleeding in a parking lot, the same girl, terrified, struggling futilely against Consequence in a park. And now, after all this time?

She is the one to mention that mad midnight first, vaguely, and then we never speak of it again. Ever.

This, then, is how I meet her, Jimmy's very own test-tube prodigy: Sonar Debbie Dream.

She descends the narrow stairs that lead up to street level, ethereal waif shrouded in gauzelike shadow and delicate wisps of smoke. Black hair like spun jet or liquid basalt, one long braid porphyritic with crystal beads, beautiful, alien, ephemeral, shamanic, skin so pale that its translucence is a playground for the black light and strobes of this place, an underground after hours club off the beaten track, below a billiards hall whose claim to steel city fame is a murder committed there three months ago. It was a stabbing, dull rage resulting in enough wounds so that the victim's contents made its way through the floorboards to the club itself, a vast dark stain on the ceiling that crept in a serpentine arabesque along the natural slope of the sagging boards.

The club owners, two Quebecois sisters, knew their clientele well. They simply put a masking tape silhouette of a body on the ceiling. Later, Debbie told me she was there when they did it—one of them, she told me, stained her knuckle on the dark splotch itself. While the other was tearing off little pieces of tape to negotiate the tight arch of a hand, she raised the stain to her mouth and licked it. Debbie simulated this, seizing my wrist and running her long tongue slowly, caressingly, over one of my own scarred knuckles. She laughed humidly at my incredulity, my discomfort, my poor attempt to laugh it off.

But that was later.

Jimmy accompanies her, he is proud of this, smiling serenely in our direction. We are gathered around our usual table drinking bottled beer—no draught pints here. Derek and Ewan help Tribal construct a monstrous joint. They have rolling papers all over the table, the glue strips carefully torn off to use as a supportive exoskeleton. It's designed to hold an eighth, they say, just for hay-weed, cheap low-end pot, but that doesn't mean much to me. I don't smoke yet. "It's a midget's cock!" Derek beams, childish with glee over Tribal's project. Ewan contributes, he folds and tears, but Tribal is the lead engineer. His are the hands of the Maker.

My eyes are on the girl, who I recognize in a déjà vu sort of way. She already knows, smiling at me and at Tribal, but he's too busy to notice yet. Jimmy is satisfied with my expression, whatever it is, taking it for something else. Surprise or envy (or Envy), maybe.

But Debbie doesn't operate on a discernable frequency. Instead, she surprises Jimmy. She reaches out and touches my hand. Hers is cold, like silk-soft bone, long nails jet-black and glimmering with tiny constellations under the strange lights.

"I never thanked you," she says.

Now Tribal looks up, compelled by something in that voice that haunts his memory, even if she never uttered a single discernable word that night almost a year and a half ago at the Cinder Block North. He's quicker than I am—he knows immediately.

"Holy shit," he says, wide eyed, like he's just seen a ghost.

This is one of the Hammer's well-kept secrets, the *Caverne d'Araignée.* The Spider Cave. That's what this club is called, officially. Well named, I suppose: dank and threatening sort of place, claustrophobic because of its black walls and ceiling sagging with the sad weight of old brick and concrete above it, billiards hall plus five ugly floors of dirt-cheap tenements above that.

I'd spent time in one of those grimy little hovels, Jimmy lived up there for a while with a menagerie of street accessories, a small squat house tribe. The *salon des refusés,* our twin sister hostesses called that apartment, amused in a distant, star-cold sort of way. Elevator was always broken, of course, so you had to take the stairs. A depressing trudge up old concrete slats, the dull hint of stale urine and week-old vomit lingering in the filthy corners, accompanied by the occasional assault of ammonia when the owners of this makeshift outhouse made a vague show of exorcising these stubborn spirits of past bodily evacuation—the owners themselves occasionally haunted by the Board of Health, I suppose.

But the club itself is an entirely different animal. Clusters of small round tables line the perimeter like squat, wax-caked stalagmites, each with its own candle. We all play absently with the wax, mesmerized because idle boredom and fire are good bedfellows. In the club's centre is a circular clearing, a dance floor where black-clad Goth girls writhe in sinuous detachment with their stick-thin androgynous dates. The strobe lights fragment them as they lose themselves in the heavy and relentless beat of German techno, sometimes live and crammed into a tight corner a fist-swing from the bar or, like tonight, pounding through the stereo sound system.

There are sub-woofers installed under the floorboards as well, the bass tickles your feet if you stand still on the dance floor. I used to wonder why some of these night freaks spent portions of songs crawling on the floor, grinding against the worn wood. Jimmy explained that if you watch, there are clusters of prone Goths around the places where the speakers are entombed, drawn like black moths to invisible lights, the thump thump thump of each telltale heart pounding away below the surface.

This is The Cave. We come here every so often for variety—it's good to people watch and Goths are a pretty entertaining lot, in a morbid sort of way. We play this club once or twice a month, too. We bring in a different sort of crowd—the Goth girls still show up, but their vaguely male companions stay home, huddling I suppose in fetid, lightless basement flats until they know their cavern is free of boots and targets, James jackets and 2-Tone. Not that we cater to that crowd in particular, but we do play some Ska and I insist on at least a few covers from my own comfort zone—The Jam, Purple Hearts, Kinks, Small Faces, High Numbers, and—of course—The Who.

Tonight, though, we're just here for a little communal solitude. That is, this club isn't on the official radar screen yet and the billiards hall crowd has been pretty subdued since their little incident. We're all under age—or, at least, most of us are—but this is a small detail that doesn't overly concern the Coven of Two behind the bar. They don't discriminate: they don't care how many years a hand holding dosh is lacking.

Debbie's sudden acknowledgement of a past and intimate encounter with Tribal and me throws Jimmy into a small cosmic crisis, but the Catfish in him—reliable, calm, sanguine, adaptable—compensates for this new weight of information, pulls Jimmy back to the surface. I see it in his eyes, a brief flicker of confusion, but only because I know him better than the others.

"Didn't know this was a reunion," he says in slightly baffled amusement.

She slips her thin arm around Jimmy, eyes still holding Tribal's in place, and shrugs slight shoulders.

"We haven't met officially," she admits, "only in passing."

Jimmy catches the hint.

"Ah! I see," he says. He gestures to Derek, Ewan, and me. "Well, you have the dubious honour of meeting my band-mates. This is Lead Guitar, this is Drums, and this is Rhythm Guitar." Then he points at Tribal. "And the chief engineer and winner of the Worst-Joint-Ever-Rolled trophy is Brother of Rhythm Guitar."

We all laugh. Jimmy is himself again.

"Gentlemen, this is Debbie Dream."

She smiles and says hi. Then she excuses herself and slips off to the bar.

Debbie Dream. Probably Jimmy's fabrication, I say to myself, but a fitting one: there's something unreal, otherworldly about her—it must be her eyes, I think. But that isn't it, this is only my trite attempt to compartmentalize her. A natural gut reaction: we all try to rationalize what we don't understand, de-clutter our own personal orbits.

Definable boundaries. That's what we like.

Debbie returns with a reservoir glass of green fairy, stirring in the sugar cube with slow rotations of her finger.

"Hold this, please," she says, handing the glass of absinthe to Jimmy and slipping into the dance floor circuitry.

Tribal has shaken himself loose of the past by now and works with renewed vigour on his hayweed sheath. Derek helps him roll it, his fingers far more deft than Tribal's. Ewan watches absently, not as invested as he was, fingers drumming a soft but rapid beat on the table in time with the music.

She's back almost immediately, small square triumph in hand. She holds it up between finger and thumb, a playful smile on her lips. Jimmy nods in mock approval, a proud father, patting her gently on the head as she defers to him, eyes lowered bashfully, a shy child proud of herself. A confusing pantomime.

Jimmy takes the small flat square and drops it into the glass, swirling it carefully until it dissolves. I feel considerably out of my league, whisky and beer connoisseur that I am. Absinthe has its own stigma, mythic defamation well established long before any of us. And all of it shite, I assure you, it's as harmless—or as harmful—as anything else out of a liquor bottle.

But there's a reason Jimmy likes the Cave. Some emaciated caver with a cutting issue always has something retro, some common street drug that passed its fashionable prime among the mainstream. Quaaludes, mostly, but sometimes you stumbled upon an old acid stash—and blotter from the early '80s averaged over a hundred micrograms of LSD per hit. That would skull-fuck you right proper. You really wanted to cut it in two and share, or risk a trip fraught with serious thoughts of cosmic fucking annihilation. Not anything like the infamous Bicycle Day of godfather Hoffman (who said the Swiss never came up with anything better than the cuckoo clock?), but reasonably surreal by standard reckoning.

With this lot, this dangerously lonely crowd of urban misfits, the escape mechanisms of the past had a soothing reminiscent quality, like childhood memories. And most of the blotter paper was liberally decorated with cartoon characters. They cling to them with a desperation that we can't quite grasp. And it's expensive, even if we intimidate them without meaning to.

It's the Mystery Machine Debbie is after tonight. And its keeper is out there on the dance floor, clad in black except for his Shaggy-green shirt, sign well displayed, clearly open for business if you knew how to read, a sign language slightly beyond the liminal threshold.

In it goes, Jimmy swirling clockwise. "Just winding it up," he jokes, and they take turns, conservative and careful sips, savouring each one.

This isn't an unfamiliar concept, just an unfamiliar combination. We hang out occasionally with a black lace skinhead crew or two, Trojan skins—as I said, followers of the true skinhead spirit, pride without prejudice—and purple jesus is still a popular pastime beverage. I don't mean the pussy frat-boy variety purple j of grape Kool-Aid and grain alcohol: these crazy bastards spike it with microdot. Jimmy carries a fair supply for sale or barter.

Not too much LSD in microdot—maybe 15 or 20 micrograms—but there's a shit load of Benzedrine. Vehicle is strychnine, I think, but I'm not sure. Whatever it is, the delivery's pretty violent. Like you've been hit with a mail truck, Jimmy says, a tired joke that's funny mostly because he won't let it die.

Tribal's monster is complete, a fat and flaccid oblong obscenity held together by soggy glue strips and mediocre luck. Gravity clearly mocks its structural integrity, the earth's core tugging playfully at its tiny magnetic field. A small lump of stringy weed rolls out of the end and falls into a puddle of hot wax.

"Jesus dog-walking Christ," he growls. "C'mon, gimme a light before the fucking thing disintegrates."

Jimmy sips serenely away with Deb, ignoring the clumsy spliff as it makes its ponderous way around the Three Architects.

Me, I go get another beer.

That same night, the dream starts.

It is the same dream. It takes place in Westdale, Steph's neighbourhood. I'm with Tribal and we're in a rush, but I know I've lost something. I keep looking behind me, down the road or sidewalk, but Tribal won't stop. Jimmy's there, too, but in a little brick house. He's drowning behind a window.

I will have this dream for years.

Chapter Two

Debbie is elusive, accompanying Jimmy that spring to the occasional practice, the occasional gig. But nothing more.

I ask Tribal in confidence, see if he has any insight.

"So," I begin. He's half hanging out the only window of the single miserable room we share, muttering and cursing as he works to splice our upstairs neighbour's cable. We rent the room from an old Italian couple—they own the four-storey building and rent out every possible square foot, from the vintage clothing shop at street level to an illegal makeshift firetrap of an apartment tucked into the goddamn rafters.

"Pass me the pliers. No, other ones. The red handles."

I comply and try again.

"So, what's your take on Debbie, eh?"

"What you mean, 'my take'?"

"I mean, why isn't she around very much?"

But Tribal pulls himself back in and gives me a long hard look.

"Don't you have a girlfriend?" he says. Then he crawls back out onto the sill.

A warning, and well meant. Staying faithful isn't what Tribal means, that sort of thing not really a pressing concern amongst our lot. It's about staying loyal, a reminder about crossing lines. Jimmy's claim is ambiguous, but it's there.

As for the girlfriend comment, this is not exactly true. Not yet, anyway. But close, I think.

Happened two weeks ago, the tail end of March. A steel town fairytale kind of thing, Yours Truly sweeping in for the rescue. Sounds like utter shite, eh? But that's the way it was. Not like Debbie, thank Christ, my encounter with Eira just a minor but meaningful intervention on the first warm and dry spring afternoon after a miserable winter.

Right on King, actually, Eira and two friends emerging in their private school uniforms from the city bus, flushed and tense because they ditched classes early for the first time in their lives. Real wild and rebellious life choice—they scrambled out of the open bus door and made their way right quick toward the Jackson Square entrance before the army of fucking truant agents lurking in their imaginations spotted and reported them to the Great Wigs upon the Mountain.

But not fast enough. Ambushed by the squid, a tall and wiry skater kid turned thrash punk, maybe seventeen or eighteen. We used to see him when he was younger, intense and reckless and pretty goddamn good on a board, handy with it too when backed into a corner. But one thing led to another, the squid eventually frying a fair number of synaptic connections beyond repair.

Tribal squawks about it, disdainful and cruel, maintaining that vast quantities of T. Leary's snake oil made a magical tragical mystery tour through the squid's wires, but Jimmy knows better. A piss-poor attempt at Dexamyl he tells me confidentially, sadly, an east-end basement chemistry experiment gone wrong. Purple hearts was the original name, an inspired combination of amphetamine and barbiturate, but no one knew what the fuck these imitations really were. As far as street drugs went (Jimmy told me), amphetamines were hard to come by because dealers ran out fast. It was the promise of wiring you up right sharp, clean and focused without the drowsy intoxication of alcohol or the muddy haze of pot or hash or oil. So, a good choice for maintaining and even improving reaction time on a board flying down a crowded sidewalk.

But the squid kind of transformed, or maybe declined is the word, over a pretty short period. From a sharp and hard-shelled street denizen to a soft and bleary, barely sentient accessory. Just another kind of signpost, Jimmy said. Our own Epimetheus, he means, collapsing lighthouse on the shoal, one dim warning lamp barely flickering for those still navigating that particular sea. But this is cause, not effect, the bottom line being that the squid could be an annoying fuck because of boundary issues.

Which is why he threw himself at the penny loafer-wearing dork leading the charge toward the shelter of the underground mall, Eira and the other girl following closely in his wake. And Penny Loafers wasn't much use to anyone, you could tell from body language of course, the squid looming over him in gangly unconscious aggression, shredded jeans and oxblood 14s so scarred and filthy that no one ever bothered to roll him for them, foot-tall mohawk a concoction of electric blue dye and industrial glue.

Harmless, though. He just wanted a smoke, it's all he ever wanted from anyone (and everyone). And now Penny Loafers was caught, held firmly in the squid's clueless grasp and he leaning in close and personal, mouth a stinking hole of brown nubby fangs, shouting.

"You got a smoke, man? Just a smoke, c'mon!" tugging playfully on Penny Loafer's school tie, too, the kid shaking and starting to panic a bit, red-eyed not with annoyance or anger, just fear.

"Gimme a smoke, fuck!" more insistent, tugging still, not so playfully.

Penny Loafers couldn't even answer, the poor bastard. He was a delicate looking kid, blond and willowy, knees starting to soften and lower lip quivering.

The girls were at a complete loss, neither of them very assertive, though they didn't abandon Penny Loafers. But these possum tricks were making the squid, impatient.

"Fuck!" he bellowed, "Gimme a fuckin' smoke, faggot! Hey, faggot! How 'bout that smoke, eh? C'mon I said please!"

Because Penny had that look, but shite like that wasn't cool, which is why I stepped in at all. That, and Jimmy looked at me through a ratty foliage of dreads. *Do the kid a favour, eh?* Just a pained glance as it shifted from me to P. Loafers.

"Before he pisses himself," Jimmy added.

I sighed, a bit put out. "A'right," I grumbled, and bulldogged my way between P. and the squid, giving the latter a friendly shove hard enough to send him sprawling. Good skater reflexes still functioning, however, no one falls on pavement as softly as a skater. He was back on his pins in a flash, bony fists clenched and wild-eyed.

"Hey, fuck you, asshole!"

But I knew the incantation to dispel this street ghost, harmless as he was at heart and more pitiful than anything else.

"Asshole, is it?" I asked casually, teeth clenched and snarling smile. "Those fourteens are shite, but I'll take 'em anyway."

I would never have hurt the squid, not seriously anyway. He hesitated, shit-sure that Loafin' P. was holding out on him, and too far-gone to tell if I was serious. Nothing six inches of straight blade didn't clarify, though, the squid suddenly abandoning the field at a gangly loping run.

So, there it is, more-or-less. My blade disappearing as fast as it appeared and Jimmy smoothing over the shock by playing the gracious host, jack-of-the-road charm and catfish smile in place, inviting the three of them into Jackson Square like he was proprietor of the place. He liked the girl—the friend, not Eira—and assumed responsibility for the intervention.

And rightly so, I guess. I would have meandered by in oblivion.

Penny was quiet, humiliated I suppose. From his mumbled, grudging thanks and inevitable avalanche of I was going to's (confiding his intentions to the girls, not to us) and finally the clumsy attempts at camaraderie in my direction as if all were to assume that he was just about to yank out his own lace slitter from its trusty resting place, I guess he passed for tough in his world. Jimmy and I traded smiles.

We headed to the food court, Jimmy passing the time in lighthearted banter and even winning over P. Loafers before too long. But not Yours Truly—I was all eyes and ears, even in the comparatively calm waters of Jackson Square. Bull's-eye in place, it was best to stay on top of things in close quarters. Of course, Eira—so tragically out of her own environment—interpreted my stony silence as cool indifference, probably the most addictive demeanor to any insecure teenage girl, the emotional rewards of elevating yourself from invisible to a point of interest too compelling. She bolstered herself up and took the plunge.

"Hey, thanks for the rescue," voice timid, a touch shaky.

"Huh? Right, yeah. No problem," eyes still hunting.

"No, really, we were totally freaking out!" Then, timidly, "I'm Eira."

Fuck. Three bomber jackets hung on chairs, but I didn't recognize the skins at the table. We were still outside of the triangular space occupied by the food court, and the skins hadn't seen us yet.

"Oi, Jimmy, who the hell are they?"

Jimmy stopped dead. "Don't know," he said, confused because he knew everyone. "Want me to do a walk-by, find out?"

Too late. A fourth approached the table with a tray, and we were right in his line of sight.

"Fuck it," I said. "No point now, eh? Let's see it out." And I started forward again.

Eira's friend, the girl—I forget her name, doesn't matter—was the first to voice their confusion.

"Um, like, what's going on? What's the problem?"

"The problem," Jimmy said patiently, "is that mods and skinheads don't always get along. That, and my bull's-eye wearing friend here has a fundamental problem with common sense. It runs in his family, I've noticed."

"Running's for pussies," I growled, then felt bad. "No offence," I added, looking at Penny.

But if Loafin' P. took issue, I never found out. Because it was at this moment that the skin alerted his crew mates that I was approaching. The other three turned to look.

And then the skin with the tray sat down.

I was at a loss, Valkyrie wings beating fiercely in my ears, the wyrd laughing and pointing. Down.

Then I noticed, Jimmy already at ease. Black laces and SHARP insignia—Trojan skins, thank the gods, though sometimes that didn't mean shit.

"Close call, eh?" I said to Jimmy. "Where from, d'you figure?"

"Oh, Toronto, most likely. I'll leave a calling card with them and see what I can find. See you in a bit."

Jimmy headed straight on and I herded my wards a touch to port toward an open table across the way. I watched furtively as Jimmy shed one persona for another, every bit the catfish now with a sample of Benzedrine or acid or maybe just a marble of foil-wrapped hash already concealed in hand, a friendly gesture to welcome newcomers.

All this was too much for Penny and the girl. They saw the drugs emerge from beneath Jimmy's poncho and panicked, they were all for moving on, coaxing Eira along with a frantic barrage of excuses as to why they suddenly weren't hungry, but she didn't want to go. *Back to school*, they urged, *gonna be late for the* but I'd had enough and figured it was time they had a right proper education. Or at least a small taste.

"Hey, Penny Loafers," I said, quiet but hard, "don't get your vagina all in a knot. You and Valley Girl sit down and shut the fuck up. I've about had it with your whining. You. No, not you, the pretty one—Eira, is it?—why don't you go grab yourself something to eat."

She got up immediately, smiling and flushed.

"Okay," she said. Then she turned back and added, "Um, you want something?"

Warning glances and a short sharp hiss from the quivering duo.

"Nah," I said. "I'll wait. You could grab a couple chicken balls from the Chinese place, though. Penny here seems to have misplaced his."

And that was the end of it, really. Nothing happened, the skins having migrated from St. Catharines up the Queen E. to Hamilton in search of greener pastures and happy to have met Jimmy, steel town distributer of medicine lodge magic. Eira came back just as Jimmy did. One of the skins came with him to say oi but just to me, the others invisible to him, and Jimmy recounted the mundane details of their migration. Eira squirmed in a schoolgirl's fantasy over even this as the skin and I shook hands, curious bristling moment of aggression and respect.

Christ, I thought, if something worth repeating had actually happened, she probably would've cum on the spot.

So, alone again, I asked for her number, but she wouldn't give it up. Asked for mine instead, which I thought was a line. Surprised the hell out of me when she actually phoned, mostly because I had to give her specific times I'd be in (and by "in" I mean times I'd be within earshot of the payphone outside the library), altogether an awkward end but there it is.

There are closer payphones, of course, but Hamilton Public Library is on York Boulevard. Not too far from downtown, really, but it might as well be on the other side of the planet as far as our lot is concerned. Not meant to be an insult, it's just that reading isn't exactly high on the boot culture priority list, and the library's not on the way to any of the regular Hamilton haunts. Unless you're going to the occasional farmers' market held in the six-storey parking garage across the street. And can you see a couple of skinheads, street scrap boots laced tight and length of chain slung over one of their shoulders, carefully picking through the beefsteak tomatoes?

Me neither.

So, a refuge. I slip away when I can, make my way into the angular concrete monstrosity and then into the stacks. Only a few know of this strange habit, this incongruous addiction to reading. Just Tribal and Tina and Jimmy. But then, Jimmy was the one who showed me the library in the first place. He has that gift—he just seems to know what you need.

Or maybe he has an affinity for identifying addictions.

So, the payphones. I wait for a call, leaning indolently against the rough concrete inside the vestibule and enduring the disapproving glance of the occasional old crone that shuffles by. True to Eira's word, it rings at the appointed time.

"Hello?"

"*Hi!*"

"Hey. So. Uh, how are you?"

"*Um, fine. You?*"

"Yeah, fine. Great." I'm clearly awesome at small talk. Christ. "So, this weekend—think you can make it? Should be a pretty good party." Now that the weather's warming up again, house party season is upon us. She's nervous, though.

"*But whose house is it? I mean, is it a friend of yours?*"

"Well, not exactly. More a friend of a friend." Of a friend. Of sorts.

My kind are predators that hunt pretty aggressively for this sort of distraction. It's another way to slip away for a few hours into a foreign world. It works like this: a clueless kid from the suburbs occasionally has the house to himself because daddy and mommy are off opening up the cottage and want a little time away from Junior. Independence decides to throw a discreet Saturday evening get-together with a dozen friends, maybe beg someone's older brother to buy some beer. News travels to us by way of a predictable migratory path—host tells friends, friends mention it to other friends, and friends of host's friends spread the news until it gets, inevitably, to Fallen Friend. This is the outcast, expelled or maybe a dropout. He's *our* friend.

Or by more direct means. Mentioned, for instance, by some high school kid who buys from Jimmy.

But it becomes clear that Eira doesn't operate on this frequency.

"Look," I say, "it's just a house party."

"*But I've never been to a house party before.*"

"You—wait. What?"

"*Some of us have pretty strict parents. You know,* totally *protective. Don't yours care how late you're out or where you go?*"

"I—" don't even know what to say. So I try the truth. "Nope. My parents don't care at all."

"*Wow! You're really lucky.*"

We attend, it's a pathetic gathering in Westdale and if it weren't for the company it would be a wasted night. At least I'm mobile now because I bought Derek's truck from him in the winter. '80 Chevy G20 Extended, real cargo van elite. Six years old and not exactly a comfortable ride, but I'm one of only a few with a vehicle. A man of property. As for a license and insurance, well. Someday, maybe.

Eira complicates things with machinations so far out of my realm of experience that I feel like I'm in some kind of surreal film—drop off and pick up times and supposed intermediary rides by friends' parents to work on geometry or a science fair project, and then a final pick up time at the Tim Horton's on the corner of Route 20 and fucking Mud Street, up on the Escarpment. We rarely come up the mountain—that's what Hamiltonians actually call the Niagara Escarpment, "the mountain"—so it's all new territory for me. I pick her up in front of the downtown library, however. Lie number one. Science fair research.

She waits on the corner, preppie-style blouse and jeans, light sweater tied around her thin waist. I pull over and roll my window down.

"You waiting for anyone in particular, or will I do?"

She smiles, bright and innocent. Blonde hair and blue eyes and one piercing per ear, tiny gold cross on a chain around her neck. When I told Jimmy and Tribal I was bringing her tonight, they'd looked at each other and then laughed. But I'm flattered by the sheer amount of fabrication it took for her to keep this date. Until she explains it to me as we drive off down York Boulevard.

"*All* my friends do it. They cover for each other all the time. Otherwise no one would *ever* have any fun." Then she kind of takes stock of her immediate surroundings. "Is this your dad's? Like, a work vehicle?"

"No. It's mine." Then, "I don't have a dad."

"Oh my God, I'm so sorry, I didn't mean to—"

"No problem. Never knew him, so no big loss, eh?"

She's quiet for a bit, idly plays with a loose flap of upholstery.

"So, just you and your mom, huh? Got any brothers or sisters?"

A stellar opening to this date, to be sure. Pretty much everything Jimmy said would happen already has. Of course, he also reminded me that the house party will likely end the way they all do: with cops and running. Eira's wearing slip-on flats. Fuck it, I think. All in.

"Okay, Eira, here's the thing. And I want you to know this because if we're together you need to understand where I'm coming from. There's no father. But there's no mother either. My mum," I still use the Scottish pronunciation for her, I don't know why but maybe just habit, "she hasn't been in our lives for a while now, eh? My brother and me, we split home, four years ago. Things were—"

A fucking nightmare. Her drinking was out of control, her bedroom might as well have had a revolving door.

"Things were pretty bad."

I brace myself for a barrage of clueless pity and ridiculous, schoolgirl bullshit followed by a quick drive to that Tim's at Route 20 and Mud. But instead a tear slips down her face. Just one.

"My dad's pretty great," she says softly, "but my mother, she's—she hates everything. *Everything*." Her voice drops to a whisper. "And it's like living in a prison."

She gathers herself, I can feel it.

"I hate her."

It's a reasonably cool Westdale evening, but dry for April. I drive at a respectful pace down wooded streets lined with old two-storey brick houses, every one of them different and yet looking identical to Steph's.

I park one street over, and perfectly. That is, I can look up the driveway and through the backyard of the house I'm in front of and see the back of the host's house. One low courtesy fence separates their backyards. That means an easy escape route, even in Eira's slip-on flats. And judging from the crowd we saw driving in, we'll need it.

I don't mention this to her, though.

When we get to the front door, Eira reaches for the doorbell. I take her hand, twist the handle, push.

Already it's pretty packed. Plastic cups mean keg, and that's a good sign because we arrive with nothing. Eira did ask after our quick dinner if we should pick up a host-gift, which was fucking adorable, and I realized right then and there that I would need to mind how I handle myself tonight. By which I mean no fighting. But that's rarely an issue in these situations, because it upsets the herd.

Jimmy materializes from the crowd congregating in the kitchen, two full cups in hand.

"Saw you parking from the back deck, saw you had someone with you," he says. "Thought I'd save you the wait."

"Appreciated. This is Eira."

"Hey." He hands us the beers and rises to his full gangly height, stares bleary-eyed over the crowd through his forest of dreads.

"Who you looking for?" I ask.

"Tribal's here somewhere, so's Derek. Ewan, too, but he won't be with us for much longer."

I roll my eyes. I'm not carrying his drunk ass out of here tonight. A month ago we were at a party up on the escarpment and the cops showed up on the early side. We found Ewan in the basement, passed out and curled up half in the dryer, just his scrawny legs jutting out. Fucking drummers, eh?

Keg's in a tiny washroom just off the kitchen, idiotic placement because you can't gather around it watering hole-style and fill several cups at one go. The locals—all Westdale dwellers, privilege pulled over their eyes like fleece—mill about, waiting patiently for a turn at the trough. First party or no, Eira slips into place at once. These, I realize, are her lot.

Then Tribal. He bulldogs through, all leather and heavy pewter rings and purpose. Wordlessly, he hands me his plastic cup on the way by and cleaves his way through to the narrow washroom door. A few of the more assertive ones offer a complaint, but Tribal brushes them aside, too.

Thirty seconds later, the keg is in the middle of the kitchen.

He joins us, double fisting. A wary no-fly zone forms around us, but we've become accustomed to this treatment in these sorts of neighbourhoods. Nervous disapproval. I suspect Eira notices it, but I can't read her expression.

"Fucking stupid," Tribal mutters.

"Yeah. This is Eira. Eira, Tribal."

"Hi!" she chirps, smiling and chipper as shit.

Tribal gives her a cursory nod, then turns to me.

"How do I let Jimmy talk me into these things? No one's here."

"Wow, really?" Eira scans the mob, waves excitedly to a pair of lukewarm girls by the door to the deck. "Who *isn't* here?"

But before Tribal can douse her clueless enthusiasm with venomous disdain, Quinn staggers into the room, sees Eira, and bellows a happy hello. They go to the same private school.

Quinn we know.

Surprised and giddy that Eira's at this Westdale gathering, but he immediately turns stoic when he sees Tribal and me. Nods as cool and casual as he can, feigning indifference.

"Hey, how's it going? Didn't know you guys were here."

I give him a nod, Tribal not so much. He never had much use for Quinn.

"Is Eira—did she come with you?" Clearly our proximity to her confuses him.

Tribal clarifies, stabbing a thumb in my direction. "She came with him." Then he leaves.

Eira watches Tribal as he disappears around a corner. "Did I do something wrong?"

"Nah," I say. "This just ain't his scene, eh?" But Tribal made his point.

"Hey, uh, can I borrow Eira for a minute?" Quinn points to the deck. "Some people saw her come in. You know, people from school. They wanna say hi."

"Sure. I'm off to find Jimmy."

Eira, however.

"Don't you want to meet my friends?"

"In a bit," I say. "I'll be back in a few minutes." It's getting loud, though, and I have to shout. I grab Quinn and pull him in close. "Keep her on the deck, eh?"

I find Jimmy in the basement.

He's been here long enough so that the rec room looks like an upscale opium den. Twelve or fourteen people sit in a circle on the floor in various stages of far-too-stoned, thick fog gathering on the underside of the drop tile ceiling. Another half dozen are draped over the furniture—a couch, a loveseat, and a couple of recliners that didn't make the cut for upstairs. He's traded out the regular lamp bulbs for soft orange and purple, his calling card at house parties. Increases sales, he says.

He meets me by the stairs.

"I'm cleaned out." Grinning, too—this has been a lucrative evening. No squabbling over prices in Westdale because the sources are few and the dealers know it. "Wouldn't want to give me a ride back, would you?"

"I'm not alone, remember? Said I was bringing that girl from Jackson Square a couple weeks ago."

But Jimmy's eyes, bloodshot and all hazy-gazing, open wide. "*That's* who that was? I thought you were kidding, man! Tribal seen her?"

"Yeah."

"Ah."

"Yeah."

It gets worse. Out on the deck, Steph has cornered Eira. Not surprising that she's here, since she lives two streets over. But Quinn, in his persistent effort to raise his own sad street credentials, must have made it abundantly clear that Eira arrived with friends of his from *downtown*. Of course, this is Steph's own pet niche and she's an only child, not really into sharing. The ridiculous "I've got *real* street friends" thing, I mean.

It isn't Quinn she won't share with, though. It's Eira. And, of course, I assume that Eira innocently added fuel to the fire by recounting the details of how we met.

"She's so *cute*," Steph says. "She was just telling us all how she met you and Jimmy."

"Oh," says Eira, "so, you know each other?" Still all smiles, but her eyes not so much.

"Yeah—" I begin, but Steph's having none of it.

"For *years*. They're *always* at my place." Always, right. About six times in total.

Jimmy sorts it out, stepping in to smooth things over in one of his oblique ways. But he is distracted suddenly. He cocks his head, listening.

"Steph," I say, "is there a fucking problem?"

"Problem?" she asks, all cutesy Betty fucking Boop. "Why would there be a problem?" Then to Eira, "Why haven't we seen you around before? I mean, you know Quinn, right? Don't you go to that fancy school on the mountain?"

"Um, sure. Yes, but, I—" Eira's floundering. "I guess I—I just don't go to parties. Too often," she adds. Lamely.

"Hey, man," Jimmy says.

"Really? I mean, your, um, *friends* over there say you've never even been to a dance at your school." Then a look, a simulated revelation. "Oh. My. God. Is this your *first party*? This must be *so* exciting for you!" Then Steph hugs her.

"Hey, man—seriously," Jimmy tries again, hand shaking my shoulder.

Released, Eira stands awkwardly, face flushing red and eyes dropping. She's going to cry. I have no fucking idea why, but I see it.

So does Steph.

"Sweetie, are you okay? Maybe that beer was too much."

"Or maybe," I snarl, "she's looking at that hack mark on your face. How did that happen again? Something about a skingirl punching the fuck out of you?"

Drunken Quinn leaps in, oblivious. "I know that story! I *love* that story!" He starts that story. Loudly. And like I said, Steph is pretty self-conscious about that scar.

"Hey!" Jimmy shouts. Jimmy never shouts.

"What?"

"Cops are here, man, I've been trying to tell you."

I grab Eira's arm. "C'mon. Time to go."

—

And about Quinn.

He was older than us by maybe a year or two and not part of the Hamilton scene, a private school kid from up on the escarpment who wandered around the downtown area—walking a tight line on King between Bay and Cannon, and only during daylight—with a few select friends. They smoked cigarettes with shirts un-tucked and ties askew. Real rebellious shit that drove Tribal crazy, he being all for intimidating a pack of smokes or some dosh out of them every time he saw them, because of the sheer unfairness of things. They were just harmless, though, occasional fixtures who comported themselves in a way that was meant to draw attention from the respectable set while remaining invisible to people like us. Incredible: they practiced being blatant and invisible simultaneously.

Anyway, there must have been some appeal to the boot culture groupthink, because he'd finally decided to throw in an oar. Unfortunately, the silly bastard didn't do his research. He showed up one mid-week evening downtown in brand new oxblood 14s, the AirWair tags flapping about in the back, laced like work boots. Mail order, right from Carnaby Street in London. He'd gotten himself a classic poser part-time punk haircut, too, something that could be spiked, but fell neatly into New Wave acceptability when necessary.

Fifteen minutes. That's how long it was before Quinn was hunched up in a doorway, dazed and confused and in his socks on a Wednesday evening. Nice night, at least. No rain.

Of course, he missed the warning imbedded in the traditional opening line right before you get rolled for your boots. Simple enough explanation, he didn't speak the language. It was a pair of skins, red-laced Nazi pricks. They'd ambushed him on the stairs leading down to a head shop. Didn't take too much to reconstruct the scene:

Skinhead #1: "Nice boots." Sly and oily smile.

Quinn: "Thanks, they're new." Chipper and innocent.

Skinhead #2: "Take 'em off." Hard snarl, smile now absent.

Quinn: "Wha—what?" Confusion, disbelief, nervous smile just in case it's a joke.

No joke. Just a fist into the soft belly and a scared grunt as he falls down. Practiced knife work, a pair of tugs, quick rummage through the pockets, and they're gone.

It's a long walk in socks to Carnaby Street (so the adage goes), but Quinn was no quitter. Bad luck, he reckoned. Six weeks later, he was back downtown in a brand new mail order pair of oxblood 14s, still laced wrong.

Fifteen minutes. That's how long it was before Quinn was flat on his back between two cars in a parking lot, split lip bleeding and eyes welling up with tears. Mods this time, three tickets from the Dundurn and Aberdeen area. Nice guys, good scrappers. Again, a reconstruction:

Mod #1: "Nice boots." Sly and oily smile.

Quinn: "C'mon, guys, they're brand new." Voice wobbly with the wyrd, but weak smile just in case.

Mod #2: "Take 'em off."

Etc.

No, if anything, Quinn was determined. Six or seven weeks later, brand new mail order oxblood 14s. Back downtown, determined to fit in at any cost. Too bad about the social smoking, because he couldn't run for shit. That said, he did manage to improve his time by around five minutes, because twenty minutes from the bus stop at King and James, Quinn fell into the clutches of the exact same two Nazi skins who rolled him the first time. And, predictably,

Skin #1: "Nice boots."

Fuck it, Quinn must have thought, and without so much as a word he took them off right then and there, handing them over.

The reason I knew anything about this was that I ended up with a pair, I was wearing them that day Jimmy found Teddy in the alley, in fact. Easy come, easy go, I guess—not much of a story, Tribal and I finding the skin on the edge of unconsciousness just off of John Street, drooling Dramamine all over the front of his flight jacket. He didn't even know we took them at the time, the idiot. I kicked him in the face anyway, of course, a steel toe calling card. Asked around, though—always nice to know your boots' history—and those questions led me back to Quinn's name.

To be perfectly honest, I never understood the mentality behind private school. Even if Quinn serves as exhibit A in its defence, its purpose is still to charge its clients a shitload of money for an education you can get for free on the street. I mean, three pairs of Doc Martens, all from the U.K.—must have been close to five hundred bones, which Quinn ended up paying to learn not to talk back on King Street. Jesus.

Story went around through the usual channels, Derek and I hearing it together from a rudeboy named Seamus who never went anywhere without dressing right proper, pork pie hat and switchblade included. He always dressed like he was ready for a Selecter album cover photo shoot, but most of the 2-Tone skaboys did anyway. They were more at home with the so-called fashion mods than we were, there being a fair bit of snobbishness on the fashion mods' part concerning us (street mods and Trojan skins, that is), and more than a little disdain on our part concerning them.

They saw us as a vulgar and violent lot, and we saw them as overly sheltered and barely sentient mannequins. The skaboys, they were a nice medium through which we could communicate our mutual disapproval of one another.

Happy ending for Quinn, though, as Seamus relayed to Derek and me over beers at a basement keg party up on Aberdeen. It came to pass that Quinn had thrown his lot back in with his upper middle class peers and become Carnaby Street window dressing. French cigarettes, three button blazers, acid jazz, even a Vespa—nice, safe, elitist environment in which to strut and preen.

"Peacock petting zoo," Derek offered, and we laughed. Turtle aquarium more accurate, I thought, but didn't say. Because there was a sideline activity gaining popularity among the skinheads in the mid-'80s, at least in our area—they would roam about in a box van, hunting outside of malls or through suburbia. When they found a cluster of these army parka wearing wannabes, they'd leap out like poachers and nab as many of the flock as they could, packing the terrified little bastards into the van and screeching happily away down to one of the piers. There, without too much ceremony, the skins would chuck their catch into Hamilton Harbour to the amused wonderment of dockworkers and tanker crewmen.

"Turtle tossing," the skins called it. And hate them or not, it was still pretty funny.

But this doesn't put much in perspective, Quinn's past of timid tragicomedy. It was, finally, music that determined trajectory and impact, without consequence, or so I thought back then. Jimmy was right, though—I couldn't read for shit. Teddy's bag of butterflies should have taught me that much, a single wing beat and everything can change. But maybe that's more butterfly affect than effect.

An all ages club called the Four-Nine-Four, we played there regularly, everyone in the band but Derek underage anyway. Like I said before, I insisted on some covers from my comfort zone, Derek in full Trojan support. Jimmy didn't mind, so long as most of each set was original, and Ewan just loved to be behind the kit. Others sat in with us back then to fill in the missing parts—hard to do ska without brass, for instance—and Funhouse, a monster of a Jamaican rudeboy, used to show up with his cousin who could dub right proper to anything with a steady beat. We did some good shows—pretty primitive back then, to be sure—but upbeat and with enough boot culture in the room, a skanking crowd could turn mosh in a drumbeat. That's never bad for reputation, just for cheekbones and noses.

Anyway, Quinn and his new mates would show up for the occasional gig, especially if we were opening for a proper ska band or a group with some circuit longevity behind them. They were confused, you could tell—they'd dutifully memorized every straightforward measure of the revival bands. The Jam, Purple Hearts, that sort of thing. They'd twisted and crawled through the labyrinth of second generation ska (2-Tone, that is). But mostly, they'd committed themselves to every syllable and inflection of *Quadrophenia*, The Who's ultimate mod tribute album.

And missed the fucking point. The only things mod about that album were the details entangled in the lyrics—the music itself was a rock opera, and an exceedingly complicated one at that. Wouldn't have mattered anyway. We had guest horns on stage for a Madness cover, for instance (mates of ours in the headlining band), and Quinn's lot stood in a tight group squawking for "5:15." Ever looked at the score of any song Townshend wrote for *Quadrophenia*? Forget it. We just didn't have the talent to pull it off.

It was after one of these gigs that we crossed paths with Quinn—just stupid luck, we all maintained, but the Catfish smiled and shrugged. Derek had a van, the same one I have now, and we made a run into the North End after dropping off the equipment. Jimmy had made arrangements, so to speak, and a parcel waited for him in a snug and dark little corner just off of Burlington Street. Jimmy never asked for help when picking up drugs, so his quiet request took us by surprise. Ewan bowed out, but Tribal and Funhouse joined us, as did Rob, a Trojan skinhead mate of Derek's and a great monstrous lug to look at. Didn't say much, either. Tribal at least got a smile out of him, asking (after introductions) what tractor plant he'd been assembled at.

So into the North End we went, the time of night making all vehicles too conspicuous and those that stopped under dark bridges even more so. We pulled up beside a sedan parked tight against the bridge footing, tense and ready for the possibilities, but all went smoothly. We never saw the exchange itself, Jimmy taking care of all that by climbing into the back seat of the car and then, thirty seconds later, climbing back out again. The car cleared off immediately, slowly and without headlights, until well away from us. We did the same.

Jimmy revealed his clandestine purchase once we were underway. It was a brick. Still too early for me to fully appreciate that much hash in one place, but the others were pretty giddy, schoolgirl excitement over the myriad possibilities this thing apparently offered. Jimmy told us that he only owned about a third of the thing, the rest belonging to four other dealers who also forked over for this little business venture. Still, Jimmy assured the general company that everyone could expect payment in kind for accompanying him on this transaction, grams (he grinned) that would come from the others' shares, since he, too, risked legal life and limb retrieving the thing from dark and mysterious forces under a murky bridge. Tribal grinned, too, in shameless greed—he knew I'd give him my cut, having no use for it myself. Yet.

But we'd barely left the pickup point when a familiar utility van flew by us, black with Iron Crosses spray-painted on the back doors, Skrewdriver blasting out of the open windows, its obscene audio stench trailing in the van's wake. We knew where they were heading.

In all fairness, we didn't really object to the turtle toss. But the opportunity to turn the tables on some upstanding members of the Fourth fucking Reich was too much to pass up—we all sort of looked apologetically at Jimmy who was cradling his massive lump of narcotic like a baby swaddled in cellophane, but he just shrugged in his serene and passive way.

"Just a passenger on the Journey, man. Do what you feel you have to do."

Derek grinned a malicious and hungry grin, turning hard and speeding up.

We caught up to them just as they were lobbing Quinn's bony frame off the end of the pier into the cold and stinking soup that perpetually reeked of dead fish and marine diesel. He was putting up a hell of a fight, too, and against (of all assholes) Billy Hardcore, that sidekick of his (Angel, wasn't it?), and two other goose-stepping idiots I didn't recognize. Nonetheless, over Quinn went, screaming for help before he even hit the lightless surface below.

We'd pulled up to within about thirty metres, lights off, and doors already open. The other two had gone over without too much complaint, just Quinn crying and screaming as if they were chucking him into a pool of sharks. As we were unloading, though, Jimmy grabbed my sleeve, comprehension in his eyes.

"Hey, that last one, he can't swim—"

Christ, I thought, running to catch up to the others. Now what?

The skins turned in time to see us flying at them, but only the one named Angel made any pretense of running, the others too hardened to let bad odds get in the way of pride. I gave the Nazi pricks a hand, by lightening their burden: ran straight through them and skidded to a stop at the edge of the pier, staring into the blackness for signs of splashing.

Between the four of them—Funhouse, Rob, Derek, and Tribal (no one expected Jimmy to lower himself to violence)—the skins were outmatched. Still, I must have looked pretty daft teetering on the edge of the abyss, bull's-eye taunting them from the back of my shell. But I must have looked right bloody insane when I suddenly threw off the shell and jumped—boots and all—into the Harbour.

Just a feeble flash of foam and a whimper, that's all I got, and I jumped at it. An instant of air between wharf and water and then it was oily lake, violently cold, crushing me as I plunged below the surface. I was up and almost instantly had a handful of material, pulling it toward me and kicking hard for the concrete wall of the dock. He struggled, clawing and clinging as if I were buoyant. Which I wasn't, of course. He would have drowned us both if it hadn't been for the ladder bolted to the concrete and running up between two of the monstrous tires hanging over the wall as bumpers.

Luck, I guess. I really wasn't much of a swimmer.

Once he had safely entangled his arms through as many rungs as he could, he calmed right down. I climbed over him and got myself back to the top, a little embarrassed by the whole thing. But I needn't have bothered, Billy and his mates beginning their involuntary descent (not Angel, no one could catch him) as I cleared the top rung. Quinn was right behind me, followed me up, although I didn't notice until I heard him breathing in short gasps right behind me. The other two kids were already climbing up another ladder about eight or ten metres away—seemed at least one of them had taken a swim before, I guess, to know right where to go in the dark.

Tribal, shiner starting under his left eye where he got clipped, looked at me in utter confusion.

"Uh, why the fuck did you just turtle toss yourself?"

"Yeah," Derek chimed in from the driver's door of the skins' van, "not sure I understand your timing. There was a scrap up here, you know." He pulled the keys from the ignition and lobbed them over the edge. "Hey, Billy, catch!" Kerplunk.

But I wasn't in the mood, jerking my thumb back at the soaking wet and shivering beanpole behind me. "Kid can't swim," I snarled and, picking up my shell, I walked back to Jimmy and the van.

"Hey!" This from Funhouse, rummaging through Hardcore's shit and holding up a half-quad bag of weed, "Dey got dagga! Ah, skinhead no get di herb . . ."

Derek dropped Jimmy off. No point in hauling that much hash all over Hamilton. Then we drove our soggy charges home, right into suburbia. It was a tense ride, not helped by the fact that the van was filled with the toxic stench of marine diesel. Tankers run on this sludgy crap about one step up from asphalt, so it tends to sink into clothing pretty efficiently. Fish don't like it much either, but Hamilton never gave much of a fuck about the fish.

The only good part of the night for me was watching Funhouse fuck with upper middle class white preconceptions. He walked each kid to the front door, ringing the bell and informing a flabbergasted father or horrified mother that we'd fished their son out of the Harbour. Polite as shit, too, leaving each dripping mod with sage advice about avoiding the wrong type of people, each pasty white and shell-shocked parent nodding along in earnest agreement.

Fucking hypocrites.

Chapter Three

And now, Yours Truly is last year's creature of summer heat turned post-vernal castaway: the way is barred—Stephanie will not forgive. Nor will she forget.

Jimmy delivers this edict to me as we descend the rickety fire escape, the only reliable means of getting in and out of the room above the thrift shop that Tribal and I still rent. A mid-May morning, light rain and Jimmy's news no more of an inconvenience than the mildly inclement weather.

"Happened a few weeks ago, actually. Day or two after that party, but I kept forgetting to tell you."

"I figured as much, eh? No loss."

But Jimmy doesn't respond. We reach the alley and he retrieves a pack of smokes from under his light wool poncho. He offers me one.

"I take it you disagree, " I say.

He exhales. "Strata, brother. Burning bridges is bad karma."

"That was bullshit, though, eh?"

"Maybe. C'mon, man. We're supposed to meet Deb at noon."

We drive across the city and into the east end in comfortable silence, Jimmy scribbling away in his beaten old moleskin booklet—repository for his cosmic contemplations, lyrics mostly—and I mull over my supposed loss. I try to remember how many times I'd actually been in Stephanie's house, but the memories blur together.

Fragments, though, fierce and insistent.

Because time, that tumid river, flows on without pause, ebb and flow duly noted. Just illusion, just fabrication by those who rage against it. Pointless, really—time is nothing more than patience, perennial and indifferent to our struggle to dam its progress, to divert its course. Words are the only anchor we have, cast into that relentless current to snag and hold.

So, fragments. I feel left behind somehow, pieces of me lost along the way.

In the four months since Jimmy brought Debbie into the fold, I've slipped away more often to read, sometimes just to think. And I dream that same puzzling dream.

And driving toward Debbie now, Jimmy humming quietly beside me as he works out his poetry, I consider all the words I've ever read or heard or spoken. They, too, left behind. Tossed overboard into the river's current. Or past.

I try Jimmy.

"Hey, can I ask you something?"

"Sure, man. What?"

"I'm not sure how to put it, actually." But I'm rarely if ever self-conscious around Jimmy, and so. "I guess it's a question about, well, words."

"Okay. What about them?"

"When you write down, you know, like lyrics or poetry or whatever, what happens to how you feel at the moment you wrote them? I mean, what you wrote just now. You seemed pretty in tune with something, eh? But what will those words mean tomorrow? Or next month?"

But the Catfish smiles, muses a moment.

"Brother, these words?" He holds up the weathered little booklet. "These words are already lost, man—we left them at the intersection of Main and, like, Sherman. You want to know what I was feeling when I wrote this?" He points to a scrawled line, but I can't afford more than a sideways glance. "Go ask the Jimmy of five minutes ago. If you can find him."

I laugh, then have a thought. Memory, actually.

"What?" he asks.

"Nothing. Just—I was thinking of Teddy. Remember? That bag of his full of dead butterflies."

Jimmy considers, pulls at his goatee.

"No, you have it—that's essentially it. Better than a bag full of live ones. Easier to read."

Words, then.

Jimmy's head and hand and little black book—they conspire together to keep a running record, a neatly catalogued mental history. Otherwise, what would Jimmy's lysergic lyrics or philosophical ramblings be but a bag of flies, each word an insect eager, impatient, witless, unaware of the tight opening, unless is tumbled upon in aimless spurts of frantic flight?

Fitting analogy, by the way. I become suddenly and acutely aware that time, like writing, is just a type of flypaper. That's what I would write, if I could: flypaper prose. Each black speck is a moment, a word, dying or already dead. How old? Do we compare with cold calculation the rates of decay, carbon-date for accuracy? What about for validity?

Because I need my words to mean something—not what I say, I don't say much worth repeating. I mean what I read. There is meaning there beyond the days and nights of circuit gigs and pointless fights and empty sex and petty politics.

This is why Stephanie's "edict," as Jimmy calls it, means nothing. Or probably something less.

We make a left on Ottawa Street and head north toward the Lake.

Debbie's place is a dark and claustrophobic flat above an imported fabrics shop in the textile district, just off Ottawa Street. She works for one of the merchants, though not the one she rents from. Deb minds shop for a short, fat Lebanese man and his wife, also short and fat, but with a worried and weatherworn face so unlike her perpetually grinning husband.

He seems to like us, waddling in undignified and acquiescent haste to the door on the rare occasions we visit Deb during daylight, nodding and grinning and gesturing us in. "Yes, yes, yes, Debbie here yes, you come!" he'd babble, pulling us by our sleeves through a chromatic labyrinth of heaped cloth and middle aged white women digging through the tiers, scrutinizing each layer of the strata.

"They're like archaeologists," I once said in amusement.

"More like grave robbers," Debbie had countered flatly.

In the cluttered little office at the back heady with the thick fragrance of exotic coffee, of honey and incense and cedar, among the myriad photographs of a home so far from this place (markets and family and beaches and trees and ruins in a confusing mosaic, modern Beirut through the eyes of a maudlin Canaanite) is a grainy photo of a man, thin and fit, proud and hawkish, and his young wife, dark eyed and modest of her beauty, small baby in her arms. He pointed it out to me the first time I visited Debbie here, pointing not to the smiling man (himself), but in pride to the young woman. She didn't smile then, either, apparently. I had nodded and gaped and gawked with the appropriate mix of approval and envy, endearing me to the strangely magnanimous proprietor of this place.

But I had pointed to the infant after, raising my eyebrows questioningly. The smile quivered a bit at the mouth corners, the dark intense eyes flashed with water, with confusion, and he had said merely "Ah Ah Ah" just sad intervals of sound. It was enough, though. I felt terrible for even asking. Civil war refugees, then, with their own deep scars, their own heavy and silent stones to bear.

Death by water. I recall this fragment of poetry, then I see him crossing wide waters with his broken eyed wife, part of them left behind forever in that land of Phlebas, soul's flesh stripped, bones picked clean in whispers by that sea's current. Terrifying chiasmus, T.S., for in this deep-sea swell, for them, it is profit to loss and then loss to profit. But empty profit.

And I will add something more: *Empty cradle filled now with dead fabrics.* This will I add.

Just words, though. I am poisoned by the same poetry I find entombed in quiet stacks across the city.

When she isn't behind the front counter, Deb is usually in the back office, talking quietly to the worried wife and she listening intently in solemn and mournful silence. But today the missus shoots us a hangdog look and slinks away as we are hand delivered by her smiling and oblivious husband.

Debbie sits cross-legged on a sinuous and painted stool, sipping away at a mug of pungent tea. Our host points at an open box of cookies, smiling and nodding, pats Jimmy's shoulder, and then exits after his wife.

"We interrupt something?" I ask, watching him go.

Debbie smiles sadly. "Spring is hard for her."

I turn to the wall of pictures, but the one I'm looking for is gone. Debbie watches me, a distant and curious look in her eyes when ours meet again. Jimmy meanwhile tugs absently on one of his dreads and runs a finger over the Arabic script of an open newspaper.

"This is beautiful," he says. "Looks like music to me. You know how to read this, Deb?"

"No. Well, a little." She nods toward the door. "She's taught me a bit."

I glance at the clock by the door.

"You're on lunch, right? Wanna go?" To be honest, the merchant's wife makes me uneasy. I feel she's out there somewhere, skulking between the heaps of fabric, quiet curses and evil eye at the ready.

Debbie reaches into her tea, fishes out a leaf fragment with a long nail.

"Look, I appreciate you two making the trip, but now probably isn't a good time. I should go find her."

"Yeah," Jimmy says. "We should split."

I hold my tongue, this sort of thing happening (it seems) more often than not. Maybe that's a part of it. Why she drifts, unbidden, along the ragged edges of my thoughts, a barely perceptible daydream ghost. I watch her now as she transfers the tealeaf from nail tip to palm, but it's like I'm already outside again with Jimmy, standing in the rain. Debbie looks up, smiles at me.

We drive back along Barton Street, a long and shallow grey wound that cuts through the flea market aesthetics of north end Hamilton. Discount industrial cleaning supplies, appliance outlets, thrift shops, mission soup kitchens. Or the secondary signs of the Hammer's lifeblood—steel workers' union hall, truck service stations, warehouses. I am tired, worn thin. Music and shell and boots seem superfluous here.

Jimmy notices, of course.

"You alright, brother? Pretty quiet."

"I'm fine."

"Uh huh." He offers me a smoke. "You wanna hack a dart, buddy?" He's teasing me, trying to make me laugh. He knows I find the rural Canadian skid-slang ridiculous, but I smile in spite of myself. And, yes, I'm aware of my own hypocrisy.

"Huh? Buddy? Dart?"

"Piss off."

Now Jimmy smiles. I take a smoke anyway and reach for the van's cigarette lighter. Such as it is—it broke about five minutes after I bought the van from Derek. Tribal fixed it for me, duct taping a plastic Bic to the end of the original lighter.

"Hey, man, you mind turning on Gage? Drop me off so I can look at that Hammond."

"Are you fucking kidding? Not that goddamn thing, Jimmy, seriously."

Jimmy has an arrangement with an all-girl punk band—Quaaludes for equipment. We borrow stuff from them a couple times per month. They don't do well on the circuit, mostly because their sets consist primarily of caterwauling and feedback, but they have more gear than any three bands combined. They hole up in this run-down detached garage you can only get to by way of a nameless alley that runs along the backyards of Primrose Avenue.

"C'mon, man," Jimmy says, "what do you have against the retro sound of a Hammond?"

"I have nothing against the retro sound of the Hammond. I *love* the retro sound of the Hammond. It's the fucking tops. However, there is the small matter of it being completely covered in neon pink faux fucking *fur*!"

"So what?"

But there's no reasoning with him. I find the narrow alley opening and hook a left, drive him down to the sagging building.

"Can't stay, man—I gotta pick up Eira soon."

"That's alright," he says. "Can you come back tomorrow and grab the thing? Assuming it's working. I'll let you know." Jimmy knows this is an awkward request because not long ago I slept with the band's bass. Not the bassist, the actual bass—passed out hard after a party, right on top of the fucking instrument. Had a rude awakening later, courtesy of a punkgirl boot to the ribs and some intemperate language aimed at Yours Truly. Still, my van's the only thing the Hammond will fit in.

Eira waits at the corner of Garth and Fennel, but not in the bus shelter. She stands in the light rain, close to the curb.

"Didn't want you to miss me," she says as she climbs in. Still in her school uniform, too, kilt and blouse. I give the upholstery a cursory swat with my hand, but that doesn't do much more than stir up the crumbs and dirt and smut of past passengers. I cover the seat with my parka shell instead.

"Thanks," she says, clearly relieved. I suppose you don't take kilts down to the coin-o-matic.

"Yeah. Sorry 'bout the mess," I offer, but she just shrugs.

"Where to?"

"Don't know, actually. How long you got before you have to be back?"

"The bus leaves at five." She means the school bus. Home is way the hell out in Caledonia, mostly cornfields and dairy cows and tree farms.

This is how we manage, a relationship of stolen segments—a half-hour, sometimes ninety minutes—arranged ahead of time. Not every day, only a couple afternoons per week, after classes of course. Weekends are more difficult.

Tribal found one of Eira's schedules tucked above the visor not long ago, bubbly innocent script written out like a tea party checklist.

"What the fuck is this?" he'd sneered. "You *still* dating that chick?"

"So?" I'd countered.

Tribal tucked the thing back where he found it, shaking his head. "Not a good line to cross, brother. You know that."

And I did. Jimmy said as much, too.

Still.

Eira and I drive down Fennel and turn onto Upper James. There's a coffee shop not too far from the intersection, a short drive, but she feels compelled to fill the time with trivial details. I hear about a paper she's writing, about how boring calculus is, about a French test.

I have nothing to contribute. This relationship is a dreamscape of sorts, a strange otherworld where I feel more passive observer than active participant. Like I feel around Debbie, in a way, but with Eira something is missing. Then it hits me.

Urgency.

That's what Debbie stirs to life—capricious and fey, Jimmy's sonar gypsy. *Dull roots,* I muse, stirred to life by the spring rains. Nonsense thoughts, dangerous thoughts. Loyalty is what defines us, Tribal's cutting inquiry upon me now: *don't you have a girlfriend?* Debbie is Jimmy's find, not mine.

At least, not anymore.

Eira intrudes with an inquiry.

"So what do you think I should do?"

Fuck.

"Uh—just do what you feel is real, you know? Don't bog things down with, like," what? Wait—got it. "Politics."

"Wow," she says, "you really *get* this!"

"Yeah," smooth and smarmy now. "It's a gift."

This is how it works, our relationship a cocoon of sorts beyond the reach of Tribal's venom, Jimmy's concern, or even Debbie's capriciousness. It gnaws at me, too, because there is no logic whatsoever in what I feel for Eira, our worlds so distant that sound and sight should be meaningless, all words lost in the empty void between us.

But.

I hate her.

Eira's quiet confession on the way to a Westdale party—my last. This is the narrow span upon which we meet, not because of a shared enmity (at best I distantly pity my own mum), but because this simple act of bravery, exposing something that raw to someone she just met, was a revelation. Because it's not what we do, sometimes not even to blood. I mean, I'm luckier than most. I have Tribal. I have Jimmy. But there are still things that go unsaid, thoughts we see in each other and know better than to intrude on.

Eira, though, she just opens up, innocent and warm and accepting, and I begin to feel that I can do the same. No shell, no bluster, no street-hardened cynicism. Just me.

—

The weekend is warm, a Saturday far from her supposed research downtown. We are parked at the end of a gravel road at the edge of an abandoned quarry. Bolt cutters did for the gate chain, but I arranged it so it looked undisturbed. A few hours, that's all we have. But it's enough.

I'm in no rush, and say so.

"I want to," she says. Her blue eyes are intense, determined.

"You sure? Not like there's any going back."

"I know." She pulls off her shirt, unbuttons her jeans.

"I mean, we've only been together for," what? Six weeks? What the hell is wrong with me? In my world, six *hours* means Not Happening. Still.

She climbs over the seat and into the back of the van. She slips out of her jeans, just panties and bra. They match—I almost laugh, but bite my lip in time. Slender, pale, fragile, unsure, pretty, kneeling now, thighs parted and shoulders back. This is scripted, memorized, and flawlessly performed.

But she's coming to the end of Act One. Act Two, I realize, is meant to be improv.

I oblige.

Chapter Four

But two weeks later, jumped. Happens to everybody eventually. Still, circumstances point accusingly at Yours Truly for what was, in retrospect, an unforgivable lapse in reason.

A revelation that comes as Tina dabs gently at the split just above my right eye.

"You'll need a couple stitches."

"Yeah. Funhouse can manage."

"Where'd it happen?"

"Catharine Street and King William."

"You were there *alone*? Jesus, what were you thinking?"

Couple of skins from one of the white power crews, young, hungry. But they didn't do it right. Just a glancing blow with a length of pipe because I saw it coming and jumped back, the other one got too close for his mate to line me up right proper. Sudden siren blast, though, and they were gone, shogging across a parking lot at a good clip. Just a cop warning the intersection that he wasn't slowing down for jack shit, it turned out—certainly not for us.

They were after my boots, of course, attracted by the shell and target. Like wasps.

And me? I didn't even get a swing in, not one. What worries me more is that I'm not even that angry about it.

Thing is, I've been going places more and more without the shell. Today was an exception, and a clear indication that head and heart just weren't in it anymore. Stupid mistake, not one I would have made even a couple months ago. But as Jimmy said last summer during a Westdale café conversation, the bull's-eye and I didn't have much time left together.

Tina's was closest, and so.

"Since when are you that careless? You coulda been really hurt."

"Yeah, I know. Thanks, mum."

"Fuck you."

I smile, and then pull away because she pushes too hard.

"Ow! Careful, eh? I'm delicate. Where's Funhouse?"

"He went out for milk." Funhouse loves milk—he goes through about four litres a day. "Should be back soon."

Tina moved in with Funhouse after she came home to find the two rooms above a pawnshop on Catharine occupied by a half dozen Bosnian men in their twenties. The other girls were gone, no trace at all. Tina didn't even try to recover her shit.

Funhouse and Tina and four or five other flat-mates live below a record store on King. It's not spacious, but it's cheap because it isn't exactly up to code. And it's safe because it's right on the main drag.

"Anyone else here?" I ask. It's a little before noon, too early for a visit according to squat house etiquette, but the place seems empty. Still, I feel bad because I definitely woke Tina up.

"Everyone's out, I guess," Tina says. Leonard's bony frame is stretched out on the same couch I'm sitting on, but he doesn't count. He's rarely conscious—like an emaciated hibernating island lizard, connected somehow to Funhouse, but I forget the details.

We can hear Funhouse above us now, floorboards overhead creaking as he enters the record shop and greets the clerk, loud and animated, then the squeaking of old stair treads as he descends. He and his milk come through the narrow door.

Takes one look at me, bloody mess that I am, and rolls his eyes. Wordlessly, he crosses the room to the rusty old fridge, puts away his milk, and grabs a shoebox from one of the two cabinets still attached to the wall.

Tina fills him in as he fetches his surgical needle and thread from the box.

"Kiss me rass! Wah mek yuh wear dat?"

"English, Funhouse. Rough morning."

"Wah mek—why wear da shell, an' alone?" His tone—admonishing, disappointed—makes me smile.

"Hold still," he rumbles.

Funhouse is a rudeboy of the first order. He looks like a giant black bear, powerfully built and a formidable fighter, a right proper mate to have in a scrap. Close-cropped hair topped with a pork pie hat, tight Fred Perry shirt, black mohair trousers and brogues—he dressed the part. Much of the cramped flat was covered with his clothes, all stored in plastic like dry cleaning to protect against the smoke. Suits and shirts hung everywhere, from pipes and from nails, or they were carefully draped over the backs of chairs.

Funhouse inspects his work. He is satisfied. Rising to his full height, he points a long warning finger at me.

Then he heads for the fridge.

And what concern presses its way to the forefront? Eira's reaction to a pair of stitches. Not that this is the first she's seen in our few months together—bruised ribs, split knuckles, some minor and meaningless abrasions. She took them all in stride, fascinated but finally at a point where she didn't hound me with questions.

But recent news, a university acceptance letter, has changed her. By which I mean that Eira finally screwed her courage to whatever fucking sticking place she could find and asked me drive her home Friday afternoon. No end-of-the-school-year bus for her, she would arrive by way of shabby white stallion.

I pick her up right in front of the hallowed institution itself, no Fennel Ave. drive-by's or edge-of-the-field waiting games. Front door service. I park my wreck in the space marked "Headmaster" and wait.

Eira emerges, triumphant and happy. I pull out and drive over to her.

Her smile disappears as soon as she gets in, though.

"Oh my God! What happened?"

"Nothing. Small dispute over property rights."

"But your face!" Her voice wavers and I realize she's actually closer to hysterics than she's letting on.

At least I'm respectable otherwise, the mod street gear of my misspent youth nowhere in sight, though the 10-holes and short-cropped hair remain. She coaches me all the way down the dead straight country highway that leads toward mother, that taut umbilical cord of asphalt time itself wasn't likely to sever, frantically repeating instructions that I don't really hear. I yeah yeah yeah as she talks, but my mind is elsewhere. Gig tonight, party afterwards, that sort of pointless tripe.

"And if she asks, can you just say you, like, walked into a door or something?"

"Sure. Door, got it."

"Wait—that sounds so stupid! What about hit with a baseball? You know, while walking past a park?"

"Ball to the gourd. Got it."

"Or maybe—" And so on.

We approach the isolated Caledonia country abode, a lonely and austere house far removed from city sins (and not one sin is venial, I assure you), a temple in which certain handpicked virtues survived so long as they adhered to the narrow definitions imposed upon them by the Matron herself.

A prison, Eira calls it. But Eira's older brother escaped, moved on. Lives on the west coast. Eira herself is next, preparing to slip through the perimeter come autumn, off to the University of Western Ontario. That's in London, an hour-and-a-half west of Hamilton.

I pull in to the long gravel driveway slowly, respectfully, stopping beside the three-car garage where Eira's father tinkers away on some obscure project.

"So this is he, is it?" he asks by way of saying hello, a pleasant tone, devoid of judgment. It becomes immediately apparent that Eira is at ease around her Dad. I am, I realize, one of their many little secrets.

"Nice to meet you," I say, shaking hands, but squinting into the darkness of the garage. "What's that, a TR-6?"

"Right!" dad replies, a bit excited at my interest. "The motor's over there, still a work in progress, but the body's coming right along!"

Tribal knew a bit about cars, not me, but the cat is so fucking pleased that I'd identified the model that I have to fake it as best I can. I only know what it is because of this poster my brother had on the wall for years, first at home and then, later, in our own place. Fortuitous, I suppose.

I ooh and ah a while as Eira stands in front of the hood watching me, pleased but unsurprised by this development. After all, the man strikes me as next to impossible *not* to like. Just one of those guys.

In the next few minutes, I get the basics. He's a history professor at McMaster University, but every moment he can spare is spent with that decrepit fucking shell of a car, or on one of the other mechanical messes he has squirreled away in there—a disemboweled lawn tractor, an ancient fridge, a 1960s pinball machine. "A work in progress"—he says that a lot.

And if even half of what Eira has told me about her mother is true, then here is the real victim of this farcical tragedy, the poor bastard doing the hard time. He has himself a life sentence—no parole, no reprieve. But we're disparate spirits with a kindred cause, of sorts.

"So, Eira tells me you're a musician. Guitarist, right?"

I smile. "Yeah, that's right."

He looks over at the van. "I suppose you get the honours of the mule work, too."

"Of course," and I laugh.

"You know," he says, "I was in a band myself at your age."

"Dad," Eira whines.

"What?" he says disarmingly. "The French horn is a noble instrument!"

"Dad, *please*!"

"Now hold on," I say, jumping to his defence. "If it's good enough for John Entwistle, it's good enough for anyone."

"Exactly!" he chimes. "It's like Ian Anderson and the flute. And, as a matter of fact, Entwistle was an influence of mine in the late '60s and early '70s."

Then he frowns, considering. "You'd, uh—better go up to the house."

Eira sighs. "I know. C'mon."

And as we walk from garage to front door, I see a curtain rustle. Then another one. Eira's mother has been waiting, lurking to be more precise, assessing every discernable signal and sign.

The door swings inward silently and there she is, a squat toad of a woman in a hideous pant-suit the colour of diseased liver, eyes like cold, dead stars trapped between a tight, graying perm above and loose flaps of jowl below.

"Pleased to meet you," I lie to break the considerable ice, holding out my hand.

She takes it briefly, a clammy touch for the sake of fulfilling custom, placing that trembling eel-like appendage in mine before pulling it away, a moray recoiling into its lair. Fitting, since the sleeve of the gruesome jacket is too long, swallowing her hand up to the pudgy knuckles.

"So," she begins, "How long have you been seeing my daughter?"

It's more an accusation than a question, but I've been coached ahead of time, on this one.

"Not long," I lie again. "Two weeks tomorrow, to be exact."

She's quite literally plugging up the door to her home, furious portal guardian of all entrances under her domain.

Too late for one door, though, and I think she senses it. A tiny apoplexy crawls wildly about under the soft flesh of her face, like some mad and miniscule mole.

"Two weeks tomorrow, you say?" she repeats calmly, her small mouth tightening against all probability into a stone-hard line in that doughy sphere of flesh. She glances beyond my arm at my van, grey with dirt and shabby, but at least it has windows in the cargo bay so it doesn't look like the lair of some pedophile gone mobile. She isn't overly subtle about it.

"I can't say I approve of *that,*" she says, jerking her head in the van's direction. "What does a young man like you need with so much space, hmm?"

And then, without waiting for a response, she uncorks the door to allow us in. Which is appropriate, since that van is where her daughter let *me* in, as it were.

After this, we met when and where we could, same as the spring, really, but this time under the dour scrutiny, the smoldering awareness, of Mother.

Jimmy and the others found the entire situation hilarious, of course. They still didn't understand what I was doing—Eira had a certain innocence about her that sets those mired neck-deep in street politics on edge—and they definitely didn't understand my stubbornness when it came to locales. But I couldn't exactly bring her along to one of the squat house communes inhabited by the shiftless street trash tribes (us included) of boot culture Hamilton, could I?

Funhouse jumped to my defence one night, unexpectedly. Tribal opened up on me because I was going to skip a house party to spend what little time I could with Eira. Funhouse, though, he put a heavy paw on my brother's shoulder.

"Leave it be, mon. How he gonna bring her back to mamma stinking of di herb?" He drew out the last word, a generic Jamaican idiosyncrasy that some of the younger 2-tone white kids tried to mimic. (Once.)

But Tribal pressed the issue. He resented Eira, and Tribal was not one for hiding how he felt. He hated it when I missed gatherings.

"What the fuck, Funhouse—you condone this shite? He doesn't even *smoke* it, my man! If my brother's gotta bring her, then he can just hover outside, in the yard. Naught but the keg and cigarettes out there, eh?"

"An' 'ventually di babylon," Funhouse added with a sly wink, "an' di running, zeen. Remember, mon—you like dat bit. We don't."

Tribal exhaled, disgusted, and looked around for support. This evening, however, there was only Leonard on the sagging and stained chesterfield, awake for once, and Tina in the tiny washroom, applying makeup—Funhouse's other flatmates had all drifted off to their various nighttime haunts.

Still a skeletal piece of human wreckage with a rat's nest of dreads and a sallow tinge to what little flesh was stretched loosely across his skull—chronic to his carcinogenic core—Leonard nevertheless added his bit this time, parting his withered lips in a slow and gruesome grin, grey tongue moistening the desiccated borders of his mouth with gluey saliva before running itself over the snaggly remains of his upper teeth.

"Di boy in love," he croaked, pointing a shriveled stick finger at me, and giving a leaky wheeze. "Hey mi yute, she a put Obeah pon ya, uh? Heh heh heh!"

Funhouse smiled, even while trying to quell this withered zombie's mirth.

"C'mon, Leonard. You no helping, mon."

"Mi? Ha, ha! Mi nuh kya. Hey, Tribal, wa'ppun, rude bwoy? Mebbe she need a put Obeah pon ya, too!"

"A fuckery dat, Leonard!" Funhouse scolded.

Leonard laughed again until he was coughing in throaty heaves and went back to his fucking dagga. He let it be after that, offering Tribal a hit to show he was just joking.

No harm done. We still couldn't understand a fucking word.

Summer crawls along, hazy and slow. Gigs are plentiful, and we're competent enough to secure some regular slots at good venues. The Hamilton music scene is alive and well, a thriving entity whose tentacles stretch aggressively along the main drag and then reach into smaller clubs, basement bars, corner pubs, underground afterhours haunts, and outward still. Out into the countryside, bands play bush parties. There is talk of a festival. The tentacles even reach into midweek and earlier—we nab a regular slot every Tuesday night at the Hound and Hare.

Through it all, I see Eira two, maybe three times per week, only because her dad made shit sure she had her driver's license and her own car. Nothing too impressive (says the guy with the '85 rust box), just a Chevy Celebrity, but it's a way to get back and forth from London. And driving to and from Hamilton is meant to be good practice behind the wheel. Even mother couldn't argue with that logic.

But Eira's different, somehow. More confident in how she handles herself. Our talks, once so candid and effusive, are now conducted as if we were passengers on a bus. Guarded, slightly aloof, coded.

Distant.

Sex, too. Still intense, I take strategic advantage of my experience, but it lacks that shared cathartic connection. As if we were sharing the space instead of the act. Afterward, she dresses quietly, pondering something light years away from the floor of the van or the blanket laid out under a copse of trees. No longer does she trace an idle finger over my tattoos, my scars.

She has stopped asking questions.

Mid-June. That's when it began, I think. Maybe I felt the rift and took steps, or thought I had. A fool's errand, as it turned out.

Eira and I met outside Hamilton Public Library, my idea—nostalgic, most of our early dates having started on that very stretch of pavement. Once, I even made sure I was there in time to be busking when she arrived. Her dad had dropped her off and she didn't know quite what to do, lost between pausing and passing. But dad wasn't a worrier—he drove off, and Eira asked for another song after I finished the one I was on.

Anyway, she arrived a little late and a touch put out.

"Why did you want to meet here?" she asked.

"I just—I want to show you something."

Then I led her to my corner in the Public Library. I felt like I was introducing her—not to family, but to something familial. Or familiar, at least, this hidden alcove my own mechanism of escape. I thought Eira would understand, she'd read things, knew the means of prying secrets out of words, while I could only feel my way through language—groping blindly through that land of vibrations. For me, language was mostly a tactile journey.

Trembling, intent, I led her a little too quickly through the lobby and up the stairs, beckoning her on as if something else might distract her before I could show her what some small part of me huddled against a vast and consuming emptiness needed, wild-eyed and shackled by desperately lonely necessity. Who else could I share this secret with? Only Jimmy, but for him all things were transient. Tribal knew but didn't care. Tina, too, but she didn't understand.

So, there I was, a ludicrously self-important hypocrite—streetwise and violent and fiercely independent, broken-nosed and scar-knuckled and weary of the vigil it sometimes took to navigate even from street corner to street corner, taking in stride a day or two without food or a month without hot water, trembling with insecurities and excitement over—what? Soft-bellied exposure? This well-guarded weakness emerging bat-like, gentle winged and blind (*the eyes are not here*) to what Jimmy (*there are no eyes here*) called the strata?

Eira and I crossed the aisle and I led her through the stacks to my corner, chair nestled in the angle between the concrete wall and the large window overlooking the street below. I smiled, self-conscious and suddenly at a loss for words.

"Well, this is kind of it," I heard myself say. "This is where you can find me . . . " this last bit limply offered. I suddenly felt like a dog, waiting for approval on the porch.

She didn't really react, just a small nod and polite smile, eyes distant, vacant, in a way I'd never noticed before. *She'll get it in a moment,* I thought, *she'll feel what I feel. These things she knows, they are familiar, real to her.*

But I was wrong.

Eira took up a slender copy of Kafka's *Metamorphosis*, but only because I handed it to her. Polite, you know? She held it limply in uninterested fingers, gaze drifting instead through the window and down to the street.

"Um, I don't . . .I'm not sure why you brought me here. I thought we were getting some dinner."

"Yeah. Right, dinner." I took the book back, tossing it onto the chair, both of us now standing there awkwardly.

"So," I said, at last, "where you wanna go?"

She smiled and shrugged.

"I don't know, anywhere, I guess. Just not—" and here she smiled again, but in a way at once incredulous and condescending, "not to the *library*. You really hang out here?"

I had to rein in first, momentary maelstrom of words and images like a flash flood raging, tenuous and trembling (but not with tenderness, lips now dead, having made a supplication, a prayer to this broken stone—*the eyes are not here, there are no eyes here*—a mantra, whispered without sound, calming, I regain control).

"Eira, I *can* read, you know."

"Oh, *please*—that's not what I meant!" Bullshit. "It's just that, well, I never really pictured you hanging out in a—a *library*."

"Yeah, I guess," I said. "Let's go."

And revelation? It too came with this, my whimper of submission. *Let's go*, and no more ever said about it.

See, I suppose what I wanted was for her to take up Kafka's nebulous labyrinth of words and images and say, *This is what it means*, or *Here's how you're supposed to read this*, or *This is the secret to how it's done.* She had to know, I figured. That school on the escarpment, after all—private school, they do that sort of shite, right?

But what the fuck did I know.

There was nothing at stake, I guess, no required response or report to make on the doings of Gregor, a young man with shitty parents and a useless sister waking up to discover that he was a monstrous vermin. I had devoured the words, ravenous for meaning, balanced on a precipice overlooking a vast and bottomless sea, whose nameless depths I couldn't make myself jump into—I'd never really understand, I just knew that I'd never ride the deep currents below the surface. That cramped and shabby five-room flat in Prague where Gregor suffered stoically, pathetically, pointlessly, among three human parasites. Hollowed out, one page at a time.

I remember, too, how I both loathed and loved it—I grappled with the book like an insubstantial mist, meaning (whenever it took form) as fragmented and painful as shattered glass, and it frustrated me to tears, I'm ashamed to say, until I finally let go, feeling as if Kafka himself had wrenched it from me. Just a single choked gasp and hands pulled fiercely across my eyes, looking up again to hunt for witnesses through a blur and guilt but finding just one old librarian watching me surreptitiously, her practiced hands replacing books on nearby shelves.

It was because of Grete, Gregor's own selfish siren, whose final, cold betrayal outraged me beyond reason. Or without reason, maybe, seeing my outrage lacked substance too, just another sort of mist. The image of Gregor reduced to a broken beetle at a shop girl's feet. He alone comprehends her, failing mind decaying under latent insect/incest fantasies telling her how he alone must have her, love her, own her, at last a true parasite among his (This is how I struggle, a fool's shabby collection of emotional refuse. I read, I am ravenous, I even dream of these things, but then these tiny worlds are lost to me when once again I return to the rootless drift, the orbit-less trajectory of my) own kind.

And so I'd handed Eira that book feigning a detachment I didn't feel, waited trembling for her verdict, but what I really wanted was that cliché connection. Not a beetle, maybe, but a spider—blind and crippled, leaning out recklessly over the Precipice of, what, *this valley of dying stars,* is it?—and hurling strand after silken strand into emptiness, the vast spaces that separate us all, hoping to make one substantial link.

But all she did was smile impatiently at me and put it down. First test Eira ever failed, though neither of us realized it at the time. We are, all of us, blind and tiny worlds hurtling through a lonely and endless void—a dead land.

A cactus land.

Chapter Five

And later, under a street lamp in front of a dormitory, she would play for me a rehearsed and tired song. And I, too wretched and too overwhelmed to argue, would turn and slowly crawl away, just a hollowed out shell.

Late November gathers itself for the mockery of months to come.

And me? I pound whiskey out of a paper bag, propped up like salvage against the cold wall of the library. My guitar, discarded carelessly on the sidewalk nearby and with two broken strings, gathers beneath it the shadows of the cold afternoon.

I compose a letter, *Dear Eira*, not committed to paper, though. Just to memory.

Dear Eira, this is just to say

Late afternoon library patrons sweep by, incensed or amused, taking stock of this sad drunk on the sidewalk, but I greet them all with bleary-eyed indifference. *Dear Eira*, (I begin again) *this is just to say*

And so it goes.

Drove home pretty late that last night, huge fight the whole fucking way. Yelling, swearing, wild gesticulations, the lot. Mostly for show, though. You weren't in the car. Those I passed must have thought they were seeing some music fiend bellowing away to the radio.

True, in a way—I was singing to you.

As I entered the modest broadcast radius of Hamilton's university radio station, though, I calmed right down. It was the opening riff of an acoustic guitar—mine, drifting invisibly across the ethers, broadcast to a handful of late night listeners. A surreal experience to hear yourself between commercials and the pseudo-sultry voice of a university DJ. She played two songs in a row off our only CD, following the tracks with vague praise—she called them short and sweet, adjectives oddly offered—and a special hi to Derek.

Then I remembered. Derek had slept with her two weeks ago, a house party hook up in Westdale. If I remember correctly, that encounter was also followed by the same vague praise. Still, she played the songs and that was something. Maybe an apology, Derek's ego took a pretty vicious beating, after all. Fuck it, though: beggars can't be choosers.

It was the first time I'd heard us played on the air. We'd had tracks played before, the others had heard them, either whole songs or pieces cut in compilation style to advertise the Hamilton music scene, but this was it for me. Virgin no longer, a pleasant and cerebral audio fuck that soothed me into quiet contemplation, sweet tranquility even if it was short-lived.

Then I thought, shit, maybe she's right, this midnight DJ: short and sweet might be exactly what it is. But infuriating, too, because I wanted you to hear it, I don't know why. As if hearing that song—the song Jimmy wrote about us—from an objective source would somehow validate it. Or me.

Stupid, really—just a senseless late night rambling thought, but drowning I guess you'll grab hold of anything, even (or maybe especially) the desperate and frayed ends. Just segues without substance.

Eira, this is just to say

November. A shite time of year to get dumped, but there it is. She'd stockpiled her own armament of adjectives, and although she waged full-scale warfare with them, at least short and sweet were not among my list of crimes.

Distance gave her strength, or maybe perspective. I sure as hell didn't have any. Once Eira realized that she was no longer that timid girl in ethical shackles struggling to open her legs, ankles still woefully bound tight by Mother's authoritarian apron strings, the real measure of distance became the space between her matron's cold and disapproving stare and the frosh party in the dorm next door.

Mother was finally far enough away not to burst in unannounced. Far enough away so that she couldn't (I swear to God) seize at hands—Eira frozen, mortified—and eagerly sniff at fingers like some feral bloodhound seeking illicit musk, or feel over and under the sheets for telltale signs of dampness. Jesus fucking Christ, the matron of Eira's world was, to put it mildly, the proverbial hatter.

I learned right fucking quick not to spend too much time in the house. After the first finger-smelling incident, Eira couldn't look me in the eye for a week. I'd laughed it off, for her sake. Still, it wasn't anything worthy of repetition, so I stayed the fuck out. Which I think might have been the point.

But that was still summer.

Not that I'd ever coerced her—quite the opposite. I guess I'd developed some variation of a Pandora complex, if such a thing exists. Some things should remain closed, but the lid to this vessel was membrane-thin and in the possession of a girl teeming with pent-up resentment. She never put her true motivation into words—I don't think she could have—but when she finally laid out her points as to why we should have sex, well organized and concisely delivered, it boiled down to the two of us making love while, simultaneously, fucking Mother. Her decision to have sex was an act of self-inflicted terrorism. Eira convinced me to breach the levy, to break through the most precious wall in her mother's otherwise impenetrable defences.

But the dual nature of this act came naturally, since I'd been living two completely separate lives our entire relationship. What I mean is that I was faithful to Eira, but only when we were together. The rest of the time—after gigs, at parties, wherever—casual sex was just a part of the landscape, no one took it seriously. At least, most of us didn't.

Witless fool. I helped her to throw open that box of maladies, everything released save what fool's gold hope remained within.

Dear Eira, this is just to say.

The rest tumbled downhill, propelled by inertia, beyond my control. Nothing left to protect, she slipped away from me soon after she got to university. I'd done my bit, performed my task in her evolution, she could breathe the air now.

To her credit, she at least dumped me in person. Outside the dorms, ten at night, under the incessant insect buzz of a streetlight, its post plastered with photocopied ads for roommates and keg parties and frat events. This was her choice of venue, dorm behind her a thunderous cacophony of music and laughter and shouting.

"I just think we've drifted too far apart."

"But, I don't—why?"

"Look, you know it, too. This year has been really great, but we're just not right for each other."

"But why not?" I heard myself ask, unmoored, roar in my ears drowning out the din behind us. Like I was a passive observer to a discussion between two strangers, just a member of the audience.

Eira considered, glanced behind us at the dorm. She was eager to return, body language clear. In a way, she was already there—just this final performance to go, for the sake of closure. "Listen, it's not like I'm not grateful. You really opened up a whole different world for me, but I just can't see us growing together." And then, of course, "This isn't your fault, honest, it's totally me."

Followed by another quick glance behind. And I realized in that moment that somewhere, peeking timidly or maybe just anxiously out of a dark upper window, was my replacement. Things clicked together, I'd met him a few weeks before, slope-shouldered disheveled guy, soft-bodied with close, weak eyes and a severe overbite. *Fuck me*, I thought, *you must be joking.*

"Eira," I whispered, "I can't—it's too, I still love you. You said you did, too, you can't just stop. Maybe there's something I can—"

"You need to go now, it's over. Goodbye." She turned and walked her narrow line back into the dorm. I was dumped.

Carefully rehearsed and coldly performed. Act One was over. And Act Two? Improv.

Broken, set adrift, I clung to my wreckage and headed home.

That is, I obliged.

Dear Eira.

Now slouched against the library despite the November chill, I swig whiskey from a paper bag like the flotsam we throw change to over on

King and James. And of all fucking people, she's suddenly looming over me: Eira's mother—two books firmly trapped by those sausage-like digits, imperious sneer spread across the doughy sphere, at once livid and smug.

"Well," She drawls, "isn't this a pleasant sight? I *warned* my daughter not to get involved with your *type*."

"I'll bet you did," I slur. I've been here a while.

"You can be damn sure I did. And now," and here she smiles, venomous derision visibly dripping from every bared fang, "Eira tells me she has a *new* beau, an *engineering* student with a future, instead of a worthless drunkard with a van. Things worked out *quite* well." And then she galumphs her fat carcass up the stairs and into the library, her triumphal ascent, I guess.

And for once, nothing comes to mind, nothing I can say can penetrate that self-satisfied carapace and get at the sullen fury beneath. I just watch her waddle off, impotent and outraged and wounded and confused there on the concrete with my 40 in its paper cocoon. I don't say a goddamn thing.

Not even when she reemerges fifteen minutes later, serenely pleased with herself, the cops arriving almost upon cue to take away my half empty bottle and issue me a 53.75. Ticket, that is, the fine for drinking in public. All under the smug gaze of that obscene manatee, the fat fucking bitch.

They're cool, though. Just the ticket. Should haul my inebriated ass off to the copshop, but I don't think they like her much, either.

But I sink, weighed down by the weary hours and then days I have endured without phone calls, thin and brittle time like onionskin collecting around my feet. *I will convince her otherwise*, I vow, *I will construct*, but it is all too pathetic and transparent, my only weapons are words. And I already know that a word is unreliable, same as everyone and everything.

I am numb. I drag my guitar into my lap, wipe off some of the cold mist that clings to the battered wood. And then, late afternoon hangover setting in with a vengeance, I skulk into the library and lose myself among the stacks before retreating to my corner.

On the sill beside the chair, is a copy of Tolstoy's *The Death of Ivan Ilyich*. Not put there by me, though. I've already read it, but I throw myself into the seat and pick through it anyway, this darkly humourous and biting attack on pre-comrade yuppies and their filthy ilk.

As I read through it in bits, though, I remember: Ivan's marriage to his vapid wife—like his life—an ocean dotted (sparsely) with islets, brief moments of joy. But Tolstoy got it wrong. He should have said it was a desert dotted with mirages, empty journeys from lie to lie, fabrication to fabrication.

What joy, my ass, Ivan. You should have yelled out *What shite.* But who the fuck am I to criticize? Nobody. I'm not (how did that liver-coloured *vache* put it? Oh yeah) the *type.*

Later, I decide, I will pass it by Jimmy. See if he likes the sand better, too. But he'll just agree out of hand, a supportive mate. See what I mean? Just a goddamn illusion. And so, once more into the breach.

Dear Eira, this is just to say

this is just to say

That there's nothing left to be said.

Yeah. That feels about right.

—

Jimmy heard about my little encounter outside the library from Tina. She's the one who first found me after I returned to the library steps, bottle-less and ticketed. He asked around but no one knew where I'd disappeared to. No matter—he knew where to look.

Across Hamilton Harbour is a small parking area with a couple of picnic tables and a tiny stretch of stony beach. Directly across the wide stretch of slate grey water are the immense steel mills, themselves slate grey and green and black and dun as they hover, as it were, through fog and filthy air.

But at night, the whole place transforms. To the left is the monstrous arc of lights, the Skyway Bridge, with its myriad pinpoints of binary stars (white pairs falling, red pairs rising) making their steady way across the span. To the right is the dim and steady glow, pinkish-orange and soft, of the city at night. But directly across the water, silk-black mirror in the darkness—ah, that's the real reason for visiting this little corner of the wealthy and suburban north shore called Burlington. Because at night, the smoke stacks that rise above the yawning furnaces tucked into the bowels of each steel mill belch forth towers of fire, huge conflagrations of fierce light that set aflame both sky and lake.

Jimmy arrives during daylight, materializing it seems from out of nowhere. I'd spent the last three days sitting or standing quietly by the gently lapping water, talking in circles to myself, trying to rationalize the random and unconnected events that led me to this place, my only companion on this mournful and pathetic soul-search a dead and bloated carp decaying on the stones an arm's length away, so I jump a bit when he finally speaks. He's obviously been assessing for a while before he committed himself to interrupting my companion and me, the two of us immersed in a fierce, silent debate over what I could have done differently under the streetlight that final night.

"Alright," he says quietly, "you're done." Then he kicks my mate into the lake with the toe of his boot.

I watch as the carcass bobs along with each small wave.

"Maybe I'm not," I say, sullenly.

"Oh? Figured anything out? You and your friend come to any conclusions yet?"

"No. Not really."

"Then you're done. Now let's go, it's fucking cold out here—and suburbia doesn't approve of whisky straight from the bottle. They have props and rituals and I think occasionally citrus fruits to legitimize their whisky drinking. C'mon, mate, up you get. And I'd better drive."

"You don't have a licence," I manage.

"And you don't have any depth perception. Gimme the keys."

"A'right. Where we going?"

Jimmy thinks a moment.

"I have just the place."

And he does.

Debbie opens the door.

"Oh. You found him. Still drunk?"

"Still drunk," Jimmy confirms.

Debbie takes my hands, smiling sympathetically at my pathetic state.

"Leave him here," she says softly. Jimmy hesitates, then nods and disappears down the narrow stairs without a word.

"Well," Deb says gently, "What are we going to do with you? No—" I've already moved a bit into her doorway, but she stops me. "Take off your boots."

I comply with some difficulty, leaving them behind as she leads me into the shadowy recesses, through a beaded curtain and into her tiny universe, a confusing maelstrom of sight and sound and scent.

Debbie's tastes, like her sense of humour, lie somewhere between the macabre and the comically blasphemous. No pseudo-hippie tie-dye in this (micro)cosmic leg of her celestial sojourn, instead a wild menagerie of religious iconography caught in the loving embrace of the Goddess Kitsch. Or the mass-produced elevated to religion, like her stuffed Warhol doll nailed to a miniature rocking horse. It's hard to tell.

I sit down heavily on the low futon in her small living room, flanked by retro lava lamps (red and green) tucked into the laps of matching seated Buddhas. Her small television is in front of me, always on but just noiseless flickering white static—and upon its hot surface lounges her only roommate, Lily, a quiescent metre-long iguana. On the wall above the lizard hangs a large crucifix, naked body in tortured repose upon a plaster cross. But of the head only the thorny crown and poorly painted brown hair is visible, the rest covered by a black and white mask of Timothy Leary's serious face, cut out from a magazine and tied in place.

"Listen," she begins, sitting cross-legged on the floor in front of me. Her head blocks out the television screen, pale static halo, a silver sunset obscuring the details of her face. "You have to accept it. This mourning of yours, it's self-destructive, a dead end." Debbie turns briefly to check on Lily, more earth mother than maternal, then back to me.

"But you, well. You're so linear, just like Tribal. That first time we—" She looks away again, this time just a quick glance at a mannequin in the dark corner behind me. "That first time we . . . we met—that time in the park, a million years ago—I knew you were brothers, even then."

She shifts slightly, her face invisible in the blackness of her own eclipse, pellucid and silver static. Above her head floats Lily, seemingly legless now in the glow as she, too, shifts herself into one long and sinuous line, neck craned and tail extended in placid pleasure.

"Listen to me, this is important." Her voice, as opiate as ever, caresses me. I stare into the shadow searching for a glimpse of that bewitching mouth, but the darkness deepens as she talks, my eyes blurring with the strain.

"Time is really, well, just an inaccurate convenience we use to map things out. What I mean is, you've spent all your time considering the 'what ifs,' right? Well, in your self-induced world of speculation, the possibilities are endless. And meaningless, by the way. Think about this: what might have been and what actually happened both point to the present, to the now. So what are you going to do? Wait—" She stops me before I can interrupt, word unuttered, breath suspended there in the sudden silence. "Because tomorrow is already determined, we simply fulfill our natures. Your only real choice is how you get there."

"So . . . you're saying every path leads to the present," I mumble.

"Yes."

I look at her, drinking in her outline.

"Deb?"

"Mmm?"

"From where I'm sitting, it looks like you're wearing a lizard hat."

She smiles, or at least I think she does.

"I think," she says softly, "I'll make a choice for you." She rises, one fluid motion against the very laws of gravity, like mercury rising, and reaches out a slender hand.

"Come with me," she says, gesturing at her dark bedroom with a slight nod of her head.

And one thing more.

I still keep the bowl of rose petals she gave me afterward, a small clay bowl on the table by her bed. I took the proffered gift from her hands in silence (*they too,* I thought, *those thin fingers like mercury too*). Confused by the gesture, forever a victim of the same error, *Impact without consequence*, that erroneous echo skipping dangerously across the strata too rapid to catch or to see (Jimmy says *You forget*) and here, again, I am blind to the sigil, to the sign (Jimmy says *You forget that we live between the strata, not just on the top layer,* these coffee shop words, at least, I remember).

Still, sometimes I remove the small bowl from its place and gently insert my fingers, eyes closed, into its silken depths, soft caress though each brittle petal is coated now with dust like a moth's wing. Or a butterfly's.

There I feel, or believe I feel, or *need* to feel so urgently that it becomes so much an echo of the moist and inviting folds that this vessel once held, humid petals that once clung to my fingers, as they slipped beneath the soft and yielding surface.

I still collect fragments, and a late night phone call from Tel Aviv will change us all.

Debbie Dream.

Emerged out of the night when we were kids and disappeared into a night years later. In that brief span between, though, Debbie shaped us—transformed us with nothing more than her passive presence, her passive distance.

Patience, though. Her story will come in good time, tragic and beautiful and brief—our wayward intergalactic gypsy, a shooting star.

Or falling star, maybe.

Yeah. Falling.

PART THREE

the river bears no empty bottles

Chapter One

But eventually, a lighthouse.

Although it is nonsense physics, because—lost and lightless on the sea, after blindly groping through the days and nights that followed my one brief respite with Debbie—the lighthouse finds me, not the other way around.

Out at the Point on a bitter December evening, and I standing still as stone, overlooking the frozen water below. Tribal emerges from the deepening grey of twilight, footfalls hidden by the hiss of falling snow.

"There you are," he says. "Been looking for you all afternoon."

"Oi," I return absently. "Got a light?"

He looks over at the small tent of wet and snowy sticks enclosing crunched up balls of soggy newspaper. I'd built it hours before, then forgotten about it.

"That ain't gonna burn, mate." He reaches inside his leather. "But this will."

Looking at that crooked monstrosity of a spliff, I think *why not? Why the fuck not? What harm can it possibly do me now?* Lost and lightless, after all—time to shed one shell for another, renew, restructure.

"Yeah, alright," I say.

Tribal is taken aback for a moment, then smiles, pleased but serious—he, too, knowing the difference maybe between recreation and re-creation. He lights it, working it into a reliable and steady burn.

"Gently," he instructs, "hold it in your mouth for a second before breathing it in. It gets hot—"

But, of course, I choke half to death on it anyway.

"You cold, man?"

Tribal's voice drifts into awareness, detaches itself from the slow pulse of snow. I hear each snowflake as it slides across the wind-churned surface of the frozen ground, granular and independent voices like a vast crowd engaged in a thousand content and civil conversations. I am contemplating winter as Tribal speaks. I love it, suddenly and fiercely, this frozen hiatus from the weary shift of seasons.

"Hey, know what pisses me off?" (I lean in, a confidential secret.) "People who have to point out buds on tree limbs and new leaves and shite. They're the same fucking people who have to constantly point out fall colours like the rest of us are blind or something."

"Uh, yeah, that's real shite. You getting cold?"

"But winter, man—winter's different 'cause there's nothing for them to latch onto, you know? Like a flower or a new leaf, that's one thing, eh? You can point that out and say 'hey, look at that fucking flower' or 'there's a new bud on that branch' or 'ooh look, I found a goddamn red leaf on the ground' but winter, what can they say? There's a snowflake? There's another one? I mean, it's too vast—the best they can do is say 'shit, it's snowing' and then go drink hot fucking chocolate 'til spring."

But Tribal smiles, experienced shift of position.

"Uh, yeah, I like winter, too, man. Ground is hard, everything freezes solid, ice starts in your toes and fingertips and works its way up—you feel it?—creeping up your limbs, yeah, hot chocolate sure would be good right now, imagine that sliding down your throat, eh? Or a coffee. Coffee would feel right fucking sweet, eh?"

"Yeah . . . yeah, you're right, man. We should go, eh? It's getting cold."

"You think?"

"Shit, yeah. Know what? I wouldn't mind something hot to drink."

"That's a good idea, my man, a good idea. Let's go."

Initiated. Newest disciple of this weary mystery cult, I perform my part. I descend, climb down into the darkness to listen to the clandestine whispers, the hissing snow secret-speaking clearly with Tribal's reassuring voice, and for the first time I feel the vibrations between the strata—too subtle for sight or sound, too gentle for crude hands to hold. This, then, is what Jimmy means and what Debbie implies and what Tribal knows. A spectrum not of any one sense or combination of senses, but a mere state of mind. Just a small shift in perspective, really. It's been there all the time, sensibly and quietly waiting for me to notice, an invisible lighthouse beckoning to weary travelers stretched too thin from life's proverbial trip.

—

Tribal, then, dragged me back from whatever edge I was dangling over, my brother and dog-loyal mate. None better. His cure was, well, the predictable cure of the self-appointed shaman: the medicine man in the lighthouse assessed the situation and said, Yeah, it's peace pipe time.

Gotta say, though, artificial or not, it gave me some insight into what I'd allowed myself to become over that wasted year. Winter had been unbearable. After Eira cut my mooring line one November evening, there was no way to mark the twain, and I was adrift in the unfamiliar waters of that undefined next stage.

My lighthouse? Ah, the heater of that first smoldering joint, my first ever.

Hey, land ho.

And now, April. The cruelest month.

Spring rain stirs dull roots to life and I resolve to burn anything I can—love letters, scraps of sentimental paper, birthday card, all the combustible tripe that serves as evidence of who I had become since last March.

"About fucking time," Tribal says, sick of looking at it, or maybe weary of watching me brood over it.

"I know." I store everything Eira ever wrote me in a stolen canvas Royal Mail bag. "Don't know why I've kept this shit around so long."

"Well, if you're all done being a twelve-year-old girl, I got an idea."

Out to the Point for this one—only Westdale woods and water would do as the setting for this particular cremation.

We set out just after dark, I immersed in sullen self-pity (pathetic), he irreverent and loud—joking, teasing, encouraging—supportive in his own way. But the woods have their own etiquette, and after a while we drift through the blackness, too familiar to require light, in comfortable silence.

When we reach the Point, though, we aren't alone. A thin silhouette sits on one of the logs surrounding the lifeless fire pit. Tribal notices her first, heater of a cigarette drifting in tight arabesques through the darkness.

We walk down the hill, the last ten metres, in unconscious silence. Experience has made this an automatic modus operandi, but it takes our guest by surprise. Here in body but not in spirit, as it were.

She starts, sharp intake of breath as we drift into her awareness, but remains seated. Our eyes are well adjusted, but under the trees, even in the narrow clearing, it's still too dark to make out more than body language. We drop the kindling we've collected on the way into the pit.

"Apologies, little sister," I say to break the silence. "Didn't mean to startle you. Mind if we build a fire?"

"Go ahead," she says as nonchalantly as she can, the timbre a touch shaky.

"Right. Cheers."

Tribal fetches a few larger bits from the stash we keep close by while I arrange the kindling. I try for casual conversation during the process, but without the appropriate cocoon of bar, pub, or party, the artifice is glaringly obvious. At least to me.

"Haven't seen you out here before. You alone?"

She doesn't answer at once, weighing my words maybe. In retrospect, the last bit was unwise (my personal m.o.), but I've underestimated her: this girl isn't afraid of shit. Yeah, her voice shakes, but only because she's been there for three hours in the damp and then in the dark and she's freezing.

"Mmm hmm," she finally offers. "I'm new to town. I'm not even entirely sure where I am right now . . ." She laughs. "I just sort of followed a path I found a few hours ago and then got to thinking. Next thing I know it's dark. Need a light?"

No, but a fire should always be a communal effort. I hand her an envelope, letter still inside. She hesitates, then shrugs and lights it, slipping it into the slot I left in the arrangement. *Delivering it*, I muse.

"I'm Sarah," she says as the flames catch.

She's beautiful. Sculpted cheekbones, flawless make-up, long brunette and braided hair, pierced navel, short skirt, high boots, something in French across her sleeveless top. A Montreal café dwelling stereotype, right down to the sinuous neck and insouciant and unconscious disregard for the world around her.

My brother appears as if on cue, dead branches in hand, and we introduce ourselves.

"So," says Tribal as soon as he's comfortable, "what happened? Decided to take a night hike on the way to the club? You ain't exactly dressed for the woods. You must be fuckin' freezing, eh?"

She just smiles, but it's pretty clear that she's already concluded that this little stroll wasn't her wisest life choice. Though the fire helps, her teeth chatter audibly.

I start to take off my jacket, but Tribal beats me to it. He comes around and drops his own leather, scarred and heavy, around her shoulders.

"Thanks," she says, seemingly more grateful for the gesture than for the warmth.

She figures we're alright after that, I guess, because we fall into easy conversation and she opens up a bit. From Toronto, she tells us, a Bloor Street West girl. She's only been in Hamilton a few days, looking for a little space (incognito) to clear her head after breaking up with a long-term boyfriend.

"Why Hamilton?" I ask. T.O's a sprawling monstrosity, pretty easy to lose yourself.

"My dad lives in Hamilton," she says. Then, "Or that's the last place I heard he was, anyway."

So, beautiful, yes, but just like the rest of our orphaned or abandoned or forgotten tribe.

I was partially right about Montreal: that was the ultimate destination—all she needed was the dosh to get settled. She had a job already in a Jackson Square boutique and an apartment, but she took a city bus on a whim, got off in Westdale, and started walking. Found the path into the woods after meandering around the quiet tree-lined streets, confused because this was one of the only parts of the fucking city not built on a grid, and for a Toronto girl, the world only exists in intersecting 90° angles. Simply put, she didn't exactly know how to get back.

"So, where's this apartment of yours?" I ask.

"Well," she begins, "I'm on King William, kinda close to Jackson Square. I know, I know—not great, just a couple rooms over a smoke shop, but it's cheap and not a bad walk to work."

Tribal and I exchange a glance. A shite neighbourhood, though not bad during the day. Still some skins about, the occasional chicken head (punk, that is), but it was the less obvious dangers that you have to watch for. Incognito.

We sit for a while in comfortable silence, distracted by the flames. Tribal retrieves one of his trademark spliffs, crooked, bulging and obscene. Around it goes as we watch the fire.

Our link, I muse, to fifty thousand years of evolutionary flatlining. I imagine our naked, shivering, hirsute and flea-ridden ancestors squatting in some dank and fetid cave, huddling around a fire identical to this one, mesmerized by the complicated mechanics, hypnotized as intense dry heat sends wave after rippling wave of movement under the skin of sticks, slowly eating away at bark and bone, cracks and sudden pops, like dry branches under foot and beneath it that hissing breath simultaneous intake and exhale and it looks so alive an intense orange tide surging up and down and up that log that branch that stick hissing even whistling a tiny kettle boiling over but that's just sap I know that what about the smoke when the smoke blows my way I know the spell the incantation but what chants would they use to coax the choking smoke from their own faces is it like us I hate white rabbits or faster I hate whiterabbits IhatewhiterabbitsIhate whiterahey hey are you listening hello anyone home

What?

Whoa. Damn, Tribal. Stuff's strong.

"Sorry. What?"

Sarah smiles, taken by a little revelation.

"I said your brother's name's an adjective."

Tribal smirks and shakes his shaggy head. "Where's Jimmy when you need him?" He lights up a second monstrosity, takes a few tokes and passes it to Sarah.

Jimmy the *scop*, the namer of things. He named Tribal, one of his typical bong water baptisms if I remember correctly. But Sarah's point is well taken.

"Oh yeah," I grin. "So's yours, though, in a way. And mine. Everyone's, really."

I mean it, too. After five minutes of getting to know anyone, most names just become descriptive accessories for people you don't really know. And never will. Without that mystery, that elusive piece of the Self, what the fuck's the point of being friends with anyone? Names—just another modifier, something to get stuck on or in. Or with. Flypaper.

She contemplates this for a bit, seems to know what I mean. Tribal isn't all that interested, though. He watches the motionless spliff, seemingly forgotten between her thumb and finger.

"Hey, there, Casablanca, you done?" If anything, Tribal's blunt (ha ha).

Sarah comes back to us. "Oh, sorry," she says, embarrassed, and passes it over to Yours Truly. But once it's safely back into Tribal hands—reserved, as it were—he's all business.

"C'mon, brother," he says, getting to his feet. "We didn't come out here for nothing. Let's get this show on the road, eh? Grab that sack of tender fuckin' memories and let's feed the funeral pyre. Casablanca here can help."

It takes longer than anticipated—there's simply too much of it for me to feed the fire piece by piece. And Sarah isn't all that comfortable with the process, feeling (I assume) like she's inadvertently intruded on what was clearly a private, cathartic moment. She helps, but only out of politeness. Must be strange destroying the labours of an unknown sister-spirit with neither motive nor malice in which to revel.

Me, though, I'm focused, like this little exercise will purge me, exorcise the ghost that squats stubbornly between me and the rest of linear fucking time. Worse, I want to let go of things in an orderly fashion. Christ, given time, I probably would have burned things chronologically, but Tribal doesn't share my patience. And it begins to look like rain.

"For fuck's sake," he says, "you've already wasted enough time on this bitch. Don't drag it out any more than you have to!"

He's right. I tentatively throw a handful into the flames. Tribal grabs a bundle and tosses it into the heart of the fire. Then more, everything into the growing conflagration, my solemn and mournful little ritual now a frenzy of lunatic activity. We giggle like idiots, provoking the fire into a ridiculous size with paper, and then with fallen pine branches, uprooted saplings, logs, an abandoned coat, someone's shoe.

And for closure? Ah, Tribal's signature act, one that sums up his very being in a single, shall I say, fluid motion. He takes a last toke, muses at the smoldering ruins of our handiwork, and says by way of farewell, "Good riddance, bitch. Get fat."

Then he pisses on the remains.

But not everything will burn.

A gold chain, two rings, small mementos from a mother-sanctioned school trip to a far and foreign land—these things I can't feed to the flames. Tribal is in favour of a burial at sea.

"Throw that shit in the water and let's go," he says.

I don't, though, dropping the pieces back into the canvas bag instead. Tribal sneers, but Sarah smiles sadly.

"Hey," she says, "we all cling to whatever floats."

However.

The following afternoon, alone this time and dead sober, I drive down Main to Ottawa Street, park, go into the closest pawnshop, and empty the small pile onto the counter. Old, dour-faced guy fingers the trinkets and jewelry, unimpressed. He likes the chain, though, you can tell, but I don't even give him the pleasure of the haggle.

"Five bones," I say, watching his meandering finger.

"For *this*?" he asks, pointing to a touristy and tiny pewter replica of a Greek helmet.

"No, brother, for the lot. Yeah, the chain, too."

He must think I'm a fucking idiot. This is what I contemplate after I take the five-dollar bill into McD's and buy chicken nuggets. I don't eat them, though: I feed them to the seagulls loitering around the parking lot on the corner.

That's poetry, I figure. Feeding mass-produced poultry by-products to the shit hawks, cannibalism twice removed. *Eating and drinking*, T.S., *dung and death*. They'll do a much better job spreading the remains of memory across this goddamn city.

Then I go on, obedient to human nature—same as anyone else who loses something of real value. Like pulling a tablecloth out from under the china. The audience oohs and aahs at the trick, all eyes on the props—the cloth, the glasses, teacups and saucers, even a pair of fucking candlesticks if the cat is good—but no one looks at the table. Cheap, scar-faced, utilitarian, there for one purpose only: to hold shit up.

And there it is: no one pays attention to what is, for all practical purposes, the most important part of the trick. It's not a fucking illusion, after all, not sleight of hand, just a tediously rehearsed act of controlled violence. A sharp and vicious tug, yet everything seemingly stays the same.

Hey, draw your own clever fucking metaphors, I've got mine.

Still, I can't get over Sarah living above King William Street. I wander around Jackson Square a week later, find her, go to lunch. She has a phone now so we exchange numbers, become friends.

It's still April. Jesus—she exchanges one handful of dust for another, as it turns out. I swear to God, this city's unreal.

I can't remember her ever telling me she regretted it, though. Come to think of it, I can't remember regretting too much, either.

Chapter Two

But April, it too just a symptom of the lifeless mechanics of this mindless stone's rotation among the spinning stars. Spring has come at its appointed time, axial tilt making its ponderous way back to the beginning, predictable as tide or time.

Reliable, like gravity.

I begin collecting up the pieces, the fragments to—how does it go, T.S.? Ah, yes—*to shore up my ruins*, the detritus of necessity. These are not pieces chosen consciously or carefully. They are incidental, situational, like Sarah. They become me.

And language, its connotations worn one upon the other, embraces me. Each word, each syllable, wrapped as in onionskin to be peeled until meaning—that other capricious and vacillating whore—exposes herself, obscene and unwanted.

"Even your pieces," Jimmy says late one night, become subject to this, the word itself is faceted. Pieces. Does he mean fragments, like dross? Or selections, like art? Or are we pieced together, like a puzzle (repaired, this implies, something that once was whole, perfectly fine, and then broken on purpose. But why? Simply) to reassemble?

Just specks in the glue, really, caught again in that sickly sweet and bone-weary trap of language.

"Even your pieces," Jimmy says. "They'll give you something to be buried under. Like us all."

It's the May Two-Four, Victoria Day weekend. We've gathered at Ragged Falls, a Provincial park in the Algonquin Highlands, 250 kilometres north of Toronto. We come here often enough, camping outside this time with May's heavy thaw coming early and the roar of water still deafening even now, at the end of this wet month. Sarah too is with us, newest addition to the tribe. But she slips into the circuitry with relative ease, wary even at the beginning only of Debbie.

We pick a place above the falls, Tribal and me, where the shallow rapids tumble by with quiet and comforting persistence. The river-worn stones are smooth and flat, but the water's too choppy to skip them, a child's pastime that we share, the others unaware. Exposed tree roots—cedar and jack pine—stretch like stairs across the steep bank to the small patch of rocky beach, the roots gnarled fingers that clutch heavy rock and thin topsoil in confusing knots. Barefoot now, the winding trails carpeted in silk-soft pine needles golden brown and the black loam beneath like sponge. Even from here, we can hear the radio back at camp where the others are content to lounge in lazy confusion, too stoned or drunk or hung over to make this hike with us. Social Distortion—Sarah's tape. The treble reaches us over the babble of water.

"I don't get this band, man," Tribal says, retrieving another crooked spliff from his pack of smokes. "It's like Billy Bragg had sex with Sid Vicious and knocked him up, but Sid couldn't turn down the hooch and Billy was all like, 'You're gonna hurt the baby, eh!' And Sid was all about quitting but late at night he couldn't keep his skinny hands off the bottle and then there's this big tragic scene at the hospital and out comes Social Distortion with—what's it called? Fetal alcohol syndrome. Fucking tragic, man. Oh, and then, like, they send him to Pogues band camp, eh? And Shane McGowan teaches him how to sing. But Social Distortion guy actually *can*. You want some of this?"

I turn it down, laughing.

"I think I've had enough. That made total sense, and that's a pretty good sign that I'm about as lit as I need to be."

"Suit yourself," Tribal shrugs, hauling on it in heavy tokes.

Derek's uncle owns a small hunting camp up here on the Canadian Shield, a decrepit shack with six plywood bunk beds, a wood stove, and no electricity. He never uses it though, just an unwanted inheritance, so he gave the key to Derek as soon as he could drive. It's not terrible, I guess, if you don't mind the twenty metres to the outhouse, or the half-kilometre walk through the woods to the small cold lake and the thick and furious clouds of insects. Still, it wasn't the arid and idle Hamilton streets of summer.

It wasn't too long after we first started coming up that we found Ragged Falls. Accessible by road, well-kept paths to the top and bottom of the water, remnants of logging from a century ago still visible—telltale pylon holes cut into the stone, immense iron spike or two jutting from the vast sheet of rock on the far side, inaccessible because of the sheer volume of water. A popular sightseeing spot for tourists heading to and from Algonquin Provincial Park. They swarm over the angled slabs of stone that form a giant's egress down to the bottom of the falls themselves, massive and crooked steps that cradle wayward cedars, stalwart jack pines, occasional birches.

But tourists are a fickle tribe, so we camp higher up, following the river until the paths grow thin, and then forge through the brush of saplings and ground pine until we reach a pale of fallen and weather-rotten trees that diverts the casual hiker. These we climb and continue upriver until the forest thins out a bit, small clearings wide enough for a few tents, a good fire.

"So, how 'bout it?" Tribal breaks the solitude, as we stare with meaningless intensity across the river. The music has changed, Social D replaced by something softer, inaudible.

"How 'bout what?"

"Sarah—how 'bout it?"

"C'mon, man. We just met her, eh?"

Tribal rummages around his leather for his lighter, the heater having fallen off his cigarette and into the river without warning.

"What's that got to do with it? Didn't stop you the last few months, after gigs and at the—what, two, three?—anyway, the parties you actually showed up for. Figured you were over the other one." Her name is taboo now.

"That was winter," I mumble.

"Yeah," Tribal agrees out of habit, not really hearing me. "But Sarah ain't hard to look at, eh?"

That's true. Sleek, elegant, even up here in denim and a borrowed lumber jacket. Obeah voodoo enigma. Like Debbie, really, but somehow more real.

"Sarah. Yeah. Sarah's . . ." I clutch at words through the haze. "Beautiful."

"Yep!" Tribal is content to just stand and talk, the end becoming his own beginning in this cyclical conversation, a mindless seasonal rotation.

"So, what 'bout Sarah, eh?"

"I told you, man. Too soon."

"It's been, like, a month, eh? How long you gonna wait? Girl like that won't be around for long."

I reach for the spliff, world too close, now that we've been here a while.

"It's not that, man, it's just—here, take this thing—it's just that I really like her, eh? You know, as a person. Sex just fucks things up, confuses everything."

Tribal is dubious, throwing a sidelong glance at me before he turns to face the distant campsite.

"That's shite, man. Can't live like that."

"Okay, then what's to say she's even interested to begin with, eh? Not a one-way street."

"You are one blind fuck!" Tribal laughs.

But Sarah and I, we've talked often enough in the short time since meeting to understand the lines, the past still too palpable to ignore just yet. She's more of a closed book, terse and quiet answers to my questions a totem against probing too deeply, while I'm the proverbial information kiosk. I come with pamphlets and a goddamn map—Jimmy's observation, not my own. Sympathetic hand on my shoulder, asking in his gentle and chiding way where the souvenir shop was. But that, too, was during the winter.

Souvenir shop closed, ladies and gentlemen. We had a small fire, I'm afraid. All goods were lost.

Tribal and I loiter on the way back to camp, collecting firewood as we go. It's always been a bit of a sore point with us both, this task falling mostly into our hands for no good reason. Derek's not a fan of manual labour ("Hey, man, it's my cabin—I'm providing," he says defensively, even though we haven't spent a night in it in two years, preferring it here in the woods). Ewan is never in any shape to do much of anything, baked beyond even the fundamental boundaries of interpersonal skills within an hour of arriving. Jimmy will sweep the immediate area, but he's more druid than drudge. And, besides, he at least cooks for us. Pretty good, too. The girls are exempt, chauvinists that we are.

There are others on occasion, depending upon the season, but not this time. A small group for this sojourn—just the five of us and the girls, Debbie and Ruby Tuesday (Rebecca, that is, Derek's girlfriend), and now Sarah. But when we get back to the campsite, there's a fair heap of dry wood, divided even into kindling, bigger sticks, and logs. We look at each other, surprised and pleasantly confused, but Jimmy unveils the mystery.

"It was Sarah. She's been busy since you wandered off. Said she was bored and needed the exercise."

We drop our own small bundles, pathetic beside the mountain of wood she's dragged back from the forest, and thank her for saving us the trouble. We stress the *us*, but it's lost on the others.

"Oh, no problem," she says, off-handedly. "You said we needed wood before you left, right? Just doing my bit."

Derek shifts uncomfortably, and reaches for his guitar. Jimmy rummages through the cooler for dinner. Debbie, though: polysemous smile drifts across her face, ambiguous after all—as equivocal as thought.

"She's quite energetic," she says, "I'm exhausted from watching her."

"You were welcome to join me," Sarah returns, pleasantly. But we all sense it, the stirring of an evil seed, roots creeping relentlessly downward, soon to be firm and deep. Poisonous flowers, their cloying fragrance rife with decay—that will be the only fruit of this day's sowing, rootwork rising.

Debbie smiles sweetly back, bewitching and dangerous. Her small pink tongue darts out and across her lips—whetting them, as it were. Tasting the air, subterranean predator blind and out of her native element. We are denizens, all of us, indigenous to the steel mill city to the south, not to this wilderness of wind and water and feldspar and jack pine. But Debbie is, of all of us, a true alien—stranger in a strange land. She is, on the few occasions she comes with us, not really with us at all. Detached, just a minor error in temporal displacement. She sits on the edge of a cooler or in one of the folding beach chairs we carry in and watches us with bored indifference, tolerant smile playing at the corners of her lips, her eyes.

"Like she's waiting for a bus," Sarah says to me later, frustrated by Deb's refusal to offer anything in return, even a retort to Sarah's comment. I brush it off, though. I know nothing of these things yet, I can't see Debbie, still blinded by an unspoken past in a dark parking lot. Sarah's just jealous, I figure, because Debbie, too, is beautiful.

"C'mon, Sarah. This is supposed to be relaxing, eh? You're gonna go back all stressed out over nothing. Where's—Oi! Tribal!"

"What?" Tribal's found himself a rustic throne, pine needles heaped up beneath a blanket, his back against the soft and ragged papery trunk of a cedar.

"Got a bone handy?"

"Yeah, but you gotta come here, eh? I've, uh, kinda grown roots."

Sarah feels it below thought, though. And in the end she's right, of course. Debbie can't see up here in the woods, not in the same way she sees in the city.

But she can taste Sarah.

Debbie just smiles, patient as stone.

This was my fault—I was hoping Sarah and Deb would each find the other. You know, kindred sister spirits and all that shite.

Jimmy had smiled at me, simultaneous sympathy and mock in the long-fingered hand that patted my shoulder, after I told him I'd invited Sarah up to Derek's.

"Strata, my brother," he had said, "Learn to read the strata."

I didn't know exactly what that was supposed to mean, but I knew I'd fucked up again. *Sightless*, I think now, *my eyes not likely to reappear as the*, what, *perpetual star*, is it?

Ah, the shallow hope of empty men, eh?

Sarah and Debbie's first encounter had more-or-less set the tone, I suppose, with me inviting her out to a band practice in mid-May—barely three weeks after meeting her—to introduce her to one and all. She had arrived with Tribal, dressed in punk-chic—tight and provocative, tall boots and short skirt, perfect skin and that long hair, dark with just a hint of auburn beneath the harsh fluorescent pulse of our third floor makeshift studio.

But Debbie, cloistered away with Jimmy, had stopped mid-sentence, her silken words falling like dead leaves shaken unexpectedly from a branch, shadows of what she'd been saying quietly collecting about their feet.

Jimmy's face had told me first, a furrow across the brow as he gauged reactions. Debbie had stared in amused curiosity, though, as if she had walked into a dressing room to find a funhouse mirror. Because it was at this inopportune moment that Yours Truly finally made the connection.

They could have been sisters.

I had received my wish, after all: they found each other, alright—unfortunately, the animosity was instant. And mutual. Stony stares, a meeting of medusas, or maybe a pair of ill-tempered vipers growing out of different sides of the same head.

Me, I'd forced a weak smile and made introductions.

And memory, heavy too, sinking as if broken-backed and left to drown out here in dark waters, lightless and cold up above the falls. Because I feel it sometimes, a substratum destination reached by slow and steady descent.

Jimmy and I discussed it—Sarah, and her effect on the chemistry of our little group, because things *have* changed. Stretched just a little too tight, now, that epidermal sphere that contains our small tribe, stretched too thin now to accommodate this impromptu addition.

"Like one of those self-contained fishbowls at the mall," he said. "Ecosystem in perfect balance—you know, just the right proportion of water to air to plant to fish. You know what I'm saying, right?"

Sure. Some alchemist had cast his hermetic spell over each delicately balanced sphere of elements. A seasonal trend, maybe—just one more oddball curiosity that catches the momentary attention of the herd as it mills its way aimlessly through shop-lined corridors, picked up and studied and put down again. Fickle crowd, just like the tourists.

But Jimmy was serious. He worried, I know, about cause and effect. Birdsign reader, streetwise soothsayer. "What is it?" I asked, concerned. "What exactly?"

Jimmy frowned, tugging thoughtfully on his facial hair.

"Don't know yet," he said. "Something, though."

"Is it, like, attitude? The others say anything?" I looked over at Sarah now, sitting by the river with Tribal and Tuesday and Derek, laughing. Nothing seemed out of place, but I wasn't exactly the best judge.

"No, no, no. Nothing like that. I like her, we all do." By unspoken agreement, we avoided naming the exception. "But there's just something stirring that I can't put a finger on yet."

"Relax, brother," I said, trying to joke with him. "Probably just the adjustment, eh? One more piece to fit into your grand and cosmic Plan, and here you were thinking the puzzle was all done." I smiled, facetious and proud of myself.

Jimmy smiled too, but vaguely—he wasn't really listening. Musing, recalculating, retracing steps to find the divergence. Then he shrugged, resigned to ebb and flow, time alone solving this microcosmic mystery. Because as it turned out, it was something beyond his control.

The descent, then. Slow. Steady.

The Catfish, whiskers twitching, vainly searching the lazy currents for the scent of change and frustrated, too, because it isn't Sarah at all—yes, one more than necessary, invisible shell taut, straining not to tear—but not *because* of her.

Deep below the surface, below the liminal reach of even the Catfish's senses, this is what Jimmy felt. Below even the depths, subterranean, an earth-borne bathysphere containing the first fetal movements of something unanticipated.

The Illiterate, stirring.

—

Debbie reaches over for my cigarette, the small glow as she inhales illuminating the delicate curvature of her face, porcelain and flawless. Even her eyes, translucent stones from another world. She exhales, a steady stream of smoke at once visible and invisible, dissipating at the terminal end into the ethers.

"What part of me is in that smoke, do you figure?" Her questions, whimsical or serious, carry the same implication: the world is just an accessory to her existence.

Practice is over, more or less, unless Jimmy experiences a late night revelation. It's a good space, a room wide and open and empty on the third floor of a hundred-year-old brick building in the east end. Industrial area, no locals to piss off, just barebones small industries—plastics, abrasives, tool and die makers, cabinets. Shops like that occupy the ground floor and half the second floor, but no one's up here on the third. At least, not yet.

This is what the landlord told us when he agreed to lend us the room, implying that if someone wanted to stick a drill press in the middle of our practice space, we were shit out of luck. Old guy, real Hammer Town blue collar to look at, but rich as hell. He owns a bunch of industrial and commercial rental properties, including the downtown building presently housing the Hound and Hare.

That's how we got such a great fucking deal, though—it's this old cat's son who owns the Hound, and we're the house band. For now, anyway, a gig Jimmy secured three weeks ago at the end of May. Within days of returning from our camping trip, actually, and welcome news because the pay is solid. But it isn't because the ancient coot is a philanthropic patron of the fucking arts, just simple sentimental economics: we bring in a good crowd, and they spend a shitload of dosh on slightly overpriced pints.

A solid practice, though it's almost 2:00 a.m.—a bit late for a Tuesday night with work for most of us in five hours. Sarah stayed until just after midnight before she made her excuses and took off, even though the shop where she works doesn't open until 10:00 a.m. on Wednesdays. Of course, Debbie materialized around eleven, coffees and bennies a welcome change to our diminishing beer supply.

So, Sarah managed an hour of enduring Deb before she left, longer than usual. Fortunately, Quinn's been haunting our practices a couple times per week, too, supposedly as a fan but really to fawn over Sarah. A bit pathetic, he's hardly subtle, Sarah handling it well, patient and distant and kind. Quinn was on his feet before Sarah had her first goodbyes out.

"I'll drive you home, I have to leave, too."

"Yeah? Cheers."

As Sarah put on her coat, our eyes met. *When will he take the hint?* they said. I smiled, sympathetically I thought, but Sarah's eyes became suddenly distant and she left without another word.

"What the fuck?" I said, under my breath. Jimmy was watching, his own smile just as sad and sympathetic.

We stand apart from the others, Tribal and me. He helps me wrap up patch cords and stow them in one of the dozen milk crates we use for hauling all the random odds and ends—mic cords, extra strings and bridge pegs, hex keys, pliers, screwdrivers, effects pedals, picks, drum sticks, nuts and bolts, new springs for floating suspension, input jacks and jackplates, paper and pens, amp fuses and tubes, copper wire, a soldering gun—not one fucking crate organized for shite, but by now we know where everything is without too much digging.

Derek and Ewan stand apart as well, cloistered away in the far corner and surreptitiously sharing a nubby little joint. Tribal looks over at Debbie, amused look on her face as Jimmy's tongue does its Morris dance, a mummer who missed his calling. She laughs at his quiet antics, a silvery shiver. A performer through and through.

Tribal shakes his head, contemplative tonight. He offers me a swig from his mickey, but whiskey and I had a recent falling out. He shrugs and takes a pull, still watching them.

"What the fuck is it about her?"

I watch her for a bit too, now, Deb perched lightly on top of the bass amp as Jimmy entertains.

"Don't know." I say. "She's—"

"Not really here, if you know what I mean."

I shake my head. "Nah, it's like she just kind of dropped in—you know, extraterrestrial gypsy with some time to kill before she moves on." I take a swig from Tribal's bottle anyway and grimace. Tastes like fucking screech. "But have you ever noticed how she makes you feel, like, a bit unreal yourself?"

"What you mean, like you feel stoned?"

"Yeah, I guess that's close, but I mean she makes me a bit more aware of what I'm . . . like, feeling." Lamely offered, and Tribal flashes a toothy smile.

"That's a little gay."

"Yeah, maybe a bit," I grin.

"You're totally gay for Debbie, man."

Yeah, maybe a bit.

Can't sleep.

Time crawls by, Benzedrine still racing through the pipes, and I imagine each interval, each minute a small black beetle that scuttles up one wall and across the flaking ceiling and down the far wall, tiny lightless suns scrambling across the celestial confines of this corner of the wretched tenement that Tribal and I share, our seventh (or eighth?) place since we left home.

And that about five years ago.

There was a legal scrap, attempts to hold us down, make us stay with her. Our mum, I mean. And then more shite with foster homes and threats of youth detention programs, but neither of us took any of it seriously. They'd split us up, we'd find each other in under a week.

Then they did get serious, because some fucking pervert foster fuck tried to get close and personal with Tribal in the kitchen, like the System was a buffet line for child molesters. But, Tribal being Tribal, things didn't work out the way this douche bag planned. And, of course, Tribal found a creative way of dealing with the situation, grabbing the first thing readily available—a large unopened can of baked beans—and splitting the idiot's face open with it. Took his hits in the scuffle that followed, knuckle marks across his forehead, nail rakes down his right arm, bruised ribs, split lip. But when he found himself slammed up against the counter, Tribal pulled open a drawer and grabbed blindly. Hand came out with a can opener, one of those silver double-ended ones, which he crammed sharp end first into this asshole's mouth. It slid along the upper gum line, carving a nice jagged trench in its wake and exposing roots before lodging itself somewhere in the back.

Cops took their sweet fucking time trying to sort that one out, System reps throwing their oars in too, but in the end it looked like Tribal went feral, bit the hand that fed him. This would-be rapist walked, and it looked right fucking bleak for my brother.

Tribal told me about it, grim and quiet, once we met up again at our regular spot, a dumpster behind a pharmacy on Parkdale, a bit north of Main. I didn't have too far to go, because they stabled me with a welfare case living in an apartment building on Gage. She was nice enough, but I was fifteen and having none of it.

I remember how Tribal stormed around the corner, saw me, and came over to squat beside me against the wall.

"You good?" I asked. He was clearly furious, eyes of stone and mouth set hard and fierce under the ugly orange streetlamp of twilight.

"I fuckin' hate this shit. I ain't going back in."

"What happened?"

"Fucking court. Stuck me with a pervert. Had to clock him and they blamed it on me. On *me*!" He was close, I could tell, minding the levy with rage. Tears for Tribal were not an option, even that young.

"Jesus Christ! How'd you get here?"

"No problem. Third floor in that place in St. Catharines, you know it?"

"Yeah. They gave you a fucking lawyer, eh?" I'd been there once, too.

"Oh yeah, real winner. He had to make a fucking phone call or something. Gave him a minute then I took a look. Nobody around, so I opened the window at the end of the hall and went down the fire escape."

Sirens on Parkdale and we sprung to our feet, but just a cop passing by. We were skittish back then.

I opened up my bag, handed Tribal a roll and a package of ham. He took them, ate savagely.

"You hitchhike?" I asked.

"Yeah. Hid until nightfall, then got to an onramp for the Queen E. Didn't take long—this university kid gave me a ride. How about you?"

"Nothing, just walked out. Gotta find a squat for the night—don't want to spend it here."

"I got some money."

"Yeah? From where?"

Tribal smiled, humourless and cruel. "Legal boy's jacket was hanging on the back of his chair. Took his fucking wallet after he left."

What the Province took, Providence provided, and we found the means to find each other. Tribal took the brunt of it, the System infallibly finding a string of dysfunctional idiots to abuse him in small ways. Or not so small.

Suffice it to say that I got lucky by comparison—one well-meaning lot after another—so when I fucked off it just looked plain ungrateful.

But that was five years ago. At nineteen and eighteen, we're well beyond their reach now. Retired escape artists, both of us.

And so time, insect feet clicking away, a time bomb mechanism. Pale light too, the early summer moon making its slow and steady way across a cloudless night sky, playing at shadows. I watch a narrow black form on the patch of peeling linoleum floor to my right—a beer bottle's shadow, a makeshift ashtray left on the windowsill—watch its measured journey as the shadow pivots, the lonely hand of a broken clock. At once torpid and tireless.

I watch TV for a while, flipping through channels aimlessly, volume down to little more than a whisper. Tribal's a light sleeper (by necessity originally, now by nature) and he startles easily. And the cable is stolen, spliced from the neighbours, and as of yet undetected. Which is good, since they hate us in the same way they seem to hate everything, including each other.

We'd moved in a year ago, five months before that street lamp conversation with Eira left me stranded and, for a while, unaware of time. *I remember her shadow, too,* I toy absently with this memory, *it too a lone hand of a broken clock, how it pivoted violently as she turned away toward that children's asylum,* leaving me without even the echo of where she once stood. And sometimes, late night television recalls these things, summoning the small and delicate demons of this old and nagging addiction.

Because I'd driven home that night she dumped me to find the place empty, Tribal out and not likely to return before late morning. So the TV kept me company, a parade of wild-eyed televangelists, shouting Aussie salesmen, financial gurus, monotone news reporters, reruns—all kept vigil this night with me.

Eventually I found a grainy late night movie, some kind of '70s porno kung-fu fight film set in Memphis, Tennessee. After it was done, the star—much older now—came on to say hi to fans like me, late night voyeurs sitting broken and aimless in the dark. She had crow's feet around her eyes, the skin of her cheeks and around her mouth just a bit too flaccid, a touch too soft to defy the tug of gravity. She was there to be interviewed by a "specialist," some kind of researcher of old smut, a collector of sad and demeaning relics.

He was a piece of work, too, this researcher. Fat, sweaty neck squeezed up and out of his starched collar in an obscene bulge, comb-over of stringy black hair barely covering his splotchy scalp. Body language, too, a pathetic example of cause-and-effect human nature, he leaning forward in his cheap studio chair to lay a supposedly friendly hand on her knee, and she stiffening slightly as if he'd just slapped a lump of cold wet ham on her leg, groped I guess one too many times in her life by this type of greasy and lecherous parasite.

He asked her the sort of questions you might expect out of some lonely and half-naked bastard calling up a sex line, questions designed to expose and humiliate, but in a disturbingly clinical way. And she did her best to maintain her side of the conversation, but you could tell she was there because she needed the dosh. Or maybe the attention.

This poor used and wretched whore from a bygone decade, clutching wildly at some validating moment when youth and beauty and promiscuity had ensured her last-minute inclusion at the parties of certain porn industry pioneers. Just a fleeting instant, and she talking as if it were some lost Golden Age she'd somehow left behind.

That night, sitting alone in my decrepit flat while Eira was, I had no doubt, being groped awkwardly by my ecstatic replacement, I wished I could phone that late night porn star up and commiserate. My shipwrecked sister, marooned too on a lonely island, sea-drift washed up by the relentless tide.

But then I thought, no—she's just flotsam. Hers was not a tale of calculated betrayal, except by time. Nothing malicious, even in the capricious whims of late seventies meat-peddlers. She just got too old to land leading roles, and was left behind by mistake. Adrift.

But me? Jetsam. As in

jetsam (n) \'jet-səm\
Etymology: alteration of *jettison.*
Date: 1591.
1: the part of a ship, its equipment, or its cargo that is cast overboard to lighten the load in time of distress and that sinks or is washed ashore.

According to my (stolen) Merriam-Webster dictionary, anyway.

Chapter Three

June is capricious, none of us quite knowing what to do with our time. And idle hands, they say.

We stay in the city. Yes, for the gigs and because of day jobs, but also because the Canadian Shield is intolerable in June: mayflies in their last frantic throes, mosquitoes, deer flies—not worth the effort of camping. We'd be trapped in Derek's uncle's cabin, held hostage there by tens of thousands of suicidal insects.

And so Debbie and I share the warm darkness of a late June night close at hand, out at the Point, the others drinking down at the Hound and Hare and unaware that we've slipped away for a while.

I had come across Debbie earlier, late afternoon downtown and sitting by herself on a bench in Gore Park. Or seemingly alone. A dumpy middle-aged guy in a shit-brown tie stood off to her right, working hard at small talk. I didn't need to hear what he was saying to see that he was building up the nerve to solicit her.

"You good?" I asked when I was close enough.

Deb looked up, as if noticing her surroundings for the first time. She smiled at me vaguely, sadly.

"I'm just thinking. Needed some space."

"No problem." Then to the would-be john, "You can fuck off now."

He paused, stuttered. Did his best to act incensed.

"I'm entitled to use this park!" he declares. "I'm not doing anything wrong! Who the hell do you think you are?"

Didn't accuse him of anything, so I took it as a declaration of unspoken intent. I helped him out a bit.

"Excuse me!" I shouted to the park patrons in general. "This dumpy fuck is looking for a hooker! Any takers?"

The poor bastard bolted, but Debbie wasn't impressed.

"That wasn't nice."

"He was—"

"I know, but it still wasn't nice."

Deflated, I slumped on the bench beside her and tried not to sulk. After a while, Debbie smiled playfully and offered me a cigarette.

"I didn't say it wasn't appreciated."

"Hm. Still need your space?"

"Yeah, but I don't mind sharing it with you. Got anything on you?"

"Maybe."

"Good. Wanna go somewhere?"

"Sure. Where to?"

A warm night. I prod what's left of the small fire absently as Debbie tells me for the first time—slowly, tentatively—about her past. Her family's, rather, her parents emigrating from Israel to Canada because her mom was pregnant and didn't want to raise a child there.

Why not? I ask, what's the difference? But she just smiles and looks up at the stars. She's hard to see. I built the fire earlier out of habit, just something to pass a joint back and forth over, and by the time she began talking—really talking I mean—it had died down to embers.

She mostly tells me about her grandmother, a Christian Armenian whose childhood began in Turkey and ended somewhere in the slums of Aleppo, a child survivor of the Armenian Genocide. There, in that northern and impossibly ancient corner of Syria, she was married by sixteen. He was a Jew, also lonely and displaced. Young, they let love and impulse override prejudice, but this sort of thing was rare, people didn't understand. They stuck it out, though, and she was thirty-one before she'd had a child of her own who lived past the age of three—Debbie's mother.

This was later, in Poland. They had left Syria for Europe, because her husband was promised work there in the mines by a relative. So, in 1937, in one of the worst fucking times and places to be Jewish, Debbie's mother was born.

For the second time in her life, Deb's grandmother found herself trapped in the senseless grip of hatred and mass hysteria, not because of her nationality this time, but because of religious beliefs. Not even her own, but that didn't matter. Just another world-weary manifestation of the same monstrously tragic joke history had been playing on her husband's people for millennia.

She didn't survive the Holocaust, and neither did her husband. Statistically, the odds of their survival were astronomical.

"Like having only one chance to point to a star that supports life, and getting a bullet through the brain if you choose poorly. That one," she says, pointing up at a dim cluster of lights a million lifetimes away. "Just to the left of the two that look like they're touching."

She cries, quiet tears that catch the silver flicker of the moon, newly emerged from the clouds, or maybe it's the reflection from headlights on the High Level Bridge. I reach out for her hand, but she pulls it away. I build the fire back up instead, both hands busy for a few moments.

Debbie tells me about her mom, then, barely more than a baby when she first went into the camp, and a half-feral child when she was rescued by American G.Is in '45: a tattooed seven-year-old, branded calf at a slaughterhouse. A type of felt, a fawn's coat, had grown over the bulbous joints of her stick-like arms and legs, starvation's work—evolution's cruel idiosyncrasy.

And it is for her mom that she weeps, a small and skittish woman who lives daily with emptiness, that deep and indescribable sense of loss. A daughter without a mother—a subtle and poignant cruelty, especially since that mother was taken away by a world of fathers, blind and rabid sons of the *Vaterland*.

This is the first time Debbie has ever mentioned her mother. I remember, vaguely, that surreal night three years ago, Tribal and I leaving her alone outside a hospital with a handful of coins and a few parting words—*go call your mom*—and then slipping back out into the dark circuitry without so much as a glance back.

We never spoke of that night again, not really. Maybe she told Jimmy about it, but I kind of doubt it. Even Tribal and I leave it be—the one closed door, locked and ignored, along that shared corridor of memory.

But Debbie reaches out and takes my hand as I grapple with these ghosts, hers and mine, holding it now as if making up for pulling away earlier, wrapping it in a tight and steady grip around my own clumsy paw. With one deft and tiny finger of her other hand, she lightly traces the silvered scars across my knuckles, a slow exploration.

"Reading my future?" I ask, piss-poor attempt at a joke.

"Are Tribal's knuckles this scarred up?" she whispers.

"Worse. Much worse, actually. As kids, he liked getting into the sort of shite that led to bleeding knuckles, eh? I didn't."

My eyes drift unbidden to her own scar, but that thin line—barely visible by day—is indiscernible in the unreliable firelight. She knows, though, watching me.

Then, leaning forward, she puts her lips, soft and cold, against my knuckles and kisses them, barely as if with just breath itself. Gentle, a flutter as of moth wings or the secret caress of a quiet spider, perched upon that precipice of skin and scar and bone, blindly casting silken strands out into the dim night—what tiny worlds will these lines connect? And, once bound each to the other, around what centre will these binary worlds orbit in their mad rotation, spinning in wild circles like hand-linked children on a dance floor, submerged utterly in the moment of laughter, the rest of the room no more than an insignificant blur of colours and lights and shadows, as if it never really happened?

I am helpless, enthralled by my alien companion, tiny hand holding my own, lips fluttering over my fist in some fervid and sudden dreamscape ritual of Sonar Debbie Dream.

A thank you, silent and sincere, for that night so long ago.

—

Because, yeah, like the poet said: a tumid river. That's time for you, a time for beginnings and ends. I always loved that second quartet, Eliot's rural ramblings. Here, then, is a confession—an ending, one that hurts even now. Incongruous, like an inexplicably recurring bruise or a word spoken in passing by a stranger, clawing at memory, tenebrous and equivocal. But it's the calluses I reopen on the occasional string, really. I press harder, though, through that sharp and prurient pain.

That's the way I will always remember Debbie: with my fingertips.

Ragged Falls is not much more than a trickle in early August compared to May's fierce torrent. Debbie and I have returned, alone and in secret, to these falls so far removed from the city sidewalks terse and brittle under streetlamps, up here among glacial lakes and rugged granite, jack pine and hard maple, birch and spruce. Wind, water, tree, and stone.

Debbie is not far below, negotiating her ascent up the indifferent rock beside the roar of the falls, perilous even in summer's gentle stretch. Timid probing with ill-shod and clumsy feet , clumsy hands also ill-shod with manicured nails—a city girl, unaccustomed to this particular kind of climb.

For me, sure-handed and caressing the fissures in granite, in feldspar (sometimes by memory alone), I listen to her jest at her own awkwardness, but I only hear the water. Somehow, it's more believable, audible in its own way.

Below, she stumbles, graceless and apparent. She jokes about it too quickly—silk tongued chameleon, this denizen of underground clubs and basement bars, and I laugh in spite of myself.

I'm not the first to stand here, of course. Echoes of footprints haunt the lichen, ghosts in the strata. Ambiguity is a staple for me, I think, as she reaches out a slender hand for help. Unnecessary, just an affect.

But I take it anyway.

Here at the crest stand the sentinels of this place: maple and oak, jack pine and spruce, unaware of our time among them—no more than a heartbeat or inbreath in the patient span of their years. *Creeping quietly skyward*, I muse, *since the seed days of their forefathers, they alone are left. Their ancestors are long gone, felled and directed down the falls to the river below and onward to the shore of the lake, where the sawmill reshaped them, transformed them.*

And I follow that ancestral path, eyes tracing down the flood, the steep and rugged incline, to the base of the falls where the river is the widest. There, the waters only whisper, exhausted after their descent.

Below, the fury is pacified, sated on the stones and perpetual driftwood. Or the water is lost in the deep crevices that lead beneath the roots of the falls.

Gathered there at the base is a wreckage, a logger's folly, a host of lost timber still caught on the stone pale that divides rapids from river.

The summer lull reveals the greatest of them, but in spring's swell most—the bleachboned remains of elder trees—are interred beneath the churning froth, entombed like chieftains, oak or ash or maple.

And now, dusk.

A breeze stirs the ground pine and she sits closer.

"Getting colder," she says and I, for my part, agree with a nod. She feels connected, in tune—waits for a reply, a confirmation, her words require a written receipt.

I can't commit myself to language, though. I struggle with the possible consequences of our sojourn, our temporary reprieve from the searing city heat and prying eyes. I watch the river (we are above the falls, now), water breath-holding in anticipation of the reckless plunge just ahead. It ebbs and swells, slipping past like storm scud.

Cradled upon its mottled surface, black and grey, are occasional leaves, too green, wind-stripped or idly plucked by careless tourists farther up river, in Algonquin itself. She in turn is obliged to add her own mark, a small stone thrown awkwardly into the current. *Not current, but past*, I think, a grim consideration. *She, like her clumsy stone, will soon disappear*.

What Debbie and I share at this one moment in time will never happen again. This is what I believe, here above the falls, watching water as it slips away into that void, esurient and insatiable.

The rings from her stone are almost instantly swept from sight, lost upon the churn of froth and foam.

And in its wake, I see it—there, there by itself in the middle, unassuming, drifts a lone branch.

Bold remnant of bygone days.

And so, on a weekend where beginnings and endings meet, near a lonely tent by the river above the falls, she standing ankle-deep in the rushing water, naked in the starlight, silver skinned, translucent, beautiful haunting waif calling playfully to the fireflies, unaware that the rushing droplets—they too silver and translucent—leap up and around her thin ankles, rise and fall like joyous fireflies themselves, beads of water each capturing a moment of starlight from a hundred million years ago.

"It ends here," she says. "Eons of travelling across that endless void to reach us and it ends here." She gestures to the river, water alive with diaphanous reflections. "Even the moon—we don't see the moon in the present but in the past, a fraction of a second in the past."

"And us?" I whisper.

"Yes, we too are in the past. It ends here."

So we resume, return to what we were before. But not as if it had never happened, landscape altered of course. Same with Jimmy and Debbie, though she gives him a bit more time. Or, they give each other more time, but Jimmy understands Debbie for what she is: an emotionally enigmatic free agent. Nothing she does or doesn't do seems to have any significance, beyond the moment—we get used to it, after a fashion.

Jimmy says nothing when we return. What is there to say? Unreliable, language can never get it right. We do our best to deal with it.

For a while the medium is acid, because eventually I, too, surrender: eyes skyward, tongue extended, Jimmy himself the guru-priest who drops this greatest of communions into my mouth. But that's just another kind of language, acid I mean—tongue heavy with thick-winged moths, unintelligible fluttering of words and wing dust blowing across just one more dreamscape.

Moth wing words, and this is how it went:

Jimmy's flat is muggy. Late August nightfall has done nothing to break the still and heavy heat of this languid steel city summer. It's a Westdale flat, rented digs usually reserved for university students, but Jimmy's clandestine business ventures make this place possible. For now, anyway. I sit by the window, watching with some concern as a small bath-robed crowd gathers on the sidewalk outside. They begin to shout at the house itself.

"What the fuck is their problem?" bellows Jimmy. "Can't even hear the TV, man!"

Neither can I, not over the stereo that shakes the very foundations, Zombie thundering through our skulls and out beyond the walls of both head and house. Occasionally we hear the beer bottles smashing off the walls in the hallway where Jimmy stands, hurling them systematically at the wooden door that leads to the basement, but that's only during the pauses between tracks.

I can't take any more.

"Jimmy, this is fucking ridiculous, man! The last thing we all need right now is a 2:00 a.m. visit to the copshop!" I cross the rubbish-strewn shag carpet and kick the power button on the stereo with the toe of my boot. It's been some time since I left the scene behind, but the Docs remain.

Sarah sits in the corner, knees drawn up to support her head. Her eyes are closed, but she isn't sleeping. Just waiting out the storm. After all, this is the other side of Jimmy—not the sly and supple Catfish.

No, this is the Illiterate.

He hurls a final bottle, a smash and then tinkle of scattering glass, audibly offensive in the sudden silence. Then he stalks into the front room and throws himself into the stained recliner he rescued a month before from a street corner. The lever doesn't work anymore, but it's still the only comfortable chair in his possession.

We hear the crowd pretty clearly now, just loud and mostly indistinct warnings, an occasional threat of legal repercussions if it happens again. Jimmy closes his eyes, smiling a grim smile, the glow from the TV screen flickering away, our only light source, volume set at barely a whisper. He muses a moment and then chants, rhythmically:

Angry neighbours have collected on the lawn,
but midnight television is barely even on . . .

He smiles again, it pleases him. The Illiterate is easily amused.

Sarah and I had dropped as well, but we split ours. House on the Hill, real old school acid that you could only get from this retro burnout downtown, and then only on the days he was wearing a faded grey tee with "salbonavita" written across it in black marker, whatever that means.

Jimmy, though, he'd taken one with the dealer and two more for good measure. Ordinarily, this sort of reckless consumption worked out, and he'd spend twenty or thirty hours straight writing and recording on his 16-track, laying down foundation tracks for later, experimenting with sounds, objects, effects.

Not this time. Instead, he'd slipped right off the fucking edge, Catfish diving deep for cover in the murky recesses of that cavernous mind of his, temporary hibernation at ten thousand atmospheres.

We'd dropped that afternoon in the park. Never downtown—sets the wrong tone and taints the entire trip. Me and Sarah, this really isn't our thing, but stepping out of the comfort zone once-in-a-while is good for the soul: walking out in the air, you feel that cosmic connection between stars and brain, right? My own personal prophet's wisdom, because I have a guru, too. Only mine's not mad as a fuck—and you can find him sensibly entrenched in Eel Pie Studios in London, not aimlessly sloshing around in a downtown public fountain.

The bubble crept up on us pretty quickly. That's what I call it, anyway, that lysergic cocoon that closes in around you, transforming every sensation—wind, water, walking, waiting—into fluid hyperawareness. Sitting on that park bench in a bubble, on a sunny afternoon. Mine was kind of tight, but Sarah and Jimmy didn't seem to mind the lack of room.

I was watching the wind, trying my best to relax and walk that thin line (there is no control, only the illusion of control), when Jimmy dropped tabs two and three. I could hear them bubble and hiss on his tongue, see right through his cheek into his mouth, watch them just sort of sink into him, syringe-like. I couldn't handle that level of detail, so I focused on Sarah instead. She seemed pretty composed, as good an anchor as any.

No Debbie Dream on this sojourn—at least, not at that moment. It was Sarah's one condition for participating in our retro experimentation with the hallucinogens of our forefathers, those psychotropic pioneers of the past. But of course our paths crossed anyway, Debbie materializing out of thin air. It was at a small café on Locke Street, another displaced Quebecois-owned place. We'd stopped in for a quick drink, and there she was.

Fact is that Sarah hates Debbie, won't have anything to do with her. But the feeling isn't mutual—or at least, Deb never lets on if it is. Pisses Sarah off, too, because Debbie will occasionally materialize at band practices with coffees or beer or even an eighth of weed, always enough to share, Sarah included. Worked into the calculations somehow.

Or she'll descend upon us, a fleeting wisp, ephemeral and unearthly, at the pub, a bar, or one of the ominous underground clubs that embraced her kind. We'll go there sometimes, just for a change of scene, a change of drugs. The Spider Cave, for instance, or one of its other incarnations, there are a few.

Anyway, as Jimmy's fond of saying, Debbie Dream is sonar—if we're there, underground, she knows. That's why Sarah's never with us when we go. The whole cave cult thing puts her off, she'll say in casual conversation, building up the foundation for a plausible excuse for not joining us on the nights we go.

But Sarah has her limits: she never misses a gig, even when we play the Cave.

Maybe it is Debbie's machinations, after all. What do we know, me or Tribal or even Jimmy, about that battleground beyond the liminal threshold of male awareness? The male world of experience is a linear and myopic road. One road, one direction. Women, well—they seem to function in peripheral zigzags.

Outside, the lawn begins to clear of angry neighbours. But Jimmy's watching the lights behind the TV set, dim flickers on the wall. "A constellation," he muses, wide-eyed and whispering, "a cityscape, a star chart . . ."

"Is he through yet?" Sarah's had enough. Her tolerance for this sort of thing is lower than mine, although she shares Jimmy's chemical love affair with sound and sensation. She attends the long stretches of audio mayhem that usually accompany his trips. Not Yours Truly, though, I can't get at the cobwebs and strange that gather in the corners, the centipede scent that clings and crawls over everything, that throbbing pulse that moves around my body, migrating up and down limbs or through my torso toward my head. It's all definable, though, identifiable. So long as it's just that, I'm fine. I know it's temporary.

"If you mean is he through waking up the neighbourhood, then yes. Well, probably. Maybe. I don't fucking know. Why?"

She doesn't answer. Eyes closed, stone still. So I start talking, just babble mostly, my coping mechanism for dealing with the centipedes scurrying about on the inside wall of my skull. Conversation is a little one-sided, though, Jimmy now absorbed in the screen static, sinking into that chair of his, Sarah uncommunicative.

It was stopping at the café that set this tone, when we ran into Debbie Dream as if by chance, acid in full effect. Sarah doesn't believe in fate, but there's only so much you chalk up to coincidence. Anyway, Debbie doesn't appear so much as she just sort of occurs.

But Debbie's arrival coincided with the crisp and sudden ascent of this trip. Clairvoyant, in tune with the waxing phase of lysergic clarity, I grappled with what had to be done, wrestling my own private salbonavita acid angel in that empty desert, stretching for lonely leagues between synaptic rhyme and reason.

I had to tell Jimmy. About me and Debbie, I mean, our early August disappearing act. He had to know what happened, and that it would never happen again.

Rhythm, though—*that* remained a café constant, I could feel it in every pulse and gesture, remark and movement. Just the acid, but it's sensation that determines any trip's destination.

So I counted out the measured beats and thought *It's time*, looking at Jimmy for his unconscious confirmation, his approval, his support. It can't go on, there's too much invested, Jimmy's a brother. Time to stake out boundaries with Debbie, no more peripherals.

I told Jimmy then and there, but—mate that he is—he got angry at me for all the right reasons. The Catfish is no fool: he saw where this river had to empty.

And sometimes it's better to leave the truth alone.

So: back in this sweltering Westdale flat, nine hours after that artificially erudite exchange, I ramble on about anything—music, food, drugs, books, movies, people—with Sarah listening in stoic silence and Jimmy staring deep into the static. Then I get careless.

"Think it's too early to phone Debbie?" Just a reckless thought, only half serious, but Sarah shoots a quick and cruel glance in my direction.

"Prefer Debbie's company?" she asks sweetly, and my skin crawls in warning. Not centipedes, so much, as a futile attempt to shut down the vocal mechanism. Too late. Mutually exclusive operational systems—my mouth and whatever part of my consciousness houses common sense.

"C'mon, Sarah, she's cool—you just don't give her a chance, eh?"

"Really?" she responds. "You're so fucking clueless sometimes."

"Yep!" chimes in the Illiterate, still seemingly absorbed in the TV static in front of him. "Hey," he continues, "my life is just like a chair . . . that reclines!" He giggles madly.

But I miss the portent, blind to birdsign. I forge ahead.

"Sarah, what the fuck are you talking about? Look, we've been mates long enough now—speak plain. What is it about Deb you don't like?"

But the linear road is not for Sarah. "Just not my cup of tea," she says.

"Hey," Jimmy says, "yeah! Acid in tea! Acidit-tea, get it?" He's pleased with himself, grinning foolishly. "Where's that remote? Gotta change this channel . . ."

But I'm an idiot, still no discernable grip on the big picture.

"You and Debbie are pretty similar in a lot of ways, you know. I've known Deb for a long time and . . ."

"Yeah, you 'know' her, alright, but fucking *her* doesn't give you insight into *me*!"

Silence.

But Jimmy's found the remote. He's been pointing it at us, frantically clicking.

"Oh well," he sighs. "Too late."

Chapter Four

Flypaper, though.

Jimmy and I are mired in what Debbie and I shared, neither of us fully willing or able to face facts directly. Frozen there in time, sideshow curiosity for those who paid admission.

Or maybe just attention. In other words, just Jimmy and—dense and daft fool that I am—Sarah.

But love and loyalty, fierce and anchored in the inescapable past, shake us free. Not that Jimmy or anyone else could really stake a claim to Debbie—wild as wind, storm scud, and fickle—but for the sake of friendship (mine and Jimmy's, that is), the gesture has to be made.

Debbie, at least, made things clear in August up there by the falls, the water little more than a ragged trickle (*here is no water but only rock*) in late summer's lull. She spoke of us as if we were already back in the city, already physical strangers again—she a slender arabesque naked and silver in the moonlight, ankle-deep in the rush of that luminous river. Behind her, half-hidden by the deep shadows of the shore, I squatted there watching her, naked too, a primate on his haunches too daft to see past or future. Even the present was little more than silver and shadow and whispered words only half-processed, Debbie Dream, little more than what her name implied.

Most confusing of all? It was Jimmy, of all, people who'd triggered this in the first place, shoring up my drunken ruins by delivering me to Debbie's doorstep himself after fetching me from the lakeshore that cold November afternoon almost a year ago. He must have known there was a risk of something happening between Deb and me—after all, he knew there was a hidden history there, unspoken, lurking beneath the surface of everything Deb and I said and did together.

And after she and I returned from that final weekend up in Algonquin, my late summer attempt to end what was already over or was never really there, Jimmy and I smoked the proverbial peace pipe back out at the Point.

Neutral ground and late September. Time, I think, to clear the air.

"Jimmy."

"Hmm?"

"Why'd you do it?"

"Do what?"

"Take me to Deb's that afternoon, you know, last November? Why not to Tribal, or even back to Tina? Or just straighten me out yourself?"

He takes a series of tokes, rapid draws of smoke cooled by the autumn air in his cheeks and stored in quick stages in his lungs. Standard method, I know, but weed always makes my head feel it's expanding, a flexible flesh and bone balloon, and then the heaviness sets in. It is setting in now, anyway.

Jimmy exhales, jet stream of depleted exhaust, and passes the bone over to me.

"You remember that dream you told me about, the one you started having when we were sixteen or seventeen?"

"Uh, yeah, sure, the one about the brick house, and looking for something I never find. But what—"

"Well, I figured out what you were looking for."

"What? How?"

But Jimmy reaches over for the joint instead, doctoring it briefly before taking another toke. The last one, too, a flick of his fingers and off it sails into the darkness, a dying firefly.

And no answer. He asks a question, instead.

"When's the last time you had that dream?"

"Shit, Jimmy, I don't know, eh? Lemme think. I guess it was . . ." but I can't recall.

"The dream stopped after I took you to Debbie's that afternoon." He smiles, sad-eyed with memory. "You were a right fucking mess, you know."

"Yeah," I say. "I was."

Jimmy retrieves baggie and paper from his jacket pocket, rolling a second spliff with practiced grace.

"Tell me the dream again," he says, and lights up.

Dusk. A quiet street in Westdale, simultaneously familiar and elusive. I emerge from the woods, presumably from the Point, and walk the shifting silent roads perplexed. Tribal is with me, a quiet companion. He sets the pace, which is too fast because I am looking for something that I lost in the woods, I know it slipped away and drifted into Westdale—familiar and elusive as this street, its name and shape impossible to recall. *It is small* this I repeat to myself as I search, *small and hard to see.* I look behind me often and alarmed, as if But my search is interrupted, a frantic muffled pounding from a small house to our right, a little red brick house with no door and only one window. Inside is Jimmy. He strikes at the window with his fists, room behind filling up with water, a rapid and torrential deluge pouring down the stairs behind him. The water is to his waist, he flails and pounds but his face remains perfectly serene. It's his eyes (*look*, they say, *keep looking for it*), detached from the horror, water now up to his chest, and still those eyes (*it is there if only you'll look*), Tribal calling to me now from the corner to hurry up, no time to stop and talk, he yells, got to keep moving. . . .

Jimmy and I finish the second bone. We feel in tune and by unspoken agreement will not risk a third—there is a fine line between the lucid state of communion we have found, and the weighty obtuseness of the kind of body-stone likely to occur if we partake any further. Sometimes it hits you later anyway, cement seeping in unnoticed, until you're too heavy to move anymore.

"Maybe it's some*one* I'm looking for, not some*thing*, eh?" I am fishing now, but Jimmy maintains radio silence. He has grown serious, business-like. "No? Okay, then maybe it's a key of some sort, or something to break the window. You know, let the water out before you drown."

He smiles at this, slight and sardonic.

"No need, brother. You can't drown the Catfish."

I laugh.

"Oh yeah, good point."

But Jimmy's smile fades in the dwindling light, brow furrows, and he shifts slightly on his log.

"I think," he says quietly, "it's time you filled me in on some of the missing pieces."

"Eh?"

"The missing pieces, brother. It's time." He looks up at the small patch of evening visible through the treetops. And then back at me.

"Tell me how you and Tribal first met Debbie."

So, Jimmy had already pieced it together, this puzzle of the past. He knew from the moment he introduced us all officially at the Cave when we were seventeen that there was a ghost in this Machine, her eyes and mine haunted by things we didn't speak of, by mutual agreement. Neither did Tribal, but he's more resilient—to him the past belongs there, no point in dwelling on it.

"Or in it," he said to me once, not long after that surprise evening Jimmy led Debbie down those dark club stairs. Destined to descend—Debbie, a falling star in the quiet hour of a desert night, time rushing her toward that silent drop through the terrible emptiness, Jimmy the only witness to this disappearing act *just blink* she might have said *blink and I'll be gone* and she ending her voyage on the sand below, just dry salvage, as if this was how we were meant to meet her again.

As I said, descending.

At the time I grappled with this image—that girl struggling hopelessly in the park, that girl drifting effortlessly down the stairs—and I couldn't get this bizarre coincidence out of mind. I called to Tribal as he rummaged through the meagre offerings of our fridge.

"But what are the fucking chances—"

"What I say?" Tribal said sharply. "Leave it where it is, eh? Leave that fucking ghost in the grave."

And so I did. At least, until Jimmy arranged this little séance in the woods three years after the Cinder Block, two years after the Cave. Because, as it turned out, a séance is all this was.

So I tell him. A confession, I guess. I tell him about the Cinder Block, and the skinny girl frightened and bleeding in the parking lot, and the same girl later that night bleeding again, but this time terrified beyond mere fright in a dark corner of a park. I tell him what we did, boots and bottle and bat, Jimmy nodding slowly and watching me with those steady grey eyes, processing. I tell him about the tense and silent walk down Barton to the hospital, and about leaving her there in ruins with nothing but a stolen trench coat to cover the tattered arras, the torn remains. And the handful of coins.

What the fuck were we thinking?

Jimmy is still in the deepening gloom of evening, quiet for a while and watching. Something large—an owl, maybe—lands in one of the treetops above us. He sighs and shakes his head.

Me, though. Firmly in the wretched grasp of memory.

"But that was, like, three years ago, eh? We were sixteen! Not *even* sixteen, in Tribal's case—and his hand busted, the entire goddamn *Oi* movement on the warpath, a fair shog behind us and another still to go—"

I pause to light the fire. We'd built it when we first arrived, but waited to light it until our faces were lost in the darkness.

"And here's the other thing, eh? If we'd stayed with her—you know, seen her through until they'd had a look at her—cops would have had us back in the System, and separated. Again!"

"Assuming they even believed you." Jimmy says this quietly, his first words in a while.

"Exactly! I mean, what the fuck, Jimmy—"

"Relax, brother, relax! It's all just paths to the present—you did what you did and here we all are, right on schedule."

"Yeah, I think Deb told me the same thing." I recall this vaguely, words of wisdom in the small cave to which Jimmy brought me that November, mystery cult magic just another layer of the strata.

"So," he says more to himself than anything, "that's the missing piece."

"What missing piece? You mean the dream?"

"No. And yes. The missing piece in the corner."

In Debbie's flat, he means. A dark corner, occupied only by a slender dress mannequin—armless, legless, headless—suspended in shadow by a thin steel pole. Hanging from its lifeless hips are the torn remains of a houndstooth mini skirt. Around its thin shoulders is draped a small, ripped and buttonless blouse, once white. Beneath the blouse a bra, it too torn, held in place with a safety pin.

And at the mannequin's base, barely visible in the sultry and perpetual dusk of Debbie's tiny world, a single saddle shoe, tiny and forlorn. As if it were meant for that lonely pole. Its sister, I know, lost along the way—it was small, hard to see, left behind as we gathered her up and propelled her forward toward the glaring fluorescence of a late night emergency room.

That one shoe. Lost between the cracks in the road.

Chapter Five

So rock and no water, just a sandy road to trudge along, connecting one fucking wasteland to another. Another summer, then, our second with Sarah. A starting point, I guess.

And to sand, as it turned out, was exactly where that road led.

Tribal and I meet Sarah outside Dundurn Park at one of the gatherings growing in frequency in southern Ontario, a festival wrapped in the threadbare shawl of an earthy, grassroots sort of thing. They're all the same, though. Griot-inspired Caribbean mento on this stage, deadhead cover band on that, line after meandering line of tents housing trinket peddlers, drug paraphernalia merchants, cliché tie-dye T-shirt makers, incense hawkers—all the usual shite.

But that's not what I mean. They're all the same because it's all bollocks—all of this canvas and alpaca wool and patchouli a vaguely adequate veneer for what is, in all honesty, a commercialized money-grab. Want proof? Try busking one of these fucking things. The festival organizers—who rarely resemble the drug-rug draped migratory hippie-wannabes infesting the stalls—are all over your ass about licencing, and all that other bullshit.

But maybe I'm just jaded, twenty years old and too world-weary now to fall for the slogans and hype. That, and I didn't apply for my busker's licence in time, so I'm technically poaching.

Except I know Quinn. In some ways, he's the same skinny kid from the old days, but now taller, not quite as thin. Calm, cool, and collected. Almost finished with university, Quinn floats about festivals like this under the aegis of his father—or, at least, his father's money. An organizer now, young and energetic, a sincere believer in these things as an ethical business venture. Dad sits on this board and that, fingers in every steel city pie there is.

Quinn doesn't care, though. People know him. He's popular.

Tribal, Sarah, and I walk around the festival for a while, watch some other buskers at work, drift in and out of stalls. People-watch, mostly, but eventually we, too, slip into the lazy, counterclockwise current.

Sarah realizes it first. She's all for exploring, figuring out what's at the exact centre of this little lakeside solar system. She reasons (facetiously) that the gravitational pull seems to be culture-specific, and as we are not part of the organic fiber wearing, vegan-endorsed hive, we can safely enter the stratosphere at a steep angle without burning up like disobedient satellites. But it starts to cloud over as the afternoon wears on and she isn't exactly dressed for rain. She glances skyward, irritated.

"Got plans for dinner?" she asks, retrieving a cigarette from her purse.

Tribal gives her a light. "We're meeting up with Jimmy and Deb," he says, neutral as shit. Then, "Wanna come?"

Long drag and exhale, eyes fixed on some distant object. "No thanks," she says. Distantly.

Tribal and I exchange a glance but hold our tongues. There's value to remaining neutral. And a word for it—cowardice, I think it's called.

Then Quinn himself emerges from a glass bead stall, sees us, and smiles.

"Pardon me," he begins in mock haughtiness, "but do you have a busking licence?" He taps my guitar case with a disapproving finger.

"How 'bout I tell you the same thing I told the last guy who asked?"

"Never mind," Quinn says, holding up a hand. "Your bluntness precedes you."

Sarah stretches her back, looks around. "Well," she says, "it's getting cold and I'm not really dressed for it. And," a quick glance around, "I've about had it with hippies for one day."

"Going home?" I ask.

"Yeah. Bus should be by soon."

"I'll take you," Quinn says, a bit too quickly. "You moved, right? Just off Aberdeen?"

"Cheers," she says. "That'd help."

Fucking Quinn—a silver spoonful of snake oil in that slippery mouth of his. We say our goodbyes, and they're off.

"Me too," says Tribal. "Gotta grab my jacket and some dosh from home. Let's go, eh?"

"Naw. I'm good. I'll meet up with you later, before we head out for Deb and Jimmy."

I don't much feel like sitting on our dingy secondhand couch and listening to the neighbours through the thin wall that separates our small flat from theirs. In particular, Saturday afternoons are never good—the guy next door works nights, so on the weekends with his old lady home from work too they're usually in a right proper scrap by midafternoon.

Honest to God, these people kill me—they fight over the stupidest shite. One Saturday, it was a screaming match over some coupon she supposedly lost. The week before that, it was over dosh he'd spent on a tattoo. Then over the wrong brand of smokes. A lot of yelling and door slamming and pretty hateful shite coming out of both mouths.

"Just like living with mum again, eh?" Tribal said, a couple months after we'd moved in. He was staring at the shabby blank wall as if it were a movie screen, grappling quietly with wild-eyed memories, each one an intimate resident in a crowded asylum. *Younger*, I thought at the time, watching him. *Harder adjustment for him.* Still, better in the long run—we've done a better job raising ourselves.

Anyway, with nothing better to do and not much feeling like busking alone—or at all—I decide to follow through with Sarah's plan solo. Find the centre, the eye of this storm. Or centre ring of the flea circus, at least.

Hard to pinpoint, but I make an educated guess based on one of those visitor maps I pick up on someone's table as I forge inward. Past the main venue stage, bead sellers, hacky sackers, incense peddlers, henna artists, the standard shite you'd expect while trans-navigating this particular oceanic gyre.

I find a narrow open space between the backs of two rows of canvas tents, tense lines running to the heavy spikes these hippies had pounded into Mother fucking Earth. A corridor.

I'm not alone, however. A stringy cat in tie-dye and ratty jeans is having it out with his girl. She's a good head or so shorter than him, pretty heavy, and red-eyed. Her pudgy little fists are clenched at her sides, tight against the soft bulk of her heavy, patch skirt-covered hips. He's giving her the what for right bloody proper, in sharp undertones, but the idiotic tassels on his knit hat keep bouncing around as he punctuates with angry jerks of his head. I should let them be, I suppose, but I'm an explorer: I can't let adversity stand in the way of science.

My new deadhead companion isn't too pleased that I've intruded, though. He gives me a cursory glance, just a half-second before turning back on the girl.

"Hey, fuck off, man. We're busy."

Yeah, he probably should have taken a better look. I don't really take shite very well, too close to the old times: the King Street days, the east-end nights. I put the guitar case down.

The girl has a better grip on her surroundings, though, and comes to the swift conclusion that Wheat Germ is about to get the boots put to him Oi style. She turns toward me, makes eye contact (so swollen, so red, what the hell did he accuse her of?) and says, simply, "Please."

Nothing more forthcoming from Wheat Germ—I suppose he suddenly figures she has it under control.

And she does. What could I do? Have to respect the chunky little thing—I nod to her, pick up again and pass by. A quest is a quest, and I'm close.

The end of the corridor opens up into another cluster of vendors, and I figure whoever's nearest to my edge of the clearing has to be my epicentre—not a perfect science, I know, but we all do our best and my primary tool is a shitty hand drawn map. I make an objective scan of the terrain and settle on three aging relics of the early '70s, sitting cross-legged on the grass like eastern idols around one of those rough-knit multi-coloured blankets made of alpaca hair or some such shite. It's spread out before them, a makeshift display surface for their wares. I meander over, bit disappointed—I guess I want a sign of some sort, and this looks like more of the same.

Curious assortment, pretty eclectic: little collection of beads, some handmade jewelry, a couple of hash pipes, a neatly folded drug rug, small cardboard box of loose tea bags, pack of used tarot cards, six or seven sheet music books (Dylan, Cohen, The Guess Who), worn and weathered paperback *Kama Sutra*, and a milk crate with a few cassettes and a CD or two in the bottom.

My three Buddhas stop mid-sentence when I walk over. They all look up, staring at me vacuously, mouths still slightly open but silent. The middle one smiles reassuringly, nods his head slowly. It's a bit disturbing, hard to look into those weathered, scraggly faces for some reason. I reach into the milk crate and fish about for a cassette.

I expect anything from Gregorian chants to the Mammas and the Pappas. What I get, however, is a homemade tribute to an all but lost facet of the Hamilton music scene: The Dik Van Dykes. Live.

Besides Jimmy, nobody likes the Dik Van Dykes.

There's a pamphlet stuck to the cassette case, though, a glossy travel brochure dangling from one corner. I'd pull it loose to open the case, tearing off a small paper triangle in the process. With the cassette in one hand, I turn my attention to the brochure. Just a quick glance for no other reason than I'm still holding it.

Visit The Holy Land! it said, bold white letters superimposed on a desert sunset, all rose and orange and red and golden sand blanketed in uneven swathes of deep blue shadow. An advertisement for some company that does group tours of exotic locations, with stops at all the major points for its pilgrims. Including an *exciting two-night stay in Tel Aviv*, the lucky bastards.

Jimmy loves the Diks. I fork over the three bones they want for it and wrap it in the brochure for a joke.

Some joke, eh?

Karma's whores, all of us.

We meet for dinner at the appointed time, downtown, Tribal and me, Jimmy and Deb. I hand Jimmy the poorly wrapped and impromptu gift, Jimmy opening it and smiling, pleased and surprised, holding the cassette up so that Deb can see, too.

"Where'd you find this? They're pretty hard to come by!"

I just shrug, though, maintaining my hold on this minor mystery. Had no idea I'd stumbled on a rare recording, though, not knowing too much about the Diks myself. Jimmy babbles on happily about concerts he's attended and random trivia he's picked up over the years, Tribal chirping in on occasion, but Debbie picks up the crumpled and torn brochure, smoothing it out carefully on the table with her long and slender fingers. I watch her, absently curious, as she seems to slip away into the glossy sunset picture fractured by a spider's web of creases.

"Ever wonder what it's really like?" she asks, as if from a thousand miles away, her voice soft and somehow unreal. Jimmy stops mid-sentence, catching something in the transmission that Tribal and I miss.

"What what's like?" he asks.

"This," she responds, turning the brochure around so that he can read it, see the picture of the Holy Land through the myriad fragments made by the cross-hatched creases and folds, a sunset behind broken glass.

But Jimmy just stares deeply into the image without speaking, almost instantly as strangely lost in the thing as Debbie.

"Yeah, I never—" his voice trailing off, Deb just nodding solemnly, in tune, while Tribal and I float clueless and abandoned on the surface of this dark and mysterious sea into which they have so suddenly submerged.

And that's dinner, Tribal now avoiding eye contact with a girl across the food court because he slept with her last week and me poking absently at a small puddle of gravy that's spilled onto my plastic tray, congealing into something almost discernable, maybe readable. *Like tea leaves* I think *or maybe viscera is more appropriate, although this shite is about six times removed from an actual animal.* And Debbie's words weaving their way around Jimmy, his eyes wild with a tempest of possibilities but face intent and stone-still, as if he were trying to see her lips form the words from behind a tulle veil.

Or a pall.

PART FOUR

Chapter One

It was a dark and stormy night.

Seriously, though. Now autumn, and slashing sheets of rain and black as a Welshman's asshole (Jimmy's expression). We make our plodding way down King, Westdale-bound, heads held low, eyes squinting tight against the wind and wasp stings of half-frozen projectiles that pelt down enthusiastically. One fist is clenched and numb from holding my jacket closed (broke the zipper), the other a rigid claw because of the guitar case, hard and heavy and engulfed in a black plastic leaf bag, a clever last-minute innovation. The pile of dead foliage I emptied onto the sidewalk some blocks back will be a minor mystery in the morning, something to occupy the dull and tired mind of an early commuter on his way to the office, a conversation piece that might interrupt the monotony of shallow and mechanical evening exchange, the *How was your day, dear?* and *did you pay the hydro yet? no, I thought you did,* and *is he done his homework why is the tv on he always leaves the math until the last minute* and *how was the casserole fine just fine as always well I'll go read in bed if you're going to watch the game sure alright goodnight I'll be in later*

Because when he returns, numb from the cubicle, the leaves are still there to be raked up, spread now by the late afternoon wind, but damp and heavy, they don't drift far, to be bagged again, the original vessel vanished into thin air it seems. *But where,* he will think and then ask her, *where did it go? Who would take it? Why? Ah, Gnomes!* he will declare, smiling at his clumsy humour, *Yes, yes, you must be right—gnomes* she says, smiling too, it feels good to smile together, new and undiscovered words now on their tongues, combinations not thought of before, this foreign meeting of convoluted imagery—gnomes and leaves and bags and theft—and real imagery, too, he scraping up the leaves in his tie in awkward sweeps, avoiding his suit with the sopping handfuls he stuffs into the new bag, and she out there with him—the first time in years—helping, holding the mouth wide open for his hands and their heaps of wet pulp. And imagery there, too, or the stirring of imagination at least as he thrusts heavily into that opening, words now clumsy and timid *Hey, it's been a while . . .* and she, too, *it's been so long since we talked—*

And in that violet hour of renewal, homeward these two might sail.

I don't deserve this, I think, meanwhile, *this fucking rain on the threshold of sleet. I've done my bit, I've stirred the dull roots to life, so how about a break?*

And so it goes, my mind occupied with such rubbish as I trudge along, stupid with cold.

Tribal's beside me and behind us walks Jimmy. Tribal is sullen and resolute, trudging at a steady pace. We missed the last bus because of him, though neither Jimmy nor I say so.

Jimmy keeps pace, covering ground, though he seems to stroll. Not in stride, but in attitude. He muses at the rain, somehow detached from its effects, he contemplates the heavy blackness, distantly fascinated by his surroundings. As if cold and drenched and tired were novel experiences for this traveler from some distant planet where these things do not exist.

Me, I'm just fucking miserable.

It was a good gig, though, a decent crowd. The Gallows is a great venue to play, a spacious pub with a good stage. Some places are brutal, the band crammed into a tight corner where you dodge table edges and elbows. Afterward, we'd loaded my van while Jimmy settled with the manager. Derek and Ewan took it, though, gave Sarah a lift home too because Tribal and I wanted to catch the last bus with Jimmy into Westdale and crash at his place. But Tribal was hammered. He wouldn't leave someone's girlfriend alone, and the guy got pissed.

And, of course, when I tried to intervene I took a left hook to the cheekbone. Not on purpose, it was meant for Tribal, but Jimmy jumped in and smoothed things out right quick, supple tongue and tone slipping through the blustering and posturing and other primate antics before we could get into it, and Tribal furious that I took the shot though it was no big deal.

Took time, though. And as Jimmy negotiated this petty peace treaty, the last bus came and went unnoticed.

"C'mon," Jimmy had said once he'd convinced the guy that, right motives aside, moving on would probably be wiser than standing his ground against me and Tribal. "It's a good night for a walk—we'll shog it into Westdale."

It hadn't been raining then.

Jimmy's intervention came at exactly the right moment, the boyfriend saving face because he got to punch somebody, me saving face because at Jimmy's urging he beat a hasty retreat, after offering a semblance of an apology. That left Tribal to take the blame for the misunderstanding, which he did at first, with drunken grace. But as we made our way down King Street, I could see him playing it over in his head, memory muddled by vodka—Tribal's worst choice of beverages—and I knew that all he really saw was me catching it in the Chevy Chase (as the saying goes) and him not returning fire. And by the time we'd crossed Locke Street, Victoria Park just a vast black void on our right, Tribal's myopic vortex of recent memories had tightened down to this: his brother took a hit, and he did nothing.

A tangential karmic adventure, I decide. We need something to pull Tribal out of his downward spiral, or sullen self-pity will set in until he sleeps it off. Vodka, what a pain in the ass.

Then, as if on cue, the monstrous cathedral looms before us as we cross Dundurn. Perched upon a hill, it overlooks the 403, the western portal to the city. You could see the bulky spire from as far back as the corner of King and Queen South, but by Dundurn its gothic tower—bathed in fierce white light that cast its long, vertical niches into impenetrable shadow—demands attention without compromise. An idea emerges tentatively from the murk, centipede scent sharp and sudden—a warning, I've learned since.

We could explore the cathedral, I suggest, furtive malice spilling out at the corners of my stupid grin. Pry into its niches and alcoves, into its dirty little bone shard secrets or withered bits of flesh squirreled away in golden cages. You know, antiquated fragments of saints or petrified slivers of wood. I'm just curious, really. I mean, what's the real difference between a saint's finger bone enshrined and a desiccated, two-headed snake in a glass case, like at any carnival sideshow? Jack shit, that's what.

"I'm sure it's locked up," Jimmy says. "It's two in the morning."

"Worth a look, though," I counter. Just a slight swerve to starboard and we'd be on the dark road that leads to its cavernous double archways. Easy enough.

But Tribal isn't interested in debating the finer points of my impromptu plan. Without so much as a word, he jumps the guardrail and slides out of sight, the cold, dead grass slick with rain. We hear him land with a thump, immediately (it's a tiny hill, barely four steps down). Smiling, we follow.

There's a single car in the parking lot, a lonely and dismal sight, the rain hammering out a steady, relentless rhythm on its drab surfaces. Tribal ignores it, intent on the looming building itself. Jimmy and I do a walk-by, though, just to make sure it's empty.

"Thought we'd stumbled on something worth interrupting, eh!" I joke.

But Jimmy just smiles absently, water streaming down his face. He places his hand on the hood for a moment. Then he crouches down, reaching deep under the front fender.

"Jimmy, what the fuck you doing?"

Squatting there in the downpour, one hand thrust under the car, he peers into the darkness after Tribal.

"Engine's still a little warm. Someone's in there."

"Fuck me!" I growl, "C'mon!" And I shog it right quick, toward the church.

Too late. Tribal's already discovered an unlocked door at the top of the wide stone stairs and slipped inside. I follow, vague guilt already mingling obscenely with the thrill of this wee hour invasion, though my only objective is to find Tribal before he does anything too obvious. Last thing we need is to run into some midnight priest doing fuck knows what in some shadowy corner. *What then*? I ponder.

Inside, it's quiet as a tomb. I grope my way past a giant stone bowl of water and find another door. *Has to be where he went*, I think, and I slip inside.

Into what appears to be a monstrous cave, columns of granite soaring skyward into the gloom high above. And I stand there, jaw hanging open in stupid amazement, gazing up into the spidery network of stone veins that run in confusing perfect symmetry across the ceiling, eyes caught (as it were) in that web of distant and delicate lines. It's my first time in the cathedral. My first time in any church, as a matter of fact. Bit humbling, really, but in a vaguely irritating way, if that makes any sense.

At the far end of the long cavern I see the warm and eerie glow of candlelight, shadows dancing around the edges. Low voices, too. I set the guitar down close to the heavy door behind me and slip quietly through the stone forest, sliding along one of the countless wooden benches that connects one wide aisle to the next, make my way to the massive wall on the far left.

The benches are tight packed, though, foot room restricted by long and cushioned rails that make walking awkward. Rows and rows of them, too, seating for hundreds and maybe even a thousand. Like the waiting room of a giant medieval bus depot.

But all the sneaking and creeping and wariness are pointless. When I finally navigate my way down the length of the cathedral, there's Tribal, standing beside a bald and droopy-shouldered guy of about forty. They're in front of a pile of candles arranged in rows as well, only sloping upward. Stadium seating, I guess.

I stand unnoticed behind them just at the wobbling and jagged edges of light, still and silent. Then Jimmy materializes from the thick invisible air behind me, he too a silent spectator to the cloistered conversation before us. We stand there patiently, happy at least to be out of the rain and wind for a while.

What a pair, Tribal in drenched leather and straggly hair, jeans and boots soaked too, and our host, dry and dressed as if he's come straight from the office but three days ago, shirt and trousers wrinkled and stale. They talk, or rather our host talks and Tribal listens to a low and broken voice, both of them facing the bank of candles as if this gaunt and shabby shade were actually addressing the flickering lights instead of the dangerous and unpredictable spectre to his right that chance has thrown his way this miserable night.

Like Tribal's some kind of manifestation, avatar embodiment of a saint or spirit or ghost, voice just a hollow and wretched echo in this night cavern empty of everything, even faith. Because the words, detached as they are, issue from a mouth I can't see (it too an empty cavern) in that face (just imagined) a right mess of stubble and dark sagging circles under each watery eye as he talks his way through the labyrinth of senseless circumstances, looking hopelessly for function behind the form.

As this ruined ghost gets through his tale, dead voice from a dead mouth, Tribal beside him listening, words I once read by Hemingway surface unwanted beneath the implications of what he's just said. Six simple words—

For sale: baby shoes. Never worn.

Christ, what the fuck kind of god can there be if it drives a harmless man like this to seek solace in a hollow stone shell, after witnessing his own baby die? He'd come straight from the hospital, his wife, broken and still unconscious from the accident, didn't even know yet.

That's for the morning.

Meanwhile, this poor bastard comes for comfort to this place—layman official, a keeper of keys, meek and humble and hopeless search for an answer from the Great Triagonal Myth to which this monstrous pile of stones is heaped, while the whole time the three of us weep. Compelled to, for we are human—water is stronger than stone. We weep for him, in our own ways.

And what of our Host Proper, looming in the gloom above us, giant wooden man nailed to a giant wooden cross—the only one of us in any position to see all four faces—dangling in stony silence, but eyes closed tight and lips sealed? Come, all ye faithful, and keep the faith. Keep it, and keep it close.

But me, I don't want it—to grovel on calloused knees to your sticks, to your stones, to your withered totems of archaic flesh and petrified bone, knuckle or finger joint rust-brown and fibrous and splintered with age, or a tooth of man maybe or beast (saint or pig or goat), and in the end there will be only (*a time for the wind to break the loosened*) pain.

I step forward, not sure why I cross that jagged candlelight threshold, only to feel Jimmy's hand fall quietly on my shoulder. I look back at him, but he shakes his head slowly. *No, brother*, he says, eyes wise and sad, *let it be.*

And so.

Under the gentle weight of Jimmy's hand, I stand my ground, the ruined figure by the candles still unaware that we're behind him, and watch as Tribal unknowingly echoes Jimmy's gesture, laying his own hand on that defeated shoulder. A couple of ragged breaths and then a deep sob, heart-rending and vast in its emptiness, filling all of this hollow space to bursting with something real. Even compelling wood to weep, it seems, with we three helpless in its wake.

But if there's any help to be had here, any comfort to be offered, it doesn't seem to answer from the shadows. Sticks and stones, naught but shite, faith a shallow handful of cheap glass beads exchanged for the only thing we have of any true value: time.

A voice, then. Just a whisper.

"I have to go. Back. To the hospital, I have to go."

He straightens himself up, turns to reach for his coat and sees Jimmy and me for the first time. He's not surprised, though. Maybe for him, this place is always populated, on some level. He picks up his coat from the bench, and something heavy and metallic slides out onto the floor with a clunk.

I don't see it, our host stooping quickly to retrieve it, but Tribal says later it looked old, like something officers carried in World War One. Family heirloom, he ventured.

Embarrassed then, eyes glancing up shamefully at Tribal's as he hides the thing away.

"I—"

"It's alright, mate," Tribal says. "We understand. But that ain't the way to see this through."

"It's why I came here," he whispers, remote, hollow. "But then you came. I—I would've. I think I would've. But I can't now."

He coughs in shallow, tearless gasps, as though he might laugh.

"I think you might have saved me."

And then he walks away.

Tribal shakes his head.

"C'mon," he says, "let's get the fuck outa here, eh?"

Quick look back for me, though, one glance of mocking derision at the giant scarecrow, phantom straw man of this cannibal cult of flesh and blood, keeping the birds at bay with his manmade mechanics.

At least we did something, I think. *Where the fuck were you?*

But in the wooden lines of agony, in the contortionist's suffering, there's a hint of something.

Smugness.

And then the possibility dawns on me.

"You clever bastard," I whisper.

Then off, back into the storm.

—

But in this violet hour, renewal for me as well, I suppose, this tangential lapse in the long rainy walk shaking my own convictions. You never know when that next test will occur, ambushed by some combative and persistent vision sans sermon in whatever desert you're traversing. For me, it is a moth-winged Valkyrie emerging from the musty shadows that gather between the book stacks.

This will not do, though, because whining about the unfairness of things is for the weak. And so, later that same autumn we stumbled into the church, still bleak and cold, I find myself unprepared for that proverbial bell.

Round one. Ding.

"Excuse me . . . excuse me, young man? Young man, we're closing now."

"Hmm?"

"I said we're closing now. Are you alright?"

"Huh? Oh. Uh, yeah, cheers. I mean sure, thanks."

"It's . . . it's just that you were asleep. This is the third time this week—"

"Right, yeah. Sorry, but—"

"Yes?"

"Well, it's just that it's warm in here. You know, quiet."

"Oh. Oh, I see. Listen, I . . . I don't mean to appear intrusive, dear, but do you have . . . someplace to go? You know, a . . . home?"

"Huh? Yeah! Oh, no, I'm not homeless or anything, eh? I just, you know, I like to read. And it's warm in here, and . . ."

"And quiet, yes. So you said. You're in here quite a bit, aren't you? Always in this corner."

"Well, yeah, I guess. It's where you keep the good sh—stuff, eh?"

"Why, yes, I suppose it is! There aren't too many people your age who seem to agree with you, though, are there? Oh, my. When I was your age, books were everything to us . . . Who were you reading today, not more Tolstoy?"

"Um, no. I finished that lot. This is . . ."

"Eliot! I think I've seen you with that collection before, haven't I?"

"Uh, yeah."

"I don't think they'll let you borrow it now—the desk is closed, I'm afraid."

"That's alright. I don't have a library card, anyway."

"I see . . . Are you *quite* sure you have someplace to go, dear?"

"Yeah! Yeah, I'm good, cheers. I just need to, like, grab my things."

"Shall I put this aside for you? I assume you'll be back tomorrow."

"Nah, that's alright. I know where to find it if I want it. Night."

"Oh. Oh, of course, yes. Goodnight, dear . . ."

I wait for her each night on the corner of York and MacNab, meek librarian, grey-haired and quiet. But she doesn't know, never has.

I watch as she leaves the library, making her way to the bus stop through the heavy rain, umbrella held awkwardly to block the wind (right cold, it is mid-November), canvas tote bag bulging with (I assume) paperback novels, ten or twelve, a couple weeks' worth.

I know that Conrad's dark novella lurks in there, too. It always does. Though not the library's, her own. She carries it everywhere, I know this, too, our secret.

Or my secret. Another thing she doesn't know.

It haunts her, that slender tome, I too knowing what it means to have that particular terrifying journey lurk in the corners, just out of reach. Each object, each image, every one of them cloaked in implausibly haunting prose. *Here is a river*, the pages seem to say, *here is a broken pipe, a sabotaged hull, a grove of death, a mournful cry* but without solidity, without real meaning. Hollow. Just an emotive refrain, as if you read it bat-like, aware only of echo, not image. A mere handful of fluttering pages, but they surrender nothing.

Until the end, of course. This, I know, is what she worries over. I've watched her pore over the final ragged pages again and again, slight frown creasing the thin, papery skin of her forehead, eyes strained with consternation behind bifocals on a thin gold chain.

Frustrated, dissatisfied. Behind her desk, she reads between interruptions, or at the bus stop between arriving and departing, or even sporadically when she comes across a copy hidden in the stacks. But the shelves are just another type of sepulchral city, populated by the Dead—listed and organized and catalogued. A decimalized Erebos where the numberless shades gather in memory of what warmth the cold and lifeless words once offered.

Which is where she found me, one day. Hidden in those same stacks,. She's more curious than the others, I see her surreptitious glances as she passes me by. I know she must look for me when I'm not there, on those days when I don't slip away from the scene, my own quick intermission away from the dirt and the anger and the rootless, fickle acts of my own kind.

But this is only supposition.

At the corner of York and McNab is a parking garage, shadowed and sheltered, a good place to watch from. She doesn't know I wait for her as she makes her way to the bus stop, oblivious to even her most immediate surroundings.

Which is the problem. That, and her naïve curiosity about certain occasional library patrons better left alone—panhandlers and other rootless travelers, all looking for a free place to wash up or warm up or sleep. Not that they don't deserve the roof or the rest, far from it, but some of them don't exactly have the firmest grip on reality.

And she was just one of those people, you know? The kind you like immediately, without knowing why. Because she was so utterly harmless, I guess, a frail-framed spinster stereotype, graying hair pulled up into a severe bun, those bifocals on a thin gold chain around her neck, plaid woolen skirt falling to the exact place just below the knee that makes a plaid woolen skirt so unattractive. That sort. Clueless and sweet, alone without the burden of being lonely.

So when she took a passing interest in Murray, I knew it was only a matter of time. Wasn't really her fault, all she said was hello and tried to engage him in a little light conversation, but that was enough for Murray. In the murky recesses of his tragically fucked up mind, he would translate her casual attention as an invitation. And Murray liked to touch, groping his way into one incarceration after another, first the lockup and then, sick of seeing him, to the asylum on a dozen charges of indecent exposure.

Hard to miss him, even on a crowded street. He was tall, well over six feet, but stooped over and slow because of the sheer volume of flaccid, bloated flesh that pulled at his frame. He wore the same greasy and stained and ratty brown overcoat all year round, a shapeless tent he found in a dumpster, and his lower jaw hung open as if the hinges were loose. He drooled on his chest flab and he muttered to himself and by God he stunk like an overused public restroom, vague minty understatement of urinal cakes through the pungent reek included.

Jimmy felt sorry for him, but Murray was too goddamn pathetic. When he begged for change, he just shambled up to people and shoved his meaty flipper in their faces, vacuous gaping expectant smile on his filthy fat puss. Annoying as shite.

Tribal straight up hated Murray, pissed at him for pawing away at a couple of the girls on Emerald and knocking a friend of his down some stairs (by accident), and Tribal's prejudices often rubbed off on me.

Murray loiters in front of the library, also waiting for her to emerge. He's been hanging about, following her to the bus stop every day for almost a week. Anyone else would have noticed—he's got the stealth and stalking skills of an overfed walrus—but she can't seem to tune in.

She steps out of the glass doors, moving in spritely obliviousness toward her stop. The minute Murray sees her, he reaches down the front of his voluminous grey track pants and starts working furiously at whatever he can reach under that bloated pubic paunch. He begins his awkward shuffle toward her, momentum slowly building.

I move across traffic, determined to cut him off, keep her clueless. Others on the sidewalk veer away from him, disgustedly amused, or just stare, shocked.

I dodge a bumper, hop a bench.

I'm between them now.

Oblivious librarian and the lumbering sack of shit named Murray, *the young man carbuncular*, I muse, here on this crowded street, inconspicuousness impossible, so I figure fuck it, I won't bother trying. The icy rain helps, though, people moving with purpose and self-absorbed, focused on immediate sensation and not peripheral sight.

I shift so that he has to manoeuvre around me, an elephant seal trick, and he lumbers to my right, dull eyes locked on that silver bun of hair. Guitar case in my left hand, I look for someplace to land a punch, but even this is ludicrous. Though I'm hardly small, I feel comically miniscule compared to this wayward moon, my fists of little use against this planetary monstrosity.

His feet flap through the puddles, sandals held together with twine and bits of electrician's wire, blubber pushing out on each side of the makeshift bindings like wet dough rising, red with cold. And the limp, left leg a bit gimpy.

That's it, then.

So I step aside, a bit to the left, to let him pass. Simple plan: guitar case held low to block casual view, I'll give the back of his left knee a savage steel toe kick to buckle it while his weight is still on it and down he'll go—*with a soft umph*, I imagine, *right hand still jammed awkwardly down his pants and suddenly trapped by the folding fat as he falls forward, left arm thrown out but too little too late, felled like a tree his left knee slamming into the pavement first followed by the rest of him, giant brown sack of jelly, greedy embrace of gravity sudden and urgent—*

But there's no need—I'm not the only one keeping vigil this evening.

Just a quick flash of movement, passing headlight glint off metal. A cop, plainclothes, badge hanging from his belt and momentarily revealed by the jacket flapping back as he steps out from his own quiet corner and into the drizzle.

And now two more, also supposedly in disguise. Crew cuts, yes, but it's the uniform predatory intensity that gives them away. They've already got me queued up, the first one watching me, eye contact followed by a slight warning shake of his head—imperceptible—he sees intention in my own shift and shuffle.

Step aside for real, no need for me and my tangential interference, just quixotic now. Let the so-called professionals handle it.

And they do, efficient and brutal. They wait until Murray almost has her, though, shambling up behind her in the bus shelter and reaching around those thin arms to paw heavily at her harmless breasts, leaving greasy smears across her blouse, the fucking animal. And I—outraged at these bastards' cold methodology (these small house agent's clerks, these silk-hat fucks)—fly forward, but late, too late for either of us.

Murray is down. He bleeds and bleats, Hamilton's finest working contortionist tricks on his flabby limbs until he is properly trussed and a paddy wagon materializes—I didn't see it, either. Then he is hauled up (bodily moved, the strength of these right brutal bastards!) and out of sight, two cops left behind to take down names and numbers in their little pads, consoling with tired and unconvincing words a frightened old woman alone in a bus shelter.

And in this place the loneliness must finally consume her, holding it together until after the cops get what they want and fuck off (assuring them she's *fine, no, no, I don't want to be a bother, the next bus will be along soon, really, officer. I'm perfectly fine, I have your card, thank you for your help*). When they're finally gone, a slight shudder and then the quiet tears, face turned away, grief carefully concealed.

She doesn't want to be a bother.

I move then, or feel myself in motion, propelled or pushed. I too enter the bus shelter, dripping and haggard and weighed down by water and a vague and nagging guilt, not really sure why I even care.

But to every action there is an equal and opposite, so they say, and her reaction is immediate, hyper-focused now on her surroundings, a frail and thin world with an eye quick to spot and fearful of orbiting entities. Sharp intake of breath, she turns to me with those scared and swollen eyes, after which recognition washes over her.

She knows immediately that I saw the lot, humiliation creeping up her neck and into her thin face despite the attempt at a polite smile.

"I'm sorry," I say, hand lightly on her arm, tenuous, cautious. "I tried to get to you first, but the cops beat me."

This makes no sense, how can she know that they allowed Murray to strike? But she looks down, head nodding absently, as if she agrees with me.

"Look," I say, "how 'bout some company, eh? You wanna grab a coffee?

Or tea? A cup of tea?" I drag out a handful of change and jingle it, a pathetic attempt at humour. "C'mon, I'm loaded, I have, like, tens of cents here. It's on me . . ."

So, Yvonne.

Named after her mother, a Scottish immigrant. We have heritage in common, although unlike me she's serious about it, in touch with her genealogy, her roots. She tells me this and an avalanche of other personal details over tea, the two of us cloistered away in a corner café late into the evening. It begins carefully, me coaxing her out of her frightened shell a bit at a time with mundane questions or filling in the silence with more piss poor jokes (clean and harmless) or editing to dullness the details of my own life for her.

It's the bag of books she still clutches tightly that finally breaks down the reserve, and we delve (so to speak) straight to the bottom and into the pages of Kafka, comfort food for her. She opens up, a little at first, and then—a breeched dam—it pours out, a torrent, a deluge, life flooding finally the wasteland of squandered years. Caught now in the whirls and eddies of this surge, I realize how wrong I've been, assuming for the four or five years of our parallel coexistence that she lived in voluntary solitude, content and introspective.

Here, then, begins my sojourn into an older world, Generation X traitor on temporary hiatus. And what I wanted so desperately, the secrets I tried so pathetically to harvest from Eira—clumsy and blind fool, a witless harlequin's folly I realize now—are given to me freely.

Yvonne, then.

We become friends this night, a friendship at first restrained to cafés and aimless walks when the weather permits. A ludicrous pairing by the limitations of society, of course, the gentle spinster and the ex-boot culture refugee.

But both lonely, both longing for something more than the shallow passing of time marked by the slow and reliable pivot of a tree's shadow, a building's—or by the turning of pages, the sequential processing of words. We cling to each other in unconscious desperation.

We all cling to whatever floats, as Sarah had said to me the April we met, hardly eighteen months before. I guess that's true.

And in the quiet hours, the lazy twilight time between two worlds—the narrow landscape of mindless day labour (concrete block factory automaton) and the wild cosmic dreamscapes of Jimmy's musical visions—there is a time for talk, a time to slip into our own pattern. She instructs. No pedantry, just a gentle coercion disguised as conversation. Because she doesn't yank back curtains to reveal the charlatans in the shadows, there are no grandiose gestures here—and I, for my part, begin to see the vastness of my own ignorance, my own loss.

I listen and learn with a child's enthusiasm, self-conscious at first, as is to be expected. Weakness is unacceptable, the fatal flaw of a dismal and narrow world to which I still feel some connection.

But this, too, is childish. I soon leave it behind as well.

I realize now that I've begun to mark time's passage through a sequence of sidereal drifts: summer's impromptu festival gift wrapped in a brochure, Autumn's tangential confrontation in a midnight church, November's discovery outside a bus shelter—an unexpected friendship. And onward into the following spring. My own vernal calendar.

Chapter Two

"Behold, the Pillars," Jimmy says dryly, from the passenger seat.

We drift between them on Main Street, the Spectator—Hamilton's newspaper building—looming above us immediately to our right and, off to our left and beyond King Street, the Basilica Cathedral.

"Mighty proponents of all things True," he continues.

"You're in fine form," I say.

But Jimmy falls silent, cracks the window and lights a smoke.

I catch quick glances of the church spire before it is lost behind us, obscured by fast food restaurants and billboards and the black branches of leafless trees. It haunts me, that mountainous stone cairn. Five months ago, and I still think about it.

I worry about Tribal, too, a sealed vessel, that wee hour encounter in the church shaking loose the wainscot—the past, I mean, our baby sister Maggie's ghost still among the myriad things we haven't properly faced.

It was good to see, though. Tribal's hand falling gently on that broken shoulder in the candlelight.

But Jimmy, well—he'd merely filed the encounter away, one more signpost on the cosmic journey, the single-minded path he's been walking since last summer. Because soon after my impromptu food-court present, he and Debbie entered into a clandestine partnership, quiet necessity working the mechanisms, both of them enigmatic puppets in a street performance these many months. And now, with churlish March bulldogging its way into spring proper, I sense an end to this reckless road.

By which I mean Deb has been dealing, too, and fearlessly at that. And she can go where Jimmy never could, prowling the makeshift Westdale frat houses and even the dorms—a spider in the network, venomous in her own way. Raves they attend together, psychotropic stash depleted quickly—through washroom stalls, stairwells, even strobe light transactions on the dance floor.

Gigs, too, Jimmy finding more work than the rest of us really wanted, because we now all have day jobs. But none of us ever get around to saying no because the money was decent. Until he spoke casually of touring last October, testing the waters, I suppose. Emphatic no, however, and the matter was dropped.

"Plenty of venues here, eh?" Ewan had said. "No need to go near Toronto or wherever."

"And besides," Derek added, "we got a good thing going here—regular slots on the circuit, eh? We leave for a bit and we'll get replaced."

I held my tongue, never disputing with Jimmy in front of the others (ah, politics), but he could tell I agreed.

"Just a thought," he'd said, casually, shrugging.

But the touring idea was more impatience than anything else—wanderlust had set in, I could see it. Not so much in his interactions with others, or in his chosen topics of conversation. It was his hands: Jimmy began to fidget.

Autumn slipped away and winter crept in, dour and slow. Jimmy and Derek began to feed on each other in a way that took Ewan and me by surprise, the bickering and minor clash of egos that had been a weary and reliable part of our years together and now suddenly replaced with fierce mutual respect—the playlist grew quickly, new material, but also old songs reworked into mature compositions.

And success (relatively speaking) became an unintentional bi-product of so many damned gigs. We had a small following, friends and friends of friends, even some from the old days of bull's-eyes and shaved heads. But this crowd began to transform as well, a tide of new faces, migratory and consistent: by the end of August, we had to leave the Lion's Head behind, too small a venue and a pity because we loved the place.

Then Quinn came through for us, unsolicited and unexpected—got us an interview with a respected writer for the local music scene. The article was flattering (vague descriptors like "compelling", "enigmatic", "complex"—shite like that), but we got asked to play a short set live on the radio (the university station, that is) not two days later. By the end of the week, we had an invitation to play a university pep rally. The last one was pretty intimidating, the venue being outside and in front of about five thousand drunk and stoned students, but paid better than a month's worth of gigs combined.

It all started to get that unreal feeling, that too good to be true sort of vibe. Which was about right, of course. Derek had begun actively planning creative ways of telling his employer to go fuck himself (he really hated work), and I'm pretty sure Ewan was rehearsing behind locked doors for his exclusive with Rolling Stone.

Me, I saved dosh like a bastard, I knew what was coming. After all, Jimmy wouldn't let anything as insignificant as success disrupt the Plan: when they could afford it, Jimmy and Deb were shogging it to the Middle East. Every fidgety fucking finger told me this, as if his hands were desperately communicating to the outside world in their own coded sign language. And it wasn't as if this was a big secret anyway. I told the others what to expect, they just didn't believe me.

Now, with the March thaw upon us, Jimmy had asked us to join him for an afternoon drink. So, past the Pillars and into downtown proper. I find a parking spot a stone's throw from the Hound and Hare and we enter the pub together. Derek and Ewan are already there, two pints in, so Jimmy and I grab our own pints from the bar and join them, settling into a comfortable corner next to the stage. Then, without too much ceremony, Jimmy announces that he and Deb are leaving for the Middle East.

Derek, predictably, loses his gourd.

"You're fucking *what*?"

"Leaving, man. I told you guys last summer."

"You were *serious*?" Derek's a good size, still has a shaved head and he's pretty inked up, intimidating enough under normal circumstances.

Jimmy reaches for his pint, lifting it a fraction of an inch off the table.

"I mean, what the *fuck*, Jimmy!" Derek slams a fist down on the table, hard. Ewan's empty glass, too close to the table edge, bounces off and smashes on the scarred wooden floor. The rest of the glasses jump and slosh.

Ewan just sits there, blank and unreadable. Me, I work at containing the beer spill spreading across the table.

"Things are fuckin' great right now! Airtime, shitload of gigs, that fuckin' CD—and you wanna piss off to the goddamn Middle East? Why? *Fuckin' why?*"

But Jimmy weathers the rage, a hermit on the mountain, as if all Derek's fury were little more than an empty and futile storm. Simply pulls out that fucking pamphlet I wrapped the Dik cassette in last summer, my impromptu joke.

Derek snags it and stares in angry confusion, but if the answer lies beneath the crumpled gloss of chromatic sand and sunset, it evades him. Jaw clenched and red faced, he crushes it in his meaty paw, throwing it back at Jimmy.

"Fuck you!"

Derek stands, table lurching violently, and storms out. Ewan rises quietly and follows. Not one fucking word.

Jimmy. That head of his a hut, a portable bone medicine lodge, his mad dream to pack his entire world into that cage and transport it through time and space to a place where past and present and even future are as meaningless as the remains of sand leaking from a broken hourglass.

I'm the first to break the silence left in Derek's raging wake.

"When do you leave?"

"Tomorrow."

"Christ! Tomorrow?"

"Yeah."

"Fuck!"

"Yeah."

"You might have told me, at least, before now." I feel a bit hard done by, and it shows.

"The others would've seen it in your face. That something was up, I mean. Would have meant days of Derek's temper and Ewan's moping. Better this way, I figured. And besides," he adds, after a sip from his pint (the one thing still upright on the table), "I was up front from the beginning. They knew this was coming."

"Why the Middle East, though?" I never really understood that bit. "I mean, the *Middle East*? Why not B.C. or even Europe?"

Jimmy slowly retrieves a smoke from his pack and lights it. I wait patiently until he's had his first drag, but he still doesn't speak for a while.

Instead, he squints as the smoke rolls gently up his face, contemplates the thin and steady glowing ring that creeps in tiny increments down the cigarette, ash left in its wake. Feather soft, that growing cylinder of ash would disintegrate at a touch, but Jimmy lets it be.

"Did you know," he asks, "that when you're cremated, that little urn you get isn't really filled with ashes?"

"Uh, no. Thought it was."

"More like pebbles. Just the bits of bone that didn't burn up, petrified really. Much of the body evaporates because we're mostly—"

"Water, yeah, I know."

"Right." Another drag. "Man, I don't want my life reduced to a handful of fire-blackened gravel. Experiences and memories—that's what life's about, you know? There's just *gotta* be more to it all than *this*." He gestures at the pub vaguely, but I know what he means.

"So, tomorrow," I say.

"Yeah. And, uh, we'll need a ride into Toronto, too."

"Of course you will. What fucking time?"

"Around five."

"Alright. I'll be at Debbie's after work."

"Actually, I kinda meant the other five . . ."

"Christ! In the *morning*?"

"Yeah."

"Fuck!"

"Yeah."

—

Jimmy's hiatus.

We limp along as a band for maybe another month. Coherence and chemistry, though: two and two, necessary goddamn conjunction. With Jimmy gone, the music crawls along behind us on dry bones, on broken feet, none of us willing to admit that our absent enigmatic midnight prophet was the one who truly gave substance to sound.

We do our best to carry on without him.

Small gestures, carefully offered. This is what we become, Derek and Ewan and I. We mind the eggshells underfoot, Jimmy's name a taboo now, as we creep reluctantly toward the end of this stage. Still, we cling to the remains out of habit.

For instance.

I meet Derek after work and we go to his place, a small basement flat under an east end house that he shares with Ruby (his girlfriend). It's tight, but they've made it into a pseudo-psychedelic grotto that any experienced midnight toker would appreciate. Ruby works at a daycare, but she also teaches after school art classes for little kids at the Cultural Centre. Mostly just that plaster you harden in milk cartons and carve away at with popsicle sticks, or papier-mâché on chicken wire. Anyway, she's pretty talented herself and a wall in the one main room of their place is covered with about three-dozen mâché masks, each one painted intricately.

It's pretty ominous, actually, sitting on one of the giant beanbags and staring at this host of disembodied faces. Before Ruby moved in, Derek had painted the wall black and draped it with Christmas lights, the little multi-coloured ones, and Ruby just hung the masks by tying them to the wires. When the lights are on, most of the masks' empty eye sockets glow red or amber, blue or green, a bizarre eclectic electric death mask portrait gallery. Freaks me right the fuck out.

She's not there when we arrive, though. Five months pregnant, Ruby works as much as she can to build up some dosh for when the baby comes. Derek's already quietly lamenting his place—too small for a family, he tells me, but it's really Ruby's issue with the landlords. They live upstairs, a pair of Bosnian brothers who drink heavily and play Euro-shite music until the wee hours for the six or eight other countrymen that plague the place, arguing politics or whatever in loud, unintelligible drunken gibberish. A fucking refugee camp, it is.

Anyway, I'm there to pick up one of my guitars, a secondhand classic Fender Strat that I found at a pawnshop in Toronto. It was pretty beaten up, and the cat clearly didn't know what he had, so I traded him a Peavey bass amp and thirty bones for the thing. Straight to Derek's for a facelift.

Like Ruby Tuesday, Derek's a hell of an artist. We took it over to his dad's place—he has a woodshop in the garage—and I helped him remove the hardware and strip the paint and sand it down, but then he threw me out. That was two weeks ago. And now? Ah, the great unveiling.

"It's beside the stereo," he says casually from the miniscule kitchen area, "mind the speaker wires, though."

Casually, yes, but you can tell he's pretty excited. I retrieve it and bring it over to the half wall separating the kitchen from the main room because the fluorescent is on, the only light brighter than a lava lamp in the entire flat.

I lay it out on the counter for a proper look.

"Jesus Christ!" This is about all I can manage at first.

Derek grins, proud of himself.

"Yeah, turned out good, eh?"

"Jesus, Derek! It's fucking . . . beautiful!"

Which isn't exactly true, except that beauty is in the eye of and all that tripe. It's overwhelming, though, a thoroughly amazing journey, this psychedelic landscape of toadstool insanity, cacophony of colours and abstract designs. And in one spiral, he'd written lyrics in miniscule letters that receded until they were little more than blurry dots.

"Hey! These are the lyrics to—"

"—Naked Eye, yeah. Figured you'd appreciate Who lyrics on your guitar. Did them with a magnifying glass."

Then there are the facetious additions, he'd replaced the volume and tone knobs with dice and the pickup switch was now a tiny plastic figurine of Jimi Hendrix. And on the body, right above and between the neck end and the first pickup, is a cigarette lighter from a car. I poke at it and look at him in confusion.

"Push it in, it works!"

And this a fucking Stratocaster.

Ruby makes her way down the stairs soon after, finally home.

"Hey!" she says, smiling. "How do you like it?"

"Incredible! Whose idea was the lighter?"

"Mine, actually."

"Tuesday, you're a genius, too good for this Trojan lug. If it weren't for the lighter, I'd have thrown it out immediately!"

Derek smiles, happy that Ruby gets along so well with his friends. No surprise, though, she's pretty easy going. Hard not to like her. Ruby's tall and thin, long blonde hair falls in untameable ringlets across her shoulders and down her back. And because she's so thin, she's showing pretty good, firm and compact bulge not yet to the point where it's inconveniencing her too much. Great sense of humour, sensible—all in all, Derek got pretty goddamn lucky. Not that he isn't charismatic himself, but she's definitely a touch out of his price range.

So, yeah, the lighter through the body of an otherwise incredible guitar with its nine volt power source installed recklessly in the back (probably set myself on fire halfway through a set), but it's the thought that counts. He refuses the eighth I brought him as a gesture of thanks, but not too hard. It soon finds its way into his homemade bongo drum, the inside of which is lined with jean pockets he'd somehow tacked in there. Except what he kept out to smoke. Protocol, after all.

But then Tuesday comes home, and though she doesn't object, she's touchy about secondhand smoke and the baby. I pinch off the heater and hand the remainder of the joint to Derek to stow.

"So," I say, packing up the guitar, "tomorrow night. Nine-ish?"

Derek doesn't answer immediately, eyes drifting to Tuesday's belly.

"Nine-ish," he confirms.

"Alright. I already got Ewan's kit in the van. Can you bring Ewan?"

"Yeah." Softly.

The following night, Sarah meets me in front of the Thistle, an older pub-turned-sports bar on Argyle Street, Caledonia's main drag. Terrible venue for piss-poor pay, but there it is: scrounging as we try to adjust, dwelling now on the peripherals of the music scene. Caledonia, too—Six Nations territory, no place for outsiders to play a gig. We're intruders, unwelcome for what are probably pretty solid reasons.

"Our entire relationship," I tell her in a spliff-rendered reverie, just before we go on, "is based on the fact that one of us is attracted to the other."

And of course, she raises a perfectly sculpted eyebrow, smiles, and asks, "Oh? And which one am I?"

"We both know that," I say, smugly. "Why ask?"

And so, the final gig.

Passively hostile crowd, but it's early. We opened for a straight up rock-a-billy group who act like they're regulars at this dive. Behind the bar hangs this massive Canadian flag, but there's a mounted warrior superimposed on the maple leaf. Plains Indian, too—full feather headdress, long spear held high, war paint, real horse-culture elite. That dude's about as Iroquois as I am, but the locals seem pretty smug about it.

I put my guitar in the case and help Derek with the amps. It's bad form to take off before the headlining band plays at least their first set, but we figure fuck it. Restless crowd, and it isn't even ten o'clock. This isn't technically reservation territory, but I'm not one to get into the politics of land disputes. At least, not here.

I'm determined to finish my beer with some dignity, however, by which I mean while seated. A woman two tables away calls to me, though, gesturing me over. She's Mohawk and with her boyfriend, or whatever the hell he is—skinny white guy with greasy hair, scraggly goatee, and that haunted look that white guys get when they're in a mixed relationship. She looks older than him, anyway, far more sure of her surroundings. I sit down.

"That type of music isn't ours," she says, in a deadpan voice. There's something of a smile about her eyes, though. Amusement at my discomfort, I guess. The white boy just stares sullenly ahead, avoiding my eyes altogether.

"Yeah," I agree. "I see that." An apology, automatic and unwanted, jumps to mind, but fuck her and this whole venue, I figure. I'm not going to apologize for shite.

"Our music is older," she pursues, watching me with that piercing, bemused stare.

"Well," I say, "the headliners are blues-riff rock, I'm pretty sure."

"No. You don't get it. Our music is older."

Moron. How the hell did I miss that? She's no music critic—she's provoking a full-fledged race issue. I smile sheepishly, embarrassed.

"Sorry—I see what you mean." Apologizing for race is second nature when you're white, out before I can stop myself.

She smiles now, crooked, nicotine-stained teeth bared. "It's okay," she says, magnanimously. Then she touches her scrawny companion. "You're like this white boy, here. He don't get it sometimes either." Another smile, wide, teasing, intentional.

Ah, but the artifice, the eyes. I finally get it. It isn't about me at all, or about the next band or the music or race or land. It's about emasculating that poor fuck beside her. Not suddenly, not one crippling blow. No, this is a process, this is attrition.

And there it is, him, me, all of us. I'd been right there, too, once, but I'd learned to forget, I know the trick. Peripherals, you understand. I also know the cruel and cold mechanics behind it, pity welling up inside me.

He looks at me now, though, and he knows. *Brothers*, we exchange silently.

And then I leave without another word, beer abandoned. What he's going through, not something you can really share. That road is a one-man journey.

And then she comes out of nowhere, this waif of a girl with (I swear to Christ) a feather hanging from a long and beaded brunette braid, a tourist trap dream-catcher. Says she's a Cayuga, has a thing for guitarists. Yeah, right. Pissed off at her drunken boyfriend and looking for a jealousy-triggered quick fix, but she scrawls a name, a number, and a time (her 411 she calls it, for fuck's sake) on the back of my hand anyway.

Details aside, it was the chelsea and the boots all over again. Like Jimmy says, I'm never too good with the big picture.

Later, we reassemble from our varied nocturnal wanderings for breakfast at this dive of a diner on the Escarpment. Ewan grabs my hand and blurts out, "Hey, look who's collecting autographs!"

But Tribal looks up from his coffee, assesses, smiles sadly, and sighs. Straight up pity, I assure you.

Not the others, though. Ha, ha, ha. Big fucking joke at the expense of Yours Truly, an avalanche of uninspired insults from all.

Except from Sarah.

She gets up quietly and leaves.

But the spell really was broken and we eventually go our separate ways.

We all keep an oar in, though, even if it's just on the periphery. I do solo sets or sit in with friends, Derek finds regular studio work in Toronto, Ewan fills in here and there for a number of circuit regulars.

For me, the city haunts feel empty. I miss Jimmy terribly, Debbie too.

I sometimes dream of desert sunsets, glossy and crumpled. Those of us left behind fall into the mindless routine—day jobs, bleak and futureless roads ahead.

I guess our paths lead to sand, too. Each in its own way.

Even after we disband—divide equipment up, sort out the petty debts, an amicable divorce—we attend each other's gigs or show up at the same parties or grab a drink every now and then, that sort of thing.

What I really mean is, we stay in touch.

This is the point, I suppose. Jimmy's name stays the new taboo, Derek not one to forgive and forget. When Ewan and I bump into each other, Derek's usually there, too. But when we're alone—or, at least, out of Derek's range of hearing—he sometimes asks.

"You hear anything, man?"

"Naught but shite, mate."

"You sure?"

"Ewan, c'mon."

"But you'll tell me if he phones or writes, eh? You know, about coming home?"

"Brother, you'll be the first."

So, lost—we have that in common. Sarah, too, and that surprises me. As happy as she was initially that Debbie was leaving—even if it was just a temporary sojourn—she hated to see Jimmy go. They'd grown close, opposite polarities (or maybe just compelled by Jimmy into a more complacent version of herself, lulled by the current, a salmon riding out gravity's magic. Downstream and into oblivion), or maybe because Jimmy had his own gravitational pull.

Debbie, too, in a way. Affected by Jimmy, I mean. But tethered so lightly to the mooring post that she seemed to float where she stood, a nebulous extension of Jimmy himself.

It's how Jimmy could make you feel, like you were a kindred conscience, but (simultaneously) dependent upon the direction of his thoughts. So when I finally got that fragmented late night phone call from seven hours in the future, only four months after they'd left, it scared me. Jimmy was in some sort of distress, but he wasn't making any sense—

"*Down. Gone. I lost her. In a crowd.*"

"What do you mean, gone? Deb's there, right? I mean, she's fine, isn't she?"

"*Swallowed. Sea and sand, I told you.*"

"Swallowed by what? For fuck's sake, lost her where?"

"*You aren't listening. It swallowed her! Tel Aviv. It swallowed her. This place, this place swallows everything.*"

And then dead air.

In a desert city a quarter of a world away, it was sunrise. They had been gone for only four months and something terrible had happened, and all I could do was wait.

My own phone call, minutes later. I had to tell someone.

"*Hello?*"

"Sarah. Oi, it's me."

"*What's wrong? You sound shaky.*"

"Just got a call from overseas—something's happened."

"*What do you mean?*"

"Don't know—we got cut off or something. All I know is something bad's happened. I lost the connection before he could tell me what."

"*He? You mean Jimmy, right? Did you speak with Jimmy, or someone else?*"

"No, it was Jimmy."

"*Is he okay? Was it something that happened to him?*"

"No—no. He's alright, but I think—"

"*Jesus! You really scared me!*"

"But—"

"*Jimmy's alright! Thank God for that.*"

Chapter Three

Across the Harbour in the city of Burlington is a small neighbourhood, roughly modeled on the narrow, Victorian market streets of Mother England. A clumsy mimicry, but still appealing in its own way, quaint little shops along quiet and meandering cobblestone paths. Dominating this brick and gingerbread simulation is a right proper pub, it too red brick and Victorian—the Dickens.

No place for the hooligan antics of our younger years, and we kept clear of it until well after the days of boots and bats, braces and bull's-eyes. But one early summer evening, out with a friend from work, Sarah was introduced to the place and she fell in love with it. Too much like an aquarium, Jimmy said (*or a bathysphere*, I think, *rising slowly to the surface with its unwanted cargo, pressurized water-womb*), but Tribal disagrees—he likes it, too. Calming, I guess.

A fitting place, I decide one Thursday afternoon in August, and plan an outing. Friday is Yvonne's day off and a night out would do her good. We'd had a gig that night, but the place lost its liquor licence mid-week for serving minors. Fortuitous, as it turned out, me figuring that Yvonne might find something disarming in the Dickens mostly because of its namesake, but also because of the crowd.

But it isn't the main floor with its dark wood and brass taps—it's the upstairs I know she'll love, a common room where older patrons (and every bloody one of them right off the boat) gather to drink and carouse and eventually break into song, singing the old pub tunes of their forefathers or half remembered fragments from their school days, warbling away and made maudlin with pints or spirits, smiling, teary-eyed specters living simultaneously in past and present.

I only knew about this upstairs hideaway because I'd stumbled into it a while back with Keith, a good mate and drummer for a Celtic rock band called the Gallows Swines. We were on a pub-crawl, Keith and me, celebrating belatedly because the Swines had cut their first CD and I'd missed the release party. We'd decided to try the pubs on the other side of the Harbour, stay below the radar I suppose, and the Dickens was one of the last stops.

And so, with bellies sloshing with hard cider and ale and feeling a bit like it was turning to vinegar, we followed the sound of drunken voices up the stairs and down a narrow corridor until we staggered into a warm and welcoming room of Brits, bellowing out "*down a' the ol' Bull an' Bush*" at the top of their lungs, arms thrown around neighbours and swaying recklessly on the benches while some ancient crumbly in the corner banged out the melody on a tuneless old piano. We stared in amazement, unsure at first if we'd stepped into a private gathering of ghosts, but hands beckoned us in and old men shoved aside to make room at the bench, a friendly and kind lot. We accepted immediately.

Not sure if we sang or not. I think Keith did because he knew the old songs, having heard them a thousand times at home, his own parents being right off the boat from Inverness themselves, but I don't remember too much beyond the warmth and din and mingling clash of stale body odour that clung to the old men and the heady perfume of their graying wives.

So, I figure, why not again and sober this time, introducing Yvonne to this kind crowd? And if not, if she feels out of sorts, then downstairs and borrow the pub's cribbage board, have a quick pint and fuck off back home.

But it goes better than expected.

We stay until almost one, Yvonne close to nodding off but imploring me for another fifteen minutes every half hour or so, though at no point do I ever suggest it's late—sober is not the best state of mind for this lot, but it's for her, not me, and I keep mostly to myself, all friendly nods and polite jabber when necessary.

Yvonne, though. Christ. She sings along to everything, from old school hymns to sailors' shanties, she knows the whole wretched repertoire.

And then, there's Albert.

Nervous and gentle, Albert stumbles through small talk as if at any moment Yvonne will dissipate, like a dream. About her age, too, he owns a collectables shop, old coins and rare stamps mostly, though the occasional first edition of this or that. An old widower, gentleman through and through. He is confused by me, frightened instinctively of my disapproval. He pulls out a curved piece of bone from a pouch in his waistcoat, petrified black with age. It's a tooth—a tusk, really—he struggles to impress upon me its importance in the lineage of such things, this primitive totem hidden for centuries under the dark loam of East Anglia until a labourer's spade churned it up. He points to the Pictish boar tattooed on my forearm and says something else, but they've burst into song again, something dreary and sentimental (*everybody* here remembers Vera Lynn), so I miss it altogether.

No matter. Yvonne beams, happy with this unexpected find, and this her first time out since before I was born. As we leave, she is glazed over, struggling happily to put her emotions in perspective.

"This is what living feels like," I tell her, a gentle chide. Then I recall our mutual friend and his fang. "Did he ask for your number?"

"Oh, well, no. No, no he didn't. I thought he might, but he seemed so terribly nervous . . ."

"This won't do. Just a tick . . ." and I'm back up the stairs in a flash, calling for pen and paper, finding a rectangular scrap on the way though. A playing card, waxy, too large, I hunt frantically for Albert, find him fetching his overcoat. A pen! Albert himself produces it, strange look of anticipation and fear in those eyes—a time for living, Albert (I am the wind that will shake the wainscot, my field-mouse friend), here mate, take her number and call her soon, let me write it—a Tarot card? Christ, the drowned sailor, too, then call her tomorrow and take her to dinner. What shall I get for flowers, he asks this in a daze, he too glazed over. There's only one answer, though, the card a sign, a private joke.

"Get her hyacinths, mate. She loves 'em."

—

Albert's shop is part of a small strip mall, an uninspired L of single-storey businesses made of tan brick with a continuous flat, tarred roof. Like his neighbours, he rents the space from an anonymous group of owners, sending his rent cheque to a corporate office on the first of every month. Albert's nothing if not predictable.

Yvonne doesn't drive, so I take her for a surprise visit. They've been dating now for two months now. Or, at least, they've been spending time together in restaurants and cafes, or in parks and the occasional museum, so it's not entirely unexpected. Still, she's grateful for the ride, quiet on the way over and doesn't arrange for a return trip, so I figure Albert might be in for a surprise anyway.

It's faster to take the Skyway into Burlington, but Yvonne gets nervous that high up— with anyone else I'd have said too fucking bad, but I can't seem to say no to her. Anyway, it's the old way for us, Eastport Drive exit off the Queen E. to the lift bridge, an antique itself that lives out its quiet existence in the shadow of the monstrous arch of steel and concrete beside and above it. *Strata*, I think, and then facetiously *hey Jimmy, I'm between the layers* but the bridge is up and we have to wait for some foreign leviathan to crawl through the opening, its crew like aimless ants, too far away to see much more than movement.

We enter the small shop just before three. Albert is absorbed behind his newspaper, Yvonne breaks the silence.

"I hope we're not intruding. I could always come back later . . ." her overly sensitive concern for others' feelings a natural part of her personal landscape.

"Well!" he says, looking up happily, "You came at just the right time. I was beginning to think no one knew I was open!"

I'd noticed a wedding ring that first night at the Dickens, a memento of a bygone age, but his stubby finger is free now, no longer shackled to memory, as it were. Now there's twenty minutes of light banter, animated exchange between Yvonne and Albert with me throwing in an occasional word when it seems to fit. And unlike that first awkward night, the shop suddenly fills with tension, earnest and fierce, desire hungry and urgent and open. I almost laugh but catch myself just in time, a bit embarrassed even, because the two of them are looking at each other and then at me and squirming like a pair of oversexed teenagers, unsure of just how to proceed. Definitely not to anything even remotely intimate with me standing there, suddenly every bit the third wheel. Too cruel to draw this out, Albert (I swear) with the shop keys already emerging from his trousers pocket, but I can't help myself.

"Closing up early?" Innocently delivered.

"Well, yes, I—"

"No point in staying open if no one's shown up by now, eh?"

"Exactly! Yes, not really much point—"

"So I guess I'll be off, then."

"Oh, really? So soon? Well, Yvonne and I could get an early supper—"

"—or you could order in, eat at your place! Yvonne likes Chinese, don't you, Yvonne?"

"Oh, well, yes, yes I do."

"There you go then. I'm off."

And I am, mirth tugging at the corners of my mouth as I drive back to Hamilton. Hindsight's 20/20, as they say. Should have slipped Albert a condom when we shook hands on the way out the door. Then again, I'm glad I didn't think of it at the time.

That tusk of Albert's, by the way, the one he showed me that first night at the Dickens. Couldn't hear for shite in there, between the warbling of old singers and Albert's timid voice, but he explained it again sometime later, the second or third time I took Yvonne to see him at his shop.

A family heirloom, he explained, something from his mother's side, originally unearthed at Sutton Hoo in the 1930s under the direction or patronage of the Suffolk matriarch who owned the land. Albert's ancestor was the gamekeeper or gardener, maybe he said the gamekeeper's cousin, can't remember. Anyway, someone who had access to a shovel and one of the burial mounds. The tusk was an artifact that slipped through the curators' fingers, I guess, because he said (sly wink) that it's never been catalogued. Whatever the fuck that means.

"It's pretty," he said with as cunning a smirk as he could muster, "a pretty original!"

"Oh, Albert!" Yvonne had responded, all smiles, impressed by this wittiness.

Which had to be explained to me, uneducated and dense, Pretty being the family name of the landowner who allowed the first Sutton Hoo excavation. Polite ah of revelation once explained.

He let me hold it, Albert was a strong proponent of the tactile experience. Constantly pushing things into my hands on the few occasions I was in his shop, strange oddities and only the most morbid bloody objects—a WWI field amputation kit in its original wooden box, for instance, or a brittle black and white photo of a boy laid out in a coffin—he seemed to have a pretty grisly collection stashed away in boxes, cabinets, drawers, a sort of secret and morbid bazaar. Although to the casual visitor, it was a pretty standard collectables shop, coins and old Dominion bank notes and stamps, that sort of rubbish. But that tusk rarely left his pocket.

It was brittle and pitted, the colour of dull rust, but polished smooth in places where an absent thumb had worried away the empty hours of empty days, lonely spans spent in this dusty little museum and maybe before that, school days a dim memory now and mostly remembering only the loneliness. He told me this, too, after we'd known each other a while, small and awkward and asthmatic child left out of the more rugged boys' games in post-War Toronto. Fatherless (like me), immigrant mother also like me, but unlike my drunken sot of a mum, his was too busy trying to make ends meet to notice that her boy didn't quite fit in.

One afternoon, while waiting for Yvonne to reappear from the washroom in the back of the shop, Albert pulled out this enigmatic totem again. He hesitated a moment, then tapped my forearm with the worn and weathered end of the thing.

"Do you know much about that tattoo of yours? The boar I mean?"

I shrugged.

"Not much, really. Found it in a book on Scottish history. Looked, you know, fierce. Strong. Kinda fit my mood at the time, so I had it done." I didn't add that I'd cut the page out with my knife to take with me. Derek did the tattoo, he was a hell of an artist.

The boar was from a petroglyph, a primitive symbol carved into stone around the time the Picts defeated the Scots at Dunadd in Argyll in 736 AD. Albert knew these things, reciting them from memory.

"And the boar was carved into stone soon after that victory, a symbol of their fierce strength and independence." Albert paused (for effect, I supposed) and then launched, happily oblivious, into the next bit.

Strength and independence. As reasonable an assumption as anything else, I guess.

But those twelve hundred years between us, me and him.

Twelve centuries ago, a man whose name and lineage and deeds and failures and dreams and fears are utterly lost to time's steady erosion knelt over a slab of stone to carve the sinuous, abstract image of a heavy boar. And that's it. This anonymous image, powerfully built and savage-tusked, is all that will ever remain of him. Time will erode those lines, too. Eventually.

What does it mean, then, that his art—his vision of one specific aspect of that dark and brutal world—now lives again, sunk into flesh now, a faithful reproduction of image without meaning? Why was it carved in the first place, and what personal connection did he have to it?

These things are lost as well. Only supposition remains.

I pondered it all, as Albert babbled on about geography and Northumbrian politics, the collection of sage opinions he'd rendered from reading. But just tallow, really: dim and inconsistent illumination, fatty grease sputtering as it weakly burned, lighting up little.

On he went about king against tribe and chief against chief, but all I could picture were hundreds of dim-witted, spear-wielding primitive fucks stabbing and hacking at each other over nothing, muddy patches of earth and collections of dirty hovels, or a heap of stones hollowed out enough for the most savage of them to squat in during the hard times. Just medieval bucolic boot culture, really, oi-style mass mosh murder.

I smiled and shook my head at the image. And at Albert, too, still wielding that graveyard relic as he pontificated away on the more obscure points of Gaelic history, a comical sight—slope shouldered and soft, near-sighted and delicate about the wrists, the hands—brandishing the business end of a primal and violent monster of the past, a chunk of bone that probably once adorned the human version of the boar itself, a right brutal bastard I had little doubt.

Yvonne reappeared, quietly as always, standing politely to one side as Albert finished his bit. Then he noticed her, mid-sentence, and the final fate of Eoganan the Pict was forever lost to me. Silly grin and flush as he gripped the tusk tightly, fumbling to slip it back into his pocket.

But chance convergences—those incongruous meetings of the warp of one world and the weft of another—confuse us all. Asleep at the wheel, most of us in a deep and communal coma, until we crash into each other.

Each of us groping our deaf, dumb, and blind way through the slow and steady click of days and nights until we blunder into something or someone (just idiotic luck), and fabricate a connection. Not like we can't hear or speak or see, but that we walk our paths bass-ackwards, recklessly repeating the mistakes of the previous generation. And not because we're experiential learners only (what utter shite), but because we find solace in reminiscence, comfort in contemplating the road *already* taken.

Hindsight is twenty-twenty, they say, but all that really means is that you can look back at anything and plot the course, connect the dots, splice together something meaningful out of the random convergence—and divergence—of every sightless satellite you've crashed into.

So, what's reliable, real? Nothing. Pattern seekers, that's what we really are. We each have a pet illusion, well versed in self-hypnosis, some more skilled than others at articulating an empty construction of (T)ruthless reality.

So, chance convergences.

Albert showed me one more thing that day he told me about the tusk, the two of us waiting in awkward silence again, this time for Yvonne to return from a used bookseller's shop in the same strip mall as his place. Pulled an old envelope out of a bottom drawer in a cluttered corner, a clumsy attempt to give us something to talk about. Inside was a child's tooth, a tiny yellowish and dirty nub tucked into the folds of a letter, also yellowish and dirty. Albert opened it carefully and handed it to me, but it was impossible to read, a language of blocks and vertical sticks that looked more like musical notes than anything else. I shrugged and handed it back.

"No," he said, "look at the date."

Something followed by 1915 in the right corner, legible enough, but that was all. I took a stab at it.

"A war letter? World War One, I mean?"

"Well, in a way—it's in Armenian, a letter written during the Armenian Genocide. I don't know what it says, but that tiny tooth . . . it fascinates me. Maybe a mother sending it to her husband? A love letter? But it was never opened, you see. I found it amongst some other papers I bought years ago, sealed, but I left it by mistake by an open window. The dampness—or maybe the heat. Anyway, when I finally remembered, there it was. Open."

"Never found anyone to translate?"

"Never *tried*. It would spoil the mystery."

And there it was, Albert's method under the madness, defusing horrors of the past, one fabrication at a time. His own customized bag of flies, I suppose. That letter—like his other hidden and hideous artifacts—trapped in time and space, or on the surface of the flypaper reality of his own stories, black specs like braille to be read by the initiated few, those whose entire universe is between the fingertips and the brain.

So, Albert, too. Avid and secret writer of flypaper prose.

Hey, who the hell knew?

But there's method to my madness as well, a point (or a spec on the surface) that connects one thing to another. My own idiotic and rambling attempt to construct something from nothing. Because of course she was of Armenian descent. Debbie, I mean, that late night talk out at the Point when she told me about her grandmother, her mother. Debbie's soft words and softer tears.

And soon after, our clandestine camping trip up to the falls.

—

It would be another full year before Jimmy reappeared—June of 1990. Little more than a ghost himself, somehow pale and fading beneath ruddy brown and weathered skin—materializing out of thin air right in front of me as I make my way down Hess Street toward the Gown and Gavel, guitar case in hand. Gig forgotten, we go for coffee—someplace to talk.

And there, at another small café, Jimmy finally speaks. But words (those that strain, crack and break—like the world, they will not stay still, they) are stones that cannot be deciphered.

The Catfish is gone. The Illiterate, too. Jimmy comes back to us changed, transformed. He, too, cannot be deciphered. And our roles change, we two still bound together because this brotherhood is as strong or sometimes stronger than blood, with me *When's the last time you ate something, man? C'mon, Jimmy, just eat this* and him *Later. I'll eat later* and all of us watching him waste away. He haunts the same small stretch of shore that I did one November three-and-a-half years before, staring out at the factory fires and throwing stone after stone after stone into the invisible water.

It seems for a long time that this is why he returns at all: to throw his stones and to dream and to toy with the terrible possibilities of regret.

As it turned out, Jimmy had already tried to tell me, over the phone. The only other call I got from him in that empty stretch, brief and static, four in the morning and in April, just eight weeks before he returned. It isn't something you just said, though, not over that kind of distance.

"So, where's Debbie Dream, man? She with you?"

"*No, brother, she's not.*"

"Why? What happened?"

"*Better wait till I see you.*"

But in that cramped café, Jimmy's words are ghosts, too. We claim a table, speak of her immediately, no trite pleasantries despite the cold stretch of time between departure and return.

As he finally gets through it, I become acutely aware of the heavy and relentless rotation beneath us, the earth slipping away and we two moored and timeless against the axial turn.

"Sonar Debbie," he says. "She's gone. Lost."

"Lost where?"

"Brother, she jumped. She—

smiles once, serene and obscure as the star-studded eastern sky behind her. Then, lips parted, she simply steps out in the air, weightless in that void of starlight and street sounds, slender form forever frozen there in memory, weightless and immune to time (says Jimmy, eyes closed tight to ensnare her, to keep her afloat five indifferent stories above the narrow street below choked with dust, swept with shadows) but gravity's urgent pull is stronger than time, more relentless than memory. Down she plummets, a broken songbird's note barely audible above the rush of wind.

And then she's lost from sight, lost from sound until that single small broken thud reaches upward, softly. A whisper. A sigh.

Sonar Debbie,

lost between the cracks in the road.

Chapter Four

That first year after Jimmy got back from the West Bank, I counted down the months and then the weeks, the days, until I, too, would slip away. He spent a lot of time down by the water. Just staring across the harbour at the fires rising from the towering steel mill smokestacks, or throwing stones and watching the black surface of the night play insignificant havoc on the city lights (buildings, bridge, cars), ripples that sent each flickering light into dancing fragments until the surface resettled and the light regained its place, wild modulations momentarily over.

It calmed him, those ripples. Said the lights looked like sonar blips. But there was nothing I could say, none of us could—Debbie was gone, one less light on that black and liquid screen.

Lost and lightless on the sea.

Sometimes Tribal and Sarah would come with me, but it was difficult to stand in that silence, the plop plop plop of stones at minute intervals, Jimmy uncommunicative—sullen, sad, and silent. What could I do? He was a mate, a brother: I stood beside him if he stood, sat beside him if he sat. We watched the flames or the lights or the passing traffic as it arced along the Skyway Bridge or the freighters as they slogged through the waters at a crawl. All in reflection, an upside down world caught in that moving mirror.

It came to me eventually, dense and daft bastard that I am. Jimmy was watching his own reflection, real or imagined. But how can you see yourself in the blackness? Not in water, lightless itself, and yet there he was, beneath the surface, Catfish beyond reach. He'd swum too deep.

Sometimes I could pry him out of the lull. Music helped, so did weed. Not hash, though, and certainly nothing liquid—his reflection was down there beneath the surface already, a barely metaphorical drowning. It was unwise to drown his sorrows up here, too. Reminiscence, I found out, could go either way.

"Hey, Jimmy . . ."

Plop.

"Where do you think Steph ended up?" She'd left around the same time as Jimmy and Debbie, crossing the border to the south, although without ceremony or even a goodbye. It was there on the shore, looking down at the Catfish in the water, that I had decided to move on myself. I hadn't said anything yet, though.

"Don't know. Somewhere."

Well, at least it was something.

"She used to talk about . . . Cleveland or Cincinnati, didn't she?"

"Chicago."

"That's right. Chicago."

Plop.

"We should go, eh? You know, road trip! Tribal'd go, even Sarah if she got a little time off work."

But down here by the water Jimmy was adrift in desert sands, lonely pilgrim of no particular faith, his eyes so distant that I marveled he could hear me at all.

Jimmy was in Tel Aviv's underground.

He was in the Yemenite quarter of Jaffa.

He was in a moshav on the Syrian border.

He was in a Bedouin headman's tent.

He was on a rooftop with Debbie, this ragged dreaming Jesus of ours, dreaming.

He was on a rooftop.

After a while he spoke in quiet words, barely audible above the distant bridge traffic across the bay.

"I miss her, man."

"I know, Jimmy. I miss her, too."

And I do. Fuck, Debbie, I still can't believe you're really gone.

We talk sometimes and sometimes he lapses back into silence. There's no pattern to this, just the mechanics of random components (reflections, fire, ripples, words) that either conjures conversation or doesn't.

He writes lyrics again, but not in the frantic mad midnight surges of the past when, sustained by the street chemistry pumping through his veins and visions, he would let the music utterly consume him for two and three days at a stretch.

No, he now writes contemplatively, deliberately, of something hidden beneath the stone-heavy and world-weary heap of pith and marrow he has carefully gathered up from the ragged corners of memory. "Piled up," he whispers, "in one great big heap. These are the things I should be buried with," a sardonic smile, tight and devoid of humour. "Or under."

Jimmy's heap. A cairn of misplaced keys and half empty packs of smokes and sheets of lost papers worn silk-smooth at the crinoline crinkled edges by nervous fingers, broken bottles and discarded guitar strings, stolen smoke alarms and plastic bags of clothes hastily abandoned on the run, lost shoes and wasted words words words always words.

And, of course, sand.

"What about you, Sarah? What do you believe in?"

Another night, Sarah and Tribal have joined me in my lonely vigil. We sit with Jimmy by the water tonight. A rare moment during which he asks us questions in turn, a gentle but persistent flow of etiological inquiries that fit his current mood.

"I don't know, Jimmy," Sarah says, weary of this already. "Not too much, I guess."

"So, what, you're an atheist?"

Not an accusation—Jimmy never judges. But I see it in Sarah, that surreal disconnect between sound and sense. She feels that peculiar pressure of meaning beneath the casual conversational veneer, doctor's office small talk at that sudden moment of personal crisis. Just another kind of clinical probing, sanctioned violation of (I smile) personal space.

Sarah holds her own, though. *Atheist.* She contemplates the word, poking at it distastefully, as if it were a dead fish (I smile again).

"No, not an atheist, I suppose," she admits. "Jury's still out for now. Ask me in a few years."

My turn, same question delivered in the same distant, politely curious voice. But my answer is prefabricated, off-hand, facetious.

"Me? God-fearing agnostic."

Jimmy smiles, just a slight curl at the corners of his mouth, but it's still good to see.

Tribal sees it too and pulls his long hair forward so that it drapes over the front of his shoulders. Stony-browed with out-thrust jaw, he grunts.

"I pray to Crom in his mountain. But he seldom listens."

Sarah misses the reference, but Jimmy and I don't. We laugh and Tribal misquotes half-remembered fragments in his best Conan the Cimmerian accent for a minute or two. But before Jimmy is Jimmy again, he stares back out over the water at the flames rising above the mills and slips away from us, back into a solitude where moonrise means little and our jokes skip helplessly like flat rocks across the black water.

In the long quiet stretch that follows, Jimmy begins to throw stones again—slowly, methodically.

"Words are stones," he whispers.

The breeze picks up, plays lazily with the oily surface. Then he stops in mid-throw, lowering his arm. He contemplates the small lump of fused and lifeless minerals in his palm, it rests there inert and meaningless. I watch as he raises it to his lips and whispers once again, as if to himself.

"I'm not afraid of dying."

And slips the stone into his pocket.

Sarah catches up to me as I'm opening the driver's door. Tribal still waits with Jimmy down by the shore, smoking quietly while Jimmy stands aloof, contemplating stones and stars.

"You headed back?"

"Yeah. Wanna come?"

"Yeah, cheers."

Tribal picked her up after work, driving her down to meet Jimmy and me. He'd come straight from work himself, covered in drywall dust and plaster. He loves his job, the crazy fuck, a far cry from the empty days and hooligan nights of boots and bats and whiskey and beer, as shiftless and lost as the rest of our steel city generation. But we were kids then, it didn't require meaning. And at the end of it, when we were too old for music and boots to dictate our politics, there was still Sarah out there in the woods, out at the Point.

I look at her as I drive, just furtive glances. She's changed, too, still beautiful (even more so) but somehow worn thin. There are too many unspoken words between us now, they weigh us down, a burden we share by mutual agreement—words undeclared and unsorted, as inert as Jimmy's silent stones.

But Sarah and I, we don't break the surface of anything: we build a quiet wall (or cairn), high and safe, immune to the petty and seasonal tampering of whatever we must weather. We spend the drive back downtown discussing the obvious, though, safely external, a shared and genuine concern.

"He's getting worse," Sarah says.

"No, not really—at least he smiled a bit tonight, eh?"

"I suppose. Tribal's good at breaking tension, though." Then she opens my glove compartment, catches the avalanche of papers in one hand while retrieving a tube of lipstick with the other. She closes the compartment like a spring-loaded trap while applying lipstick. All in one fluid motion.

"Uh—"

"Oh, I keep lipstick in your van. And a few other things."

"Ah. Anything I should know about?"

"No. Not really."

Sarah—a keeper of secrets from our beginning. That April evening three years ago, she witnessed Tribal and me commit every scrap of paper we could to the flames— trial by fire, Yours Truly no longer bewitched, and all my memories of Eira condemned to burn. Sarah did her bit, too, polite contributions: a few letters, a postcard. Of her own story she offered little, but of the relationship that drove her out of Toronto and into Hamilton, she offered absolutely nothing.

We all collect something, and for Sarah it is solitude. She discovered that, with us, friendship didn't require an open ledger because we didn't hold her accountable for words unsaid—she could be as alone as she needed to be in our company.

I don't know what Eira did with the meagre scraps I gave her in return, a paltry handful of letters. Burned them, too, I hope, only *Dear Eira* left behind. Burned into memory, that midnight composition my only companion on the long drive home one miserable November night.

Because *this is just to say*. Even now.

And so.

This is how I occupy myself as I drive Sarah back into the city, mind meandering, more river than road. And tumid or no, on it flows. Casting back toward a (con)tributary, I see how my own stones thrown with such angst and fury and frustration into that temporal river still tumble onward toward me, following me beneath the surface. Rolling along the bottom, urged forward by current and circumstance, this river devoid of silt and snags. We are all what we were in a way, I suppose, even if that means we wear our echoes like the ripples of a snake's loose skin.

But Sarah too has her contributing factors. Because on that late April evening she, too, contemplated with no little apprehension the rugged road ahead, that ponderous trudge toward indifference—the Promised Land, so distant from love and sister hate. And although mine began that night with fire, hers had begun with tears hours before we arrived. In the darkness, and then in the unreliable firelight as we burned bundles of letters, Tribal and I didn't notice the telltale signs.

Sarah. Quiet companion on this midnight ride away from the Lake and into the city as I think about cause. I already know the effect. She looks over at me now, I feel her watching me, hear the gentle in-breath. I wait for words.

"Getting worse," she repeats.

"Maybe," I say.

And nothing more. A wall now between us of questions unasked and answers withheld. Neither of us willing to risk our friendship for the sake of what ifs.

"You working tomorrow?" I ask.

"Yeah. Nine to six. Wanna meet me for lunch?"

"Sure."

Sarah smiles and jabs a nail playfully into the boar tattoo on my forearm.

"Ow! Don't poke the pig, eh? This pig pokes back."

"Does it?"

I take a blind stab at her ribs. She squeals.

"Yep."

Sarah pulls her knees up and hugs them, small feet on the edge of the seat. She watches the street lamps for a while.

"I'm worried about him."

"Me, too," I admit.

"But why the questions? About beliefs, I mean?"

"Don't know. Maybe he was just—"

"What, engaging in small talk?" She scoffs, shakes her head.

"Nah. Maybe just curious. Jimmy's got a lot of shit happening in the attic, eh? A hard year. He'll get through it, though."

Sarah reaches over again, pokes gently at the boar this time, nail then drifting slowly, absently, over the lines.

"Do you think he's contemplating—"

"No."

"You sure? I need you to be sure."

"Sarah, I'm sure."

Valid, though. Sarah's concern, I mean. She'd tried to draw Jimmy out again after he slipped back into deep waters, smile lost again, soon after Tribal ran out of things to quote.

Miscalculation, but understandable. She simply turned the tables, asking him if he believed in any one single truth.

But Jimmy answered her, distantly as if his voice were residual, little more than an echo.

"Yeah," he whispered. "I believe in gravity."

After dropping Sarah off, I return. On nights like this, nights that Jimmy's down by the lake, I often sit with him sometimes until sunrise. Much of his first year back is spent this way, waiting. Watching. I arrive, though, to find only Tribal squatting by the shore, absently rolling a spliff and musing at the water.

"Oi."

"Oi. Thought you might come by. Jimmy left about twenty minutes ago."

"How was he?"

"Getting worse."

"Exactly what Sarah said! Jesus Christ."

Tribal lights up, takes a couple heavy tokes, and passes it over.

"Don't be too surprised. I drove her home from work, eh? What you think we talked about?"

"Ah. He's writing music again, though, that's a good sign. I think he may want to put things together again, you know, hit the circuit."

This pleases Tribal, but the incredulity is pretty clearly marked in his tone.

"No shit, eh? Did he ask you about it?"

"Not in so many words, but he showed up to the last few gigs I played."

Unintentional words, but he winces.

"Yeah, sorry I haven't been around too much in the evenings—things are still weird with Hannah . . ."

I laugh, though. His idiot girlfriend thought she'd spice things up, initiated a threesome with a mutual friend—Hannah's a slightly desperate chick about three degrees to the west of normal—then she got all freaked out by it. Territorial is how Tribal puts it, but during, not after. Incredibly awkward pause in the midst of it all, apparently, followed by a mad rush to sort of wrap it all up.

Tribal doesn't know what the fuck to make of it, in retrospect. Says it was nothing like in porn, but what is? Anyway, I can't help him—shite like that only happens to crazy bastards like Tribal, not guys like me. So I just shake my head and laugh, ask what the hell did he think would happen.

"Don't know," he says. "When an offer like that drops in your lap . . ."

"So to speak," I chime in.

"Yeah, right. Anyway, who the fuck would say no?"

"Don't worry, mate, she'll get over it." Or not. "The point is that Jimmy's got something in mind. I've never seen him like this, eh? It's like there's something lost in his head that desperately needs to find its way out."

And it's true: he's writing music in mad fits, possessed by some driving spirit. I begin to see him downtown more often, down by King and James or in Gore Park, sitting on a park bench contemplating bystanders and buses and birds (our distant Tiresias throbbing between two lives), or shuffling alongside the bus stop queues of travelers, listening intensely to their unguarded mumbles: all echoes, all pieces of the great puzzle, links in the Great Chain of Being, or so he assures me.

Or waits in the rain for an old vagrant to finally shamble away for shelter and then quickly moves to stand in the invisible pavement footprints—echoes again, but this time in the strata—eyes closed and straining to hear beneath the loneliness and tragic warp and weft of circumstance.

Mostly he just listens. To everything it seems, all at once or selectively, hard to tell. And he writes, lyrics and music bound by the connective tissue that only he can see and touch (*scop*, weaver, shaper), nimble fingers at work inside his mind amongst the shadowy moth wing words that trouble their way around the (what does he call it? Ah, yes, the) dust and rust and other dreamscapes of his making.

Occasionally a question, clarification of obscure details with no explanation.

"What colour were Tina's eyes?" He asks this of me as we walk (he with purpose, I without) north on Queen, toward the massive stone Scottish Rite that squats ominously on the corner. "I can't remember. What colour were her eyes?"

—

I was the last one of us to see her. It was Tina, who found me outside the public library, after all, that same November afternoon I'd read *Ivan Ilyich*. Back on the steps (sans bottle) she saw me, came over to see what was wrong. I always liked her, quiet girl almost four years younger than me. Still a child in some ways, just seventeen. But this was her fourth year turning tricks, no childhood ideals left there.

"You good? Look like shite."

"Cheers," I replied flatly. "I've had a less than stellar day."

"Girl trouble?" Tina was pretty observant, pretty gentle, considering everything she'd been through.

I nodded. Showed her my ticket, and gave a brief recap of the abuse I took from Eira's matron. "I didn't even say anything, just sat there and took it like a fucking pussy."

She smiled, sad-eyed, and I felt worse, suddenly—more immediately, I mean. Who was I to complain to a girl who'd been a prostitute since she was thirteen? Christ, abusive foster homes or shelter to shelter, she couldn't read or write, she'd been through . . .

Well, a fuckload more than me. Just a goddamn breakup. And from a relationship that was, for a while (almost a year, *a lifetime* she said, though only with her eyes), healthy. Mutual. No squabbling over payment or alley rapes, or trips to the free clinic or to hospital—she'd had ribs broken, a shoulder dislocated, three fingers slammed in a car door, stitches in plain sight, stitches that necessitated almost two months of avoiding the streets for fear of reopening wounds so brutal that nine of us hunted the bastards who did that to her in abject fury, all of us beyond reason, each of us willing to do the time. But Seamus and his crew found them first.

If she didn't come home when she was expected, Funhouse went out for a walk. Checked around, asked about, waited, he was a solid mate. Didn't press her with questions if he found her down the alley crying, didn't lecture her for doing what she did to herself when she needed the dosh. Funhouse was like Tribal that way—never interfered with that sort of thing.

Except once. A skinhead named Remnant, just a fucking street soldier from one of the smaller squat house crews, decided he was Tina's pimp. This was when she was fourteen, recovering from her first set of cracked ribs. I remember, because I helped Funhouse wrap her with tensors just before it happened.

The fucking prick caught her just above Jackson Square. There's a flat bit on top, a patio of sorts, but no one's ever up there. He pulled her around by her hair for a bit, slapping her right brutal, fingers aglitter with pewter rings, cheap and sharp—skulls, swastikas—cutting her face and scalp, tearing out bits of hair when the strands got tangled in his fucking accessories. He jacked her for dosh, of course, naught but ten or twelve bones, but it's the point, isn't it?

Then he tried to rape her. Tina had a trick or two, though, even then. Funhouse made her carry a razor blade in the top of her boot, just at the lip inside (he'd sewn a small pocket into the boot lining, clever little hideaway—we couldn't imagine Funhouse, monstrous Jamaican paws, hunched over Tina's boot with a needle and thread, grandmotherly concern in every miniature stitch) and as he yanked out his heathen bit of white power for the plunge, she retrieved her bit of steel and flicked it hard and upward in terror-fed hatred, reactions on autopilot.

When she got back to the flat (panting, crying, bleeding), Funhouse went out of his fucking gourd. He got the essentials out of her and then we were off, just the two of us and half-cocked on Irish car bombs.

The silly bastard. He was still there (a failed Tereus in the Unreal City), slumped against a wall, afraid to move for fear that he'd make it worse. He'd vomited all over himself as well, so we were reluctant to get close and personal at first. See, Tina had—purely by good fortune (or good as far as we were concerned)—caught his cock right behind the head on one side, slicing loose a good portion of that purple mushroom so that it dangled, flapping about like a loose door on a broken hinge. When he saw us, tears streaming down his ugly face, he begged for help. Great heaving sobs and spittle and bile accompanied a steady stream of "please fuck please fucking help me" and other such drivel.

A piss-poor show, that. What, for instance, would the other hatemongers who play Nazi with this dumb shit say if they could see young Remnant, holding his half-severed urethra closed with one bloody hand and reaching out with the other to a giant black rudeboy and his bull's-eye wearing mod companion? "Fucking race traitor!" they'd scream, dull minds too clogged up with glue fumes and Dramamine and misquoted bullshit from Mein fucking Kampf to grasp anything as complex as sympathy.

No, we certainly couldn't have that. I rummaged through the pockets of his bomber jacket (avoiding the vomity parts) for Tina's dosh and any extra and came across a fair trove of swag, including a baggy holding a vial of liquid acid and four croutons, a dozen blues, and what I assumed was blotter. Nine or ten squares of plain white paper—fitting, the unimaginative fuck.

He soon changed his tune, though, once he realized we were picking him clean. Funhouse was estimating the size of the prick's oxblood 14s (red laces, of course), but I already had a blade out for the slitting.

"Fucking nigger!" he whined, "fucking nigger lover!"

I came at him then, cruel-eyed and knife suddenly reversed oi style for the backslash, held hard in my fist with thumb across the pommel.

But Funhouse stopped me, sudden and evil grin across his face. He had an idea beyond the simple slashing and boot party beating on my short and uncreative agenda. He took the vial of liquid LSD and, grabbing

Remnant by the chops with one hand (vomit notwithstanding), poured the entire contents down the skin's throat. This came as a surprise to me as much as to Remnant, but I saw the potential immediately.

"Leave di boots," Funhouse said.

"Why? What's the difference?"

"Patience, rude bwoy, patience . . ." he mumbled. So we stood by and waited.

Soon, the acid began to kick in, the stupid fuck spewing forth a confused mix of racism, insults, and pleas for help from the beginning.

Then it really kicked in.

Of all the bad trips possible, Remnant had the mother of them all. Some instinct well beyond the pale of his feeble intelligence had led him to apply firm and steady pressure to his nauseating wound. Now even that was gone, his hands flying about of their own accord. That's when I really saw the gaping slice for the first time. I almost puked on the spot, and even Funhouse went a bit ashen, but we held our ground.

Remnant got to his feet and staggered about, soaked through with blood and bile, and moved toward the stairs leading down to King and James. The plan was to follow at a distance, purely for the sake of entertainment, and watch him trip on LSD until someone did something to him or for him, or until he did something even more stupid to himself.

Which is ultimately what he did. Three minutes of wandering in circles and then he stepped out in front of a city bus doing a fair clip to make the light. He made a little shuddery sound just before impact, the bumper folding him violently at the shins and his torso and head smacking the engine block compartment and then ricocheting off the pavement, the splatter of wet meat audible and sickening. Just a questioning little whine and then a boom.

This is the way his world ends, not with a bang but with a whimper. Well, it was more of a whimper then a bang. Ah, we said by way of streetside eulogy, no great loss.

"At least he died with his boots on," I said on the way back, laughing at my own supposed cleverness. Wasted on Funhouse, though: cultural chasm. He didn't get it.

Oh well. Remnant, eh? Fuck him.

We got back to Funhouse's flat and cleaned Tina up as best we could, peroxide in the cuts ("not in my hair!" she complained), ice on her swollen cheek. We carefully removed her top and rewound her ribs with tensor bandages. She was a tough little thing, tried to joke a bit as I navigated under her small breasts and over the angry purple welt where her ribs had been broken. I reddened, I suppose, because Funhouse laughed at me and Tina managed a wincing smile.

She asked what we'd done, but we were vague. She pressed the issue, though, so we told her, but just the end result. Not a good idea to share details with anyone not directly partaking, just good street sense.

She was quiet for a while, absorbing it, I guess. Then she looked at us in turn.

"Good," she said. "Good fucking riddance."

Tina died on Christmas Eve of 1986, the same year Eira dumped me. An overdose. She was fifteen. She'd been using drugs since she was twelve, but heroin was a recent upgrade to her series of addictions.

Poor fucking Tina. She died at her new boyfriend's flat, a skinny thrash punk junkie (Thin, his name was) who got her hooked in the first place. They shot up while watching *Sid and Nancy* on his shitty little T.V., one of the few objects he hadn't pawned for drugs. That, the VCR, three milk crates, an electric skillet, and a stained mattress. His entire fucking worldly estate valued at about thirty-five bones.

But I'll be damned if Thin didn't bawl his orbs out as they took Tina's body away. He was a goddamn wreck—suicidal, in fact: they ended up locking him in the nuthouse for the better part of three months. But as soon as they let him out, Thin marched himself straight to the Skyway Bridge and jumped off.

Couldn't even do that right, though. Caught his foot in the fencing or something, the poor stupid bastard, and they came to fetch him, dangling upside down like a ragged bit of windblown yarn, weeping. Back in the padded cell for who the fuck knows how long.

In retrospect, though, he was the best thing to ever happen to Tina (no offence to Funhouse). She was happy for the few weeks they were together, genuinely happy, and so was Thin. Both of them found love, I suppose.

But that was after Tina—so scarred and desperately lonely—stopped that gloomy November afternoon and sat with me, listening, consoling. Then I saw those deep and utterly forlorn eyes, so absolutely convinced that she'd never have even a fraction of what I'd had for almost a year, and it was the first time I could ever remember crying.

She thought it was for myself, but it was for the both of us. Tina put her arms around me, said something quietly (shapeless sounds, soothing—actual words too insignificant) as I pulled myself together. I looked at her then, she too had tears rolling out of her dark brown eyes.

Dark, rich, chocolate brown, Jimmy. I saw her cry. But later, before she died, I saw love in them, too.

Chapter Five

Eventually, we pick up where we left off, Jimmy and me, although not entirely at first. Derek is working, found a real job to support his pregnant girlfriend—music for money is barely adequate when single, never mind attached. Ewan, too, a real job and his own place, but he still drums weekend gigs with a cover band just to keep his hand in.

I stay the course, though, the least likely to do so. I work during the day, just a pair of hands and a good back, and play solo sets at cafés and pubs or sit in with other musicians three or four times per week. I improve.

Sarah still comes (a solid mate) and Tribal, of course, and sometimes even Ewan shows up to heckle good-naturedly from the bar.

But Jimmy has other plans. Echoes of what is to come sometimes escape, travelling from brain outwards, through the secret mechanisms of the ear, a byzantine conduit at odds with vibrations passing in both directions, beautiful cacophony of image as sound.

Jimmy said once he sees better with his ears than with his eyes—crude gelatinous liars, he spat, easy to doubt. But the ear, pure and unbiased receptacle, a vessel for all sound and silence—truth incarnate, a keeper of things without judgment.

That came later, at the end of the journey. Every word ever uttered stood trial, denotative defence no match for the connotative crime.

We all collect something. So when Jimmy retrieved his equipment from storage that following spring, then began collecting up borrowed pieces (effects pedals, a mic stand, a 16 track mixing board—a dozen fragments in a dozen disparate basement and attic makeshift studios), I knew that it was only a matter of time before he started to collect up people as well.

And it wouldn't have mattered to our friendship if he hadn't asked me—at least, not in the long run—but I was pleased nonetheless, when he did.

"Just rhythm—strumming, no pick work. Well, not much. Wallpaper vibration. Nothing more—or less." This is how he asks me to join him in this project. I nod dumbly.

"Good. This will be hard work," he assures, and then he's off.

Ewan is next. Just as well, it's important to know your drummer's quirks, and Ewan and I always connected on stage. Like me, Ewan's put the time since we last played together to good use. Nothing much to say outside of a gig, but you can't have everything.

Jimmy finds a bassist, an emaciated Primus freak from the U.K. with a drinking problem and a five-string fretless he's named Evett. His own name is Syd, popular with girls because of his cockney accent, even though he's an ugly fuck. Tribal and I like him immediately, and pub-crawls seal the friendship.

Then Chloe, a quiet girl from Trois Rivières, a flutist studying at the college on the Escarpment. Sarah takes to her immediately, they're inseparable, speaking together quietly *en français,* but Sarah's success at high school French didn't include the Quebecois accent or idioms, so there's a fair bit of *lentement lentement qu'est ce que tu dit je ne comprend pas quand tu parle rapidement* and so on. Chloe's nice, but indifferent to the rest of us. Except Jimmy—they talk, serious and brooding, in smoky café corners and on park benches. Chloe's incredible, though, finding with that flute some strange and inexplicable mid-ground between backwoods Quebecois folk roots and Jethro Tull. A haunting sound, eerie, a siren song Jimmy assures me.

Finally Derek for lead guitar—a careful bit of negotiation, Derek not overly pleased at Jimmy's sudden disappearing act last year. We all hate change, but Derek's made a full-fledged phobia out of it. Fortunately, he hates work even more, music being his self-proclaimed first calling. As it turns out, though, Derek had been doing occasional studio work in Toronto, laying down quasi-anonymous tracks for some reasonably successful local singers. Good thing, too—forced anonymity to pay the bills was exactly the right remedy for his chryselephantine ego. No room for a guitar god on this trip, Jimmy says, but I guess he knows what he's doing by asking Derek in the first place.

Jimmy's collection—menagerie, really—for what he calls The Midnight Circus Project.

—

Syd smokes like a fiend, telling me his life story between drags and drinks as we sit downstairs at the Hound and Hare, drunk on stout. He's telling the entire basement of the pub, actually, because he shouts when he's deep in his cups. It's a young crowd down here, all of us in our early twenties or almost except for a few still clinging pathetically to the illusion of youth.

Syd also bellows, because Brie (the bartender) plays the sound system pretty loud, Pogues this evening and *Rum, Sodomy, and the Lash* in particular, their best album, Syd and I agree wholeheartedly, and then campaign for any takers, searching for members of one of those short-lived and trivial brotherhoods of common opinion so typical in the pub around 11:00. Brie at least assents, but in that infinitely tolerant way of bartenders. She isn't enamoured by Syd's East-End London accent, her own musical Belfast brogue trumping it as far as Hamilton social values are concerned. Green eyes, auburn hair and incredible breasts help, of course—Syd's mousy mop of hair and bony frame not vaguely comparative. Ah, the unfairness of things.

His present tack centres on a worn and crumpled postcard of a Tudor-style building somewhere in London, a tall skinny thing crammed awkwardly between bulky stone bookends.

"'Ere, you see them beams?" he roars, inches from my ear, jabbing the vertical brown lines running up the dirty white façade, "Them's made aou'a wood from the *HMS Indestru'ible*, or sumfink like 'at." This because Syd loves British naval history, his da serving in the Royal Navy on the *HMS Something I Didn't Catch* and dragging him all around the coast of Southern England and East Anglia as a boy, his mum not in the picture (*abandoned ship*, I thought but didn't say), to show him historic sites of timbered fleets and ports of call and naval defences and so on, Nelson's Column in Trafalgar Square being the centre of his da's personal universe.

He also has blurry pictures of himself as a child climbing all over gigantic black lions and up immense stone steps, the column's base, but those he showed me first, beginning of course with small fading pictures of da himself. I saw immediately where Syd got his stunning good looks and manly build. Christ.

It was good, though, to see these things. They held no real interest for me visually, but I can see right proper how close Syd is to his da. They don't have much, he told me earlier, quieter, more sober, so coming over here to study music at the University has to lead to something. More for his da than for him, it's implied. Syd won a scholarship or fought his fretless and five stringed way into some sort of specialty program. He told me that when we first met, but I forget the details.

At the time, though, Syd painted a pretty vivid scene for us: a proud father at Heathrow, tears in his eyes as he saw off his only boy. We didn't know our own da, Tribal and me—he's still in Scotland (as far as I know), our mum emigrating without him, Tribal and me still too small to remember anything of Glasgow itself. From an industrial womb to an industrial playground. Shit, you'd think the woman would have had enough sense to at least settle somewhere a little more visually stimulating. Not Montreal or Quebec, the Glaswegian language barrier was bad enough without subjecting the French to it. But at least Edmonton or Vancouver or Victoria.

"*HMS Indestructible*, eh?" I yell back.

"Aye, 'at's right! Me da called th' building' th'*HMS Round-th'-Corner-From-th'-Pub*!" And he guffaws in great braying snorts, and I join him just because he's so goddamn happy talking about his da and missing him because he can't afford to fly back over Christmas.

"Jus 'old on a tick, I got more 'ere—OI! JIMMY!" who's just come down the stairs with Sarah and Chloe. Syd leaps to his feet, listing alarmingly to starboard and waving one skeletal limb madly through the smoke. "Over 'ere, mate! 'Allo, ladies, care fer a pint? Oi, Brie! Yes please, luv, free more—nah, better make it five, 'ere's a good girl!"

Jimmy smiles, Syd pleases him the way Tribal does, reckless and open with his words, though not so prone to random acts of violence when drinking. We haven't seen the Illiterate since Syd's been around, anyway. Nothing wrong with that, as Sarah mentioned not long ago.

Jimmy reaches Brie, picking up the pints and navigating toward us. Meanwhile, Sarah and Chloe settle themselves into our chairs (gentlemen that we are) and Syd starts all over again with the pictures, happy and drunk and now happier because of a new audience.

"Jimmy! Jimmy, now you jus' 'ave a butchers at this 'ere bloke an' tell me oo 'e looks like!"

And so on.

Tribal's last to arrive this evening, making a sullen entrance just shy of last call. He's in no mood for Syd's pictures, though. *That's it with Hannah*, I say to myself. *Probably for the best.*

Ever since the threesome incident, Sarah's called him Ronny J (Jeremy, that is), half amused, half disgusted with his conduct. Tribal, equally amused and disgusted with this surprising bit of conservative morality, countered by calling her Prudence.

Sarah sees him and (a bit tipsy) yells to him. Sarah's Sarah, though: she reads Tribal from across the pub and looks at me questioningly.

"So much for the girlfriend," I shout. But it's loud, my voice lost to all but her in the din. I signal Brie for another pint and a whiskey for Tribal, his post break-up beverage of choice.

But it wasn't all that serious and Tribal will recover soon. Not trivial—I'm not saying that—it's just that he seemed pretty indifferent to her for the last two months. "Stale," Tribal called their relationship, "like a cigarette left on the dashboard too long." Sunbaked and harsh.

Chloe wants to leave, but Sarah has her hand on my forearm, absently tracing the whorls of the Pictish boar tattooed there. She's drunker than I thought, me sobering up considerably since Tribal arrived and able to see the others clearly now.

And the fight about to break out in the far corner by the dart boards. I can't hear the exchange, but body language is clear enough. The shorter of the two will throw the first punch.

"What's wrong?" Sarah asks, loudly and slightly slurred, "You and Syd sure are quiet all of a sudden."

True. It's that time of night, though, things winding down. Syd holds his empty pint glass and stares in blurry-eyed confusion at the coaster. He's had close to ten, three or four more than me (only tab will tell).

"Why would an ostrich swaller a pint?" he mumbles. "An' wha' git let 'im inta the pub to start?"

"An essential line of inquiry," I offer. "Let us consult the oracle. Where's Brie?"

"Nah, mate, no good," Syd says. 'At's a question fer a Dubliner, i'nt it?"

Jimmy calls things to order, speaking softly, like an undercurrent below the dull noise between last call and closing time. I can hear the exchange now from the dartboards—the shorter one's a Scot, brogue thick and angry. I am right. He will definitely throw the first punch.

"I've booked a gig, called in a favour for a decent venue."

"Okay, when?" I ask.

"In two weeks."

"Where?"

Jimmy takes the smoke Syd offers.

"Ta," he nods, taking the light, too. "Gage Park, in the Band Shell."

"Christ! The Festival? What time, noon on a Sunday, or was there a shittier slot?"

"Friday at eight. We're opening for the headlining band—I played the organizers the demo. Plus," he adds, "I called in a favour."

Silence. Stunned silence, actually, as we absorb the enormity of the venue. An August tradition we've attended many times ourselves, those of us who grew up in Hamilton. Gage Park is at the Delta where Main and King cross, the border of the real east end. The venue is too hard to envision for bar circuit musicians, though. Only Syd remains unfazed, drunkenly smiling in approval.

"One fuck o'a favour, mate!" he offers.

Tribal's calculating, though, his own dilemma temporarily suspended. He hazards a guess.

"You hit up Quinn for this one, didn't you?"

Jimmy nods with a hint of a smile (His eyes, though—still something broken beneath. Some wounds aren't meant to heal, I suppose. They just scar over and become part of your personal landscape, like fingerprints or voice. Or memory.)

"It was easy," Jimmy says, "considering the publicity we could get from it. But the demo's good and Quinn pays his debts."

I have my doubts. Too good to be true, I think, and say so. Two years ago, a decent local circuit band—Celtic rock, solid earners with a sizable following—lost the Festival venue to a last minute big name Toronto addition.

"Anyway," I finish, "Quinn's a solid connection, but words are just words, Jimmy. What's the guarantee that we have the gig?"

Jimmy answers by simply throwing an envelope onto the table. Sarah removes the contents and scans it, Chloe hanging over her shoulder.

"A contract? Is this legal, binding I mean?"

Jimmy nods.

Tribal takes it next, his comparatively sober eyes catching what Sarah and Chloe miss.

"Uh, this says it's an unpaid gig."

Jimmy nods again, but he looks at me.

"That's right. And we have work to do. I'll see you, Chloe, and Syd tomorrow. I've already been to see Ewan and Derek." He packs away the contract. "Don't be late."

And off he goes, up the stairs just as the fight starts.

Brie yells at them to take it outside, tired and three minutes past closing. A few regulars pull them apart and we lend a hand, hauling them up the stairs and into the parking lot, pointing out the two police cruisers sixty-nine-ing across the street ("copulating," Tribal says) and advising them to leave off. One of the cops flips on the searchlight and points it in our direction anyway. Obnoxious fucking thing—real brick-in-the-teeth subtlety—it sets the two sods right straight, though, and we disperse.

There are three stages at the festival in Gage Park: the Band Shell is for headliners. The second stage is for local mainstream bands. The third stage is hidden away in a corner for freaks and their misanthropic fans, the same lot we used to see at places like the Cave before it got shut down and *les soeurs araignées* got their asses arrested for serving minors and dealing narcotics. *Très mal,* ladies, *la fin du monde. Mais c'est la vie*, I guess.

The Shell is, as I said, a hell of a jump up from places like the Corktown and the Hound and the Lion's Head—not that they aren't great venues, but, well.

Syd crashes at my place, an insurance policy against sleeping through practice because I can't sleep later than ten. Doesn't matter though—Sarah's banging on the door at nine, hung over and excited, coffees in hand. A pleasant and welcome sight as I groggily open up.

"Thought you could use these," she says by way of hellos, "I'm off to work now, but I'll be by after. Need anything? Later, I mean?"

"Umm, no. I don't think so. We're fine. Cheers for the coffees, though."

"No problem," she says cheery as shit, and off she goes, happy and blurry eyed and dehydrated and beautiful.

"'Oo was 'at?" Syd croaks from the kitchen floor. He likes sleeping on linoleum for some fucked up reason, although I have a perfectly comfortable chesterfield.

"Sarah. She brought us coffees on her way to work."

"Awwww, 'at's very sweet o'er. Bung mine down the drain and make us a cup o' rosy while I get a bit more kip, there's a good lad."

PART FIVE

Chapter One

It's another day, Jimmy says, *of treading sidewalks.*

Just to stay afloat.

Another day of buses and vagrants and bumming smokes off of fellow friendly travelers, though he has an unopened pack in his pocket. Jimmy is solo today, research he calls it. *What are you looking for?* we ask him.

But he looks so worn thin and empty and alone when we ask that, we never ask again.

It's another day of aimless sojourns across the grid, tossed around from bus to bus. A young woman glares at him, angry-eyed, for treading on her toe. This he reports confidentially (a sigil, a sign), admitting that the geometry didn't match up, that the angles must have converged on a different bus. He is discouraged, but resolute. He will have to start again.

Why, I ask despite the deep waters. But Jimmy says it's necessary—*It's for Her*, he whispers—and I understand. This is part of it, then. The others don't know, but I see where this will lead: something beautiful and tragic. This is for Debbie.

Because Jimmy now lives by latitudes, choosing when he comes down. He dwells now in the yawning chasms between buildings, contemplating the distance, counting the steps through the air with narrow eyes, through mescaline and barbiturates and acid and fleeting arguments with gravity. And Jimmy has moved again, a migration from one tenement to another, always higher (up), ascending, progressing up a private axis mundi of his own making. Jimmy wants to dwell on rooftops, he will mark the dog star rising, the passing of the moon, wax and wane.

Far away to the east, the tide recedes from the white sands that separate one desert city from the sea. Jimmy knows this as the moon makes her way across the night sky above our own city, he grows sullen as he muses at the distant and cold craters that scar the white orb's luminous face.

There's no reaching him now, Jimmy's too far away—I can only wait patiently, speak hollow words to the breathing stone shell beside me as Jimmy reaches out across that impossible distance, stretched so thin that he's invisible.

It's another day, we gather in the yawning loft studio of Stardust, a half-feral Hamilton artist who works mostly in metal with a blowtorch and soldering iron. Just a nickname, but that's how he's introduced. Aptly named, though—he too is left-handed, head and fingers crawling with tiny Martian spiders. Clinically insane, for shit-sure—reminded me immediately of something that slid off the slab and jumped out of the screen at *The Rocky Horror Picture Show*, but he's friendly enough to talk to and extremely generous with his studio space. Still, he declines our steady stream of invitations to pubs and parties, disappearing into the ether between practices to Jimmy-knows-where, the rest of us hadn't the faintest.

The main thing is that Stardust understands Jimmy's sense of urgency. Jimmy has explained it to him, convinced him of the necessity. Stardust knew Debbie too. I remember him from the old days, a black-clad regular at the Cave.

Stardust's studio is in the industrial stretch of the north end, an immense attic above an old brick warehouse shared by a group of textile importers. It has to be the better part of half a fucking acre up there, but it fits him somehow: exposed steel I-beams and iron struts, vast walls of crudely laid bricks separated by crumbling mortar frozen into oozing bulges, unfinished pine planks each as wide as sod and stretched the hundred foot length of this cavern. Even the windows, great smoke grey rectangular planes subdivided into reductionist geometry by iron grillwork, too grime-coated to let in more than daylight's dim shadow.

Stardust himself looks as though he is a scrap yard scarecrow assemblage, lanky limbs still ragged and black-clad as the old days, flesh a pallid gauze under which thin blue sickly tapeworm veins run. Obligatory white scar tissue in parallel thin lines decorates his wrists, bracelet markers of a misspent youth.

We have set up shop in the northernmost corner, closest to the Lake. Each day we arrive, Ewan's drum kit has submerged a little more under a wild frame of steel and wire and copper, a carapace from which hang a hundred found objects. Jimmy has provided many of the pieces, pipes and bottles and small hollow parts of machines, a cacophony of city sounds and sights. It becomes the central focus of Jimmy's attention, this monstrous skeletal spider that envelops Ewan as he sits at the heart of this contraption.

Stardust and Jimmy confer for an hour or more at a time, leaning forward on makeshift metal chairs, elbows on knees, intense conversation about (we assume) form and function. Soon, Ewan is drawn into these conversations, his eyes incredulous and then (soon, inevitably) lighting up as Jimmy weaves words and Stardust sketches in rapid mechanical jerks on cardboard, nodding in agreement the whole time.

The rest of us—Sarah and Tribal, too, she excited and he bored—wait out these conversations. We play through arrangements, we fine-tune the timing, we talk about the past lightly, stories of past stupidities from our teen years for the benefit of the few who weren't there—Syd and Chloe, but Sarah too, she not being present (thank the gods) for the obtuse days of boot-culture politics and squat-house poverty. And we avoid the idiotic war stories, Tribal, Derek, and I, by unspoken agreement.

Syd reciprocates with outrageous lies about his ridiculous childhood, all of us blurry-eyed with laughter except Chloe who can't untangle Syd's guttural vernacular, though she smiles politely at the appropriate moments. She declines our invitation to share bits of her own past, though, Sarah intervening a bit too quickly and the rest of us backing off instinctively.

Jimmy now emerges from the cluster and calls us together. One last piece, an arch of piping directly over the drummer's stool, from which hang a series of pipes painted a dirty white, rust coming through in streaks. A dangling assemblage of rusting bones like fingers or femurs.

And it's complete, the frame at least—this is the centre, the heart of this project, a threatening and monstrous oddity: the thunderous medicine lodge of Jimmy, our dream-plagued urban shaman, a hundred totems ready with wild metallic voices.

I understand, the others merely appreciate it, but I understand. Ewan begins, timidly at first, a blind man probing his surroundings for pitfalls and dangers, then with growing confidence, tapping, striking, brushing, smashing out a storm of deafening noise, beautiful and uninhibited madness creeping quickly up his flailing limbs. Now Ewan is closed off, he loses contact with language, with the very floor beneath him. He knows only his hands and his feet and his lungs, madman's heart slamming out the metronomic beat in his throbbing temple.

The others are awed at the sheer rhythmic confusion exploding from the monstrous contraption, they stare at Ewan's blurred form, for this moment a feral hermit trapped in his own ecstatic insanity, willing prisoner in that thunderous cell.

Jimmy catches my eye, though, ignoring the splinters of wood that fly by him at supersonic speeds, Ewan depleting his supply of sticks at an alarming rate. Jimmy sees it in my face, the epiphany caught there, fly in the web of sight and sound. He nods his acknowledgement, serene smile lighting up his countenance, mouth and mind, eyes aflame.

It's there, beneath the wild cacophony, beneath casual awareness, it's there: that gentle trochaic chant—it whispers, over and over and over again, a heartbeat in reverse:

Debbie.

—

Here, then, is where Jimmy led us at the end of his lakeside lament, that incarnation of grief finally over. We were hopeful—progress, road to recovery (we said amongst ourselves). After all, we no longer had to sit or stand by Jimmy at the edge of the Harbour, right? However.

Here is no water but only rock. Prophetic, T.S.

6 a.m., Tuesday morning.

Practice ends and we quietly slip away, alone or in twos, mumbled goodbyes and weary smiles. Spent, utterly drained and too tired to sleep, we shamble off toward our own small corners of the city. In twelve hours, it starts again.

Jimmy has assembled us, his lonely vigil watching the factory fires by a dark lake finally at an end. Now it is rooftops, but only I know this. I join him sometimes, scaling the height by way of rickety fire escapes or long walks up filth-strewn stairwells. And from up there, above this city, I too see it all falling. Because Jimmy watches skyfall, the slow and relentless mechanics of the stars as they rotate, wheel-like, descending below the horizon. I watch with Jimmy as Sirius makes its heliacal ascent, that brightest of celestial neighbours, Dog Star rising. *But not one star*, Jimmy says (barely more than a whisper), *a binary system, Debbie's favourite.*

Their sky totem, I come to realize.

Just twelve hours. Stardust sees the last of us out the door, grim nod by way of farewell before pulling the steel slab closed and sliding the heavy bolt into place. He, too, heavy-lidded, Jimmy's quixotic shaper, this assembler of crooked and wild metallurgical anatomy. Like a meticulous and self-sufficient Adam pulling his own ribs out, constructing from the very bones of his being this obscene and wondrous skeleton, monstrous spherical lover where flesh is sound, and life—its histrionic heart—the wild and witless avatar of Jimmy's will.

Jimmy. Architect by proxy.

Because Stardust also is thrall to Jimmy's vision, exhausted yet serene as if labouring while in deep slumber, limbs moving waterlogged, waiting for approval at each stage between blowtorch and pliers. But now this morning, at last, it is done.

Sarah, too, has made good use of her time. Not once since Jimmy returned to us has she mentioned Debbie. Yet, she, too, does her part. She has sewn together from a collection of white sheets a huge shroud, a skin for this grotesquely beautiful drum cage monstrosity. She has left a part undone, though, a slit in the back through which Ewan can enter. He climbs in feet-first, sliding at an angle to where his stool is. It's a tight fit. He emerges in reverse, neck craning forward and body stretched narrow and twisting slightly to navigate the opening. But he's agile, he's soon used to the slight acrobatics necessary to climb in and out.

The sheet will cover the drum cage on Friday night until we're ready to go on. The entire thing comes apart, ingeniously designed to break down into nine pieces. A giant puzzle, really. What isn't welded or wired in place comes off easily as well, another convenience for which we are grateful. Stardust just smiles vaguely at our praise, though.

This shroud, too, histrionic. An overly dramatic flourish, and there it will be. Sudden. Immediate. A looming bulge of scrap metal grey and black and brown, infrequent points of chrome like fallen stars trapped in a metallic midnight spider's web, and the rusting white bones—those disturbing vertical ribs, those disembodied dancing femurs—that dangle from chains along the arch of piping, the apex of this (what? Found-object aura? Physical and manifest, cave womb of memory, Jimmy's last attempt to entomb her, our final performance, this) sideshow spectacle, this ragged carnival act.

This last tablecloth attempt.

And so, Ladies and Gentlemen, if you would please direct your attention to the centre ring, the Midnight Circus is now in session. Raise your glasses—we drink to the final flourish, to the last parlour trick. Sad eyed clowns assemble, tumbling and road-weary antics mechanically performed.

Drum roll, please . . .

It begins like this:

Soft low pulse, just the bass, metred beat, three-four time.

Snare slides in, gentle taps, slow ascent, then a pause.

Guitar slips now into place, haunting heptatonic scale, double harmonic blues riff—not a city's sad lament, but an empty desert's dirge. Then the flute in quartertones, *Thaat* or gypsy voices wail, keening cry of She who falls.

This is how it begins.

Just nine songs. Nine songs for Debbie, each one meticulously orchestrated by Jimmy, mad-eyed ringmaster for whom this entire performance has an audience of One. I watch him carefully from my own small place in the Plan, stage right where Ewan, Sid, and I can communicate by sight over the thunderous sound. Derek is in his own world, incommunicado and in no need of outside interference. He plays by raw instinct now, his part in parallel evolution to my own. Chloe, though, haunts Jimmy mid-stage, a waif-like shadow. Her flute and Jimmy's voice harmonic, interwoven, the wild notes of the one complementing the violent storm of the other.

Because Jimmy says.

Jimmy says what he has to say, thunderous incantations of song and spoken word and terrible stretches of silence, a performance wild and shamanic, transcendent. It builds, the steel sphere behind us throbbing now with urgency, with power, with a thousand beats that will not be contained within—Ewan is possessed, he is rage he is fury he is the mercurial clepsydra of this steel city night, shattered sticks and snapped links of chain, a miasma of debris, first one metallic scrap breaks loose, a second, then a hail of fragments.

Nine songs, woven together as one.

When it is over, I look down in a daze at my own hands, fingertips sliced raw on the strings, Derek's too, he too staring as if in sortilege at his hands. There is applause, cheering, Sarah throws herself around my neck, Tribal's hand falls heavily on my shoulder, other well wishers whirl by. Dervishes, though—I am only partly aware, things just a dream. Syd grins foolishly, holding up the dangling remains of a broken E string. Chloe is distant, Ewan is utterly spent. Jimmy, though.

Jimmy has disappeared.

It will be three days before we see him again.

—

"Happy birthday, Tina."

Tribal stands beside me at the grave, still and quiet as the night air, though cool for July. Dew has already gathered in the blackness, on the invisible grass and the polished surfaces of stones. In intervals, moonlight finds its way through the clouds that drift slowly across the summer sky in ragged tatters, wind torn and tired. It's the 22nd, Tina's twentieth birthday, but this knowledge must be carried in with us—the inscription on the small granite headstone, barely readable in the moonlight, says little.

Christina Rose Lawrence
Beloved Daughter
1971-1986

Isn't much to sum up a life. But what else could they put, repentant parents who suddenly materialized in the wake of Thin's incarceration to weep and gnash teeth and shake feeble fists at the terrible unfairness of things. There was a funeral—a few flowers, a handful of nervous relatives, a sallow faced minister. And us, her surrogate family and friends.

They had wanted a private ceremony, something inconspicuous and quick. What they got was close to fifty gatecrashers, all from one Hamilton street tribe or another: buskers and street performers, homeless girls and mothers from the battered women's shelter, sad-eyed men who called the Y home, teenage prostitutes, our lot, even Glasgow, Sean D's lieutenant. Ectogenous after all. Hey, who knew?

Mom saw nothing, swollen-eyed and puffy faced, sobbing continuously into a wad of tissues. But dad's red eyes kept sweeping across the solemn and motley mob that had quietly assembled, uninvited and unwanted, around the six or seven relatives decent enough to show up for the winter funeral of a runaway teenage junky whore. His eyes returned time and again to Funhouse, monstrous obsidian pillar who wept unashamedly, great tears rolling unhindered down his cheeks. Not a sound escaped, not even audible breath, but Christ it was unbearable to see that heavy jaw clenched so tightly, broad face contorted into an agony so profound that tears had sprung unbidden to my own eyes at the very sight of him.

Glasgow, too. Of all the heartless war dogs in Sean D's kennel, he was the worst. But there he'd been, all two hundred and eighty pounds of him, crying away like Funhouse.

It ended, wooden words having been delivered by the official with precision and practice in a tone devoid of any genuine sympathy. But, to be fair, her funeral had been arranged by strangers and attended by friends. You couldn't really blame them for not knowing what to say. No wake, no reception, nothing at all afterwards, of course. Tina's blood relations dispersed quickly and quietly, slipping away into the grey December afternoon with New Year's almost upon us.

"*Beloved daughter*," I sneer sadly. "You remember that lot, Tina's relatives? Christ."

Tribal nods, remembering too how her mom had refused to look up even once, had to be moved like an awkward parcel across the snow to their car and bundled inside. What fucking showmanship. Probably went straight home to make the goddamn New Year's trifle.

Not dad, though—he'd studied us from the beginning, embarrassed maybe at the turnout and overwhelmed. His little girl had meant something, people cared about her, she was loved.

July 22nd, Tina's birthday. We sit for a while, sharing a joint by passing it deliberately back and forth across Tina's grave. Tribal and I did this last year, too. And, like last year, we found disparate bunches of flowers gathered about the headstone when we arrived: a small cluster of wildflowers tied up with a bit of ribbon, some tulips, a white rose. The rose tells us that Funhouse has come and gone. We rarely see him anymore as is.

Tribal contemplates the sharp corners of her stone, tracing the edges absently with his finger. "Yeah," he says quietly, "I remember that lot." He suddenly squints into the blackness beyond us, listening for a moment. "Someone else out there."

"I know. Been there for a while, waiting for us to clear off I think."

"I suppose our turn is up," he says, standing. Then he leans down and runs a finger over the face of Tina's stone, catching the dew that's collected there. He brings the finger up to his lips and licks it. "Bye, Tina. Be back next year."

Then we're off.

"Did you know her dad wandered around downtown a month or so after the funeral looking for Funhouse?"

Tribal's voice cuts through my reverie as we sit together at a quiet pub not far from the cemetery. I was contemplating her last name—none of us knew it, not even Funhouse. Not until the funeral.

"Yeah, I heard. Jimmy mentioned it."

"Know what he wanted?"

"No. What?"

"He wanted to know about her life, you know, as a prostitute. But details, like what she did exactly and for how much. I mean, real twisted shit for a father to be digging around for, eh? Anyway, he finally finds Funhouse and starts in on him, no fucking hello or anything, just launches into his fucked-up questions."

"Christ. What'd Funhouse do?"

"What any of us would, I guess: gave the cat fair warning, then clocked him when he wouldn't shut the fuck up. But the stupid bastard got back on his feet, chased Funhouse and started in on the interrogation again."

I couldn't quite picture it, Funhouse looming over a flimsy, middle aged white guy with red eyes and a bloody mouth still full of questions about his daughter's tricks of the trade.

"It gets worse," Tribal continues. "Daddy starts in on the girls over on Emerald, soliciting them. And then once they're in the car, he questions the shit out of them."

"That it?" I ask, "He just hunts around for sordid bits of Tina's past?"

"See, that's the real fucked up bit, eh? Once he had a good idea of what Tina did and for how much, he paid for it. He only went after the younger girls, though, no one over sixteen or seventeen."

Takes me a while to process this, not quite grasping the logic behind the incestuous necrophilia-by-proxy fantasy this guy must have had running through some clandestine synaptic sewer pipe.

"You gotta be fucking kidding. How long? Did the missus ever find out?"

Tribal laughs, though subdued, quiet.

"Oh yeah—she found out, alright. Daddy ended up getting caught going at it with Eazy K late one Saturday night in the back of his fucking Lincoln. Cops dragged them both off to the copshop, daddy weeping and whining, K pretty much resigned, but you know K."

"Shit! Wasn't Eazy like fifteen, or something? What a moron."

Tribal smiles now, recollecting.

"Actually, she was fourteen at the time and carrying a little gonorrhea, no extra charge."

"So, he gets a court date and an STD to boot? Nice. Hard to hide the one, but just a quick trip to the clinic for the other, at least." Thank the gods for the free clinic. We've all been at one point or another.

"Yeah . . . not so much. Eazy K gave him gonorrhea, alright. Gonorrhea of the throat, and that's apparently not so easy to fix."

"Of the *throat*? I—I'm not even sure I know what that is."

"Me neither," Tribal admits, "but it sounds right fucking nasty and it made him a popular cat around the hospital. Heather's mom told her he was kind of a celebrity because of it." Heather is Tribal's current girlfriend. Her mom's a nurse. "Anyway, he got his trial date and his divorce papers around the same time. Very considerate, I guess, since he already had a lawyer handy. They could spend some time discussing how to keep the ex from milking him dry when they got tired of trying to think up excuses for why he was fucking a fourteen year old with gonorrhea in the back of his Lincoln."

I have to laugh. It's all so ludicrous and pathetic and petty and tragic. Nice tight Kingston accommodations for Mr. Lawrence—the Crown frowns rather sternly at statutory rape and the peripheral legal baggage.

We order another round, though pints after pot isn't my first choice. Tribal likes it, and so does Jimmy, but only out in the woods—blunt, blaze, beer and breeze, he says, the four elements. Spiritually sound.

Tribal takes a sizable swig and points at me with his smoke.

"How 'bout you, eh? You ever with Tina?"

Once, yes. And it rushes back, that cold November afternoon, me drunk and reckless on the library stairs. It was the only time I'd ever slept with Tina, later that evening in her small and squalid room, with Funhouse passed out and Leonard asleep in his chair and the other denizens out for the night.

So I tell Tribal about that day with me broken on the stairs and Tina there trying her best to pick up the pieces and not even with envy. I tell him slowly, deliberately, I tell him everything. I never told anyone before, embarrassed at my own bitter sense of loss when she'd never had anything. I tell him how ashamed I was, and how I didn't even know her last name until the funeral, none of us had ever bothered to ask, but Tribal sees through the static. He understands the way Jimmy would.

Should have said it all graveside, though. A much better eulogy than the one she got from that wind-up monkey of a minister.

—

But Tribal expiates too this night, a story older than mine and woven into my own before it unraveled around me. Because he slept with Tina, too—once, the afternoon she met Eira in the labyrinthine corridors of the underground mall.

Impromptu introductions, taking us all completely off-guard. She didn't understand, Eira I mean, jutting out her small pale hand in friendly and automatic obliviousness when Tina didn't repeat the gesture. They both stared at that soft and innocent extension, Tina perplexed as if Eira were gesturing vaguely to something beyond recognition in the chasm between them. I felt just as awkward, I suppose, this an unexpected meeting though downtown and in Jackson Square. Plausible, if I'd thought about it beforehand.

"Tina's hand is hurt," I'd said by way of explanation. Tina obliged, though, holding up the swollen and purple ends of three fingers.

Eira's reaction was textbook, vapidly innocent.

"Ouch! How did you manage that? It looks really painful!"

And I watched Tina processing, toying with an answer. I guess the look on my face kept her from playing dirty, though. She managed a small smile despite my terrible blunder, forcing her to face Eira's long clean hair and subtle makeup and blouse and skirt and bangles and designer shoes and purse and little gold cross on a chain—and she strung out and no trick turned yet to pay for a hit, tattered fishnets and worn boots and the filth of last night's memories still stagnant between her thighs. I was so fucking dense sometimes.

"Just a little accident, no big deal," she said, though her eyes never left mine. *What the fuck are you doing*? they asked.

"So, anyone hungry?" I figured food might give us all something to do. *So she's different*, I said to Tina. *So fucking what*?

"I wouldn't mind a bite," Eira chirped. "The food court's just down there, isn't it?"

"I gotta go," Tina mumbled.

"Oh. Well, it was nice to meet you!" Friendly wave, sincere smile.

Christ.

And despite Eira's stunted senses, she still felt my uneasiness as we sat down fifteen minutes later to share food court poutine. She began, predictably, in a roundabout way.

"So, where do you know—Tina, is it?—where do you know her from?"

Dodge and weave.

"You know, just from downtown. You start to see the same faces after a while, eh?"

"Oh," she said, clearly unsatisfied. Then she circled in a bit closer. "Is she always that . . . dirty?"

That bit annoyed me and it must have showed because she followed up pretty fast.

"I—I just mean her clothes were kind of, well, scuffed and worn and her hair was tangled and her makeup was smeared around her eyes, like she'd been crying."

What could I say? Rough and anonymous sex in an alley or in a car or in a cheap room, rape for dosh or drugs or sometimes for nothing at all just survival, these things will wear you pretty thin—clothes and hair, flesh and soul. And that hollow gaping endless void—what is there to fill that emptiness? But I summed it up anyway, flat and expressionless.

"Tina does a lot of crying," I said.

"She's a . . . a prostitute, isn't she?" Eira whispered the word as if she'd found it, dirty and unexpected, in one of her textbooks. Denotation only, though. For her kind, the connotations were mysteries beyond comprehension.

"She's a *friend*," I said, a bit too loudly, but her observation took me by surprise. "What she does with her time and why, it doesn't matter."

Eira bit her lip and toyed with a french fry for a bit, pushing it absently through the congealing gravy.

"Have you ever—"

"No. It's not like that. She's just a friend."

"Okay," she said, cowed and quiet. "It's just that I've never met anyone like that before."

"She's a person, like anybody else."

"Of course, I know that."

No she didn't. She didn't even have the common decency to suspect that I was lying to her.

But Tina left us and ran straight into Tribal, loitering outside the strip club on King and trying to communicate with one of the transient Montreal imports, she not speaking a single *mot d'anglais* or pretending not to. Tina told Tribal she didn't want to go home just then, asking him if he would let her use our shower and then our couch to sleep. Our place was a far cry cleaner than Funhouse's, Tribal being a bit anal about filth and personal hygiene. For a dingy three-room flat, it was surprisingly well kept.

But one thing led to another, Tina emerging from the washroom cleansed and naked, straddling Tribal as he sat innocently watching one of the four channels that came in on our shitbox of a TV.

—

Tribal finishes his pint.

"She was real quiet afterward, didn't say a word. She just sorta laid down on the chesterfield. I got up and made a sandwich, one for her too, but when I brought it over she was already asleep, tears still wet on her face."

I don't say anything. But I remember: she'd cried afterward with me, too.

But this night's quiet cemetery visit, just one of my goodbyes. These things I have already said, about how Jimmy returned, and I began to think about leaving. Even when he finally got around to collecting up equipment and then people (me included), I knew it was only until he'd said what he needed to say. Then it would be over for good.

So, time.

From the moment Jimmy and Debbie left, that fickle March morning in '89 until he returned to us as if by magic one warm summer day in '90, time crawled or flew or stood still—though forever inanimate, my own petty machinations lending it life, witless marionette on invisible strings—or it was forgotten in the lulls. But always (with me) that nagging sense of waste, time being the only thing of any intrinsic value, when all is said and done. Jimmy taught me that.

I have untied the mooring lines this year, one by one, those closest to me watching in helpless torpor or anger or silence or curiosity as I solved each knot with clumsy deliberateness, unsure really of where I would go or why I was going.

Even the Hammer itself has changed. Trends slip away, others take their place, the scene shifts, transforms. I put aside the bull's-eye and shell years ago, but the rest of the scene didn't outlive me long. Now the summer of 1991 and even the youngest members of old boot culture Hamilton have entered the workforce proper. The advance guard of the next generation had found our old haunts, filling them with new sounds and new forms, slovenly and grungy and casually self-absorbed and politically indifferent, like mopey nihilistic lumberjacks. Whatever. So be it.

Only skinheads remain, though rare. Both sides, the skins who stayed true to their roots (Jamaican music and Birmingham street ethics—pride without prejudice), and their white power offshoots, the living bastard abortions of Mother Ignorance.

It changes. All of it. Within just a handful of years of pulling that mad-eyed bastard Teddy from the rubbish, it all did. Stephanie would disappear without a word. Eira would cut my mooring lines. We'd lose Tina. We'd find Sarah. Jimmy and Debbie would head to the Middle East.

And only Jimmy would return from a desert city by the sea that swallows everything.

But out there—by that quiet and ancient stretch of sea, by that lonely and restless stretch of sand—what can we expect of even the most careful of plans? What would my own personal prophet say? Because I guess we're all a little quadrophenic.

Just like (I smile) Jimmy.

Chapter Two

Another goodbye, this one complicated.

Sarah and I arrange to meet downtown on Hess Street at one of the bars with an outside café. It's a Tuesday night, late summer but cold and uninviting. A pub night, to be honest, but Sarah won't go. Says she hates the smell of beer, but that's not it. A pub—especially a tight little place like the Lion's Head or even the Corktown—isn't the right venue for her ego. Puts her out of reach when crammed in with the unwashed pint-swilling masses, hidden away from the roving eye, as it were.

"Not my scene," she'd said once, years ago, when Jimmy inquired. He had been in a facetious mood, though.

"What'd she say?" he asked. "Can't be seen?"

It was funny at the time, even Sarah laughed. Debbie, now, she wouldn't have. That's essentially the difference between them.

Sarah makes me wait. I grab a beer inside but I go out onto the patio with it. You wait forever if you sit out on the patio first, even in good weather. Should have ordered a coffee, but I can't enjoy it without the occasional draught of cigarette smoke. Not that I smoke too often myself, but I always seem to drink coffee with those who do. Addicted to second-hand smoke, I think. Jesus Christ, talk about a selective addiction.

Sarah.

Our time together not the longest of roads, just over four years, but still. I guess because we went through our stretch at roughly the same time—both of us dumped by our significant others almost to the day—we found ourselves clinging (coincidentally) to the same remnants, the same scraps of emotional refuse.

Whatever floats. Sarah's own words that night we met.

Eventually, we clung to each other—we all *collect* something. Of course, there were long-term mitigating circumstances, all fallout: a moderate amount of pot, a copious amount of hash, and the odd dalliance with hallucinogens, but that, too, was later. One April afternoon four years ago, I was lost and alone—before this patio, before this phase or friendship or whatever the fuck it is Sarah and I share—and by the evening, well, still lost and alone. But at least lost and alone together. Twin phoenixes rising from the flames, I suppose.

Or at least from the ashes that collected around us as Tribal, Sarah, and I finished the last thick and crooked joint, that parchment coloured bone that resembled (I remember thinking at the time) a smoldering finger pointing out into the woods.

But toward what?

I reminisce foolishly. Sarah arrives as I am holding my hand up to my face, chin resting on the back of my knuckles, one finger thrust outward, pointing accusingly at a beer advertisement on the wall across the patio.

"Et tu, Brewti?" she says somberly, and then laughs.

"Very clever," I manage. And it is. I laugh too, embarrassed.

"What exactly were you doing?" She throws her bag and purse on the table beside us, grabs at the purse as it tips, rights it, retrieves cigarettes, and slides into the chair across from me. All in one fluid motion. Tablecloth puller, I muse.

"Well?" she pursues.

"I was thinking about joints," I say nonchalantly. "They remind me of fingers."

Sarah smiles dryly and lights her smoke.

"You mean you're thinking about your brother's joints. Tribal has no sense of moderation. Obsessed with quantity, not quality. A very male trait."

Not exactly true, but I know what she means. My brother's most public triumphs are phallic extensions. The reason, however, is simple: he rolls like a monkey. Bigger spliffs are just easier to construct. Victor fucking Frankenstein, I explain to Sarah, but she isn't really listening. Something's on her mind, and hers is a circuitous path. She starts with an unrelated object. Or so she thinks.

"That's a ponderous looking book you're toting about."

She reaches out, rotates it so she can read the spine. Then, the inevitable eyebrow of incredulity.

"*Ulysses*? Are you kidding? Who, exactly, are you trying to impress?"

Fair question. I read a lot, Sarah knows this, but this thing is a bit too conspicuous to be a casual change of pace. I tell her the truth.

"Actually, I figured I'd give it a go just to say I read it, eh? I mostly carry it around and read it when I'm waiting. Like just before you got here, but you arrived faster than expected."

"Ah," she consents. "So, how is it?"

"Pretty self-indulgent." What I really mean is masturbatory.

"Eh?"

"Well, here's the thing, I figure. Joyce probably enjoyed himself immensely writing the goddamn book, but it's a bit of a slog reading it. I feel the passive observer."

In truth, it makes me feel inadequate, but there's a limit to my sexual metaphors in mixed company.

Sarah's a solid mate, though. She actually pursues the topic, albeit awkwardly. Perhaps she feels a little inadequate herself.

"Based on Homer's *Odyssey*, isn't it?"

Trite comment, really, but it's the thought that counts.

"Yeah. Well, maybe. That seems to be the popular opinion, but I'm not seeing it so far. I might be a bit daft, though." I take a swig from my pint and add, "Then again, isn't everything pretty much a variation of the ancient stuff? You know, the archetypal journey myth . . . Fuck off when you're young, face your dragons as you grow up, lose your identity, find your identity, spend your whole bloody life trying to replace what you took for granted in the first place?"

I'm a fucking philosopher at twenty-three. I'm pretty Jung, eh?

Laugh, assholes, that was funny.

But Sarah and I nurture a careful conversation this night, the idle words—words selected carefully *because* they're idle—offered and worried over, the two of us surreptitiously obsessing over each sound, scrutinizing each syllable for tone, for intent. I poking absently at the spine of my book, she scrutinizing those who drift by us beyond the pretentious wrought iron fence of this patio—and even now, I still contemplating the past, the changes, the restructuring of things.

Flypaper prose, my chosen medium, as much a process of witless artifice as is saying that you're writing in the antediluvian tar pit with bones. Not like some prehistoric giant sloth lumbered in there to make a statement, after all. The poor bastard wasn't commenting on the condition of his kind in the intermission between ice ages. He just wanted a fucking drink and got sucked in, probably front legs first.

Talk about embarrassing. One minute you're lapping water off the top of the tar, the next minute your arms, shoulders, head and neck are completely submerged. You drown or asphyxiate or whatever the fuck tar does to you, with your giant meaty ass jutting out like a great hairy hillock.

Fucking humiliating. Giant sloth afterlife must be a place that caters to a pretty dry sense of humour.

"Hey, you're new. What'd you die of?"

"Me? Embarrassment."

Sarah, though—she doesn't feel the sticky appeal of reminiscence. No, I see it clearly underneath the casual absorption she feigns with her immediate surroundings, a febrile impatience clawing for purchase at the forced indifference of her words. It's the future—it clings to every syllable she utters, I start to feel trapped.

Sarah has an agenda.

"So," she begins, "are you really going south?"

She asks, exhaling at the same time. You want signifier and signified? There you go—hear the words, but read the smoke signals. Two completely different questions.

I'm pretty good at this by now, after all, I learned from the Catfish himself. *Mind your step*, he'd say if he were here.

"C'mon, Sarah. We've had this talk, eh?"

"Yeah, I know. It kind of took everyone by surprise, though."

True enough, but I'm still watching the smoke. Sarah casts one of her slow glances to the left, lifting her head to expose that long neck of hers and focusing her eyes (allegedly) on something down the street. She's posing, a black magic profile, for shit-sure. I already bought immunity, though. She knows, but this is one of the games we still play.

Still in profile, Sarah watches the heater of her smoke as it dances through the air in slow arabesques, a nervous habit of hers. It means she's thinking.

"Ewan's in the bar, you know."

"Didn't know, actually. Does he know we're here?"

"I think so."

Ewan—I never figured him out. Years of sitting behind me at a drum kit and the only meaningful communication we have is through a mutual understanding of time changes. Six-four seven-four alternating, watch for the chorus, fall back at the bridge. That's us at our most cognizant.

Ewan's pretty angry, though. This much I know: he's just delusional enough to believe that the band has some sort of future—you know, visions of record labels dance in his head and all that sort of tripe. It's not totally unjustified—since Jimmy got back and took the reins things have been solid: good venues, write-ups, even air time in Toronto, but for Jimmy these things are just peripheral by-products, necessary evils that interfere with the message itself. I see the end of this tunnel. Jimmy's already said what he needed to say.

Not Ewan, though. Peripherals. I guess they vary depending on who you are. Or think you are. See, Ewan's going to be a fucking superstar. He's got all the luggage packed and waiting by the door. A neatly labeled pile of prepackaged delusions all crowding the way out of his skull. Hey, all he needs now are the fans.

Sarah takes a final drag and says, "I think he's been here since this afternoon. I worry about him."

"Christ, I don't. That skinny bastard will drink anyone under the table. Give him some credit." Drummers. They're crazy fucks, like goalies. Same gene pool, I figure.

"That's not what I mean. Jesus, you can be dense."

I let it go. We both know what she means and she knows it. Smoke signals, after all.

Then the patio door flies open and Himself makes an unstable exit from the bar and into a table. Shitty timing, but what can you do?

"Hey," he slurs and aims himself in our direction. "Why you out here? In the cold, huh?"

Stagger, stagger, stagger, slump. Right onto Sarah's purse. Takes him a good ten seconds to process that she wants him to stand up again. Some awkward manoeuvring, a drunken apology, and we're off again.

But Ewan divines that he may have (literally) stumbled into an uncomfortable situation. He solves it in the manner of all proud alcoholics: drunken pontification.

"Hey, know what I say? Fuck MTV! Fuck them, eh? They're assholes, man. When I make it, man, fuck them, you know? I'm fuckin' Canadian. I'm no sellout, man."

Jesus Christ. Here we go again.

"That's great, man. Stick to your principles."

"Fuckin' A!" he yells, and falls over, taking the table with him. A man with a mission, though. Ewan glares up at me from the patio stones. *Tu m'accuse*, mate.

"We're just getting going, eh, what the fuck, man? Why you leaving? What the fuck'r you 'fraid of, brother? We need you, man! Need that guitar!"

Enough is enough, I figure.

"Shite, Ewan. Think about it: I'm doing you a fuckin' favour, eh? Get yourself a real guitarist."

Sarah scoffs. "C'mon, give *yourself* some credit. Don't say that."

I love Sarah, I swear to God. Underneath all the dodge and weave and things unsaid there's a consistency you don't usually find with girls. Chauvinistic? Yep, but admit it: it's the truth.

This ain't false modesty, by the way. I'm the weak link—Jimmy's on his own plane and the others are all pretty professional. Me? I'm a hack, pure and simple. Always have been. It's rhythm guitar, though, a wallpaper position. Just need to play the right chords at the right tempo at the right time. It's not like I'm up there building a fucking rocket or anything. I don't know what they're called. Jimmy spends a lot of time at practice pulling my fingers into contortions across the fret board, hovering over my left hand like some sort of mad scientist turned basket weaver. Talks the whole time, too, but to my hand, like it's an independent entity or perhaps his own left hand's slow second cousin.

Here's the other thing: the chemistry's faded now that Jimmy's said what he had to say. Cosmic tumblers out of alignment and the lock won't open, right? Ironically, though, I'm not the real problem. Jimmy and I, despite my musical shortcomings, work in harmony because I have absolutely no false pretenses about our relationship. It's easy, really. Musically, I'm simply the witless avatar, an extension. Clockwork man—program the chords and wind the key.

Ewan doesn't have anything else to say, I guess. He starts to nod off. Sarah, however . . . well, she never got around to saying much of anything, either. Too late now.

Thank the gods for Ewan.

"I can't let him drive home," I say. "You know how Friday night is." There's a checkpoint on every onramp to the 403 by now, the cops don't fuck around. I reach down and haul him to his feet, throwing a wiry arm across my shoulders.

Sarah doesn't even look at me. Yeah, she's pissed right bloody proper. Even under the best circumstances, she hates getting interrupted. And these, well.

She pokes my book with one long, deep red nail and says (distantly, I assure you), "Don't forget this."

I look at Jamie J's hollow and tortured face gazing up from the cover. I'm sick of hauling him around—Ewan, at least, will stagger along cooperatively. This other cat's a goddamned anchor. I make an executive decision.

"Nah. I'm going to leave it behind. Either it's utter shite or I'm an idiot." Seventy years of controversy and criticism nod disappointingly toward the latter, though. But what can I do? I can't be expected to lug about anchor *and* albatross, can I?

"Hey," I say by way of goodbyes, "coffee tomorrow? Usual place?"

"I don't know," she says, absorbed again by the dull glow at the end of her next smoke. "I'm pretty busy tomorrow."

"Ah. Well, phone, eh? Let me know."

Chapter Three

"Hey . . ."

"Yeah, Ewan?"

"I'm gonna puke, man."

"Yeah?"

"Yeah . . ."

"Can you wait till I pull over?"

Guess not.

Chapter Four

But Sarah never phoned. She never even showed up to see me off. I left and everything changed, I never saw her again. I tried phoning her from the States a couple of times, but the distance was too palpable, too real. I don't know. Maybe because it was me who left instead of her, still there in steel city exile, Montreal just a sickly-sweet dream rife with decay. Or at least a dream deferred, anyway.

Jimmy and Tribal came with me, as far as the border. They were going to hitch hike back up the Queen E, a little foil adventure to parallel my own plunge into a foreign world, Jimmy said jokingly, but the humour was forced. Tribal didn't say shit. They were supportive—solid mates—but they didn't really understand. Not sure I did either, at the time.

I pulled into the Duty Free parking lot. All ashore that's going ashore, I said half-heartedly. We all got out of the car to say our goodbyes, and it was a right bloody hot day for September, though. Tribal was still incommunicado, Jimmy still feigning humour.

But it couldn't last. Jimmy too grew sullen, even Jimmy, and we both clutched awkwardly for words. He stopped first. Instead, he reached into his pocket and drew out a ragged ball of cloth and handed it to me.

I didn't need to unwrap it—I knew immediately what lay within that dirty bit of army green fabric that still carried the scent of sea salt and sand.

Inside the bundle was his red clay bowl flute, a gift from a Bedouin when he was in the Middle East. With Debbie. You could imitate desert birdcalls with it, he told me once. I smiled, a bit overwhelmed—it was his favourite possession, the last link to what was lost. Signifier over the signified: too valuable a sign.

"Jimmy, I can't," I said. "This is too much." I tried to hand it to him.

But Jimmy pressed it back into my hands.

"Take it."

It was time. Tribal still wouldn't speak, nothing left to say, really, not at this point. But he had something for me, too. He unbuckled the old army pack he carried everywhere and pulled out a flat rectangle wrapped in a faded Canadian flag. I didn't need to open it either—I knew what it was, too.

—

I remember.

We were kids, maybe thirteen and fourteen, when we stole that sign. Upper James and Mohawk, a Saturday night. A bit drunk, a bit reckless, feigning outrage when our bus didn't show. We had the tools and the time—took it in mock protest, proclaiming the entire bus stop obsolete, and announcing ourselves minor heroes on some vague, indefinable level. We'd had the thing for years. We shared a room when we still lived at home, displayed the sign proudly between our beds—and when we split (in protest, but far from mocking), it was one of the few possessions we took with us.

Music, clothes, my guitar, that sign, and a fierce sense of loyalty to each other. That was it. I remember.

There'd been yellow caution tape on a fence a stone's throw away—we removed it carefully and wrapped the bus shelter in it. Idiotic, but we still laughed about it even years later. No one else did, though—not one of those traditional bonding moment stories people related to. No one else knew why we were so attached to what was, for all intents and purposes, a pretty mundane tale of petty vandalism.

But it wasn't the sign: it was the walk we had to endure because of the absent bus. Almost two hours' shog to the north end. For a while, we trudged along in silence, each mulling over his own thoughts but never once without the other in mind. And then, as we got to the bottom of the Escarpment, Tribal spoke.

"What we gonna do?"

"Don't know." I shifted the bus sign to my other hand, away from the street. Hamilton cops were pretty observant. "We could leave, eh?"

Tribal kicked a piece of asphalt into the road, watched it skip across the lanes until it rolled into the opposite curb.

"And go fuckin' where? We got no money, no friends with room to spare. Just end up in the System. And apart."

I knew he was right, it was a simple matter of time. Foster care was a crapshoot at best, and we weren't exactly the easiest candidates for placement. But Tribal was right about home, too: we couldn't stay under the circumstances. Our mum was drinking again, and not lightly, the shabby North End hovel we inhabited a flophouse for one wreckage of a boyfriend after another. Sometimes she'd have two of them in there at once, one passed out in her bed, another sprawled out in the kitchen or on the stained and threadbare couch.

Once we found one in our bedroom, lying in a congealing mess of vomit.

"Look at this fucking asshole," Tribal had said, rolling him over with his boot. Beneath him, we found a flattened Tupperware bowl and a puddle of sour milk and gluey cornflakes. Must have been there for half a day at least. Tribal gave him a kick in the ribs, but the sot didn't even stir.

I looked at my brother. He needed out, I could see it as he folded in on himself.

"Anything's better than living in that shithole," I said. "We'll go."

"Where?"

"Squat house to start, I figure." Even back then I knew Seamus, a Trojan skinhead and a solid mate. He lived in an abandoned machine shop, second floor accommodations in a building not quite on the condemned list.

We did go home that night, though, pushed our way through the lightless warren (hydro cut the power), through the stale reek of unwashed clothes and stale beer, the cloying stench of old cigarettes and vomit.

We had a couple candles squirreled away in a fist-sized hole in the flimsy wood paneling of the room we shared. Tribal retrieved them and lit the wicks.

In the unsteady glow, we took stock of what we were: two dirty and neglected kids with nothing to lose. Or so we thought.

"Now?" Tribal asked.

"Yeah. Fuck this place. And fuck the courts. They can't make us stay here."

We packed our meagre possessions quickly, with purpose.

"C'mon," I said. "Seamus'll let us stay for at least tonight."

But Seamus took us in for over a month. He taught us the fundamentals, how to find food, where to hide, when to fight, when to run.

The System swept us up anyway, no rock unturned. But we'd slip away, find each other again. And again.

Earlier that year, I'd met Jimmy. Young, too, but the catfish within—ah, older than we knew, wiser than us all. He'd leave home not long before we did.

Tribal and Jimmy: brothers by blood and by circumstance. Fuck, it was hard getting back into that car and driving off. I just need some time, I told them, this is just for a couple of months.

But we all knew that wasn't true.

As for Sarah, after our cold and terse patio conversation (such as it was), with Ewan sprawled out on the ground before us and too wrecked to walk much less drive, well. She never even phoned.

But I knew in time I'd phone her. Things would be alright. Eventually.

Eventually things would be alright. A sparse comfort, and one of the few things I took with me. Inevitably, I lost pieces of it along the way.

But that's the way of things, I guess.

—

And then?

Histrionic clown, I think, sad-eyed hypocrite. Because I had found my own unlikely way of slipping into the circuitry, adapting, transforming.

My road stretched westward at first, Chicago—brawling, sordid city—but it was a hollow place that reeked of echoes (false memory, déjà vu fabrications). I set myself adrift down wind-raw streets, past towering buildings grey and bleak and forbidding, and even the harbour—slate grey too—smelt somehow wrong. Too much like Hamilton, though not really because of its sprawling vastness, its fierce and unapologetic pride in its own brutal past.

But the echo was there, barely discernable, like a coin dropped on a crowded city street by a stranger. Maybe that's what brought Steph there in the first place.

East, then. Into New England, drifting aimlessly to be dropped quietly among the other glacial erratics, deposited as if by chance amongst the drumlins and great domed hills of metamorphic rock, carved out ponds and lakes, rugged landscape of gneiss and granite, maple and pine, one more migrant drifter incognito. And cities there, too, but more just backdrops for the shabby mill towns that squat stubbornly like old age pensioners in the river valleys, *I remember when* and *in my grandfather's day* and *before they closed the canal* drifting from the mouths of old men, careworn and kind, at a dozen different diners and corner restaurants, the same cheap greasy food and strong coffee as welcoming in one place as another. An easy sort of life, unpretentious and insular.

Or pristine towns with picture postcard commons occupied by narrow generations utterly oblivious to anything not within sight of the bandstand on the green, Catholic church on one side, Protestant church on the other, two congregations eying each other's steeples (one lot secretly envious, the other lot gracious but smug) while layman officials plot ways of adding on a few feet to their modest *axis mundis*.

Oblivious and trusting, the lot, in the towns and even in the few cities that dot the uneven, hilly terrain. As a regional characteristic, I mean, New England being as subject to its own quota of assholes as anywhere else. That's one thing I've learned from my own small cosmic journey: people are pretty much the same no matter where you go.

Well, except Chicago. That place kind of sucked.

And so. I read this even now, this histrionic shite (*hypocrite lecteur!—mon semblable—mon frère!*), and wonder: what would Jimmy make of me, or Tribal? What would (or could) Sarah say? Or Eira, now little more than a ghost that even memory sometimes can't recall? Strangely enough, I know that Debbie would have smiled, approving of my chameleon prank, my showmanship.

My wildly successful tablecloth trick.

Because I, too, found a way through the cracks in the road. Acoustic gigs in city dives, new sound somehow appealing in its otherness, earning me some regular slots though modest paying, and under the table day jobs offered by friendly bar patrons who knew I was looking. One night I meet a girl—pretty, waif-like, possibly adrift as well—into vintage dresses and 1920s fashion and (apparently) illegal alien hard-luck cases. She works in a small boutique owned by a family friend, antiques and clothing and strange remnants of other people's lives. So unlike anyone I knew back home, at first, that she reminds me of nothing—but this is untrue. She reminds me of all the things Debbie was not. By which I mean, all the things I wanted Debbie to be.

It is the absence, then, to which I cling.

We date. I fall in love with her, casually at first and then more so, and she (I suppose) with me, but these things are a matter of perspective.

Small civil wedding ceremony, just a few of her friends and her parents—kind and accepting people who are vaguely confused, I come to learn, by everything their only daughter does—followed some time after by a trip to Boston. Immigration processes me. Inked and interrogated, photographed and filed—entropic fossil now officially in the strata, one more foreign-born blip on the radar.

We have a small flat in a three-decker, just the front three rooms on the second floor, but it seems to be enough. There, I spend my first winter in this far and foreign land musing, and then planning. And that spring, just a year since I slipped away across the border, I tell her.

Risky, to say the least, but she loves it immediately, excited before I'm even finished outlining the details. Bold-faced deception: this is what my girl is addicted to, Bonnie and Clyde, she teases later that night as we talk in bed, entangled and drowsy and warm and connected. But I know her well enough by then—*we all collect something*, Jimmy's words drifting through that hazy veil that drifts softly over the first moments of sleep.

The rest was easy. Strangely easy, and I wonder how many before me have done the same. Of course, I had Quinn, and he provided the props. Could have been managed otherwise, but I like to maintain it never would have worked without him. His final payment, debt paid in full: I saved his life by dragging his scrawny ass out of black waters—now he gave me a life in return. I don't know how the fuck he got hold of it or what strings he pulled, but six weeks after I phoned him (innocently pompous now with his own importance) I got a parcel, signature required.

We opened it together that night, she was giddy and maybe still a bit stoned because we'd partaken before dinner, and there it was: a genuine university diploma with my name on it. And a bonus, Quinn's final thank-you gift: an actual transcript documenting four years that never existed.

I got myself an interview at a private school (disaster), and then another one. Five altogether that May and into June, and no one actually asked for any documentation, any proof. Not one school official doubted that anything I told them wasn't absolutely true. But then again, it's your personality they're really judging, not your credentials.

And at the end of this whirlwind farce? Two offers. *Two*—I actually had a fucking choice. Amazing.

This, then, is what I do. English Lit, working in a New England prep school that caters to its elite, but also to hard luck cases, kids who come from families with everything and nothing—another type of *salon des refusés*. These are the kids I get—fitting, if only they knew the truth.

But I love the little bastards—and bastards they are, in a sense, farmed out to boarding schools for substitute parenting, the biological culprits responsible for these parcels of raging hormonal imbalances, these frustrated victims of social profiling, dodging their obligations by throwing dosh at someone else. Maybe these kids sense my sympathy, my comprehension.

Predictably, I bond with the so-called worst of the lot, the kids most of my fellow caretakers can't seem to figure out. They're an odd lot, too, the other zookeepers—either fresh out of college and not much older than their wards or antiquated watch towers, guardians of the Great Weal. It's the old sots I can't seem to get along with, their condescension, their disdain, their narrowness, their intolerance for anything remotely off kilter, their chiastic dramatics: Wall wisdom, any stoner can tell you—meat before pudding, pudding after meat. Christ.

It's a small school, just a few hundred kids, tucked safely away in a quiet little rural hamlet: a green and garden-bordered common with the obligatory pair of churches, town hall, post office, library, general store, and collection of xenophobic locals brimming with the narrow pride of villagers.

The locals talk in regional euphemisms, repeating their grandfathers' sayings to each other. They discuss local politics with stern and concentrated vigour. They watch each other like fucking hawks.

I watch them, these locals, same as I watch the others, teachers and students alike. I study their mannerisms, their talk. Concerns and dreams and fears—warp and weft, I learn what I can, performing my Odysseus tricks daily on an unsuspecting crowd, subtle and guileful subterfuge. I begin to enjoy it, the web of lies I need to weave in order to sustain this farce—invented staff room stories and impromptu sideline anecdotes to provide the illusion of legitimacy.

And the Great White Fathers who run this asylum? Ah, puny man in the ominous cavern of a hungover Cyclops, blind and oblivious. To them, I am nobody, nothing out of the ordinary, my oddities of speech and gaps in grace chalked up to my Otherness, just foreign idiosyncrasies.

I learn to avoid the college guys my own age, though. Too quick to sense something isn't quite right, the distance between our worlds is too immense. So I take shelter with the older crowd, distasteful as it is. But I am a tablecloth puller, not a disguise artist. I scrounge around like a nameless beggar in the manor, while they throw me scraps of wisdom and bits of advice. Nothing too useful, the stingy bastards. They at least don't question my past—just another young nobody to them, a temporary sounding board. Like their students, I am just something to talk at.

As for the other part of this equation, it doesn't last long. The marriage, I mean. At first she plays her part well, spider in the Great Hall, spinner of tales, catcher of flies. We flesh things out, fabricate a plausible past in careful steps. She scrutinizes the details and questions me closely about my day. For a while.

But she grows weary of the smallness, the pretense of respectability wears her thin. Can't really blame her—she had hardly any role at all in the games I was playing. Waiting and weaving her own small lies, it isn't enough.

The snows come early that first year, but so does spring. And one day in late March, she disappears. No note, no warning. Just gone.

She doesn't take much with her, either, just some clothes (all vintage), and most of what little was in the bank. She leaves behind everything else: letters, pictures, small gifts and sentimental tripe, a broken wristwatch, her grandmother's earrings.

Want to know the worst part? I couldn't really get all that upset about it. I mean, I tried—I told myself she betrayed my trust and abandoned me and must be insane and was probably cheating on me and so on, but at the core of it all, I didn't really give a fuck. I just sort of shrugged it off and went on with the school year.

To hell with it, I think. *She was just a means to an end, anyway.*

Evenings are lonely, though. After a few weeks, so are the mornings.

Then her parents show up, one weekend in early May. They stand in the doorway of my dorm flat (rent-free housing! Ah, what a magician I have become!), bewildered by my casual account of their daughter's own disappearing act. She, too, is quite the magician, it seems.

"Gone," I say.

"But—you mean, to shop? To the store?"

"Nope. I mean 'gone,' as in 'no longer lives here.'"

Her father stands there in bewildered silence. Mom tears up, panic in her voice.

"Why? I mean, why? What happened?"

"Don't know," I say. "Came home one day after work and she'd already moved out. Thought she would have moved back in with you."

Mom mouths a few syllables, searches for handholds.

"We just saw her last week," her father says, slowly. "She came by for some things. She never said anything."

"Ah. She didn't tell you, then."

"No," the father says quietly.

Mom finds her voice and asks, "When did you come home to find her gone?"

I glance over at the calendar on the wall.

"Five weeks ago."

"*Five weeks?*"

"Yeah."

What can I do? I try to console them a bit, but there's not much point. I give her mom the earrings, at least, I don't want the fucking things.

And then they're gone, too. Poof, into thin air.

Strangely enough, though, it isn't her I think of in those empty stretches. Eira at first, of course, but that's to be expected. After all, it's a predictable comparison—unexpected and sudden end, I mean. Debbie, too, is a more poignant presence in those first days and weeks, but I dream about her so often anyway—terrible dreams that fall away in ragged wisps as soon as I wake, eluding my grasp, fleeting memories of her face slipping away from me and into a violent crowd of screaming angry mouths and clenched fists. I call to her, but she can't hear me. I try to follow but they won't let me through. Sometimes Jimmy is there, too, quiet and still as the mob rages about us, his voice gentle and persistent, "Look harder. It is small. Look again."

No, who I really think of is Sarah.

How long, I wonder, since we last talked?

And then I can't breathe all that well, chest tight, knees wobbly.

I dig frantically in the hall closet for my duffel bag, dormant and all but forgotten between migrations since I first came south. Inside is a sheaf of crumpled papers, addresses and phone numbers stuffed into a plastic bag. I rummage through them, regretting it almost immediately because of the guilt that accompanies this rapid excavation through the layers (*not one* I think *not one of these people have I*) and so on.

I find it. A small address book, Sarah's name and number carefully recorded on the first page. I toss the other papers onto a chair for later and reach for the phone.

Finger shaking, I punch in the numbers and wait.

But the number I have dialed is not in service. I am instructed to please hang up and try my call again. By a recorded voice.

Daft fool. I immediately phone Tribal, tenacious to the bitter end. All I really want is to hear Sarah's voice, there is an urgency to it now. It's been too long since Tribal and I talked, I've lost touch. I kept meaning to phone, but one thing always led to another. And recently I haven't been in the mood to talk to anyone since I came home to an empty flat. Understandable, I figure.

He picks up fast, thinking I'm someone else. He was expecting a call.

"*'Bout time, Vin, where you been?*"

"No, man. It's me."

"*Holy shit! I was starting to wonder where the hell you were, eh? How's life with the wife?*"

So I tell him the truth. Just the facts, like I'm giving a report. I keep it brief. Tribal commiserates as best he can, but he can't get any more upset about it than I can. Maybe he figures I'll come home now.

"Look," I say, mercifully changing the subject, "I haven't exactly been all that good about keeping in touch with people—"

"Jesus, you think? Want a list of mates who think you're a dick? First off—"

"Whoa, there, Jiminy fucking Cricket, I got it. I'm a dick. But I dug out a bunch of numbers, so I can start making some calls."

"You better start with Derek, eh? Syd fucked off back to the U.K., but Seamus is out now on probation—"

"Thought I'd start with Sarah. Her number's disconnected, though. You know where she's living?"

Silence.

"You haven't heard."

"Heard what?"

"Sarah's gone, brother. Went to Montreal not too long after you left. Her and Chloe, they left together."

"Shit! No, I didn't. I didn't know that. Did she leave a—"

"Hold on, man. There's more."

And now that old sensation—centipede scent creeping into place, scuttling feet tickling the inside of my skull. Insects, too, gathering in the dark corners, finally unstuck, free to fly.

"Okay," I say, tight and calm. "What else?"

Tribal sighs.

"Fuck, brother, what can I say? She just got married, like two or three months ago. I got a fucking postcard."

So, this is the way the world ends.

God damn it.

—

And there is no sortilege here, no scrying. No way to determine (how did he put it? Ah,) disease in signatures, biography from wrinkles of the palm, tragedy from fingers. No tealeaf sifter or rune reader or dissector of dreams could have swayed me from my course.

As far as I was concerned, everything I left behind slipped into stasis to await my triumphant return. A world in hibernation, incapable of aging while I, a light speed traveler on my own cosmic journey, made my galactic sojourn and returned—what, wiser? No. Just world-weary.

But I got it backwards, relatively speaking (ha ha). It's the *traveler* who barely ages, not those left behind. Can't even get an analogy right.

It figures.

So, this is the way, shite for *shanti* and up at dawn the next day. Classes to teach, after all. For the first time in ages, though, I begin to think of home.

Because who am I, here in this far and foreign land? Nobody (to continue the allusion)—my entire persona is a shabby mask, a careless game it seems in the sober morning light. Can't face it and I call in sick, leave a message, let the inmates have a little free time to dabble in what they consider mischief.

And real mischief, too. Some hotshot thirty-something administrator has my fucking number. Clever bastard, he sees through my smoke and mirror façade, suspects in a more insidious way than the younger teachers do, though maybe one or two of the sycophantic little fucks tuned him in. I started to feel it around the time my enigmatic partner in crime slipped off into the ethers: a greeting coldly returned by this old codger or by that secretarial crone. Or whispers in my wake, nothing too obvious yet, but still. The jig, as they say, is almost up.

I'm not playing the lamb to the slaughter, I assure you—just out of principle, if nothing else. Call it a harmonious blend of genetics and environment: I'm not one to let a little tit-measle like Hotshot take me out without a right proper reckoning.

Vengeance lurks in the bottom of a plain blue duffle bag.

I try to go back to sleep, but I can't. Routine has rewired me, I who once slept only when morning was finally upon us, the night's debaucheries shed at dawn somewhere (*between the motion and the act*, I muse), abandoned.

"Set free," Jimmy had said, one morning, "like dead leaves in the wind."

6:00 a.m., Tuesday morning.

I prepare to go instead. To quit this school, although they'll likely leave it be until the end of spring. An embarrassing error, gross miscalculation on the part of the poor bastard who offered me a contract. Can't admit the mistake too soon, though, we must save face, mustn't we?

I am right. About the timing, I mean. The call finally comes the afternoon before what would have been my first graduation ceremony. Ever.

Icy and brief, the great chief's secretary speaks—a summons to his office. "Now," she says haughtily and hangs up.

And so it begins.

Hotshot is there, too, standing behind his master with arms crossed and distantly smug. A couple more of his trusted cronies have also been summoned to the sidelines, witnesses I suppose.

"Well?" the little man behind the huge desk begins. His voice quivers with rage. "Have you any idea, any idea *at all* why you are here?"

Uncomfortable silence. I break it.

"Enlighten me."

Hackles up, the old man jabs his finger in my direction.

"I have made *inquiries*—just who the hell do you think you are?"

There is a chair behind me, decorative and old. *Fuck it*, I figure, and sit down, lean back. Might as well get comfortable. Hotshot's face falls visibly.

"I'm the guy *you* hired to teach some classes, remember?"

"But absolutely everything you gave us was fraudulent! You have no previous experience, you don't even hold a *degree*! We don't even know if this is your real name!"

The old man takes a breath, collects himself.

"So," the ring-giver concludes, "you lied to us from day one."

"From day one," I say, steady and clear.

"But surely you knew the risk you were taking?" His voice cracks. Infuriated, he adds, "I am seriously considering pressing charges!" A frail fist falls down on his desk, a feeble thump.

"I don't think so," I hear myself say. I am drifting now—a small taste, precursor to what is to follow (patience, though, soon not now but soon). "Not exactly the sort of thing you'd publicize, eh? Anyway," I add, "I wasn't half bad at it. Teaching, I mean—I did alright."

But he goes beet red under his shock of white hair. Hotshot bristles too, hackles rising. The other two shuffle from one foot to the other. My refusal to even pretend to be sorry leaves them impotent, I suppose. I'm right about the legal charges, though. Too embarrassing.

The old man reaches into a drawer and produces a legal document of some sort—a promise not to press charges if I go quietly and keep my mouth shut about it all. *What the hell*, I think, *why not*? I sign. Then I am dismissed, told to vacate before the graduation ceremony begins the next day. I am not—and they make this quite crystal—invited to attend.

But me? No lamb to the slaughter.

Traditions, I know, are sacred to these types of places, and this one is no different. The Grand Poobah (not a bad old guy, really) likes to preview the day's events with his trusty thanes over tea, especially when the event is public and requires showmanship. It's an old teapot he uses, some relic of one of the cult-deities that once lorded over the place. All properly performed, I assure you, loose tea leaves in one of those silver and perforated spheres, biscuits of some description also in attendance. And all locked up tight in the throne room.

But the ancient silver creamer, the cups and saucers. Ah, these are kept by the little sink beside the small fridge in the supply room next door, close to the 8-ounce carton of milk in the fridge below. His secretary must wash out the cups immediately after use (her master is particular), then they are stored upside down to prevent the microscopic debris of the day from settling in each gentle concave.

There are written instructions posted for this, I shit you not.

I still have my keys and the offices can be reached from the academic wing. Elevenish, moonless and black, I make my quiet way inside, unseen and unheard. Anathema now, just a minor monster that goes bump in the night. Down to the supply room I creep, heart racing, edge of hysterics, a practical joke worthy of song.

Because on the inside of each of the four china teacups, I pour a few drops from a tiny vial, a potent potion—the last of my House on the Hill, smuggled in so long ago at the bottom of a plain blue duffle bag and untouched until today, my salbonavita salvation. I swish it around until the inside is covered, a lacquered layer. Will it work, I wonder, or will it just evaporate?

So the rest I pour into that little half-empty carton of milk. A pity too, because I can't stay for the show.

Or maybe I will, I muse, *let's see what morning brings*. But homeward and right quick once I've had my fill. No point in lingering, after all.

Morning comes. A strange day, overcast and muggy. An eerie mist lingers on the open green where proud parents gather, arranging themselves in seated rows before the makeshift stage. I am not among them but in the stairwell of a dormitory, window seat to the world below. In the parking lot on the far side of this building is my shitbox of a car, packed with what little I'll take with me. I lean against the cinder blocks and wait.

But it doesn't work.

Opening speeches of welcome are given, the guest speaker is introduced at some length. My former jarl sits down to applause, my jury also enthroned upon the rostrum, still as stones as their honoured guest starts to speak.

And then, finally.

It begins. The old man suddenly bats away at something, swinging at first in small swipes and then (in time) with wild flailing arms about his head—bird-sized biplanes or maybe the wings of his own combative salbonavita angels harry him. There is commotion, a close and fierce and hurried discussion as his thanes rush to his aid.

Not Hotshot, though. Once on his feet, the stage seems to slip beneath him, tilting wildly—legs spread and feet splayed, he shuffles over to the diploma table, head bowed into the storm that howls about him—grabbing for the table's edge, he pulls violently on the white cloth and spills everything, a tumble of ribbon-bound parchment tubes and a few old trophies. He doesn't seem to mind, though. Objective reached, he climbs on board, belly-down, and holds on for dear life.

And now commotion from the front row, too, amongst faculty—an esteemed relic slowly, deliberately removes his shirt and tie and then squats gargoyle-like on his chair, his head now moving in rapid jerks from side to side, like a metronome. *Milk drinker!* I howl, *Milk drinker on the sly!* He was no tea-party guest of the wildly thrashing hatter mid-stage, I know this, just an old and bitter bellyacher, a malcontent who must have sneaked a drop of milk from the supply room.

I am in an agony of mirth, fierce stab of pain under my ribs as I laugh it out. But softly, silently. There is more to come, I am sure, but I have to go. By this time, though, the master's rimy-thighed she-thrall has washed away the evidence.

After all, there are written instructions.

I shit you not.

Chapter Five

But between the essence and the descent.

Because I return to shadows, or so I think at first, Jimmy nowhere to be found.

I return unannounced as well, just a ghost in the Machine, standing on the edge of the Escarpment and looking down at the grid and the slate-grey stretch of water beyond. I stay until the sun sets behind me, until the city lights begin to collect in the beads of water on my window and hood (it rains now) and I know I won't be here for long.

This city no longer feels like home.

Tribal takes me in, of course, though I see it will be a short-lived arrangement—his girlfriend sees me as a foreign component in an otherwise carefully balanced equilibrium. I don't say anything, but she reminds me of something Jimmy said once, when I first brought Sarah around. Something about interrupting the delicate ecosystem of hermetically sealed situations. Tribal seems pretty settled, though, and she seems right for him, so I won't rock the boat.

I return to old haunts, walk wraith-like along the same boot-worn paths of my youth, but everything has changed. Even Hess Village, that cluster of pubs and bars mid-core. Gentrification, or the beginnings of it. I meet an occasional friendly face, but not too often. Or, at least, not often enough. Young faces have taken their places at the tables, faces soft-eyed and strange, a different generation (*houses live and die*, this I know, *and there is a time for building and for living—*)

And for dying. Oh well, I shrug, farewell to the empire. Even the boot culture remnants and refugees are just memories.

Funny what you miss.

I look for Jimmy. Passively at first, and then with a vague urgency.

Tribal doesn't know where he is. Derek doesn't, either. He seems happy to see me (Derek, I mean), though he talks to me like I'm more memory than mate. Tuesday left him, took the baby.

Ah, I say softly. *I lost someone too.*

But it just isn't the same. There's no common language, no reservoir of words left from which to draw. That well has long since dried up. We part, saddened by circumstance—but it's the loss of common ground, really, that nags at us both.

I visit others as I find them, but they only remember the old me. Maybe I'm a threat to the thin veils of respectability they've wrapped themselves in, I'll maybe expose the hooliganism of the past to their better halves or small children or employers or neighbours. Mostly there are rushed introductions to young wives (suspicious or sometimes just curious) or friends followed by *I'll phone you we'll get together soon great to see you again right in the middle of something but later we can* And so on. Fuck it, I think.

Not everyone, though. Seamus has me in, sits me right down in his small north end kitchen and calls his girlfriend in to meet me, two beers on the table right quick and stories tumble out unedited, unapologetic. And he just a casual acquaintance from the old days.

Keith, too, the Gallows Swines now just another sentimental footnote in the history of the Hamilton music scene. He's married to Jen, a mutual friend from the old days, a girl who grew up in one of the wealthy satellite towns but slummed it on the weekends—part time groupie and pub rat, she is all smiles and hugs and as beautiful as ever when she opens the door. They have a house and a baby and a monstrous dog and careers. A real life.

They're right proper mates. They know me for who I was, not what. I tell them my fantastical tale, every ridiculous detail. We laugh about it and the evening hours slip by unnoticed.

"So, what is it you do, exactly?" I finally ask. From where I am, I can see a compact office, the desk littered with paperwork.

Keith smiles sheepishly.

"I, um, sell pharmaceuticals, actually. To doctors, to be exact."

"You gotta be fucking kidding me."

"Nope. I just became a regional manager. Actually," and here he looks to Jen, who smiles and nods, "you looking for something to do? A job, I mean?"

"Cheers, brother, I'm good. Quinn's taken care of it."

I forgot to mention that bit. Another right proper mate, he took care of things before I was in the city a week. Crash course in the current music scene for Yours Truly: King Street's own Dog Whistle Night Club has a new set of owners, a new name, and—apparently—a new booking manager. For a while, at least.

By virtue of family clout, Quinn owns a heavy half. The short of it is that he got to name his newest venture. And in his oddly sentimental and oblivious way, he continues to pay tribute to the highpoints of his own youth, naïvely proud of his ingenuity. But his creativity is borrowed, of course.

Like my own, I suppose. I know you'd agree, Jimmy—you, a true brother, so generous with your words and wisdom.

No, Quinn is not one to shy away from his fervent and effusive love affair with misplaced memory. He baptizes Hamilton's newest underground nightclub The Midnight Circus.

Flattering, but for me this is acuminate, a splinter caught in the corner of the eye. Or a fingertip opened up on a guitar string. But this is also a familiar and welcome pain. And after the last year's bit of dodge and weave, I've become a moderately accomplished actor. Quinn waited wide-eyed for my reaction, still eager for my approval, he stood frozen on the narrow and tenuous edge of his own self-confidence, teetering this way and that by whatever my eyes betrayed.

But I smiled, sincere and warm. I know him now—no charlatan, no fortune-hunting huckster—here is one of the few genuine defenders of what the music scene was always about. I took his outstretched hand. But for the first time forearm to forearm, a boot culture cliché from the old days. And (I swear to God) a tear flashed briefly in the corner of his eye. I smiled at that too. Why fight it, I thought, he'd probably try to make me part owner of the place someday if I let him have his way.

But this is just a stop on the journey. I will stay long enough to scavenge some of the pieces I dropped along the way, and then I have to go. Tribal asks me why I don't unpack, why I leave things in bags and stored in the back seat of my car. He asks, but he knows without me telling him.

Side note: my first booking was none other than Enter the Haggis. Not too fucking bad for a beginner.

I also booked the Rainbow Butt Monkeys, who would not long after win a radio-sponsored contest, change their name to Finger Eleven, and live happily ever after.

But the opening act for the Butt Monkeys? A Dik Van Dykes *cover* band.

They told me they had five songs ready to go. Unfortunately they played eight.

I, well . . . yeah.

—

I find Jimmy, finally. It is simple—in the end, all I needed to do was follow the trail of scattered words. Stones on the sidewalks, stones on the stairs, dropped there by those who come to listen.

Someone in the growing gathering recognizes me. I know him too, but just the eyes in that ruin of a face. I can't place it, can't recall the name, he watches me struggle in the mists, but on this river—so dark, so tumid—I have drifted too far to see the past. *It doesn't matter* (he whispers) *here take this* handing me a glistening pebble with shabby fingers, slipping an identical one under his tongue *Take it* he says, nodding, *it helps.*

And it does. Once more, just once more, a bitter sphere, familiar chemical countdown until the centipedes crawl out of hibernation. *But to listen,* he says kindly, *you have to leap.*

So I jump. I fall.

I drop.

No broken litany in this valley of fallen stars. Jimmy finally emerges, appearing among us as if from a cocoon, more transient than transformative. In his hand are words, lyrics and music and pen crushed together in a tight fist held closely to his chest between liver and lung, and Jimmy finally speaks, says that's where he last felt the thumping reassurance of his heart, unmoored and migratory (or following a secret orbit, his fist-sized cluster of valves a tiny world in the yawning emptiness hurtling through space warm and fluid) but this is only what Jimmy says.

Hollow says Jimmy, *we are just hollow men*, thin men I ask and Jimmy sees me and smiles and reaches out, touches my face. *Yes,* he says, *that too. Thin men. Welcome back, brother.*

We gather on King Street, those who can, thin men stretched too far over too much time and distance. We have come together, street tribe of thin men, to listen.

Jimmy takes his place, now a true street prophet on the steps, standing among the stones, and holds out his hands, throws his scarecrow arms wide and we follow the trails his fingers trace in the lurid air of a city summer.

Others gather too, *but they are not thin men*, Jimmy assures us, they are *they are less than hollow, just skeletons carrying their boxes and bundles, just skeletons here to point and to laugh and to make jokes about our flesh,* but we are stretched too thin, hard and hale and immune to the soft derision of the Dead. *Stone hands hurling stones at stone*, Jimmy gestures in an arc, slowly, and we nod in solemn agreement. It dispels the others, they slip away into the mundane circuitry of King Street shoppers and traffic as if compelled by the wind (or by breath). A miracle, a miracle! the thin men whisper, speak again! Say on.

We are just hollow men, he continues, the fervour builds, he believes and more than believes, *compelling thought to flight and the birds that beat within you, black and wild winged in each thin memory, shadows trapped in bone cages shall* A ragged cheer rises from the tribe. More gather, but in earnest and with untamed eyes, drawn by the hope that this one Knows.

We are the thin men, the brittle backed men, hunched against hope, here is the oasis, the horizon—but who among us is wise enough to walk that path? Life is—

Here he pauses, he muses, he has it now, he squeezes the papers tighter so that the very ink sinks into his skin, through epidermis and into the vessels and up each miniscule road to the great arterial source. Ink rises up and up and blackens his tongue with truth.

—life is this hand and this tongue, life is a dream deferred or a dream lost or a dream without hope, that is how I dream, each stone sinking into the well like coins, and I will not wish when I cast, I will dream. Life is a chance

to dream the dream of stone, words are stones and thoughts are stones and you and I dream this world through eyes of stone watching everything, the moon too, it too a stone that rises . . .

Eyes slip upward, involuntary motion, There it is, some say, there it is! Moonrise in late afternoon, sun still caught on the scaffolding—

But enough.

I see him happy again, finally in tune.

—

And later that night, Jimmy joins me at the Escarpment's sharp edge. Below us, the city is a sprawl of electric heat and grid work—high-rises and houses, smoke stacks and factory fires. And thousands upon thousands of pinpoints of light, as if the stars above—obscured by the fierce orange haze of this city's night glow—find reflections below anyway.

The Dog Star is visible. Reliable, constant, I watch its slow and steady ascent. Jimmy settles beside me and we stare out across the city for a while in silence.

"Did you find what you were looking for?" he finally asks.

"No."

"Are you here to stay?"

"No."

Jimmy lights up, offers me a toke. Below us, cars and people crawl along under the electric light of this, my last steel city summer.

He looks at me now, brow furrowed. Then he smiles sadly.

"You're not really here, even now," he whispers.

He's right. I've returned, yes, but only in a way. I return the way you recall the fleeting wisps of a dream upon waking, grasping at the tattered remains of images, of sounds, of jokes that you know were funny but can't recall the context, of fears you know were real, but can't recall the reason. This is how I return, just a non sequitur arrant, a rootless traveler who stands on the edge of an escarpment staring down at a city he once knew.

But not the same city, not even close.

"Here, brother," I say, holding out my hand. "I brought you this."

It is the ragged bundle of green and grey, the same small cloth wrapped clay flute he gave me at the border the day I left for the States.

Because I finally unwrapped it, earlier this evening up here at the edge, and after all this time Jimmy's gift was revealed to me. Yes, the clay bowl flute, but into the red clay long ago he'd carved a small "16."

And standing here, up on the escarpment above the concrete and brick and asphalt and steel that stretches from cliff to lake, it all becomes clear. Everything, all of this sediment and erosion resettles, and I reach back past patio and forest, past coffee shops and cops, even past Debbie—past that one wrenching loss when, ears roaring, I could feel the very earth shift beneath me—back to that muggy July with Jimmy in the park, watching Jonah, that mad fuck in the fountain.

Bus 16, numerical mantra.

That little clay flute, molded and baked in a desert so far from this tumid place, our last totem. All that remains of Debbie Dream.

Jimmy hesitates, his hand shakes.

"Take it," I say.

But those shamanic fingers, so accustomed to ritual, can't seem to find their way around the little vessel.

I turn his hand over, palm up, and place it there.

"Go ahead, Jimmy."

"But I—" tears now, both of us.

"It's alright, brother. Let her go."

Jimmy looks up through the blur, finds Sirius.

Then he steps forward, stretches out his arm, and lets the small clay flute roll off his fingers and over the cliff.

Acknowledgements

The short version is this: I owe my foremost debts of gratitude to James Morrow, Meghan MacDonald, Jack Haringa, Sarah Getchell and Molly Popkin—author and agent, cynic and saints (respectively).

The longer version: After I wrote this thing and brought it to Jim's attention, he advised me (wonderful mentor that he is) that nothing lighter than rhinoceros hide should be worn while struggling to attract the attention of literary agents. I soon discovered two things as I shambled my way down that miserable road: first, that agents are a cynical and reticent race unto themselves; second, that Jim is always right.

Or almost, anyway.

One agent actually took the time to write a rejection letter that was kind, encouraging, *and* pointed me in exactly the right direction—Meghan MacDonald, thank you; you're the best agent I never had. Soon after, I showed the letter to my friend and colleague, Jack. He perused, mused, and then said, "I might know someone who fits this bill. . . ." And so he did: I met Brett and Sandra of CZP at Readercon soon after. Sarah Getchell, for whom the rules of temporal physics apparently do not apply, then gave me hours and hours she couldn't really afford to sacrifice, helping me to hone the language and wrestle the components into some a semblance of order. Oh, and she came up with the title, too. Then she had me send it to Molly, an editing force of nature. Within days I had a thorough set of notes on what needed attention; apparently, time doesn't behave conventionally in Molly's universe either. Much love to you both.

Of course, the list doesn't end there. I would also like to thank Brett for initially agreeing to read the manuscript despite the slush pile in front of him, Sandra for her incredible guidance (I had no idea what editors suffer through), Gemma Files for taking on the thankless task of copy editing, my parents Nigel and Donna Baillie for their love and encouragement, my sons Loch and Grey for their patience, and my wife Darcy for being there when I needed her most. Thanks also to those who took the time to read and provide honest feedback—Amelia Erskine, Daria Cenedella, and Sean Pierson; to my brothers, Andrew and Matt, for the constant encouragement; to Linda Pruessen for her guidance; to musicians Brad Hails, Scotty Hunter, and Jay MacDonald, and to the entire Hamilton music scene of my youth—boot culture included—for the inspiration; and to Richard Evans, web master of TheWho.com, for his kind generosity.

Finally, I want to thank Pete Townshend—for his brief words of encouragement, yes, but more so for playing such an integral role in my formative years. And (more to the point) in the formative years of a nameless narrator navigating the jetsam and unforgiving streets of his steel city youth.

Cheers, all.

About the Author

The best we can say is that his editor taught him that "plot" is not an evil word. He's less of an idiot than he was six months ago.

Beyond that, David Baillie was born, raised, and educated in Hamilton, Ontario. He emigrated from Canada to the United States in 1996 to teach modern and postmodern art and literature at a New England college preparatory school. *What We Salvage* is Baillie's debut novel, a work that draws upon his own experiences in the post-boot culture music scene of the late '80s-early '90s. It is the first book in his "Sons of the Hammer" trilogy. He currently lives in central Massachusetts with his two sons, his artist / educator wife Darcy, and her two daughters.

EMB
RACE
THE
ODD

THE HOUSE OF WAR AND WITNESS

MIKE CAREY, LINDA CAREY & LOUISE CAREY

1740. Europe is on the brink of war. An Austrian regiment is sent to the furthest frontier of the empire to hold the border against the might of Prussia. But their garrison, the ancient house called Pokoj, is already inhabited by a company of ghosts from every age of the house's history. Only Drozde, the quartermaster's mistress, can see them, and terrifyingly they welcome her as a friend. Meanwhile the humourless lieutenant Klaes pursues the mystery of why the people of the nearby village are so surly and withdrawn, so reluctant to welcome the soldiers who are there to protect them. What are they hiding? And what happened to the local militia unit that was stationed at Pokoj before the regiment arrived? The camp follower and the officer make their separate journeys to the same appalling discovery—an impending catastrophe that will sweep away villagers and soldiers alike.

AUGUST 2015

ISBN: 978-1-77148-312-4 | eISBN: 978-1-77148-313-1

EXPERIMENTAL FILM

GEMMA FILES

A contemporary ghost story in which former Canadian film history teacher Lois Cairns—jobless and depressed in the wake of her son's autism diagnosis—accidentally discovers the existence of lost early 20th century Ontario filmmaker Mrs. A. Macalla Whitcomb. By deciding to investigate how Mrs. Whitcomb's obsessions might have led to her mysterious disappearance, Lois unwitting invites the forces which literally haunt Mrs. Whitcomb's films into her life, eventually putting her son, her husband and herself in danger. *Experimental Film* mixes painful character detail with a creeping aura of dread to produce a fictionalized "memoir" designed to play on its readers' narrative expectations and pack an existentialist punch.

NOVEMBER 2015

ISBN: 978-1-77148-349-0 | eISBN: 978-1-77148-350-6

ALSO AVAILABLE FROM CHIZINE PUBLICATIONS